Sight Reading

Also by Daphne Kalotay

Russian Winter

Calamity and Other Stories

Sight Reading

A Novel

Daphne Kalotay

HARPER

www.harpercollins.com

HarperCollins books may be purchased for educational, business, or sales promotional use. For information, please e-mail the Special Markets Department at SPsales@ harpercollins.com.

Grateful acknowledgment is made for permission to reproduce from the following: "A Drunk Man Looks at the Thistle" by Hugh MacDiarmid, *The Complete Poems Volume 1*, 1978, Carcarnet Press Limited.

FIRST EDITION

Designed by Betty Lew

Library of Congress Cataloging-in-Publication Data has been applied for.

ISBN 978-0-06-224693-6

13 14 15 16 17   OV/RRD   10 9 8 7 6 5 4 3 2 1

This one is for Judy Layzer.

For harmony is a symphony, and a symphony is an
   agreement . . . ;
and thus music, too, is concerned with the principles
   of love.

—Plato

Sight Reading

*I*T WAS ONE OF THOSE EASY MAY AFTERNOONS WHEN EVERYTHING, including the weather, seems to finally fall into place. Gone were the brisk winds and persistent grayish pall, the chilly discouragement of New England spring. Today's heat was balmy and real, and all along Newbury Street people were sipping iced coffees, strolling slowly and having long chats on cell phones. Shop owners and hairdressers stepped out of doors to turn their faces toward the hazy sun. At Salon Supreme—across from Hazel's boutique—women kept requesting a pedicure along with their mani and, rather than wait inside for their nails to dry, emerged gingerly onto the sidewalk to slap the air back and forth. This was midway along Newbury, past the cheap trendy stores and ice cream shops, but not yet at the haute couture end. Stepping out for her break, Hazel caught sight of the women across the street and thought, Why not? It was one of those days when everyone deserved a little treat—and frivolous treats were often the most satisfying of all.

At the salon she was ushered to a plump mechanical armchair, its footbath swirling, by a young woman named Mi who suggested a bright coral color. And though Hazel had long made a point of being well groomed (a professional necessity, really), she found it mildly thrilling, if perhaps slightly shameful, to lean back into the thronelike armchair while someone else sloughed away at her feet. Mi worked fast, applying the polish with quick little brushstrokes. Having run out of disposable flip-flops, she constructed makeshift sandals from paper plates and masking tape, so that without risking damage to nails or feet, Hazel—after tucking a 50 percent tip into Mi's slim hand—could shuffle next door to buy her afternoon coffee. Standing in line, her cheery spring bag looped over her shoulder, her leather ballet flats poking out from the bag like bunny ears, Hazel was conscious of herself as someone who by virtue of her perfectly tinted hair (more blond than gray), tapered linen dress, and thick gold earrings could transform paper shoes into a sign of propriety and good fortune.

Taking a few careful steps forward, she ordered an iced mocha from a girl with a pierced tongue. She felt sorry for the girl's mother, whoever she was, and found herself averting her eyes when the girl told her, with slight difficulty, "That's three dollars and eleven cents." Her own daughter had never felt the need to do such a thing. Hazel couldn't help being proud of that, and relieved as much as delighted now that Jessica was engaged to be married.

Hazel smiled at the thought, and at her glossy coral toenails. Life seemed for once to be progressing as it should. With the wedding season starting, things at the store were picking up, and she could count on moving some of the more extravagant items: the rocking chair carved from a single tree trunk, the oblong mica bowls. Already she could barely keep enough lilac paper and silver ribbons on hand. And that morning she had managed to talk someone into buying the last of those enormous lemon-colored vases. The woman had looked so pleased, saying, "My niece is going to love this!"—which confirmed Hazel's theory that what was one person's bane was another's savior and that, in the grand scheme of things, everything worked out in the end.

Yes, she believed that now. Only in the past few years had she come to understand: if you just let things be, they eventually sort themselves out. This was what Hazel was thinking as she took her iced mocha and stepped carefully out the door. And there, as a reminder of the many ways life might surprise you, of all the ways the world might turn itself upside down, there with her big brown eyes was Remy.

Part One

Her Hair About Her Ears

Chapter 1

S HE ARRIVED AT REHEARSAL THAT WINTER EVENING TO FIND BE-
hind the podium a young man in baggy slacks and a boxy tweed
jacket. This was Remy's final semester at the conservatory; she was
twenty-two years old and still one seat away from first chair. The man
said nothing as the other students trickled in, just nodded "hello" and
waited for them to assemble themselves and their instruments. The
air was so dry, the clasps of Remy's violin case shocked her fingertips.
She glanced at the man, whose face seemed to be trying to say that
nothing unusual was happening, no, not at all.

It was 1987, a Sunday. A room full of students not quite recovered from the weekend's parties and performances and one-night
stands. Their regular conductor, Mr. Bergman, was a short, lisping
man with rolled-up pant cuffs; everyone looked at this new one in a
tired, questioning way. His skin was fair, and his dark hair flopped
at a slant across his forehead. There was something angular about
his face, with its defined cheekbones and elegantly bony nose. Remy
tucked her violin up under her chin and tested the strings, enjoying
the sensation of each one, with the slight turn of a peg, slipping into
tune.

Not until her stand partner, Lynn, hurried in to take the seat next
to her did the man explain—not at all thoroughly—that Mr. Bergman wouldn't be back. "And so," he announced in a British sort of
accent that managed to sound both witty and bewildered, "I've been
hired as his replacement."

He was too tall for the tweed jacket, or perhaps just too trim, too laddish: Remy decided he couldn't be more than thirty. "What did he say his name was?" whispered Lynn, who as concertmistress would surely end up on a first-name basis with him. But no name had been mentioned. The man had come from out of nowhere. Remy pictured a small pile of luggage waiting just outside the practice hall.

"Well, so, in that case, then," the man was saying. "I'm very excited about the selections we have this term. *Scheherazade* is one of my favorites."

Mine, too, thought Remy, with slight bitterness. Not a day went by that she didn't wish she, and not Lynn, might be the one to portray Scheherazade's seductive voice, with that first melodious proclamation and the passionate spirals that followed. In private she practiced the solo bits as if they were hers. Lynn, meanwhile, was briskly swiping rosin onto her bow, stirring up a low cloud of sticky dust, as if this man's sudden appearance weren't at all out of the ordinary and she might be called upon at any moment to play her cadenza.

The man's eyes were bright (though there were slight shadows beneath them) and his button-down shirt, open at the collar, was visibly rumpled underneath the tweed jacket. His expression was one of bemusement. Remy felt suddenly hopeful, though she couldn't have quite said why.

"Well, so," the man announced in a cheery, English way. "Off we go."

HE HAD THEM START WITH THE SIBELIUS. REMY LOVED THE SURENESS of her fingers defining each note, and the vibration of the strings beneath her bow. The rehearsal hall had excellent acoustics; the music rose up over her, sound waves reverberating between her body and her violin, from the touch of her left-hand fingers upon the strings through her right arm down into her wrist.

The new conductor was listening, getting a sense of the orchestra and what the previous conductor had accomplished. "All right, so," he said lightly, waving at them to stop. Remy felt a surge of frustration.

She was just one of the many faces looking up at him. This late in the semester, what were the chances a new conductor might discover all she could do?

"Starting at bar seventy-four, let the phrase play itself out." He hummed the phrase, as if from pleasure rather than in illustration. "Let it come to rest, don't rush into the next sequence. It's your job to make sure the audience hears the significance of the phrase—so you need to give them time to absorb it." He raised his baton. "Let's start from there."

As they played, Remy could feel the conductor trying to hold them back, then allowing the music forward again. Mr. Bergman hadn't done it this way.

"The thing to keep in mind," the man said, tapping his baton at the podium for them to stop, "is that what the music asks of us isn't always spelled out on the page. We might need to slow down even where there's no *ritardando* written, or rush forward where there's just a crescendo mark. Tempo is about more than just speed." He said this casually, as if the thought had just occurred to him.

"It's about the passage of time, really. In our lives—not just on the page. You know how sometimes everything seems to keep rushing forward, but then at other times things are peaceful and still? How sometimes we feel stuck in time, or just plodding along day by day— and then suddenly it's as if time's passed us by, or we're being hurried along, too quickly? That's what tempo is really about. That's what we're expressing. Not just how fast or how slowly the *music* moves. It's about how fast and slow *life* moves."

His eyes widened at the thought. They were a greenish blue. For a moment it seemed he might be about to make some personal confession. But he just raised his baton and asked them to try the passage one more time.

"RASCAL, COME HERE, SWEETIE! YOU CAN DO IT, RASCAL!"

Rascal peered over the edge of the scalloped tiles, as if considering. Hazel glimpsed the little round head of soft fur and called out again, despite wishing she could just leave him up on the Duvaliers' roof—just for a bit, while she finished her packing.

If only Nicholas were here . . . But of course he was already in Boston at his new post; he always managed to escape just this sort of ordeal. Instead, here was Madame Duvalier, standing with arms akimbo, lips pursed in concern.

"Rascal: *come on down!*" Hazel called, in her best game show host impersonation, though there was no one here to find it funny or even just stupid. Gently she shook the old wooden ladder tilted against the balcony, a reminder to Rascal as to how one might proceed. The sturdy wooden shutters of the Duvaliers' windows had been pushed open, their thick blue paint a shade away from cheerful. Rascal whimpered, and Hazel stretched her arms up to indicate that she was prepared to catch him. "It's all right, Rascal, I'm here."

Jessie was running around the damp courtyard squealing "Rascal!" and every once in a while stopping to scrutinize a plump slug. For hours Hazel had been packing, folding winter clothes into battered suitcases, wrapping their few valuables in little wads of newspaper that still held the crumpled contours of previous moves. Then Jessie, scribbling with thick crayons next to the drafty window of their flat next door, had heard Rascal's frightened cries carried through the cool, humid air.

"*RasCAAALLuh* . . . ," called Madame Duvalier in that jaded tone that all French women seemed to have. The way she said it rhymed with *Pascal*. When Hazel knocked on her neighbor's door, Madame Duvalier had answered in stretchy stirrup pants and a long baggy sweater, but to step outside and try to seduce Rascal, she had changed into her usual tight black slacks, leather pumps, and maroon jacket with the enormous shoulder pads. Her lipstick matched the color of the jacket exactly. No woman in this Provençal town dared present herself in public without first dressing impeccably, applying a sheath of makeup, and dousing herself with perfume. It was one of the peculiarities Hazel had become accustomed to these past eight months. And now she would be leaving.

"*Viens, RasCAAALLLuh . . . .*" Madame Duvalier gave a sigh but then said with real enthusiasm, "*Ah, les voilà, les pompiers.*" It had been her idea to call the fire department. Hazel found surprising comfort in the fact that even here, on a whole other continent, this particular service was the peculiar duty of firemen. A universal truth, she thought, and almost laughed, though she couldn't, really, while Rascal was still stuck up there. Anyway, it was Madame Duvalier's roof; if she desired a fleet of firemen to come to her aid, that was her prerogative. She was Hazel's age, thirty or so, yet in Hazel's eight months here the two of them had never graduated to a first-name basis. Their conversations had been comically stilted, with Madame Duvalier's serious, frowning, "Bonjour, Madame," whenever they happened to meet. It was such a distant second to "Hi" or even "Hello." "Bonjour, Madame" had become to Hazel an embodiment of everything difficult and uncomfortable about her life—trailing around after Nicholas year after year, from this orchestra or conservatory to that one, the endless cycle of pocket dictionaries and air mail packages and foreign landladies shrilling rules she couldn't quite understand. Each new city offered its own awkwardly furnished flat, where there was always a trick to the shower or something finicky about the stove, and of course some laundry-based complication. Their residence in Helsinki had been met by an infestation of wasps; in Brussels the man who lived downstairs always hung about waiting for Hazel to help him "practice the English"; in Florence they'd had to relocate when, after heavy rains, their original quarters began to smell of sewage.

Here their apartment was outfitted with space heaters in every room, yet the winter had been awfully cold, the tile floors like ice, even after Hazel put down her favorite Persian carpet. No wonder Jessie was so happy today, free to run around the dewy courtyard, where weeds were beginning to emerge and a few thick worms announced incipient spring.

The firemen—there were three of them—didn't look at all put out. In fact they seemed pleasantly surprised, stealing glances at Hazel, who couldn't help smiling inwardly at knowing they found her attractive, while Madame Duvalier walked them through the cat/roof situation with what seemed to Hazel a much more complicated explanation than necessary. Could we ever have been friends? she found herself wondering. Couldn't both of us have been friendlier?

It was a small failure, probably, not to have managed to befriend this woman. Instead Hazel had spent long afternoons at the nearby park sitting alone on a bench she came to think of as "hers," sketching trees and foliage and strangers' profiles into a little spiral-bound drawing pad, while Jessie ran around exultantly chasing pigeons. The other mothers plopped their babies inside little grassy penned-in areas that Hazel had at first assumed were for flower beds or perhaps dogs. But no, that was where mothers deposited their small children, closed the gate, and then went to sit on far-off benches, where they smoked and gossiped and read, ignoring any possible disaster that might be taking place inside the kiddy pen. Hazel sat on her bench, anxiously sketching with a dark pencil, monitoring Jessie and keeping an eye on all the other children as they ate grass and dirt, and hit each other, and poked themselves in the nose and eyes and ears, and licked the bars of the iron gate—while the slender, smoking mothers paid no attention at all.

Now she nodded along to Madame Duvalier's epic narrative: yes, it was her cat, Hazel answered to the one jolly *pompier* who seemed especially ready to perform. Perhaps she enjoyed too much the little charge that came from witnessing her effect on men; perhaps she relied on her looks too much. But looks were sometimes all she had to work with—and could make the difference between being helped and being ignored.

The *pompiers* regarded Rascal gravely, conferring in hushed conversation too rapid for Hazel to follow. This particular French trait— the somber tone of expertise that everyone, no matter their age or employ, brought to their chosen professions—was one of Hazel's favorites. Earnest consultations of grocers and hairdressers, debates between merchants and patrons regarding potential purchases, long conferences that even other customers joined in when Hazel asked for advice at the wine shop. She could make Nicholas laugh just by mimicking that pouting frown of concentration, the careful weighing of options before delivering, unsmiling, a verdict: "*Ah, oui, monsieur, celle-là vous va bien*" when, dressing to attend a performance or premiere, Nicholas asked which tie he ought to wear.

Jessie was now squatting on her heels, arranging and rearranging twigs under a craggy lavender bush, while the two serious *pompiers* brought over an extremely tall ladder and propped it against the house. Rascal gave a distressed meow, as if conscious that all this fuss was about him and he had better make it worth their while. Why did these predicaments always present themselves when Nicholas was away? When Hazel had to fend for herself, in some foreign tongue not quite at her disposal? A fuse blew, or a suspicious person was wandering the vicinity. One time a pipe had burst. These things only happened when Hazel was alone. . . . But in just two days, she reminded herself, they would be on their way back to the States. She was ready, so very ready, to set up a real home, to find comfort and ease where until now there had been only hassle. Already she had begun in her mind sewing velour pillows for the niche of a sunny bay window. There were sure to be bay windows in Boston.

"*C'est votre téléphone qui sonne?*" Madame Duvalier asked, her groomed eyebrows raised just the slightest bit. There it was again, the loud clattering of the telephone in Hazel's flat. Hopefully it was Nicholas; she hadn't heard from him in a good three days. We'll watch the little one, the jolly *pompier* told her, and Hazel went hurrying back, certain she wouldn't make it before the caller gave up. But the telephone was still ringing when she grabbed the receiver.

"Hazel." Her mother always spoke in a flat, perfunctory way, but this time there was a waver in her voice. "Your father. He's in the

ICU." Hazel felt her heart plummet as her mother said, "You can come home, can't you?"

Of course she could. I'll be there, she said, just as soon as I can.

HER PARENTS WERE NOT MUSICIANS. THEY SEEMED SURPRISED, MYS-tified, even, by how quickly Remy took to her violin, which at first was a little thing of ugly orange-colored wood, shiny and hardly larger than a toy. Her future was decided on a single day, in a few brief min-utes, which in retrospect seemed to her a disturbingly abrupt way to make such an important decision. She and the rest of the third grad-ers were led into the stuffy auditorium, where Mrs. Sylvester, the music teacher, awaited with an array of battered orchestral instru-ments. The students were to sample the ones that intrigued them and make a selection, and by the following week each would have his or her very own, on loan from the school.

Remy had already made up her mind to play the flute. She had watched April Englensen onstage with the woodwinds in the Christ-mas concert tapping her foot jauntily along with Mrs. Sylvester's baton, looking more poised and confident than all the other sixth graders. In April's hands the flute looked light and sparkly, a glam-orous accessory as much as an instrument. But when Remy tried to blow into the flute that day in third grade, no sound came out. She tried altering the shape of her mouth, but the flute barely yielded a whisper.

Mrs. Sylvester put her plump arm around Remy and urged her over to the stringed instruments. Gently she placed a violin in Re-my's left hand, arranging its wooden body so that her chin nestled onto the little black chin rest. A bow was placed in the light grip of her right hand, and though there seemed, for a moment, to be altogether too many things to think about, when Remy pulled the bow across the strings a scratchy sound emerged. This was sufficient for Mrs. Sylvester to write Remy's name next to the word *violin* and move on to the next student.

"But I don't want to play violin," Remy started to say but stopped. She already knew that what she wanted didn't necessarily matter. For years she had wanted a little sister or brother, but insisting to her parents hadn't yielded any results. And she hadn't at all wanted to move away from her grandparents, hadn't wanted to go to this school, where the other children's friendships allowed no room for a new girl with unruly hair. Even her teacher, a tall thin woman whose fingernails were as bright red as her lips, had said to Remy, in a voice of disapproval, while distributing twenty-one little thin black plastic combs before the photographer came to take the class picture, "I don't know how this thing will ever get through your hair." Remy was too ashamed to relay this to her parents. And yet this was the very reason she wanted to play the flute: to be, instead of a shy, relenting girl with a head of messy brown curls, that straight-backed one happily tapping her toes along with the music, holding a silver flute as sleek and sparkling as a magic wand.

Instead, in a crooked row with twelve other pupils each Monday, Remy stood before a heavy black music stand and sawed away at "Twinkle, Twinkle, Little Star" and "Old Rosin the Beau." She had neither perfect pitch nor a flair for improvisation, and had to work to learn to read the notes, just like all the other students standing before their own heavy black music stands. But unlike the others, Remy did not struggle to draw her bow across the strings at the correct angle, to coax the right pitch and timbre from beneath her fingertips. The awkward posture, with the left hand's inward-twisted grip, quickly became second nature. Mrs. Sylvester had affixed three tiny strips of red adhesive paper, like skinny Band-Aids, at intervals across the fingerboard of each child's instrument to indicate where to place their fingers as they scaled the instrument's neck—but Remy had no need for a visual guide, easily heard what was in or out of tune, felt innately how to interpret the notes on the page, how to turn them into sound. She found the red fret lines unattractive, and scraped them off.

Within weeks Mrs. Sylvester had pulled her aside, given her new exercises and a new lesson book. Remy loved playing her scales and arpeggios, stretching her fingers, retracting them; they were becoming quick and adept, just as her bowing arm was already stronger. Across her little amber cube of rosin, a slim rut grew deeper by the week. Remy practiced so often a small bruise formed beneath her jaw, and one of the violin's strings popped; Mrs. Sylvester had to replace it, demonstrating how to thread the tip through the peg and twist it around securely.

Soon she had moved on to the third lesson book, where the staves were no longer cartoonishly large, the notes no longer magnified as if for someone with poor eyesight. By the next year, something new had happened. At home one afternoon, practicing what she would later discover was a transcription of a Bach prelude, Remy found herself not simply playing the music but traveling inside it, among the notes themselves, from line to line among the staves, sculpting a path of sound. Not that she was consciously aware of having been transported—but when she arrived at the end, she was momentarily shocked to find herself in her same house in suburban Ohio, standing there reading from sheet music propped on a folding metal stand.

She knew then, if without the words to express it, that what she was studying was not simply music but beauty, and that she wanted to inhabit, completely, that beauty—and that this was something quite different from the jaunty flutist tapping her foot to the music.

THE NEW CONDUCTOR'S NAME WAS NICHOLAS ELKO.

At their next rehearsal, Lynn told Remy all sorts of things about him—that he was thirty-one years old, that he had been a guest conductor in Budapest and at the London Sinfonietta, that he composed as well as conducted. Since she was concertmistress, she had made a point of introducing herself and, she told Remy, found out about him from her mother (a music teacher who had a hand in all of her daughter's professional affairs). Lynn, a prodigy, was the youngest student in the conservatory and still lived at home with her parents—which Remy supposed offset, somewhat, the honor of being first chair.

Until this past autumn, first chair had gone to Albert Kim, one class ahead of Remy. Albert had perfectly even fingers and the composure of a sunset, and it had been a pleasure to witness up close the way he brought an instrument to life. Yet Remy had looked forward to the year that Albert would graduate, when she would take his place. And then, just when the time had finally come, Lynn Swenson arrived.

Fifteen years old, with long, gawky limbs and a straight orange bob, Lynn probably weighed at most ninety pounds, but when she drew her bow across the strings her gangliness transformed into beauty and sound. It wasn't just her impeccable technique; it was her daring, her nerve, an inventiveness that made even the most familiar moments sound new. Remy had tried to figure out exactly how the transformation occurred, but it was like trying to decipher the work of a magician whose sleight of hand is too quick for the naked eye.

And so it was with understanding as well as awe that Remy had stepped aside, while Lynn justly claimed first chair. When Lynn played her *Scheherazade* solos, Remy watched her shifts and slides, and admired her strong vibrato (which started at her wrist rather than her fingers) and where she had come up with smoother fingerings. She felt real affection, of an almost protective sort, for Lynn—who after all was doomed to spend her conservatory years with a mouthful of metal and few friends her age. Sometimes, as they played in perfect synchrony, it was as if the two of them became a single unit, sharing not just a conductor and music stand and the same notes on the same manuscript page, but also the internal experience of those things. Remy supposed it was the closest she would ever come to reading someone's mind.

"Turns out he's a rising star," Lynn lisped through her braces, explaining that Nicholas Elko had been awarded all sorts of prizes and commissions. "My mom says he's a winner."

It was a phrase Remy disliked. After all, there could be only so many winners, and the path Remy had chosen was the sort that gradually narrowed the further you traveled, room for fewer and fewer along the way. At twenty-two Remy already knew this. Work in first-rate orchestras and chamber groups was a rare coup, and a solo career the exception, not the rule. Most students would end up pinch-hitting for this and that ensemble, supplementing their salaries by giving private lessons or playing quartets at weddings. Yet Remy had faith that if she worked hard enough she could make it to the top. She had applied for a postgraduate fellowship and was preparing to audition for a summer master class with Conrad Lesser. That was how these things went, step by reaching step, up a steep ladder.

Mr. Elko had them start with the Sibelius again. Remy watched him not as she usually did, following a maestro's cues, but as a physical being, the shapes his arms made before him, the vigorous way he pierced the air with his baton, rising on his toes, as if about to become airborne. She noted the way he shook his head, his shiny dark hair flapping across his forehead, and the way he caught the eyes of the section leaders, almost winking at them. She was just one chair away from being noticed by him.

"Let's have just the woodwinds," he was saying. Remy looked at his boxy tweed jacket and button-down shirt and wondered if he had just the one set of clothes. The collar of his shirt framed his clavicle, where his skin looked pale and smooth. Remy realized, quite suddenly, that she wanted to touch it.

She shifted her eyes in case the other first violins had witnessed her thoughts. Across her cheeks she could feel the spreading heat, a bright blush moving toward the top of her forehead.

The secret of life is never to have an emotion that is unbecoming.

It was a line from Oscar Wilde. Remy had been reading him ever since seeing *The Importance of Being Earnest* at the Huntington last month. Oscar Wilde would never blush over something like this.

Mr. Elko motioned for the woodwinds to stop. "You all know, of course, that there's more than one side to any story." As he turned to address the orchestra *tutti,* Remy felt her blush receding. "The same is true for any piece of music."

He came to the front of the podium. "I realize I'm asking you, perhaps, to do things differently than the way you're used to. But think of it as another side of the story. What are the other angles we have yet to consider?"

The girl who played the harp raised her hand, but Mr. Elko didn't seem to notice. "Our job, together, is to uncover the composer's hidden ideas. There is often more to a composition than we may first assume. My job is to discover the possible angles, and yours is to bring them to life."

Remy had never thought of music in terms of hidden ideas. Of course lots of composers liked to insert musical allusions into their work, and sometimes mathematical tricks or in-jokes, but she could tell that Mr. Elko meant something else.

"I grew up in Scotland," he said, "and we've quite a bit of rain. Sometimes it's so fine, you feel it rather than see it. It's that sort of attention we need to bring to a piece of music. That level of awareness."

He paused for a moment. "You know, sometimes, when the rain's that fine, if you're lucky you get a rainbow. Have you ever really looked at one? Not just the stripes of color and the places where it fades out at the end, but the gradations you can barely see. It's those places, the barely visible ones, that we're trying to get at. Those are the secrets."

Remy glanced at the sheet music on her stand, as if it might contain a secret code. "It's a useful metaphor, actually," Mr. Elko added. "Not bad, that. We're trying to convey *the entire spectrum* of color. The sky as well as the earth. The celestial and terrestrial together. All points of view. The complete musical perspective." He said this not as a grand pronouncement but with a lightness, as if chatting over coffee.

For the rest of rehearsal, whenever the first violins weren't playing, Remy observed the rest of the orchestra, to try to see what Mr. Elko saw. Did he, too, find the percussionists comically grave, all three of them with hair short in the front and long in the back, counting precisely, their brows furrowed, before lowering a mallet or striking a single, starry note on a triangle? What did he think of the sad-faced girl who played the harp, and the hefty boy underneath the tuba, cheeks puffed out like balloons? And what about the entire brass section dripping saliva onto the floor, and the clarinetists with their overbites? Then there was the third chair cellist, who always looked like he was in pain when he played, writhing and grimacing, so that it was a wonder his playing didn't sound tormented. Did Mr. Elko think that, too? It was the first time Remy had felt the urge to see the world the way someone else might see it.

"I DON'T SUPPOSE YOU, TOO, NEED SOME AIR AFTER THAT?"

Nicholas looked up to see Yonatan Keitel—a horn specialist and the one other faculty member his age—leaning into his office. They had just been released from a department meeting at which nothing had been accomplished. Yonatan was from Israel, trim and Mediterranean-looking, and grinned as though he and Nicholas were in cahoots about something. "You don't have to stick around here, do you?"

"No, not right now. A reporter for the *Globe* is coming in an hour."

Yonatan raised his eyebrows. Nicholas explained that the newspaper was going to profile him in their Arts section.

"That's great," Yonatan said, without quite looking like he meant it. Nicholas decided not to mention that this was his second press interview this week; since arriving in Boston he had been made to feel like something of a celebrity. He told Yonatan, who was already turning to go, that he would join him for a spell.

"Call me Yoni, by the way. Let's get out of here."

Nicholas followed him out without grabbing his coat; Yoni's very tone suggested it would be wrong to need one. Like Nicholas, Yoni wore just a wool jacket and pale slacks, as if warm weather had already arrived, though he kept his hands tucked into his pockets. For days Nicholas had witnessed this stubborn urge for spring, the way people ignored the latest snowfall and instead of knit hats wore baseball caps. In a span of just two weeks, his female students had shed the short rubber-with-leather boots that appeared to be union issued and now wore equally ubiquitous white tennis shoes—though filthy snow still lined every curb and lay in black puddles at street corners. His colleagues, meanwhile, bicycled to work and sported spring parkas open at the collar.

Outside the air was cold, but the sun warmed their foreheads. "You all right after Bill's little dig there?" Yoni asked.

Nicholas laughed. When the chair of Composition asked for Nicholas's input at the meeting, the director of Wind Ensembles had made a loud comment about asking the opinion of "someone who has been here for all of two weeks and whose appointment wasn't even unanimously approved by the Faculty Committee."

Nicholas had weathered petty jealousies before and told Yoni so—though really he never could help feeling mild shock at being anything but adored. As a child he had charmed at the piano. The only reason he had chosen to attend a university instead of a conservatory was for the continued pleasure of surprising people with his musical gift. Hard work came naturally to him, with effort but without sweat. At the university, he studied music history, writing his thesis in one intense, flurried week—an epic poem explaining the development of exoticism in the Western choral tradition. Other undergraduates pumped out long, dull papers of interchangeable style, but Nicholas's essay-in-verse was immediately sent on to a university press. By then he had begun conducting, one of the few who, perusing a score, could envision multiple interpretations even before the first run-through (foreseeing, too, the possible difficulties and how much rehearsal might be needed). The first time he stood in front of a full orchestra, rather than becoming overwhelmed by the enormous sound, he quickly discerned the various instruments' voices, and never once lost control of the players.

It was around that time that he discovered his gift for composition, little pieces for fun, a bagatelle here, a badinage there; it helped to think of them, like his thesis essay, as poems (though less difficult, since they needed no words). Then came the string quartets, woodwind quintets, preludes, fugues. Ideas presented themselves while he showered, while he dreamed, and he accepted them with gratitude, hearing melodies in the hiss of radiators and the dripping of faucets. Even in the fortnight since his move to Boston he had begun a new composition—a sort of tone poem about the Scottish seaside town where he had spent his early childhood. He worked on it every night (since without Hazel and Jessie here he had an abundance of free time), immersed in hurtling gray waves and cool-spittle air and gulls lifted by scrappy winds.

Nicholas asked about Yoni's work and his training, learned that he was something of a jazz buff and owned an apartment just a few blocks away. When they turned onto Newbury Street, a tall slim girl in jeans and a big slouchy leather jacket sidled up to them, and to Nicholas's surprise Yoni slung his arm around her waist.

"Fancy meeting you here." He gave her a peck on the forehead, but then she leaned her face up to him and they performed a lingering kiss. "I thought you were going to the library," Yoni said.

"I'm foraging for food." She gave a flick of her long blond hair. "Your fridge is practically empty."

"Nicholas, meet Samantha. A woman of discerning appetite."

Samantha shook Nicholas's hand incuriously. She was his same height and lanky like a boy. "Shouldn't you be at work?" she asked.

Shouldn't you be at school? Nicholas wanted to reply. She looked about eighteen. It occurred to him that she might be one of the conservatory coeds.

"We're playing hooky," Yoni told her. "Care to join us?"

"That's okay, I'll see you tonight. I'm going to get a sandwich." Nicholas was impressed, somehow. As the girl turned to go, Yoni gave a lingering wave—and Nicholas saw that his hand seemed to be missing part of a finger. Something was wrong with the thumb, too.

"Be good," Yoni called, and plunged his deformed hand back into its pocket.

For some reason Nicholas immediately felt ashamed of his own hands, and shoved them into his own pockets. "She's very young," he said of the girl, not in judgment so much as observation.

Yoni seemed to understand this. He paused to formulate. "After their teens they just don't look as good."

Nicholas laughed out loud. "I beg to differ." He envisioned Hazel's shape, the elegant curve of her hip, the dip and rise of her breasts, her smooth buttocks, and the way her stomach had rounded ever so slightly after giving birth to Jessie. She was his Grace Kelly, his Catherine Deneuve. She was lovely, lovely—Nicholas's love for her was inextricable from her loveliness, her golden skin and lively smile and the thick-as-honey hair she wore in a bandeau. She nearly sparkled, as American as they come. When he met her in London in the student housing office, he literally tripped over his feet when he saw her; he caught himself by grabbing onto a chair, which knocked against a table so loudly, Hazel and the woman behind the counter turned to see what the commotion was. Hazel's eyes had laughed at him, though she seemed accustomed to this sort of spectacle, a man falling over himself because of her. Nicholas felt a flash: I want. I want that. That brightness, that laughter. Even now, Nicholas sometimes had to look to Jessie—whose looks were a precise mix of Hazel's perfectly shaped features with Nicholas's coloring—to fully understand that he and Hazel belonged to each other.

"Are you married?" Yoni was asking.

"Yes, but she can't join me here yet. Her father had a heart attack, and now there's some additional trouble with his lungs. So she's gone to North Carolina to help her mother. Our daughter's down there, too."

"I'm sorry to hear that. Though her parents must be grateful to have her there. The longer I'm apart from mine, the more I realize how much they mean to me."

Nicholas nodded, though it was nothing he himself felt. His mother had died in an accident before he was a year old, before he had any memory of her. In the last existing family photograph, she was a frail-looking woman with dark circles under her eyes, sitting next to her young daughter and holding the newborn Nicholas in her arms; her husband stood over them all, looking worried. After her death, Nicholas's father—already something of a misanthrope (or so Nicholas had been told)—had become even more withdrawn. Even now, living on a sparsely inhabited Scottish isle, the man had little to say to his two offspring. A series of aunts and great-aunts had taken care of Nicholas and Glenda until they were sent to boarding school, first in Edinburgh and then in London.

Nicholas mentioned none of this to Yoni. Whenever he did divulge some slice of his past, people reacted with pity—even after Nicholas explained that none of it had been a trial. It was simply the beginning of what had continued to be a peripatetic existence: so many places to explore, new people to discover. But according to Glenda (a social worker employed by the British military as a trauma therapist, who could supply a psychological explanation for basically anything), both she and Nicholas, denied the unwavering love of a true family, relied on their talents and charm rather than connecting genuinely with others. Deep down, she insisted, Nicholas harbored profound pain and fear of intimacy. It was the sort of thing she had to believe, since it kept people like her in business.

To Yoni, Nicholas said simply, "Well, yes, it can be difficult to be apart."

Yoni sighed, and together they continued on their way.

HER TINY TRIUMPH CAME THE FOLLOWING SUNDAY, WHEN LYNN WAS absent from rehearsal. It was snowing—one of those demoralizing

March snowfalls, big wet flakes that splattered as soon as they hit the ground—and as Remy made her way to the concert hall, stubbornly without a hat or scarf, the dusky streets glimmered, and even the complaints of car horns became a sort of music. When she took her seat in the first violin section, her hair and even her eyelashes were wet.

All day she had been humming melodies from the repertoire, envisioning the subtle alterations of expression that occurred in Mr. Elko's face. She liked the way the muscles in his jaw flexed, and the slight squint of his eyes when a passage wasn't quite there yet. A single eyebrow raised just so meant "and now the piccolo calls out ever so faintly," while a downward tilt of his head, brow frowning beneath his sweep of dark hair, meant "here comes the rustle of the cellos, underfoot, menacing." After he had been conducting for a quarter hour or so he would remove the tweed jacket and, after a few more minutes, roll up the sleeves of his button-down shirt. The way the muscles of his forearms seemed to pull him right up into the air made it seem all kinds of wonderful things were possible.

Like Oscar Wilde said: *Success is a science; if you have the conditions, you get the result.*

The stage lights warmed her, drying her curls. When it became clear that Lynn would not be coming to rehearsal, Remy fastened her hair into a thick ponytail and moved over to first chair. How good that simple movement felt, the easy taking of something she had wanted so badly.

Now it was Remy Mr. Elko nodded to, and she felt more alert, somehow—felt the spark of comprehending his sign language, his hands articulating his thoughts about the music. For *Scheherazade*, she played Lynn's solos as though they had been hers all along, experimenting with dynamics and rubato yet remaining attentive to the orchestra, to the way Mr. Elko coerced this united sound, sweeping them all together under the arc of his arm. The sensation of the other instruments converging around her was rapturous—the merging of so many voices into something greater than themselves.

"Excellent job tonight," Mr. Elko said afterward. Remy was loosening her bow as slowly as possible, waiting for him to say just that. "Truly beautiful. Thank you for filling in."

"My pleasure," Remy told him, surprised at how suavely she said it, as if she were used to filling in, as if she were used to compliments.

Mr. Elko nodded with approval. Remy placed her bow back into its slot, then reached up to free her ponytail from the hair elastic. Released, her curls seemed to her no longer unruly but proudly untamed, in a natural, perhaps even beautiful way.

Mr. Elko's eyes seemed to rest on her for a beat longer than necessary, and when he looked away Remy understood that he had finally, truly, seen her.

Chapter 2

*H*E BEGAN COUNTING DOWN THE DAYS UNTIL HAZEL AND JESSIE would arrive.

Two nights before they were to fly in, he joined Yoni at a jazz club. Groups of friends sat around the horseshoe-shaped bar and at little tables off to the side, smoking and ordering drinks and nodding reverently at the performer—a blues singer who looked to be about eighty years old. Yoni and Nicholas sat at a table in the corner.

The singer had begun the second set when Samantha showed up, and with her another girl. She always had a sidekick of sorts, probably a remnant of some initial pretense (just a couple of students hanging out with a favorite teacher . . .). There had been a different friend last week, when Nicholas joined Yoni at a café in Cambridge. It took Nicholas a moment to realize that tonight's girl was one he knew. She looked different, her long brown curls hanging freely; in orchestra she had pulled them into a ponytail, a curly burst atop her head.

"This is Remy," Yoni said when there was a moment of relative quiet.

"Yes, right, we've met." Nicholas was pleased to have remembered. Remy, what kind of a name was that? Americans gave their children all manner of names. And yet "Remy" did seem to suit her. He told her, "Thank you again for filling in the other day."

Remy's eyes lit up as she said something in return—but the blues singer launched into another song, and Nicholas couldn't hear her. He immersed himself in the music instead while Samantha leaned back in her chair, slung a leg over Yoni's lap, and managed to look supremely bored, smoking a series of cigarettes while Yoni ran his hand lightly up and down her shin. It was the damaged hand, missing the tip of the thumb—no fingernail at all—and the top two knuckles of the first finger. The skin of the thumb was a darker color than the rest. Nicholas marveled that it hadn't affected Yoni's agility on the trumpet. Or perhaps it *had* affected him. Maybe that was what had prevented him from achieving greater renown.

Nicholas had finally asked him about it, at Club Passim the other night. "Army injury," Yoni had said, looking away. "Well, off duty, actually. Wish I could say it was an act of heroism. But it was just a stupid accident." He gave a little shrug, as if to downplay the episode—but Nicholas saw a flash of something else in his eyes. He decided not to probe.

The odd thing was, ever since then, whenever Nicholas allowed himself to glimpse the damaged hand, a wave of something awful passed over him. It seemed a reminder, almost a recollection. Nicholas would find himself looking at his own hands, surprised to discover them intact. Only since asking Yoni about it had he felt this way.

Yoni and Samantha were kissing again. These professor-student romances always struck Nicholas as cliché. At the Budapest conservatory where he had been composer-in-residence, it seemed half the instructors had flaunted a precocious student girlfriend. Tonight, though, something like envy swept through Nicholas—of Yoni and Samantha's closeness, their easy connection. There was something nearly mocking about it, though he wasn't sure what he meant. He didn't need a Samantha; he had Hazel.

And with Hazel, well, theirs wasn't this lazy sort of affection. There had been pure excitement, the shock of attraction. *Tripped over my own feet* . . . He still recalled the surprise of it, finding her there in the musty-smelling housing office, where she was negotiating a residence problem and Nicholas was posting an advertisement for a room in the house where he lived—a dilapidated Victorian that his landlady was always threatening to bequeath to him. In Hazel's case there had been some confusion with the paperwork, and the room she had been allotted was still occupied. The university had put her up in a bed-and-breakfast for two nights, but on that fateful third day of her semester abroad they were hoping to assign her more permanent quarters.

"Well, now, that's serendipitous," the housing woman had said, seeing the notice Nicholas asked to tack to the bulletin board.

Nicholas gave Hazel an apologetic look. "As much as I'd love for someone like you to grace our doorstep, I'm afraid you might find it . . . less than comfortable." Saying so, he missed the corkboard and stuck the tack into his finger. The notice dropped to the floor.

Hazel laughed. "Is it worth looking at, though?"

"Absolutely. It'll make the next room you see look like the Ritz." Though he knew that the place would never do for a bright, beaming girl like this, at least he would have the pleasure of accompanying her there.

On the way, he learned that she was an art history major, spending a term in London before finishing at her college in Virginia next spring. Nicholas told her about his own program, and the piano duet he was composing, and by the time they arrived at the house, had offered to take her to the Tate some afternoon.

His landlady, Mrs. Pitt, didn't realize that Hazel was with him. "I just got back myself," she called from her usual spot by the fireplace (which was never lit, since there was a problem with the flue). "Had my annual checkup, and do you know what the doctor said? Said I've the body of a forty-year-old!"

Then she noticed Hazel, and narrowed her eyes. "See you've brought company."

"She's looking for a room, actually."

"I don't take female tenants." It was a policy she had just then thought up.

"I'm afraid I didn't note that on the advertisement," Nicholas said to her.

"That's all right, dear. Don't you worry, I'm still leaving the house to you."

When he and Hazel were once again outside, and Nicholas was deciding to offer her lunch, Hazel said, "She's fond of you, isn't she?"

"Mrs. Pitt?" That she could suggest this about his landlady gave him hope for Hazel's own feelings. "I suppose it's because I help her out a bit."

"She didn't seem too happy to meet *me*."

"I suppose she's jealous," Nicholas ventured to say, "because you're so pretty."

Hazel gave a joking shrug. "But *she* has the body of a forty-year-old!"

She had been like that then, lighthearted, happy. She didn't need him, it was clear, just as she didn't need Mrs. Pitt's rented room. Instead she took a tiny single in one of the halls of residence, on a floor with twelve other women and only one bathroom. "It's amazing," she told Nicholas on their first real date, the following week, as they walked leisurely circles in the park. "I was sure it would be a problem, all of us wanting to shower at the same time. But the others barely shower, ever!"

She seemed to find everything about life there delightful. On their wandering walks she exclaimed at the quaintness of door knockers and the curling hinges that pinned back shutters. Even the university's stodginess, the white-haired men staring from oil portraits in the halls, charmed her. She loved the tidy parks and the polite coldness of people on the Tube, the considerate way they avoided one another's eyes. "I mean, where I'm from we always smile and say hello, but this is civilized, too, isn't it?"

She found the curving roads and crooked alleys sweet, the cars comically small, the sound of their claxons adorable. And she adored Nicholas, too. It happened quickly, the way the best things do. In January she flew back to Virginia to finish up at her own college, but as soon as she graduated she returned to Nicholas. In six months they

were married, and six months later began the long years of Hazel trying to become pregnant. But until then she had been content.

Well, Nicholas told himself, while the blues singer slowly shook
his head at some irreversible mistake, circumstances can't be helped.
It was hard on her, the constant moving, never knowing where they
would be next. At first she had focused on her sketches, filled notebook after notebook with drawings she planned to turn into an exhibit of sorts. But each time it seemed the project might come to
fruition, some small hurdle put a halt to things. Nicholas rarely dared
ask about it. Hazel was quiet about her plans, shy, even, when it came
to discussing her art and what she envisioned.

These thoughts wove in and out of the music. All the while Nicholas was aware of the girl, Remy, sitting there stubbornly in the corner
of his eye. He decided to go home.

But a voice came from behind him. "I *thought* that was you!"

It was a woman he knew, a conductor with whom he had studied
in Finland. He waited for her name to come to him while she said,
"You weren't at the festival last year. I looked for you." Anna, that was
her name. Nicholas asked if she lived in Boston.

"Oxford," she told him, looking disappointed at his not remembering. But how was he to keep track of such information? His ac-
quaintances ranged the globe, from his student days in London and
Helsinki to conferences and arts colonies and orchestras. He maintained friendships lightly, knowing that in relationships it was best
not to be needy. His sister had been that way back when they first
went off to boarding school—followed the other children around until they grew tired of her. Even as a small child, Nicholas had taken
note. He viewed friendships as akin to plants; they flourished most
healthily when not overly tended.

"I'm here just for tomorrow, then off to New York," Anna was
saying as Nicholas recalled something specific about her: She claimed
to be able to translate any tempo she heard into specific counts on a
metronome. "Perfect tempo," she called it, the way others had per-

fect pitch; Nicholas thought he might mention it now, to prove to her that he remembered her. "I'm giving a lecture at the Athenaeum tomorrow morning," she said, "if you're interested." She gave a nod to the scene surrounding them. "I was told I absolutely had to see this place."

"Here, have a seat," Samantha said, moving onto Yoni's lap so that Anna could pull the empty chair over and plunk herself down between Nicholas's seat and Remy's.

As the music started again, Anna made a confidential-looking face at Nicholas. Yoni and Samantha were lightly nuzzling, and Remy was watching the singer. Anna made the secretive face again, and then again, until Nicholas made his own quizzical face back—but she just made the same face as before, a tiny pout and a raised eyebrow, so that Nicholas was thoroughly perplexed.

All he wanted was to go home and lie between his wrinkled sheets. That way he could wake early and get straight to his new composition, the one about the seaside at Hopeman; he suspected it might not be a tone poem after all but, rather, one movement of a larger piece. "Well, thank you all for a lovely evening. It's time for me to go snore loudly."

Yoni said, "Early to bed, early to rise . . ."

"Nice seeing you," Samantha said indifferently. Remy told him, "Good night," but her eyes slid away from his. Anna said, "I should go now, too," and followed him up the stairs into the chilly night. "Will you be at the festival this summer?" she asked.

"They've invited me, but I'm not sure I'll go. My wife wants us to spend more time together once she gets here. Getting settled, you know. She'll be arriving the day after tomorrow."

Anna's face seemed to change briefly. "Well, maybe you'll come to my lecture tomorrow," she said. Nicholas said he would try to make it, then flagged down a cab for Anna before heading for the T.

He slept late the next morning and, rather than attend Anna's talk, got right to the Scottish piece. This wasn't a decision about Anna or her lecture. He simply had work to do.

ONE OF THE FIRST THINGS HAZEL DID HER VERY FIRST MORNING IN Boston was lay out the Persian carpet. Nicholas had left it propped in a corner, still rolled up and covered in dusty plastic. Who knew how long ago it had arrived. As soon as Nicholas headed off to the conservatory with Jessie—as eagerly as a student to show-and-tell—Hazel pushed aside the coffee table and lugged the carpet across the wooden floor, past the piano, and over to the sofa. Only as she stepped carefully past the antique mirror (still leaning against the wall, waiting to be hung) did she think again of the woman at the hospital.

She fought the thought away—ridiculous, really—and tugged the thick plastic from the carpet, watched the carpet roll slowly open like a yawn. The winding vines of orange, blue, and pink, the bold stamp of what looked like golden butterfly wings, the deep red flowers filling the border . . . Hazel found it comforting, something familiar and lovely in yet another new place. She patted down the edges and made sure it was straight.

Ah, there. The carpet really was beautiful. Her parents had given it to them as a wedding present, and laying it out turned anyplace into home, no matter where in the world they had landed. Yet each time she unfurled it, desperate for it to work its magic, the same thought crept up: there was something petty in her lugging the carpet from here to there, something wrong with such emotional investment in a mere object.

But that was why beautiful things mattered: their ability to alter the space around them—though to say it probably sounded shallow. Nicholas had no need for the carpet. He could spend weeks with nothing on the walls, claimed not to have noticed the apartment's scratched floorboards and dirty bathroom tiles. Even the mediocre piano (Nicholas said it sounded tinny but would do) didn't bother him. Well, it was just temporary, until they found something better. In the meantime, she wasn't even going to bring the cat here; she had left him at her parents' house, chasing birds from window to window.

For now, she concentrated on dusting, washing, getting things off to a good start. The crate with their photographs and pictures hadn't yet arrived, but she still managed to fix the place up, wiping down the windows, rearranging the furniture. It felt good to keep busy, keep her mind off things. Only when she went to hang the antique mirror did she again think of the woman at the hospital.

It was from stress, Hazel told herself. Yet it was hard not to wonder. It had happened right after she dropped Jessie off at the day care area, while Hazel's father was still up in the ICU. In the waiting area outside the playroom, on the other side of the glass partition, there was a woman sitting reading, her blond hair in a bandeau just like Hazel's. But then the woman put down her magazine—and it *was* Hazel. Same wide-set blue eyes and pink-lipsticked mouth. Looking right past Hazel, she gave a little wave to someone in the playroom, then stood and smoothed her skirt.

The sight had stopped Hazel in her tracks. But the woman just turned and headed down the corridor.

Only now did it occur to Hazel that the woman must have been waving at Jessie. The thought nearly took her breath away. Ought I to ask Jessie? But no, that would just be confusing. Anyway, sometimes people just look very alike. Just because someone looked identical and was even wearing the exact same skirt with a butterfly pattern on it didn't make her the exact same person. But she wasn't even really *there,* Hazel reminded herself—it was just some momentary mental glitch, from being overtired, from traveling with a small child, from worrying about her father (who was back home now, recovering just fine).

Yet she knew what people said about doppelgängers, what they might portend. Which was why she hadn't mentioned it to Nicholas. She didn't want to worry him. Anyway, it wasn't real—just some sort of mirage, from a tension headache, probably. No point in telling Nicholas.

By the time he returned with Jessie, Hazel had cleaned the refrigerator, wiped down the kitchen shelves, oiled the cabinet doors, and lined the drawers with contact paper. She looked up from where she was crouched over a stain in the linoleum to see Nicholas with Jessie asleep on his shoulder. He winked at her and went to put Jessie down in her bed. When he came back, he sniffed the air and said, "Smells like lemon."

"Orange," Hazel said. "Even the walls were grimy. I had to disinfect them. How was it?"

"Jessie was an angel." And then, "I invited some people from the department over tomorrow evening. I thought you'd like to meet them."

Hazel felt her lips pursing. "You did what?"

"Just a small gathering, nothing special." The way he said it, lightly but defensively, made it clear that he was fully aware of what he had done. After all, this was not the first time he had inflicted a roomful of guests on her at the very moment their home was in shambles and the fridge empty.

"Nicholas, you know I'm not prepared to entertain! Look at this place!" Hazel stood up and, instinctively, began to look for the feather duster.

"It doesn't have to be anything posh. We'll just buy some cheese and crackers and some drinks. Please don't get upset."

"How can you tell me not to get upset? I'm the one who has to get everything ready."

"That's not true. I'll do it."

"Oh, you will?" Hazel nearly laughed. "Do you have any idea what needs to be done? Have our dishes even arrived yet?"

"We can buy paper ones."

"Paper ones!" Hazel felt a familiar tension climbing the back of her neck. She tore open another cardboard box and found it full of cooking utensils. How like Nicholas to have left it sitting here for weeks.

"Just cocktails," he said now. "So my new friends can meet you."

Annoyed as she was, Hazel felt that old warmth rise inside her, knowing that Nicholas wanted to show her off. But then she recalled that her one box of clothing she had sent by ship, to save on the cost; it wouldn't arrive for another two weeks. Anything elegant—her silk dress and sling-backs and the skinny chain belt—was either down at her parents' place or crushed in a trunk somewhere on the Atlantic. She had packed for Boston too practically, no heels or blouses or festive skirts. Even Jessie's toys hadn't yet arrived. Her head throbbed with the thought.

"Really," Nicholas said, "you won't have to do a thing."

"Ha!" Hazel began plucking implements out of the cardboard box. In moments like this, it was clear Nicholas didn't understand a thing—about her, about life. She would have to work very hard to make the apartment presentable by tomorrow night. Why, she wasn't even sure that the kitchen was in full working order. Yet already in the back of her mind she had begun planning a light menu: Wheat Thins and good French cheese, some carrots and celery with home-made dip. A tomato and mozzarella salad. Mixed nuts with the big silver nutcracker—oh, good, here was the nutcracker, at the bottom of the box. There was so much to do.

REMY WAS STILL IN HER FIRST YEAR OF VIOLIN LESSONS WHEN MRS. Sylvester called on her parents, explaining that they should invest in private lessons and music camp and eventually a better instrument, since their little girl had talent, and talent was not to be ignored.

Her parents regarded her with an astonished pride, as if they had won some lottery they hadn't even put in for. "Have you practiced enough?" they began asking daily, though already Remy had calloused fingertips and a purplish streak where the violin rubbed her neck. That summer she attended orchestra camp, her first time apart from her parents for more than a few days. She was one of the youngest; the older violinists already knew how to play vibrato and didn't have to reach up on tiptoe to feed coins into the pay phone to call home. At camp's end, everyone was given a record cut with the orchestra's final performance, the Khachaturian on one side, Mozart on the other, and at home Remy listened to it over and over, amazed that sounds she had created had been captured in the grooves of black vinyl.

By then a private teacher had been hired, a tiny Estonian woman named Mrs. Lepik, whose violin captivated Remy. Its scroll, unlike Remy's simple swirl of brown wood, had been carved into a small head; looking up over the neck beyond the peg box was the chiseled face of a man with a short-brimmed hat and curly beard. Remy wondered what it would feel like to be Mrs. Lepik and always have that little man behind her hand peering at her.

"I'm glad you not a whizzy kid," Mrs. Lepik announced at Remy's first lesson. "This way you grow up normal, much better."

Remy would have preferred to be a prodigy, actually, to more easily fulfill Mrs. Lepik's demands. She was to commit all pieces to memory and play not just straight scales but their relative minors. Her sheet music was ordered from a shop in New York, since only specific editions by specific publishers would do. Mrs. Lepik was exacting and could spend weeks on a chosen topic. Much of Remy's first lesson was devoted to proper posture: feet firm on the floor, no unnecessary movement. "No, too stiff! Bend a little the knees. Not so much! No sway, just little bouncy in the knee."

The following weeks were spent on using the full length of the bow. "Bow is as important as left hand! Maybe *more* important! Fingers create pitch, but bow allows you to *sing*." On her violin with the old man watching, Mrs. Lepik demonstrated perfect control even at the very bottom of a stroke. Even when she played very slowly, the bow didn't slide or angle or tremble at all. "We must create illusion, one long line that never end!" Yet as soon as Remy had mastered this long, smooth, never-ending bow stroke, Mrs. Lepik switched to staccato, and Remy had to play her scales and arpeggios with staccato bowing, to learn a down-bow staccato as controlled as her up-bow. . . .

Her life was practice, lessons, and rehearsals, seasons marked by recitals as much as holidays. Her memories were pinned to specific pieces—the winter of Waxman's "Carmen Fantasy," the spring of the Haydn quartet. School was simply the place from which she dashed every afternoon to her parents' van, which delivered her, with two other students, to the town where the All-State Orchestra rehearsals took place. By high school she was making a small salary playing in pit orchestras for musicals nearby. And so a split occurred, the sense that, while school just got in the way of things, her real life was elsewhere. All her energy was spent moving toward that other place. Her life was one of perpetual preparation.

"REPETITION NEED NOT BE *BORING*," JULIAN SAID TO REMY. HE HAD BEEN her teacher for the past four years and could say this sort of thing without hurting her feelings.

"You've got a lot of repeated phrases here"—he pointed to a section of the Bach partita she was preparing for her senior recital—"so you're going to have to find ways to keep them interesting. When things become too familiar, we lose interest."

"I made the repetitions softer," Remy said, "like it says in the score."

"Yes, but that, too, becomes predictable once you've done it a few times. How about making some of them louder?"

"They're marked *piano!*"

"It doesn't matter what the score says if it's not helping the music come to life."

Remy recalled Mr. Elko saying as much. She hung her head—at being someone who always followed instructions, always did what she was supposed to do.

I put all my genius into my life; I put only my talent into my works.

She, too, wanted to live brilliantly. Freely, decadently, like Oscar Wilde. Like Samantha, who always managed to have fun and though she wasn't even the most beautiful student here had somehow—through her confidence, her carriage, her long blond hair—convinced everyone that she was.

But decadence was impossible for a serious-minded musician. The long hours of practice were the very reason Remy excelled, why she might, with luck and more hard work, succeed. No, she was no Anne-Sophie Mutter—but one needn't be a celebrity to be a success.

Samantha, on the other hand, barely even practiced her viola anymore since deciding to go for a degree in music therapy. Though she was younger than Remy, she had already had an affair and an abortion and was moving to New York straight from graduation. How would it feel, Remy wondered, to be that carefree? What would that sort of letting go feel like?

"If you're uncomfortable changing the dynamics," Julian said, reaching for his pencil, "then let's change up the fingerings. That'll help alter the sound. Nice haircut, by the way."

"Oh—thanks." Remy reached up to where her curls ended. She had cut them short, impulsively, into a bob. She was tired of being (as she had been, so pointedly, at the jazz club with Samantha) the girl no one noticed, the one with no real haircut, no real style at all.

But the haircut hadn't made her feel any different. Peter, a clarinetist who lived on her hallway, said it made her look French—but he was probably just hoping Remy would make out with him again, as she had at a party last month. Just the other day he'd played Remy a tape of a late Beethoven quartet and then declared, "Now you've been deflowered." The comment had bothered her enough that she had nearly slept with him, just to set him straight. But she'd had her conservatory flings (brief ones were all she had the energy for) and didn't desire anything like that with Peter.

"Here, give this a try." Julian set his pencil down.

Remy sighed at the new fingerings. The piece wasn't just for her

senior recital; it was also for her audition for Conrad Lesser. He had
retired from touring and was offering a summer course for a few se-
lect students. Julian said it was an opportunity not to be missed. But
no one knew exactly what Lesser might be looking for. Besides the
Bach partita and a Brahms violin sonata, Julian had Remy preparing
two different études and scales in all keys—not just straight scales
but in thirds and sixes and tenths, and with every possible bowing
combination, exercises Remy hadn't practiced since her second-year
exams. Julian said Lesser might be a stickler for the basics.

"Was that a sigh I heard?"

Remy nodded wearily.

"No time to get antsy. You're almost there. You just need to keep
focused."

"Okay. I will."

I can resist everything but temptation.

Remy brought her bow to the strings and tried the new fingerings.

THE PARTY WAS A SMALL AFFAIR. AND YET AT FIRST HAZEL HAD
trouble keeping track of who was who. For one thing, Nicholas had
consistently referred to his department head as "Jack Sprat" so that
now, meeting him and his indeed plump wife, Hazel could not for
the life of her recall their actual names. And then there was the gray-
haired man named George or Frank; Hazel heard both and didn't
know which was correct.

"Nice apartment," George or Frank said, after Hazel had taken his
coat. She told him thank you, though she wasn't sure she wanted to
take any credit for the place. She had managed to neaten it up (washed
the floors, polished the table and chairs, put Jessie's few things out of
sight, in her room, where she was now asleep), but without Nicholas's
books or Hazel's framed pictures, and Jessie's set of toddler furniture not yet arrived, the place looked only partially inhabited. "The
conservatory found it for Nicholas. Since his appointment was so last-
minute."

Mrs. Sprat was fitting herself into a chair near her husband. "Yeah, so, it's all a big cover-up," one of the younger men was saying—the heavyset, sloppy-looking one with the cracker crumbs at the corner of his mouth. "Nobody's talking, though." He was leaning back in their one good armchair, going on about some local scandal involving a city councillor. He didn't work at the conservatory. His name was Gary, and he was a freelance journalist. A few weeks ago he had written a fawning article about Nicholas, with two misquotes that Nicholas maintained were much better than what he had actually said. This evening he had already managed to mention, as if in passing, having met President Reagan and Isabella Rossellini—but Hazel could tell that "met" might be an overstatement.

"Mollusks," the other young man, Yoni, declared. "Spineless, the lot of them." He was slim and dashing and had an Israeli accent. Two girls, both of them skinny and slim-hipped, sat on either side of him on the couch. Students from the conservatory—though Hazel detected a girlfriend-y air. Something about the way they reclined there, the alignment of their bodies with his: Could they *both* be his girlfriends? They looked absolutely comfortable, as though they sat on that couch all the time. Perhaps they *did* sit there all the time. Her pulse hastened with the thought. This wasn't at all what she had pictured for the party.

"But won't someone leak the truth?" Frank or George asked. He was pushing all of his tomatoes from the tomato-mozzarella salad over to the edge of his plate. Hazel's heart sank while Gary the newspaperman began talking about press leaks. "There's bound to be something about it in the *Herald*."

A debate began about responsible journalism while Hazel served a bit of the mozzarella salad to herself, to see what was wrong with the tomatoes. "Do you think any of it will come back to haunt City Hall?" Nicholas asked, beside her on the love seat.

"Nah." Gary took a dismissive gulp from his wine. "That's not the way it works." Nicholas often collected people like this, loud, boast-

ful ones from some field he didn't know enough about. He thought
Gary brilliant simply because he wrote for a newspaper. Hazel hadn't
dared point out that the article about Nicholas, overboard in its flattery, was full of lazy journalistic quirks. No, all the love and admira-
tion she had for Nicholas would never be enough; he needed to hear
it from some guy with a journalism degree.

"Your wife's a looker," she had overheard Gary tell Nicholas after
she had been introduced. And though it had pleased her to hear it, and
to hear Nicholas say, "I think so myself," she couldn't help recalling
the way Nicholas had been early in their courtship: so bowled over,
he could barely speak. Sometimes he had even fumbled his words,
not nervous so much as overwhelmed—with happiness, it seemed,
and a sense of his own luck. Back then, he had just begun to seriously pursue composing, and there was a sense of discovery about
him. Weekly concerts, church choruses, friends' debuts, Nicholas's
own premieres . . . All were a pleasure to Hazel, just as England
itself suited her—the museums and high streets, the Bergamot tea
and crumbling biscuits, the sound of church bells and the charming
accents around her. The very fact that people weekended in Spain,
in Paris, as casually as a Virginian might drive to the mountains . . .

Gary was still holding forth on political corruption in Boston.
Mr. Sprat said jokingly, "See what kind of a place you're moving to,
Hazel?"

"I should have been warned." The tomatoes tasted fine. Relieved,
Hazel put down her plate and smoothed her new skirt. In the end she
had gone shopping at Filene's, since she wanted to wear something
nice. She had even seen a canvas tote bag with the same print as the
skirt—but it wasn't anything she truly needed, so she hadn't allowed
herself to buy it.

Yoni, with an arm along the back of the sofa so that it was vaguely
around the blond girl, gave a broad, handsome grin. "No trouble discerning the Boston accent?"

"Only yours," Nicholas joked, while the blond girl lit a cigarette.

"No," Hazel ventured to say, "but I do find the people a bit . . . cold." There, she had admitted it.

What she meant was that everyone seemed to have a chip on their shoulder. Like the man in the Stop & Shop parking lot yesterday who had rolled down his window and yelled, "You're in my way!" when she was only trying to back into a space without hitting anything. But she didn't want to offend anyone, so she used the word "cold."

"It's true, though, isn't it?" Nicholas put in, as if it had only now occurred to him. "It's not how I usually think of Americans. No one looks you in the eye when you walk down the street. No one says hello."

It was more than that, actually. In her few days here, everyone she had come across—in the grocery, the bank, Filene's—seemed to be on the offensive. Even the birds at the feeder she had set up on the little balcony had this quality, the way they fought over the plastic perches and sparred midair, ugly brown city birds with none of the cuteness of goldfinches or the chickadees she'd hoped for. The guarded manner of people on the T, the surliness of the cashier at the liquor store. Something about this made Hazel think of . . . small, yappy dogs guarding unattractive houses. But probably things just looked this way because she was tired and hadn't yet found her footing.

Gary said, "This ain't California."

Hazel said, "No, it isn't." She didn't even feel like refilling the bird feeder. But you couldn't just cut them off like that. Once you started caring for something, it was cruel, simply cruel, to suddenly stop.

Now George or Frank was telling them about when he moved here fifteen years ago. Hazel couldn't help looking again at the little hill of tomatoes at the edge of his plate. Of course tomatoes were not yet in season, but she had made a point of finding the ripest ones possible.

At least everyone seemed to like the Triscuit recipe. And the dip in the bread bowl seemed a success. The cheese board was running low. Hazel stood, smoothed her skirt, and went to the kitchen to slice more Gouda. It was peaceful there—safer, somehow—and when Nicholas stepped in a moment later, Hazel was able to smile.

"Wonderful spread, Hazel. You're fantastic." He rested his palm on her back.

"Who are those girls?" she whispered.

"Girls?"

"Next to Yoni."

"Oh, right, a couple of favorite students." He said it lightly—too lightly, Hazel thought. "Gifted musicians. Samantha and . . . " His forehead wrinkled with recollection. "Remy, that's her name."

Hazel tried not to frown.

"She used to have longer hair," Nicholas said thoughtfully. "Sort of wild. Now it's shorter."

Hazel felt an inner flinch—at hearing the man she loved note the details of another woman's looks. "It's still a bit wild, isn't it?" she said, trying to keep her voice light. The girl had corkscrew curls that came just to her chin, and every once in a while would tug on one, as if to drag it to its original length. When she let go, the curl would spring back up. Perhaps it was a nervous gesture. It didn't detract from the fact that the girl was, Hazel had to admit, attractive, with rosy cheeks, big brown eyes, and a heart-shaped mouth—features Hazel thought of as youthful and that made her feel, suddenly and for no good reason, old.

"Here, let me get that," Nicholas said as Hazel lifted the tray of Gouda. Hazel handed him the tray and followed him back out to the living room.

Gary and Yoni were discussing Boston's new music scene, while the others looked on with what Hazel supposed was relief at not having to make conversation. The girl with the curly hair was the only one who bothered to join in, telling Gary first, and then Yoni, that both of them were wrong. "Just go into Newbury Comics and they'll let you know where the best new bands are playing. You just have to know where to find them."

Yoni looked at the girl with an almost prideful smile. "Who knew our little conservatory student was a little bit rock 'n' roll?"

"It's called being well rounded," the girl said, and pinched Yoni's arm in a way Hazel thought forward. Perhaps *she* was his girlfriend, and not the blonde?

Yoni gave the girl an avuncular pat on the head, and Hazel felt a new wave of confusion. His other arm just barely grazed the blond girl's shoulders. One of his hands, Hazel had noticed, was missing a finger and part of the thumb. The skin around the thumb seemed to have been patched on. She tried not to stare.

"What *is* the rock scene like here?" Nicholas asked. "I wonder how different it is from England."

Hazel raised her eyebrows; did he know anything about the rock scene in England?

"I can only tell you about Boston," the curly-haired girl said, Nicholas nodding along as she described the shows she had seen. Well, he was their host, after all. And he had always possessed a genuine curiosity about the world.

Hazel, too, had been like that. Each time she and Nicholas relocated, she made an effort to meet people and learn the local lore. Her sketchbooks had filled with images of church spires and bustling piazzas, and then, over time, with the very people around her, their expressions and gestures, the fleeting moments of connection. It seemed to her those small daily observations added up to something, and that she might even turn her work into a larger project. The idea had buoyed her, kept her focused no matter where or how often she and Nicholas moved.

That her love of all things European had in time—not long at all, really—become impatience (with the backward ways of Old World cities, their deteriorating buildings and finicky traditions, the inefficiency and chauvinism and general hassle of almost any daily transaction) was something she never would have expected. Things she had once thought curious or romantic became simply an inconvenience.

Following Nicholas from England to Finland, Italy to Hungary, Belgium to France (with stints in Texas and Vancouver in between), something else had changed; Nicholas's love for her was no longer enough to cut through her loneliness, through the palpability of being so far away. Not to mention the growing fear and frustration of suspecting she might never have a baby. And so Hazel became less enamored of her own life.

"You have to hear this woman sing," the curly-haired girl was saying now, about someone who apparently worked at a shoe store in Back Bay. "Even when she yells her voice is so . . . melancholic I guess is the word."

Hazel turned to refill Mr. Sprat's wineglass, relieved to not have to look at the curly girl. Instead she sat down next to George or Frank, who had moved up to the love seat.

"I remember the first time a piece of music made me cry," Nicholas said. "I was still a child, and my piano teacher had me playing Bach's two-part inventions. Perhaps you know the second one?" He hummed a little line in what sounded to Hazel like a minor key.

"Each hand creates its own melodic line," he explained, for Hazel's benefit, probably, "and there are of course stretches where one hand or the other carries the melody. In invention number two there's a recurring moment where, while one hand plays the main phrase, the other does the most basic little progression." He sang four notes of a rising scale, *Do re me fa,* followed by four notes of the next scale, *re me fa so,* and the next, *me fa so la.*

"My eyes welled up the moment I heard it. It was the simplicity of that rising scale. Plodding yet hopeful, the way it keeps reaching up."

"For me it was Bach, too," the curly-haired girl said, her eyes wide. "I mean, Bach was my lightbulb moment." Hazel could tell by her expression that she thought it meant something, when surely Bach-induced epiphanies were true for lots of musicians. Hazel was glad when Yoni, in his matter-of-fact way, said, "I think it has to do with going up four steps and then having to start again from three notes below where you've just arrived." He hummed *Do re me fa, re me fa so.* "Having to climb back up all over again."

"Like Sisyphus," Hazel said, glad to have something to contribute.

"Yes, that's it exactly," Nicholas said. "Having to try all over again after being knocked down. So basic and human. That must be why it made me cry."

Hazel found herself nodding. Basic, human . . . It was the way critics often spoke of Nicholas's compositions, praising the way that, unlike many of his contemporaries, he had moved from the cerebral and atonal back to pure melody, toward the satisfaction of linear structure and chord progressions that resolved themselves. Some even called his work "deceptively simple."

Now the girl and Nicholas were debating what made a performance "poetic," cutting each other off with interjections of "But is all poetry necessarily beautiful?" and "Just because it's true doesn't make it art." Hazel's pulse quickened, as if there were some sort of crime taking place in her apartment. *Her* apartment? She hadn't had any say in it. The living room curtains were atrocious.

This wasn't what she had pictured for the party. In her imagination there had been Nicholas with his arm around her, his new friends and colleagues asking what she had been up to without him. In her mind she had them laughing at her anecdotes, about Rascal up on Madame Duvalier's roof. . . . The vision had seemed so real. Which made this scene before her all the more disappointing.

The same thing had happened to another vision she used to have. One that had seized her repeatedly in her very first months with Nicholas, back when she was still a student: she and Nicholas walking hand in hand toward the door of a house, a beautiful house, and before them two children, a boy and a girl. The vision was blurry, like a dream, yet carried with it the certainty that this was *their* house, and *their* children.

But it hadn't turned out that way.

Now Yoni was calling someone Hazel didn't know a tortoise. The blond girl laughed and flicked her cigarette ashes into the ashtray—but no, it wasn't an ashtray at all. It was one of Jessie's art projects, the little ceramic imprint of her hand they had fired in a kiln. Jessie had insisted it be displayed right here on the table between the window and the couch. And now it had become an ashtray. Hazel felt her mouth opening, to object.

"Oh, sorry. Jeez. Ah, well." Gary was leaning over, blotting at the Persian carpet. He had spilled his glass of wine.

"Oh, don't worry," Hazel said quickly, her heart in her throat. "I'll mop it right up."

Nicholas made a motion as if to help her. "No, don't you worry," she told him. "I'll get it."

She hurried to the kitchen for some seltzer, though probably it wouldn't do any good. Mrs. Sprat had followed her there, her enormous cotton dress rustling around her. "First we'll just lift it off with some paper towels," she told Hazel calmly. "That way it won't rub into the fibers."

Together they hurried back to the living room. Mrs. Sprat administered the paper towels to the swilling, sullied flowers, her dress shifting around her like a great tide while Hazel poured seltzer onto a sponge. Gary, moving his feet out of the way, asked some question about conservatory hiring policy, and each one of the men had a different answer.

Hazel knelt on her new skirt and blotted at the carpet. The wine spread into the towel with uncanny speed, so dark and red it might have been blood. And then she felt them—tears, hot and ridiculous, about to come forth. That she was upset about a spill seemed all the more unpardonable.

"All right, hand me that sponge," Mrs. Sprat said while Hazel managed, as she always did, to blink the tears back.

Chapter 3

*E*ARLY ON THE SATURDAY MORNING OF THE SPRING CONCERT, A hall-mate said sleepily that there was someone on the telephone for her.

It was early May, buds finally opening on branches. Remy leaned against the wall outside of her room, the spiraled cord of the hall telephone stretched as far as it could go.

"Sorry to bother you this early," came Mr. Elko's voice, "but there's a possibility of what some might term an emergency."

It figured that innocent, orange-haired Lynn, still living at her parents' duplex in Somerville, would only now contract the quick, violent flu that had swept through the dorms two months earlier. Lynn had been up with it all night, Mr. Elko said; she wasn't certain she would be able to play this evening. "We'll just have to see how she feels tonight."

All morning Remy practiced *Scheherazade,* trying out different accents and bowings, finding ways to avoid crossing strings where she didn't want to break a phrase. She imagined herself saving the day— and how grateful Mr. Elko would be.

She was still embarrassed about the way things had gone at the cocktail party. Late in the evening, when she went to the kitchen for a glass of water, she had somehow ended up in a debate with Mr. Elko. For some reason (well, because she knew it might prolong their conversation) Remy had put forth the notion that brilliant ideas were always inherently original—which Mr. Elko immediately pointed out to be incorrect. He laid out a number of innovations composers had brought forth over the years, how each had borrowed from the others and made each successive musical development possible. And though this of course made sense, and was expressed with a certain exasperation ("Why, even in the past fifty years . . . you can draw an arrow from Schoenberg to Webern to Cage . . . !"), Remy felt compelled to stand her ground—until Mr. Elko's wife came in and asked what was taking so long with the lemon slices.

She was gorgeous, of course, the wife: calm and blond and floral scented. Remy had felt, all over again, unkempt, unruly. It didn't matter that she had cut her hair; it was still a curly mess.

Well, maybe tonight would be different. She would be the modest, self-effacing stand-in, as calm and composed as the stars in the sky.

But of course Lynn was there for the concert. Her parents delivered her right to the door, her mother pinning a corsage to Lynn's gown in a way that wouldn't interfere with her violin. Pale and thinner than ever, wearing enough makeup to hide the fact that she had been vomiting for twelve hours straight, Lynn gave a wan smile. In case she was still contagious, she stood apart from everyone until it came time to go onstage. She then played, Remy noted, as strongly as ever.

At intermission she disappeared into the bathroom, and Remy told herself it was still possible; Lynn might not have the strength to make it through *Scheherazade*. But she did, of course, summoning her stored talents, translating emotions into crafted sound, knowing when to stretch the music or speed it up, where to increase tension or release it, and just how long to hold a fermata. . . . The audience gave a standing ovation, and even Mr. Elko was amazed, Remy could see. When the soloists took their bows, the rest of the orchestra tapped their feet more loudly than usual, aware that they had witnessed a feat of human endurance. When they stepped offstage, Lynn said a tired, "Thanks, Remy," grinned that goofy silver grin, and went to find her parents in the hall.

Only about half of the orchestra converged in the lounge, where a somewhat dull party was taking place. As always, the concert had been scheduled too close to final exams; everyone was tired and anxious and had something better to do than sit around drinking wine that came from a box. Remy's friend Jennifer had already rushed off to telephone her boyfriend, who was in the army and lived on a military base somewhere. Samantha had sauntered off to a rendezvous with Yonatan Keitle. Peter suggested he and Remy head back to the dorm together, but Remy told him to go ahead without her. Having spent ten hours thinking she might be concertmistress for the night, she was as exhaustedly giddy as if it had actually happened, and quickly downed a glass of pink wine. It was too sweet, yet she drew another glassful from the little plastic lever, and then slouched on a sofa with a bassoonist who lived on her hallway.

When she looked up from her glass, Mr. Elko was approaching, holding a full plastic cup of wine. "Remy, I can't thank you enough. You put my mind at ease enormously."

"My pleasure," she told him, but it didn't sound as suave as last time.

The bassoonist was just leaving, and Mr. Elko took his place. The side of Remy's body next to his felt as if it were glowing. And then she was engulfed—by the urge to touch his skin, to lick his lips, to stroke the floppy dark hair of his head.

"This stuff drinkable, then?" Mr. Elko nodded at Remy's glass.

"It works for me. But I guess I don't know much about wine."

Mr. Elko took a gulp from his plastic cup. "Ghastly. We'll have to get rid of it. I say we drink it all."

She laughed. "Are you a big drinker?"

Mr. Elko considered. "I do like a good Scotch, as you may have witnessed at our party. And I suppose I'm all for getting pissed every now and again. Though this wine might stop me."

Remy said, "I can never get really good and drunk, even when I try."

Nicholas nodded, smiling. "You know, I've been thinking about what you said at the party. When we were discussing originality, where it comes from. I kept wondering what stopped you from seeing what I was saying—and you know what? I figured it out. You're a Romantic."

Remy felt her ears redden as Mr. Elko explained, "The very idea of independent genius is a Romantic one. You know, the brilliant but misunderstood loner. What artist *hasn't* felt that way at some point? So I see where you're coming from." He nodded. "I, too, am a Romantic at heart."

In his eyes Remy glimpsed the humble look she had noticed at moments in rehearsal, like in the Sibelius when the trumpets called out over the low, smooth undulations of the strings. "So that's something we have in common, actually," he said lightly, as if it were no great coincidence.

But Remy felt her heart brighten, said, "It's true I tend toward romanticism. Or maybe what I mean is I tend toward the emotional!" She laughed. At the other end of the lounge, someone had turned on a radio, and some students were mock-fighting over which station to listen to. Seeing them, Remy felt as if she were in some other room altogether.

"Strange," Mr. Elko said, watching them. "Hearing that music on the stereo makes me recall something." He shook his head, as if to dislodge the memory. "I couldn't have been more than five years old. It was my first piano recital. My sister was there, too. We sat through these insipid renditions of, oh, you know, Chopin and Haydn and Bartók, brilliant pieces played poorly. The hall was on George Street—this was in Edinburgh—and when the concert was over and we could finally leave, we opened the door and there was a gypsy band on the pavement."

He smiled. "You know how it feels to finally leave some stuffy place and step out into fresh air? The music they were playing came flying in the second we opened the door. Some lively gypsy song. There was more life there on the pavement than in the whole of our piano recital. My sister even started dancing."

Remy smiled, as if she had been there, too.

"I suppose it was the first time I really felt the difference a musician's interpretation makes. That it's the musician's job to bring a composition to life. Though at the time, of course, I simply wanted to play the accordion!"

Remy said, "That must be where your instinct to conduct comes from."

Mr. Elko's eyes widened. "You know, you may be right. I'd never considered that." He seemed surprised. "And what about you? What are your plans, now that you're graduating?"

"I'm getting ready to audition for a master class Conrad Lesser's teaching this summer."

"Ah, yes, I heard about that. Quite an opportunity. I'll keep my fingers crossed for you."

She told him that either way she would be here next year. She had gotten the tutorship she applied for, would be teaching in the school's outreach program and playing in the honors orchestra. In what she hoped was a nonchalant voice, she asked, "Will you be here next year, too?"

Mr. Elko paused. "I suppose that depends. On if the school wants to keep me, for one thing. But also if my wife wants to settle here. She's barely been here since we moved."

He explained that her father had been ill. "Every time he's in hospital, he catches some infection. Then he comes home and starts smoking again." Mr. Elko shook his head. "She had to go back to North Carolina just yesterday, in fact. Help her poor mum out for a bit."

Remy nodded slowly, thinking about the beautiful woman with the blue eyes and perfectly smooth hair. Even her perfume had smelled just right. Finding Remy and Mr. Elko in the kitchen together, she had barely glanced at Remy, as if she could not be bothered.

It hadn't occurred to Remy that there might be a wife, though she supposed she ought to have known. But she wasn't used to wondering about things like spouses; how was she to have guessed? Glancing at Mr. Elko's hands, she said, "You don't wear a ring."

Mr. Elko raised his eyebrows the way he did in the Mozart when it was time for the clarinet to sneak back in. "I didn't know that was a requirement."

"A wedding ring." Remy heard how demanding she sounded, when really she wasn't even sure she believed in wedding rings.

"We didn't have the money for that. Not back when we married. My father-in-law was shocked. Right away he went out and bought her one. Gold thing with diamonds and sapphires—I *think* they're sapphires. . . ." He made a face, as if wondering. "But back when she was your age she said she didn't need a ring. She said love shouldn't be about possession—"

Just hearing him recite another woman's phrasing made Remy feel sick. "You must miss her. You look sad."

"Oh, I always feel a bit gloomy after a final performance. A sort of postpartum depression."

"Me, too," Remy said. Of course he loved that smooth-haired woman; she was beautiful, and she was his wife. Remy looked down into what was left of her pink wine. "I guess that's the way it always is after a performance. For an hour or two we're all working so well together, we create this sublimely beautiful thing, and then suddenly it's over and we all go our separate ways."

Mr. Elko was looking at her appreciatively. "You know, you're exactly right. It's not postpartum. It's postcoital, this letdown." He laughed. "That's exactly what it is."

He didn't appear to think twice about having used the term "post-coital." Remy thought for a moment. "It *is* physical, isn't it? The whole thing. Not just the way my fingertips feel"—she showed him the tips of her left hand—"and not just the way my back sometimes hurts. It's the way I feel during the performance. Like in the Sibelius, when we're playing those swirls, and the trumpets sound like they're off in the distance? My hair stands on end, every time, and I feel like someone's just stripped my skin off—that sounds disgusting, I don't mean it that way."

What she meant was that in those moments she was acutely aware of being a living being in a mysterious world, and at the same time a mere particle in the world—a world that would continue on without her, long after her heels ceased to scuff the earth. But it was easier to just describe the physical sensation. "It makes me feel exposed, like all my nerve endings are reaching into the air. I feel that way every time."

Mr. Elko looked at her. "It makes me feel that way, too."

The side of her that was next to him felt as if it were on fire. Yet it didn't matter, because there was a woman—a beautiful woman with bright eyes and smooth hair—he already loved.

Remy said, "I should get going," hoping he would tell her to stay.

He took a sip of wine and made a comical face. "Oh, yes, avoid this pink liquid at all costs."

Remy stood and gave as much of a smile as she could. "Well, good night," she said, and went home.

"SHE SAID SHE DIDN'T NEED A RING. SHE SAID LOVE SHOULDN'T BE about possession—"

Heading home from the party, Nicholas heard himself saying the words, so stupidly. The cheap wine had left a cloying taste on his tongue, as if in retribution. Around him the air, too, was sweet, the flowering trees blooming hugely in the darkness. " . . . love shouldn't be about possession . . ." With each echo Nicholas heard the self-effacement, the falseness of that statement, understood what

Hazel had done, all those years ago, for his benefit. She had protected him, by pretending not to need or want an engagement ring. How had he not heard it before? He who had made a profession of listening.

Many times he had recalled sitting across from her that fateful night, stunned by her beauty, blurting out, impromptu, "Won't you marry me, Hazel? Won't you be my wife?" Even then he had heard the dissimulation in his phrasing, the way the words, "Won't you . . . ?" suggested doubt, when really he would have been shocked had she refused his proposal. And yet he had seen the slight disappointment flash across her face, watched her as she understood that this was it, this proposal of marriage that she had dreamed of, and that there was no little velvet box to peer into.

And so he had blubbered something about how he hadn't found a ring yet, how as soon as he scrounged together a bit of money he would buy one. That was when Hazel told him she didn't need a ring, wasn't even sure she quite believed in rings, since really they were about possession, and love shouldn't be about possession. . . .

He sighed as he turned down his street, past magnolia trees where preposterous blossoms hovered like plump birds. He had taken Hazel's word without even considering who she was, a woman who understood the tactile beauty of objects, who found imagery and symbols in any objet d'art, whether museum paintings, graffiti murals, or the patterns in their Persian carpet.

As he let himself into the darkened flat, he resolved to make it up to her. He flicked on the light and blinked at the bare walls. Of course Hazel had left her mark, had doused the bathroom and kitchen counters with a purifying layer of bleach, had detonated disinfectant and soaked the stove's coils in a tubful of suds—acts that to Nicholas had the aura of witchcraft. And indeed the apartment looked, felt, even smelled new, with Hazel's apothecary jars lining the bathroom sink and her shoes tucked neat as bunnies into compartments on the closet door. Now Nicholas looked into Jessie's room, saw her picture books on the little child's desk they had purchased for her. How he wished he could lean over right now and pick her up, fill the room with her hiccupping giggles.

Restless, he went to the piano, where he had been working out ideas for the Scottish piece.

It was the first time he had looked to material from his own life. Perhaps that was why, ever since beginning the project, he found himself remembering things. Scraps of memories—sounds, images. Not always a comfortable sensation, these shimmers of moments long past.

One happy discovery was that he still knew, by heart, much of the poetry he had memorized as a schoolboy—the Kipling and Yeats and Keats, and, later on, the Scottish poets he had discovered on his own.

> God gied man speech and speech created thocht,
> He gied man speech but to the Scots gied noght

It had been a delight to discover in university that he could transfer his love for sound and rhythm and meter to a whole other vocabulary—one that needed no words at all. He took a seat at the piano and thought back to the seaside village in Moray. Even now it was poets' phrasing he heard, "the rim of the sky hippopotamus-glum" and "the lacy edge of the swift sea" and "What bricole piled you here, stupendous cairn?"

And then came different words: "a stupid accident."

In his mind he saw the nubby finger and thumb. But it was his father's voice, an angry grumble . . . *A stupid accident*. Nicholas didn't fight the sensation that shimmied through him, some other truth lurking nearby, a shadow that when you turn around isn't there anymore. It wasn't the first time he had felt this shadow—yet he was relieved when the feeling evaporated. He waited to make sure the moment had passed, and told himself that memory was a tricky thing.

Then he closed his eyes, to try to find again the village, the beach, the cry of gulls. He continued working into the wee hours.

ALONE IN THE REHEARSAL ROOM, REMY LEANED CLOSER TO THE mirror, examining the swollen purple abscess that had emerged on the left side of her neck. It hurt to touch it. In the mirror she saw that it was close to rupturing. Though this wasn't the first time she had suffered a minor affliction from intense practice, this particular grievance was new.

"I hope you're keeping that clean," Julian said when he arrived.

"It's disgusting," Remy said, still peering into the glass.

"Stop touching it! Put a hot compress on it tonight. You can't afford an infection right now."

"Tell me about it." Both her senior recital and the audition with Conrad Lesser were only days away. Plus her parents would be here for graduation and to help her move. The boil on her neck seemed ominous.

As she played the Brahms for Julian, the music sounded limp, not artful at all, her rubato mechanical, her marcato too heavy, as if she were mimicking rather than playing. When she could no longer stand it, she simply stopped and looked to Julian desperately.

"You've practiced too much," he said matter-of-factly. "Well, not too much, but in the wrong way. It's become rote. That's what's happening."

Remy felt her panic rising. "What can I do?" She whispered, so as not to cry. "I need to play it next week. Should I just not play it until then?"

"Taking a day off won't hurt you. The work you've done will still be there inside of you." He thought for a moment. "Here. Let me see that." Julian took the score from the music stand and began going through it with a pencil, marking it here and there.

"What are you doing?" Remy asked, even more panicked.

"I'm changing some of the fingerings. To keep you on your toes."

"But I can't change the fingerings now! It's too late, I—"

"Why not just try it, Remy? I'm trying to make it less familiar to you."

"But you already changed the fingerings in the Bach. I worked hard to figure out the most comfortable fingerings—"

"And now you're *too* comfortable," Julian said.

"Maybe I'm just tired. Anyway, I'm just in rehearsal mode. When it comes time to actually—"

"Rehearsal mode! Remy, please. What have I told you for four years now?"

"That each time we play a piece is an event."

Julian nodded. "Even a rehearsal is a performance, Remy."

"I know that. I—"

"Don't ever let yourself slouch, just because there's no audience. The body remembers. The *music* remembers. Today I'm your audience—even this room is your audience. The rehearsal *is* the performance."

Remy felt suddenly exhausted. "Please don't change the fingerings." She began, silently, to cry.

It wasn't the first time she had cried, in frustration, in front of Julian. He wasn't one of those teachers who forbade any show of mental weakness. Even now he just reached out and put his palm behind her head, gave her curls a brief rub. "I still remember the first time you played for us. You were this timid young thing with big brown doe-eyes. I could tell that it had been a challenge for you to get here, that you probably hadn't had an easy ride of it. And then you started playing." He nodded, smiling, and Remy found herself smiling, too.

"Remy, wherever you end up—even at your audition next week, any time you have doubts about yourself, I want you to remember something. The music is in there." He tapped Remy's upper chest. "You've got soul, Remy. No technique can give a person that. No amount of practicing. A person either has emotional depth or doesn't. You have it. That's what makes your playing worth listening to."

Remy nodded, and wiped her eyes with the back of her hand.

"Don't give up on yourself, Remy. You've made a commitment—to your talent. Don't let anything get in the way of that commitment."

"Okay." Remy took up her bow and lifted her violin, wincing when her chin rest pressed the boil on her neck. Just beyond her left hand she almost saw, for the briefest moment, the face of the little bearded man with the hat watching her.

Chapter 4

*H*AZEL STRAINED TO LISTEN TO THE ANNOUNCEMENT, BUT IT was for another flight. Hers had been rerouted. Now she and Jessie were stuck in New York rather than back in Boston, where they ought to have arrived by now.

A family of silk-laden East Indians ferried a mountain of matching luggage past her while a cluster of brightly draped African women, their nearly bursting valises held shut by belts strapped around them, made chattering negotiations with a skycap. Hazel envied the grand togetherness of these families, so many sisters, cousins, brothers. Hazel had no siblings; there had been a baby brother before her, but he had died of crib death. And though she had friends from high school and college, that wasn't the same as family—and so much moving around since then had caused her to lose touch with most of them.

She looked back at Jessie, asleep in the collapsible stroller, and tried, as she did every so often, to sketch her. Already she had sketched various other people from the waiting area: two teens sitting cross-legged on the floor playing cards, and a man reading a newspaper, and the woman behind him whose small bag contained a furry white dog. With quick little strokes, Hazel drew the pattern of Jessie's green jumper dress. She had explained to her why it was necessary to make a good impression when you traveled—which was why Hazel was wearing her favorite tunic dress and had fastened little plastic bow-shaped barrettes at the ends of Jessie's pigtails.

But the sketch didn't look right. Truth was, she felt herself growing tired of her drawings. She wasn't sure why. Until recently, she had felt an almost obsessive duty to try to capture all she saw—had considered it a vocation, in fact, collecting these glimpses and fragments of daily life. A few years ago she had even come up with an idea for a project, a new sort of cartoon, not the usual comic strip but a more realistic expression of the world around her, its small quotidian moments. But basic questions such as how to exhibit or publish such drawings proved too daunting, and she hadn't the gumption to seek out a mentor who might help her (or to even admit to others just what it was she spent her energies on).

More than once in recent years, packing for a move, she had at the last minute decided to leave behind entire sketchbooks, having convinced herself there was nothing of real worth inside. Nicholas, discovering this once—shortly after the move to France—had been horrified. But to Hazel those drawings had become juvenilia, nothing she was proud of anymore. It had felt freeing, actually, to discard them. And now . . . it seemed enough to have seen and noted, mentally, these things around her. What had once compelled her to uncap her pen had lessened.

"Attention, Pan Am Express passengers. Flight one-four-one to Baltimore is now boarding at Gate Nine."

She watched with envy as everyone at the next gate rustled to life. The man across from her, too, and the woman with the dog, went to join the rapidly forming line. A young woman dragging an overstuffed duffel followed them, tears running down her face. Airports were such receptacles for drama, Hazel thought to herself, watching the weeping girl join the others at the gate. Every one of these people had some story. There was a very old stooped man pulling a battered valise by its leather strap like a leashed dog. There was a young couple fussing over their baby in a way that didn't bode well for their marriage or for the other passengers. There was an extremely attractive woman in a stylish tunic dress—

Hazel's heart gave a hard thud.

It was she. Herself. She wore the same dress, had the same blond hair styled by a curling brush. Though Hazel saw just her profile, she knew, *knew*, it was her, and craned her neck to see more. The other Hazel continued toward the gate check, then turned her head for just the briefest moment. Yes, it was she, her own self—though prettier, somehow. Completely at ease, unburdened, no small child in tow. Smiling pleasantly—to herself, it seemed.

Hazel's limbs trembled. She looked to see if Jessie had noticed, but she was still asleep.

The line of passengers moved forward, and now the other Hazel handed her ticket to the attendant. Not a care in the world. And then she was gone, through the door that led to the airplane, strolling into some other life.

A cold feeling rose through Hazel, like a tub filling with chilly water.

She knew what such visions were supposed to mean. The thought came to her that perhaps her own flight was destined to crash.

Why not? Hazel had long maintained a niggling awareness of life's unnecessary calamities. Not just her infant brother in the crib. Nicholas's mother, too, had died in a fluke accident, her car struck at a railway crossing when a signal malfunctioned. These things happened.

And yet she did not really believe that any such disaster was about to occur. No, that was not what this strange chill felt like. The woman had strolled forward, head high, in a way that said she was done with this place, that this was the last anyone would see of *her*. Now that Hazel's pulse had begun to return to normal, the heaviness that overtook her was not of fear or dread but of abandonment. For already she knew she would not see that woman again.

At last the chilly feeling subsided. All that remained was an odd yearning sensation—of wanting to be with that other Hazel, to have followed her happily through that gate.

❦

THOUGH SHE HAD SEEN MANY PHOTOGRAPHS OF HIM OVER THE years, and watched him in live performance on two occasions, Remy was surprised to see how small Conrad Lesser was.

His assistant, an unsmiling gray-haired woman, ushered Remy in. Lesser was standing beside the piano and seemed no taller than Remy. He was in his seventies, bald and fair skinned, with a long thin nose and enormous ears. He wore a suit, no tie, and smiled only briefly when he shook Remy's hand. "Very good," he said briskly, as if relieved to be through with formalities. "Let's start with a scale. E-flat major. Scale, arpeggio, and chords, please."

Julian had been right.

Though her hands were clammy from nerves, Remy played as well as she could, and when she finished the last chord, glanced at Lesser's face to see what he thought. But his face showed no emotion at all.

"And now," he said, "what have you come prepared to play?"

"Brahms's Violin Sonata number three." Annoyed with how softly she was speaking, Remy raised her voice to say, "And Bach's Partita number two."

"Let's hear the Brahms. First movement. Lise will accompany you."

Remy handed the piano part to the gray-haired woman. Though she had relaxed a bit, her hands were still clammy as she brought her violin to her chin. She nodded to the pianist, and began.

"Stop," said Lesser.

Remy flinched.

"Your initial gesture. It's all wrong. This is an entrance, not an announcement. Try it again."

Remy lifted her bow, aware that her hand had begun to tremble. She nodded at the gray-haired woman and began again.

"No, no." Lesser waved his hand as at wafting smoke. "The sensation needs to be there *before* you play the first note. Establish the emotional connection *before* your bow touches the string, so that the emotion is already there. In the gesture *as well as* the sound. You're sending a message as much as connecting with the music."

Remy's teeth hurt from gritting them. How in the world was she supposed to establish the mood when Lesser kept interrupting her? She tried to calm herself and lifted her bow again. But now her hand was shaking so much, there was no way she could enter on a down-bow. She decided to use an up-bow and, as the top of her bow met the string, heard how tentative she sounded, as if ready to be stopped again. And of course Lesser stopped her.

Trying not to sound furious, Remy said, "I don't understand. It shouldn't matter how it *looks*. All that matters should be how it sounds."

"Ah, but the way you see yourself affects the quality of the sound. You must be in the mind-set already, hear the music in your inner ear. Can you hear it?"

Of course she couldn't. She only heard her heart beating horribly between her ears.

"You know what they say about stars in the sky," Lesser said, "that what we're seeing has already burned out by the time we see it? A star by the time we perceive it has already *been shining,* without our even being aware of it. Think of the melody as that star traveling along on a continuum, until it arrives in the first measures of your score. Only then does the listener finally hear it."

Remy tried to picture the melody as a line beginning far away, so faint that only she could hear it. Though aware of the seconds ticking by, this time she waited until she heard the melody clearly, felt it traveling toward her, and with her eyes still closed, listened to it. This time, when she lifted her bow, her hand was no longer shaking. She played the opening bars, and Conrad Lesser did not stop her.

She played the movement through to the end, emboldened, more confident with each passing bar. When she finished she knew she had done well. Awaiting Lesser's reaction, she could feel her own eagerness.

What he said was, "You don't know the piano part, do you?"

"Of course I do." Remy was both affronted and horrified. "This is the piece I played for my senior recital."

"Well, of course you've *heard* it," Lesser said. "Lise played it quite beautifully just now. I'm asking if you've tried to *play* it."

"But— I don't play piano. I mean, I've played a little, but I don't play *well*. . . ."

"You'll have to learn the piano part," Lesser said briskly. And then, just as perfunctorily: "You're playing egocentrically."

Remy felt her jaw drop. Never in her life had she been called egocentric.

"You need to understand what's happening on the other side of the music. Not just from your side. You're too self-focused. You've not paid sufficient attention to the other side, and it's coming through in your playing. You need to step outside of yourself."

Remy remembered Mr. Elko telling the orchestra about needing to understand the music from every angle. But the way he said it hadn't sounded judgmental. He hadn't called their playing egocentric.

"So, you'll have to go home and learn the piano part," Lesser said.

Despondently, Remy turned to replace her violin in its case.

"No, no—not now. I'm not finished with you." Lesser leaned back in his chair and crossed his arms over his chest. "You know what I'd like to hear you play? Something old. I mean, something you haven't played in a long while."

Remy just stared at him.

"Something you enjoyed playing," he said, "but haven't gotten back to in a long time."

The first thing that came to Remy's mind was the Paganini caprice she had played for her sophomore year exam. "But I won't remember how—I don't think—I mean, the fingering . . ."

"If it's something you loved playing, it should still live within you.

That's the wonderful thing about music. Don't worry about the fingering. Just find the piece still alive inside you."

Remy closed her eyes and tried to remember.

To her surprise, when she began to play, the music issued like a memory from her fingertips. And though a few times she found herself tripping over her fingers and having to make some awkward improvisations, the experience wasn't as terrifying as it might have been. When she reached the end of the piece, she felt oddly invigorated, as if she had just stepped off a roller coaster.

She looked to Lesser, to see if he was impressed.

But all he said was, "We'll conclude with some sight-reading."

Remy's heart dropped at how dismissively he spoke. It dropped again when she saw the sight-reading piece. E-flat minor—six flats! That dark congregation clustered together beside the clef. Remy felt a drop of sweat roll from her armpit down her side. She reminded herself what Julian had taught her, to find the spirit of the piece and not worry if she played some wrong notes, to show that she understood more than just the melody and tempo—to capture the overall style and mood. She read through the score, lifted her violin, and played as best she could.

When she had finished, Lesser said, "I don't like the sound of steel strings."

Remy swallowed hard, so as not to cry.

"And your shoulder pad is muffling the sound. You'll have to get rid of it. And replace all but your E string with lamb's gut."

Remy squinted at him. Was this just a recommendation? Or an order?

Lesser shuffled through a small stack of sheet music, found the pages he wanted, and held them out to her. "Have this ready for our first class. In tempo, and from memory. I'll see you next week." And with that, he dismissed her.

⚬⚬──⚬⚬

"WELL, NOW, WHO'S THIS?"

"This is my daughter, Jessie." Nicholas couldn't help sounding proud. "Jessie, this is my friend Yoni. Say hello."

Jessie affected not to have heard him.

"Won't you say hello to Yoni?"

She would not. She had noticed something on the floor—a trampled pen cap at the foot of Yoni's desk—and squatted to pick it up.

"Please put that in the bin, love. It would be awfully nice if you could say hello."

She looked up. "I had a Popsicle," she told Yoni in her little alien voice.

"I suspected as much," Yoni confided. "Telltale purple around your mouth." To Nicholas he said, "Popsicles for breakfast?"

"It's almost ten," Nicholas said. He knew he was too indulgent. But now that he had her back, he felt near horror at himself—for having let his daughter out of his sight all those weeks.

"I see how she looks like you," Yoni said. "Like Hazel, too. You must be delighted to have them back again."

Yes, he was delighted, thrilled to bits—though really he and Hazel had barely had a free moment together. Each day she headed off to this office or that school, finding swimming pools and day care centers, her agenda book filled with addresses and abbreviated directions; for herself she'd sniffed out a course at Harvard Extension. Her sketch pad, Nicholas noticed, had been abandoned, wedged between a bookend and the side of the wall. More than once it had seemed there was something she wanted to tell him, that she was about to say to him—but then, just when he was bracing himself for something worrisome, she hadn't said anything at all.

"Do you play a musical instrument, Jessie?"

"I go to Marching Band."

Nicholas explained that Hazel had found a music class in town. "Yesterday was Jessie's first time. I'm told she played the tambourine and the maracas brilliantly."

"With such esteemed parentage," Yoni said, "I'm sure she's a natural." He sounded sarcastic. Perhaps it had to do with the faculty newsletter announcing that Nicholas had won the Brillman-Stoughton Prize.

"I do my dancing," Jessie explained, going up on tiptoe, arms raised, to skip around the room. Nicholas laughed. The truth was, she had never shown much interest in music. Not that this bothered him. She would surely turn out to have her own talents.

"Maybe when you grow up you'll play in a band," Yoni told her. "Have you heard of Tubby the Tuba?"

Jessie shook her head.

"No!" Yoni opened his eyes wide. "We'll have to remedy that. Maybe *you'll* play the tuba."

"Just so long as *you're* not her teacher!" Nicholas said with a laugh.

"Well, now, why would you say that?" Yoni looked surprised.

"You're stern, Yoni. I hear you with the students." More than once Nicholas had witnessed Yoni berating someone in an exaggerated, nearly comic way. Apparently it was an act he was known for on campus. "It's a wonder they don't break down and cry."

"I sound stern," Yoni said now, "but I would never hurt anyone."

In fact, Nicholas had begun to view Yoni's droll imploring of students as an expression of his own frustration—not with the students but with his own professional disappointments. At the jazz club a few weeks ago, Yoni had mentioned, very briefly, that he'd not gotten the faculty grant he'd applied for (while Nicholas, without even requesting one, had been handed three thousand dollars in "summer development funds").

Or perhaps it had to do with something more painful, like his wounded hand. Though Nicholas had grown used to the deformed thumb and missing half-finger (no longer even saw them as strange, really), it still happened sometimes that he recalled Yoni's words, *a stupid accident*, and the eerie feeling would overcome him, almost like remorse—or perhaps it was just that he had been reminded of something, though he didn't quite know what.

This feeling, a deep piercing sadness, was strong enough that Nicholas had decided not to ignore it. Instead he was using it. For the sadness was somehow intrinsic, he had realized, to his new piece, the Scottish one. He had already sketched out other sections, and in the third movement things had darkened, a sense of something lurking underneath—a Loch Ness monster of sorts, Nicholas had come to think, something you may have seen or just imagined. To tease it out, he was trying to re-create the eerie feeling, the one he had become attuned to, this brief strong wash of darkness.

"It's just my manner," Yoni said now. As if hearing Nicholas's thoughts, he added, "You know, Nicholas, there's a reason we Israelis are called sabras." He hunched down a bit toward Jessie. "Do you know what that means, Jessie?"

She shook her head.

"Well, it comes from a kind of cactus—"

"I have a cactus! At Gran and Pop's."

Yoni stood up and said to the air, "The prickly pear cactus. It's not just the land we're from. My people, we're—" He looked back at Jessie and in a boisterous voice said, "Prickly. *I'm* prickly." He grinned, the lines reaching from his eyes to the tops of his cheeks.

"No, you're not!" Jessie squealed.

"Yes, I am!" Yoni said. "Rough on the outside, sweet on the inside." And then, in a wondering way, as if the thought had just occurred to him, he said to Nicholas, "The opposite of you, perhaps?"

"I wouldn't know," Nicholas said, taking umbrage at the suggestion. He had certainly never thought of himself that way.

"*I'm* prickly!" Jessie announced.

"Well, prickly," Nicholas said, "it's time we got a move on." Yoni's musing irked him. He picked up Jessie's bag of toys and slung it over his shoulder. "Thanks for letting us stop by." But he wished he hadn't, really.

❦⎯❦

"WHAT I WANT YOU TO LEARN," CONRAD LESSER SAID THAT FIRST day, leaning back in a wooden swivel chair so that his flaplike ears seemed even larger, "more than anything else that you learn in this class, is *how to love music.*"

Remy and the others nodded reverently. The class was small; besides Remy there was a pretty brunette named Barb; a Russian boy called Mischa; twin sisters named Penelope and Pauline; and a timid blond boy (the youngest in the class) who said his name so softly, no one caught it. Each of them had been assigned a new piece to learn by heart, and Remy could tell that each of them was terrified.

The blond boy was asked to go first. He had been assigned Korngold's Violin Concerto in D Major, and as he began to play, with a definite flair but also somehow too slick, Remy recalled some of the musical friends she had known who flew from continent to continent to compete in contests and had this same, overly polished air. Mrs. Lepik had forbidden Remy to follow that path; she said it was bad to always be in the spotlight, that competitions narrowed one's creative field, that by playing the same carefully perfected pieces over and over, one's playing became mannered. Remy supposed this was what had happened with the blond boy, who seemed to have modeled his playing on Jascha Heifetz; his bowing and slides, his very stance, were recognizable, almost a pose. Lesser told him to stop.

"It's very clear which recording you've been listening to," Lesser said. "A marvelous one. But what you're doing now is an imitation. A copy. If this were a math exam, you wouldn't copy, would you?"

The boy shook his head.

"Do you know why it's wrong to copy?" Lesser didn't wait for an answer. "Not just because it's unoriginal. It's that it's *insincere.*"

The boy said something too soft for anyone to understand.

"We must always, every one of us, play *from the heart*. In fact, please sit down. Let's hear from one of your colleagues." He motioned for Remy to stand.

She could feel her heart beating as she came forward. All week she had practiced Lalo's *Symphonie espangnole*, really too much to learn (and by memory!) in just a few days. Her neck hurt from playing without a shoulder pad, and her fingertips were sore from having to press hard on the new gut strings; though her E string was still steel and the G wrapped in aluminum, the other two were fully lamb's gut and heavier than what she was used to. But the pain was her reminder to do what Lesser had said: *step outside of herself,* think of the entire piece, not just her part, not just herself.

Determined that Lesser not stop her as he had at the audition, she focused on the "initial gesture"—and to her surprise he allowed her to continue. Remy liked the sound of the new gut strings, more intense than before. But as she came to the second page, Lesser waved his hand for her to stop. Stepping forward, he said, "Please let me see your instrument."

Remy carefully handed him her violin. Her parents had bought it for her when she was fifteen, a used Otto Erdesz of a soft tan color, the burnished maple of its back a light-and-dark feathered pattern; if you peered through the f-holes you could find the small white label, *Joannes Baptista Guadagnini,* in delicate, flowing script. Remy still treated it like a new gift, always wiping it carefully with her chamois cloth as Mrs. Lepik had taught her, making sure never to leave the faintest trace of rosin on it. She wondered if Conrad Lesser was going to criticize the brand of strings she had purchased.

But what he did, to her shock, was turn each of the pegs just the slightest bit, so that the instrument was out of tune.

Then he handed it back and asked her to begin from where he had stopped her.

"But it's not in tune—"

"Begin, please."

As Remy began to play, she quickly heard which strings were sharp and which were flat, and automatically began to correct for the differences, grateful for her responsive fingertips. As confusing as it was to have to accommodate this way, it was also oddly exhilarating to instinctively make the infinitesimal changes necessary to stay in tune. Before she knew it, she had arrived at the end of the movement.

The other students applauded, as did Conrad Lesser, and Remy had to smile.

"My dear," Lesser said, probably because he couldn't recall Remy's name, "may you never have to perform on an instrument as mistuned as that. But I hope you noted—that all of you noted"—he turned to the class—"the energy our young colleague generated just now. The electricity born of fright. Or rather, the electricity that results when we *overcome* fright."

Remy laughed nervously.

"Your goal for this summer," Lesser told her, "is a very basic one. I want you to play fearlessly. By that I mean with abandon. To move past your fear and free yourself—free up your playing. Do you follow? I want you, my dear, to feel limitless."

"Okay," Remy said meekly, and everyone laughed.

"Listen to that," Lesser told them. "We limit ourselves every day without even knowing it, simply by doing what we always do, falling into patterns, not pushing ourselves further. But every one of you has expressive reserves you've not yet discovered. Your dear colleague here has just discovered some of her own, by facing a mistuned violin. I want to help each of you find those reserves, so that you can tap them and go further, and give more, than you ever have before."

BY THE END OF THEIR FIRST LESSON, CONRAD LESSER HAD DETER-mined what each student's goal would be. Just as Remy was to learn to feel "limitless," the boy who played like Heifetz was to become "sincere." For the twins, who tended to play with a terse, tight vibrato, it was to "soften your touch." For the Russian boy it was to use more contrasting sounds in order to "expand your expressive vocabulary." Today's class had focused, so far, on Barb, the pretty girl who was also best in the class. With Barb, Conrad Lesser was focusing on the finest of fine-tuning, helping her work out fingering that better matched passages of the piano accompaniment, and that might bring out the ethnic and period qualities inherent in the music. Her goal for the summer was to become more "nuanced."

Yet even she looked worn out from the past half hour of Lesser's scrutiny. "Good, very good," he said, dismissing her. "It's difficult to sustain this level of effort, I know. That's why after you've worked hard and long at this level of intensity . . . then what must you do?" He did not wait for an answer. "You must *relax*."

He turned to address the class. "This goes for all of you. What we're doing here takes incredible concentration. Physical stamina and psychological strength. When we learn how to focus, we must also learn how to release."

"You mean like take a long bubble bath?" Barb asked.

"Take a bath if that helps. But I want you growing, increasing your skills and your strength. What each of you needs," he said, "is a hobby."

Remy grunted. A hobby! As if any one of them had the time.

"Preferably something aerobic or gymnastic," Lesser continued. "As I said, our work requires that we be fit physically as well as mentally. Do any of you exercise?"

Everyone sort of stared down at their feet, except for one of the twins, who said, "I like jogging."

"Jogging, excellent. How often do you do that?"

"Once a week at least. I want to do it more, but I don't always have time."

"For this class, you will go jogging three times a week. And what about you?" he asked her sister.

"I hate jogging."

"Even better. The two of you need some time apart. What sort of sport do you like to do?"

"None. I hate sports."

Conrad Lesser nodded, eyes squinting, big ears bobbing as he contemplated.

The Russian boy had raised his hand. He said, "I would like to roller-skate."

"Skating, excellent! You will tell Lise your shoe size and we will buy you a pair of skates." He nodded to his worried-looking assistant.

The Russian boy grinned. Remy was already dreading what athletic feats might be required of her.

"But back to Penelope." Lesser squinted again. "I can see that you have a quick metabolism like your sister. As part of your imperative to soften your touch, I suggest you do yoga."

Her sister giggled.

"There are books with accompanying videos," Lesser said. "Lise will find you one."

And so he doled out their new pastimes. By their next session, Barb was enrolled in an aerobics class, and the boy who played like Heifetz was learning tai chi. Mischa showed up in his new roller skates. Remy, to her horror, was handed a pair of swim goggles and told that she now had a membership at the YMCA.

"Swimming will help stretch you even more," Lesser said. "Remember, I want you to feel limitless. Sleek and floating and free."

SHE HAD NEVER WORKED SO HARD IN HER LIFE. EACH CLASS BROUGHT its own peculiar challenge, as well as some new hulking take-home assignment. When she played Vieuxtemps's Concerto no. 5, Lesser made her transpose it, on the spot, into a different key—and then had her play the violin part on the piano, to make sure she had memorized it by sound and structure, not just muscle memory. Next she studied the entire orchestral score, "to be not just a violinist, but a musician," Lesser said—and he had her hum the violin part while playing, on her violin, a figure from the accompaniment. It was all in the name of playing less "egocentrically," to hear how harmony allowed everything to fall into place. "Only that way," Lesser said, "can you comprehend the whole of the piece, of which you are just one component."

In brief moments she really did feel she was achieving a kind of omniscience. It reminded her of when a dorm friend had taught her how to juggle. At first it had seemed impossible, so many things at once, but then, miraculously, in what seemed a single moment, it had all come together. Sometimes she even thought she could feel her brain expanding.

"All right, time for some sight-reading," Lesser announced now, and Remy tensed. Who knew what he might throw at them.

"Let's start with a duet. Remy and Mischa."

Remy came forward to the music stand where Lesser had set down a score. Glancing through the pages, she saw that this was a suite of little dances: Allemande, Courante, Sarabande, Minuet, Gavotte, and Gigue.

Lise was there to turn pages for Mischa, who would be playing the second violin part, while Lesser stood next to Remy. Already Mischa's face was reddening; he always blushed when put on the spot. When Remy signaled that she was ready, they began to play.

It wasn't at all bad. Remy found she was enjoying herself even as she concentrated on learning the notes, and as she approached the final measure of the first page, and saw Lesser's hand reach out to turn it, was even able to relax a bit.

But Lesser did not turn the page.

"Turn, please!" Remy whispered as he held the page down with his finger—yet she continued, to her own surprise, to play. "Please turn!" she said again, with no notes before her, yet she was still playing her part, correctly it seemed, continuing the thematic precedent she must have already absorbed; the piece followed set patterns that she had already, she realized, internalized.

When Lesser at last turned the page, Remy searched hurriedly for the correct measure. Only when she found it did her pulse stop racing. But when, at the third page, she reached the bottom staves, and it was time to turn again, Lesser knocked the music off the stand.

Remy nearly stopped playing. She wanted to kick Lesser, to curse him—but she continued, to her surprise, to play. By now she understood the main themes well enough to briefly improvise. Meanwhile Lesser bent down slowly, picked up the sheet music, and returned it to the music stand.

For the rest of the piece, he did not meddle with the pages. When it was over, Remy glared at him, as the other students laughed and applauded with relief. Lesser gave a catlike smile and said, "Always be prepared for the unexpected."

Remy wished he had made this point using Mischa instead.

"Anything might happen while you perform," he told the class. "Your string might become loose, or the pianist makes a mistake, or"—he looked at Remy—"your music gets blown off by a breeze. Perhaps you forget, for a moment, what you've memorized. We never know, my friends, what life might toss at us."

He nodded, and his ears seemed momentarily larger. "Not only must you be able to continue, but you must not be afraid of such things." To Remy he said, "My dear, you are learning to play without fear."

And when she headed home from class, exhausted, Remy wondered if it might somehow be possible that she could begin to lead her life, too, fearlessly.

Chapter 5

BESIDES THE MASTER CLASS AND HER JOB AT THE LIBRARY, REMY had joined a quartet that made good money at weddings (an opportunity that came by chance, when the second violinist moved to Connecticut). They often played two or three events in a weekend, and so the summer seemed to pass even more quickly.

She was working up her physical stamina, from the swimming, and had begun to look forward to those sessions in the water, the one point during her day where she could let her body fully release. She took one lesson each week and on other days swam laps. At first she had done so just three days per week, as Lesser had suggested, but very quickly she had begun to crave those sessions in the pool, where she could switch her mind off and just glide through the water. Her body felt both stronger and lighter, as if it had been stretched. There was also the fact that, as Lesser must have known would happen, the regime of hard work, physical exertion, and mental relaxation seemed to have created the intended effect: Remy was improving.

Her nights off were generally quiet. One evening in July, as she lay on the couch flipping through her roommate Sandy's *Cosmo,* aware that the summer was already half over, Remy felt suddenly glum, that she was home alone (Sandy was attending a night course) perusing the thin, inconsequential pages of a magazine instead of doing something exciting.

The previous week's heat wave had broken, and there was a light, cool breeze. A perfect evening to be out with friends, at a dance club or just out somewhere. But it was the middle of the week and there were no parties to attend. Remy decided to go to one of the concerts at Jordan Hall, where programs took place every week during the summer session, all of them free. She might find someone she knew there.

It was cool out, and Remy found herself dressing with attention: her favorite jeans and T-shirt, and her denim jacket, which had finally begun to fray at the hem in the acceptable way. Her hair had grown longer again, so she held it back in a thick elastic; Sandy said that when she showed off her cheekbones she looked sexy. The ponytail made a thick bouquet behind her, and Remy pulled a few strands forward from her temples, to lead the eye to her cheeks. Fully assembled, she stepped out into the bright, cool evening and headed for Jordan Hall.

She took a seat close to the stage, then cast her gaze around the room, searching for someone she might know. And then she saw him, striding into the hall as if aware that something wonderful awaited him there. Without thinking, Remy stood from her seat and waved.

Mr. Elko beamed back and came to her aisle, as if they met here all the time. "Hello, Remy. Fancy that."

"Hello!" she said, unashamed of her delight. Just seeing him made her cheeks feel warm. And yet she wasn't nervous or uncomfortable. When Mr. Elko sat down next to her, the warmth of the space and the golden lighting and the rustle of the audience settling into the old wooden seats made her feel at ease. It struck her that she had overcome her schoolgirl crush, that she was no longer the young, crazed undergraduate she had been just months earlier.

Mr. Elko was chatting lightheartedly, asking Remy about her summer. Yes, he told her, he would still be teaching here in the autumn.

"Then your wife likes Boston after all?"

He nodded but said she'd had to fly down to North Carolina; her father was having health troubles again.

"I'll be here next year, too," Remy told him, reminding him about her tutorship.

Mr. Elko congratulated her. "If we're going to be colleagues, you should probably start calling me by my Christian name, hmm?" He said to call him Nicholas.

The lights dimmed and the soloist, a violist, stepped out onto the stage in a long dress. The first piece was Schumann's *Fairy Pictures,* warm and wise and nostalgic. Remy closed her eyes and listened so intently, she almost—just almost—forgot that Mr. Elko was beside her. Not Mr. Elko: Nicholas.

"Your same old tweed jacket!" she noted when the lights went up for intermission and the summer students, having put in their required appearance, escaped to more entertaining activities. "Don't you know it's July? You need to dress accordingly."

"This belonged to my grandfather," Mr. Elko—no, Nicholas—said with mock pride. "That's why it fits me so poorly. He was a stocky man. Probably not even a blood relation, actually. They say my grandmother had three admirers, and a child from every one of them."

They didn't stand up or walk around the way they usually would have, stretching their legs, yawning. Instead they sat side by side, and Remy told him about Conrad Lesser's master class. "He's been helping me play with a broader understanding of the music, just like you were trying in orchestra. To get us to see a piece from all sides. He says a great artist is someone whose interpretation of the world allows for new perspectives. And that there are endless possibilities, that our only limits are ourselves." She realized she was nearly breathless. "He says his greatest goal, for all of us, is for us to 'learn how to love music.'"

"A very worthy goal," Mr. Elko—Nicholas—said.

She told him about the new piece she was learning, César Franck's *Sonata for Violin and Piano,* that the more she worked on it, the more she felt herself falling in love—with a piece of music! She told him about the swimming, that she understood, now, the link between mind and body.

All the while she felt a warmth emanating from him. And though she still felt the urge to bite his cheek, his neck, something had changed. At first she thought she might be imagining it, but the feeling continued throughout the second half of the performance, so that Remy's heart began to pound, so certain she was that this warmth was real. Yes, she understood, finally, what was different. It was that her own warmth was being reciprocated.

When the concert was over and the lights had come up, Nicholas Elko asked, "How about a drink, then?"

They found a place on Mass. Ave. that was dark but not too crowded. Sitting across from each other at a small, sticky table, they drank Irish beer and talked about things that didn't matter.

When they were onto their second beers, Remy reached across the table and put her hand on Nicholas's. In Sandy's *Cosmo* she had read that it was seductive for a woman to place the palm of her hand on the back of a man's. (Placing the palm underneath his signified something else, though Remy couldn't remember what.)

Looking down gravely, Nicholas said, "You don't know what you're doing."

She said, "Yes, I do," even though she didn't, really.

The grave expression remained on his face a bit longer, but then he seemed to forget about it. "You have beautiful wrists," he said. "I find myself noticing them." His tone was one of observation more than flattery. It was the first time anyone had praised that particular part of her body. Remy felt both thrill and comfort, a strange combination she had never experienced before.

"I suppose it's time we went home," Nicholas said quietly when they had finished their beers and the hour was late.

The "we" made it sound like "home" was something they shared. Only as she stood from the table did Remy allow that that probably wasn't what he meant. But the thought of leaving without him was awful. How could they just say good night?

"I want to come with you." She meant to be assertive and was surprised by how mumbly her voice sounded.

Nicholas frowned. And then, decisively, he gave a small nod.

Only when they arrived at the apartment where she had been once before did Remy allow the fact of the smooth-haired wife to find its way into her thoughts. But the wife was far away, and Remy had spent so many years being good. *When we are happy we are always good, but when we are good we are not always happy.*

Here she was, so close to something she wanted so badly—as much, even, as she had wanted to be first chair. What would it feel like to refuse, this time, to step aside?

Nicholas was taking off his grandfather's tweed jacket. His clavicle was smooth and beautiful. She reached out and touched it.

THE NEXT MORNING SHE WOKE UP SMILING. IT WAS THE FIRST TIME in her life that she had woken up that way. She knew she must look ridiculous, lying there grinning, with her curls all around her head. Next to her, caught in the tempest of sheets, Nicholas was still asleep.

Remy rolled to her other side and took in the room that she had barely noticed the night before. The window was open slightly, admitting a breeze. With the slight movement of the window blind, sunshine swung in like a wand. Scanning the tall bureau and the Paul Klee print and the books and laundry in haphazard piles, Remy turned to the little bedside table and saw a photograph.

At first she thought she would wait until he woke up, but she found she couldn't contain herself. "Who's that?" She knew that if she spoke loudly enough he would wake. "Nicholas? Who is that?"

"Hmm, hello, love." He rolled over and kissed her neck and cheek and shoulder and one of her wrists. "Good morning to you."

"Nicholas, who's that little girl?"

Nicholas turned and, looking at the photograph, produced a smile that Remy understood to be one of infinite, inexhaustible love. "That's my daughter."

All around her, walls crumbled. "You didn't tell me you had a daughter."

Nicholas looked perplexed. "But surely you knew? I thought . . ." Then he seemed to understand that it was nothing she had realized. Remy was horrified at having failed to note such a crucial piece of information.

"I miss her," Nicholas said lightly, as if it were not a particularly unpleasant thing to miss someone. "But luckily she'll be back at the end of the month."

The way his voice dropped told Remy that "she" meant "they" and that this was what being a mistress entailed—being with someone only partly, not entirely, not wholly. Just enough to make a mess of a family.

She wanted all of Nicholas. She wanted everything and despite what she knew of life still liked to think she might get it. "I've got to go," she mumbled, trying to free herself from the muddle of sheets.

"Already!" Nicholas grabbed her and held her. "Is that it, then?"

Remy nodded, furious at him and at herself. Not just a wife, but a *family*.

"Don't go," Nicholas said. But he made no move to stop her.

She tried not to look at him as she plucked from the floor each item of clothing that with such care she had chosen the night before. Now she felt an almost sympathetic tenderness toward her roughly discarded jeans and her Live Aid T-shirt tossed carelessly in the corner, as if they were all that remained of the girl she had been—not this new careless one who had made a selfish mistake. She dressed silently, mournfully, and at the last minute let her eyes find Nicholas there in bed, the sheets in ripples around him. He looked as if he had seen a ghost.

HE WOULD FOLD HIMSELF BACK INTO HIS LIFE UNTIL EVERYTHING was as it had been before. After all, it was just one night, one brief lapse, he told himself as he washed and dressed and made his first decisions of the day: black coffee (since he had again forgotten to buy milk); toast with a swipe of margarine; and an egg cracked onto the one small skillet, gaping at him accusatorily until he finally swept it onto his plate.

Really, nothing earth-shattering had occurred—even if he did feel, oddly enough, quite altered. Terrible, actually. But he told himself everything would soon be back to normal.

He tried to focus on his work, on the progress he had made on the new composition. This seaside thing (as he had come to think of it) was indeed turning into a big orchestral piece, had grown to a full four movements. Though he had never written a symphony before, already in brief snatches he had glimpsed the arc of the work as a whole, the waves as they would reappear in each new incarnation, from the smallest ripples, like the wake of a cormorant, to great splashy conniptions, like the tide smashing against the rocks at Hopeman.

And yet in the days that followed he found he could not work. Nicholas blamed the apartment, this place where that girl had solemnly plucked her clothes from the floor as if the very wood might have contaminated them. Her presence in his bed . . . *thorough* was the word. She had bitten him, used her teeth on his shoulder, his biceps, his neck and earlobes, and had slept with her body draped over his. How natural it had seemed, so that he had forgotten, during the night, that what they were doing was unjust. The curls around her head were abundant. Nicholas had gently pulled the elastic from her ponytail, freeing her hair as if unleashing everything within her. With his forefinger he had traced the small red streak below her chin, where so many years of her violin had scarred her, and had kissed this perpetual scar, had tasted the sweet saltiness of her neck, before moving his head down to her chest, her small round breasts, her smooth flat stomach. Slowly he had done this, and slowly, in the days afterward, his mind repeated the motions, remembering how it had felt to place his hands on her breasts and bury his mouth between her thighs.

In his chest something bubbled gruffly, an unfamiliar sensation, he could not have said what, though it felt similar to fear. But what had happened that night was a slip, an aberration; Remy had confirmed this. Clearly it was nothing to look back on or be tempted by again.

He had always been faithful to Hazel. Probably he shouldn't even be surprised at what had happened. And she would be here soon enough. That was all Nicholas needed to snap out of this odd state. Yet in certain moments panic seized him, and he had to follow the entire thought process yet again, in order to convince himself all was well.

On the third afternoon he went to campus, where he might better concentrate. Reading through the printer's proof of his duet for flute and clarinet kept him busy for a bit. It was a pleasure to work like this, fast, without pressure, not allowing any other thoughts in. And yet there was that other feeling beneath it, like a rough current under still water . . . and Remy silently retrieving her clothes from the bedroom floor.

One could really speak one's mind, with a person like that. One could really *be,* fully—really fully be—with a person like that. This was how Nicholas phrased his thoughts, how he positioned himself each time she reemerged in his mind. "One feels something, somehow. One feels a connection. . . ."

"Ah, good, you're here!" It was Yoni, leaning into his doorway. "Please, do me a favor. Come box my ears."

"It can't be that bad." Nicholas laughed. Yoni was teaching a summer session for gifted high school students.

"They left their passion at home in their bedsheets! Their souls they forgot along with their nail clippers!" But then Yoni's tone brightened and he said, "I'm happy to say, though, that I've just taught my last lesson of the summer. And I demand that you come celebrate with me."

Nicholas was grateful for the distraction.

"There's something else I'm hoping you can do for me, actually." Yoni slipped into the office and took the chair across from Nicholas. "You know the Leoni festival next month."

It was the summer music festival Nicholas had attended a few times, a small yet prestigious one held every August in Tuscany. He told Yoni, "I've been there, yes."

"Right, of course you have." Yoni gave a fatigued look. "I had to cancel on them, unfortunately. But I happened to mention you, and they wondered if you might fill my spot."

"I already told them no for this year, actually," Nicholas said. "I've spent so much time apart from Hazel, and if all goes as planned, she'll have just gotten back that week." He felt guilty just saying her name.

"Right." Yoni nodded. "I just thought I'd ask."

"Well, perhaps I could go for just a few days."

"I'd go, too," Yoni said, "if this other thing hadn't come up." It was a memorial service back in Israel, he explained—and Nicholas was surprised to see him become visibly distressed. His uncle had died of a heart attack. Only fifty years old. "So, anyway, if you can cover for me . . ." His voice trailed off until he regained composure.

"Hazel would probably understand. Well, I'll see." Saying it aloud nearly convinced Nicholas that what he said was true. He wanted to help Yoni, felt quite bad for him, actually. Not only had he lost his uncle, but clearly he had been looking forward to the Italy trip; he didn't get as many invitations as Nicholas did.

For now Nicholas agreed to go with him to the jazz club. It was early yet, and the place hadn't quite filled up. The musician, a guitarist, was playing soft breezy pieces that wafted around the room. Directly in Nicholas's view an older man and woman, their arms linked, leaned on their little table together, swaying to the music. Nicholas recalled sitting in this same room with Remy at the corner of his eye, watching the blues singer.

He had managed, during the walk to the club with Yoni, not to think about her for entire stretches of time. But now, as he watched the couple with their arms linked, he allowed himself the thought that if he didn't see Remy again, he would perish. If he did not see her, did not see what became of her, what she was becoming, he wouldn't be able to continue living. He had no idea where this notion came from, but there it was; he would topple over and die. Then again, if he did see her again, he decided just as quickly, surely that, too, would be enough to kill him. No, he assured himself, these thoughts were ridiculous. He barely knew her.

He ordered a second gin and tonic. It occurred to him to ask Yoni where Samantha was.

"Oh, she moved to New York." Yoni took a slow swallow from his beer. "They all have to do that, you know. They graduate and go to New York." He gave a smile. "Actually, there's a very good music therapy program she'll be attending there."

Yoni didn't look as if he missed her at all. Well, Nicholas supposed, he must go through this sort of thing often enough.

"I've seen her friend," Nicholas ventured to say.

"Which friend is that?" Yoni asked. Then he laughed. "That Samantha. She always needed a sidekick, didn't she?" He swallowed more of his beer.

Nicholas found himself unable to say Remy's name. Instead he toyed with a few phrases that might allow for an impersonal discussion of the topic. But in the end he simply asked Yoni, "How do you do it?"

"Do what?"

"Negotiate your relationships." Nicholas swallowed the last of his drink. "It sounds like you have quite a bit of experience."

Yoni began laughing.

"What?" Nicholas asked.

Yoni, laughing, said, "*You're* asking me?"

"Well, yes, what's so funny?"

Yoni shook his head, still laughing. "I assumed your cluelessness was an act. Don't tell me it's true."

"I don't know what you mean."

"All the women trying to catch you, and the way you appear not to notice! I thought it was an act, that you were an old pro! Like that woman who came here that time. The conductor."

"Who? Oh—Anna?" Nicholas wondered what had given Yoni that idea. "Now, there's a funny one. Has what she calls 'perfect tempo.' I've never quite understood. . . ." As he prattled nervously, a lanky teen with spidery eyeliner, deep red lipstick, and buzz-cut hair approached their table. She gave Yoni a nip on his ear.

"You're here," Yoni said, returning her bite with his own. The girl wore tight black jeans and a thin white tank top, no bra, just the smallest upturned peaks for breasts. She introduced herself to Nicholas, and he told her hello. He decided it probably didn't matter whether or not he remembered her name.

CONRAD LESSER HAD THEM PLAY CHAMBER MUSIC THAT DAY.

He did this every so often, wanted the students to grow attuned to the demands of this more intimate form—an in-between form, as challenging as playing solo, yet requiring the listening skills and self-deprecation of group playing (without hiding among a large orchestra). "It helps develop a certain sensitivity that not all of you possess. Because it's about give-and-take, about listening to another person, really listening, without compromising your own virtuosity."

It was four days since her night with Nicholas. Remy lifted her violin listlessly. She and the twins and the boy who played like Heifetz had been given Telemann's Concerto for Four Violins. The first violin part went to the Heifetz boy, probably as a concession; he hated sharing the spotlight and had even said (out of earshot of Lesser) that only if he failed in a solo career would he ever deign to play in a group. Lesser seemed to sense this and, after handing them their parts, said, "One cannot remain self-involved when playing in a quartet. You must pay very close attention to each other. If you have a whole note, count out second notes, not just your own. Attend to one another!"

Though her heart still hung low from the fiasco with Nicholas, Remy found she was able to free her mind of its sorrow by listening to the others as the four of them played. Together they concentrated—on the notes and on one another. It was not the first time she had managed to cheer herself simply by playing her violin, yet it astounded her, all over again, that she could be so content and so heartbroken at the same time.

Was this what it meant to "know how to love music"? That this feeling might overtake her other emotions?

When class ended and everyone packed up to leave, Conrad Lesser pulled Remy aside. "You played extremely well today," he said. "It seems you have a real talent for small group work."

Remy told him about the quartet she had been playing with all summer, that she must have been training her ear all this time.

"Not just your ear. It's a mind-set, I think. You seem to excel when playing closely with others. It's something to consider, I think. For your future." The way Lesser said this, gently, caused Remy's heart to sink all over again. She understood what he was saying—what was being said between the lines.

She would never be a star violinist, that was what he meant.

Remy had known it already, probably, knew it each time she watched Barb play, had known it all year, sitting next to Lynn—aware, always, of being not quite as good, and that the difference between them was not a matter of dedication or effort but of some intangible quality that Remy simply did not possess. No, she would never be a virtuoso performer with a recognized name, with a manager to negotiate contracts with promoters, and a double case to carry two violins at once. There would be no audience in awe of her trills and double-stops, no reason to practice how to walk on and off the stage, or how to properly take a bow or accept a bouquet. There would be no recording career; she would not see her name on a record label nor be asked for her autograph. She would just be Remy—a girl who had learned how to love music.

"Some of the very finest musicians are chamber players," Lesser said, and gave her a conciliatory pat on the back before going to confer with his assistant.

Returning her violin to its case, Remy wanted simply to go to sleep and never wake up.

She left the building feeling such heaviness, she was sure she was moving more slowly than usual. Was that what this summer was about, then? Striving so hard toward that one goal—only to realize that it had never even been within her grasp?

Maybe it wasn't really so bad; maybe it was just that her mistake with Nicholas made everything feel worse. After all, Remy was still a violinist, an excellent one, with a fine future ahead of her. There were some very successful chamber groups. She could still make a name for herself.

Why, then, did she feel her life was over?

Because it wasn't enough.

Loving the violin, knowing how to love music. Remy understood what Conrad Lesser meant, but it wasn't enough.

The thought came to her, clearly, as she crossed Boylston Street. Her dedication to her violin meant she could love something complicated and demanding and extremely difficult, and that she could do so with enthusiasm and without resentment. It meant that she knew what devotion was, and commitment, and the sublime satisfaction of working hard at something until she had accomplished it. She knew how it felt to achieve what at times seemed like miracles; she had witnessed beauty that left her speechless. She had known amazement up close, knew the glorious things this world held for anyone who chose to stop and listen. But it wasn't enough.

Because music wasn't a person. Her violin was not a living thing. Her talent was not a human being. She wanted to love someone, to love another—and for that other person to love her, to love Remy, back.

This was the thought in Remy's mind when she saw, walking toward her, Nicholas.

She wanted to shout and hold him and slap him all at once, to kick him and bite his neck. That this feeling was love she had no doubt.

"Remy!" he said when he noticed her there. "Hello!"

So, already he had forgotten that she was angry with him, that they had done something contemptible together. She stood silently, unable to speak, as the expression on his face changed to a look of worry. "Remy," he said again, this time in a low tone.

Remy reached out and took his hand. For a moment they simply stood, quietly. Then Remy said, "Come with me."

With Nicholas at her side, she continued toward her apartment, turning the corner and walking the two blocks to her street. Nicholas followed along as she climbed the narrow back stairs of her building, as she slipped her keys into the heavy lock, unclicked the pin, and felt the bolt snap open.

"I've been thinking about you," Nicholas said in a quiet voice, and followed her into the apartment.

Recalling the photograph in his bedroom, Remy felt again how utterly wrong something could be. She began to cry.

"Oh." Nicholas seemed unprepared for this. "Remy, love." He reached his arms around her, but she threw them off. "Okay," he said, "all right," and backed up a step. "Look, I . . . I'll just . . ." Clearly he didn't know what to do. He looked around the room in a worried way, and his gaze landed on Sandy's record collection. He said, "I'll put on some music."

He went to where Sandy's albums were packed tightly in a long low row against the living room wall, and bent down to read the spines. Remy wiped her eyes. For the briefest moment, as Nicholas hunched down to look through the records, she saw Nicholas as an old man, stooping.

Just as quickly the glimpse disappeared. And though there was nothing romantic in what she had seen—Nicholas old and hunched— Remy felt, eerily, powerfully, that she had glimpsed the future. *Their* future.

That was all it took. As Nicholas selected an album, tugging it out from the shelf, Remy removed her clothes, right there in the living room. Quietly she wriggled out of her T-shirt and satin bra while Nicholas carefully slid the record from its cover and placed it on the turntable. As the stereo released the opening strains of an electronic keyboard, Remy kicked off her brown leather sandals, her cotton shorts and underpants, and stood naked. It was not the pose of a seductress; she did not feel alluring. She felt sad and proud, declaring that this was all there was, the bare truth of her.

"Oh, love," Nicholas said when he turned to see her. He came close and leaned in—carefully, as if to breathe the scent of a rosebush. The first thing he kissed was her wrist, one and then the other.

Chapter 6

"THIS SATURDAY'S LECTURE BY VISITING CONDUCTOR NICHOLAS Elko has been canceled due to a death in the family. Our thoughts are with him in this time of sadness."

Nicholas dropped his travel bag, felt his skin grow cold. The flyers were posted all around the little train station, and though they were written in Italian, he didn't need his years of study in order to translate; his love of opera meant he was used to words like "death" and "sadness" being hurled back and forth. His heart began a frenzied pounding. Who had died, and why hadn't he been informed?

A wreath of sweat broke from his scalp. Jessie, in an accident at day camp? Hazel, run over by a Boston driver? Awful possibilities raced before him: his sister at her military outpost, attacked by a traumatized patient . . . His demented father lost in the Paps of Jura . . . Now he was fully sweating. He ran to the ticket window, where a man with a curling mustache smoked a cigarette as if the world were the same place it had always been. That's me, Nicholas explained, his voice shaking as he pointed at one of the flyers and tried to discern the source of this news.

Only hours later, when from a clunky pay phone at the post office he had called all possible relatives across three continents and two islands and found everyone to be living, did Nicholas understand that there had been a mistake. An official at the music festival slowly uncovered the mix-up: it was another composer—the one from Barcelona—whose relative had died. Sorry for the confusion. *Mi dispiace.*

Nicholas looked past the boxy telephone out to the peaceful green hills and accepted the apology. He retrieved his bag and suit jacket and made his way down the town's one road, past bobbing poppies and tall, scrappy weeds. Only as he approached the little hotel where the festival had booked him a room did it strike him as odd that the notices would have been posted at the station. Shouldn't they have been at the lecture hall instead? Typical Italian inefficiency . . . Well, it wasn't worth blaming anyone, he told himself as he followed the innkeeper, a gray-haired woman with two pairs of glasses dangling around her neck, down the hallway to his room.

The woman spoke in a rapid, rote way that Nicholas didn't quite follow—something about the outside door locking at eleven p.m.— and handed Nicholas a metal ring with four small keys. It lay in his palm like an awkward insect while the woman indicated which key would let Nicholas into the building should he be out past that respectable hour. The other three keys she dismissed, explaining, as far as Nicholas could make out, that any key at all could open the door to his room.

With that she left him. Nicholas removed his travel clothes— acrid with dried sweat—and lay naked on the thick, coarse sheets. Taking deep breaths, he listened to his heartbeats and tried not to think about the train station.

He had nearly confessed to Hazel, right there on the telephone, so relieved was he to hear her voice. But the awkward half-second delay would have made such a conversation even more painful. What mattered was what they had been spared. Everyone was all right.

Yet even now, as the evening sun began its descent, Nicholas felt the echo of something dark: the heartache of a widower, the mourning of a father, the suffering of a brother, of a son. No matter that the misunderstanding had been cleared up. It was as if every one of those possible tragedies had occurred.

Nicholas told himself that it was over now, everyone was fine.

He had been swallowed by an abyss, tossed back up, and survived. Everything would be all right.

It was what he had been telling himself ever since quitting Remy. He'd had no choice but to end it, now that Hazel was back. That he had allowed himself to become that most unexceptional of creatures, a cheating husband . . . The very banality of it bothered him as much as his own wretchedness.

When his pulse had finally slowed, Nicholas rose and bathed and dressed for dinner. He was to dine with the festival's director, a man named Lothar—a German businessman who had lived in Italy for decades and fancied himself a musician. Nicholas had dined with him in this tiny town twice before. A village, really, known only for its music festival and for an old castle that, in an effort to win a Michelin star, had years earlier been restored to its original decrepitude. Walking to the restaurant, Nicholas even noted the same village idiot from his last visit, an old man who greeted pedestrians by waving menacingly and saying nasty things about their mothers. The man was as much a fixture of the festival as the fading purple banners that lined the narrow street; as the string quartets popping up all over and at all hours; as the Polish opera company that performed the complete repertoire of Mozart's operettas; as Lothar, who attended nearly every concert and made sure that at the week's end each performer received a souvenir—always some useless, unattractive object that looked to have been mass-manufactured at a German factory.

The restaurant was filled with festival-goers, and the waiters were making the most of the extra business, flirting with everyone, showing off. A week from now the festival would be over, and the town would again be sleepy and quiet, with nothing to do but wait for next summer. "I'm so glad we were able to convince you to join us again," Lothar said in his practiced English as he and Nicholas tucked themselves into their little table and joined the din of the low-ceilinged room. "The festival missed you last year."

There wasn't much chance for detailed conversation; with so

many festival members in evidence, Lothar had to keep getting up and shaking hands and winking at people. Aspiring composers pulled cassettes from their pockets and handed them off swiftly, like drug dealers. Nicholas gnawed happily at the tiny grilled birds he had ordered.

"Fancy running into you again!"

Nicholas looked up to see his old classmate Anna. "How's Boston?" she asked.

"Oh, hello. What a nice surprise." Really he felt annoyed, recalling the night at the club in Boston, and, more recently, what Yoni had said about her. It was as if he weren't being permitted even this brief break from that other life. Anna seemed to sense this and looked somehow offended.

"Ah, my two favorite people!" Lothar called everyone his favorite. "How are you, Anna?"

"Late for dessert, I see." She glanced back at her table. "But I'll make sure to catch up with you later."

Nicholas was relieved when she walked away. Lothar sat down and took up his abandoned food. "You've grown up," he announced as he dislodged a bird from a skewer. "There are lines at the sides of your mouth. Yes, it's no longer a boy's face. Even you have been aged by life, then?"

The image that came to Nicholas was of her wrists, and her curls, and her wide brown eyes. His jaw had trembled when he explained to her that they had to end things.

"Well, it doesn't matter," Remy had said flatly. "I still love you." And though Nicholas had nothing but contempt for the way Americans said "I love you" all the time, hearing Remy say it, he felt an urge to speak, though he didn't know what to say. There was a horrible stretchy feeling in his chest.

"I love you," she had repeated, defiant. But Nicholas managed to keep his mouth shut, and walked away.

Nicholas described to Lothar his move to Boston and his busy summer schedule. He slid from his wallet photos of Jessie and of Hazel, and launched into a detailed description of his job at the conservatory, and the various commissions that had been coming his way. Talking soothed his nerves. He drank more red wine than usual and found himself telling Lothar about the posters at the station.

Lothar listened carefully, then said, "To me it sounds suspiciously like a dream. You're sure you didn't dream it?"

"More like a nightmare," Nicholas grumbled.

Lothar nodded. "It has all the elements, doesn't it? A foreign location. Panicked phone calls. A symbolic death. And, most interestingly, that momentous question, now that you've lost someone important, perhaps the most important person in your life: Who *is* that person?"

Nicholas frowned. Psychoanalytic rubbish. As bad as his sister. "I don't go in for dream analysis," he said. But a bad taste had risen in his throat. The afternoon's scare was still very real and nothing he was prepared to analyze.

"Well," Lothar said briskly, "I'll see to it that by tomorrow the last of those flyers will have disappeared. You'll forget you ever saw them. And your lecture will be well attended, don't worry."

Nicholas wasn't worried at all, though he hadn't yet prepared his lecture; he would do it tonight before he went to bed. But the thought of the flyers still troubled him, somehow.

At the end of the evening, he wished Lothar and Anna good night and walked back toward the hotel. There was some sort of discotheque up at the castle, and from over the high stone wall, like a shower of noisy stars, came the tinny sound of pumping dance music.

Those posters at the station, of all places.

And his poor mother at the railway crossing . . .

Ah, right, yes. Nicholas felt almost a dolt for not having thought of it sooner. After all, the association must have been there all along, in his mind. Trains, death. How odd that they should come together this way again—though really Nicholas had never consciously made the connection. He loved trains, loved travel. And rarely thought about his mother at all. Her death wasn't anything to dwell on (though as a child he had sometimes found himself imagining it, in slow motion, as in an action film).

At the hotel, the front door hadn't been locked. Filled with the reassurance of imminent sleep, Nicholas made his way down the dark hall and let himself into his room. Only after he closed the door did he notice that, by mistake, he had used his house key from home.

THE DAY THAT NICHOLAS LEFT FOR ITALY, THE WEATHER GREW SUD-denly very hot. Remy's room became close, stale air caught in the eaves. Worse than that was the ache that had started in her wrists—a dull pain that increased during the night and woke her from sleep.

The next day the pain was even worse. Remy felt tightening around her a chain of fears she had never before considered: that she had some awful disease, that she would become a cripple, that she would have to give up the violin altogether. She recalled her old teacher, Mrs. Lepik, forced to end her concert career when physical therapy and cortisone shots failed to relieve the tendonitis in her elbow. In class with Conrad Lesser, Remy had to make an effort not to let the pain show on her face.

Somehow the pain seemed shameful, a sign of something worse than mere tendonitis. Something horrible was happening. Even as she worked her hours at the music library, and swam at the Y, and performed with her quartet (not daring to mention the pain, fearful they might think she couldn't work anymore), and managed through it all to chat and laugh as usual, behind the chatter lurked this new, frightening pain.

She allowed herself to wonder if Nicholas's kisses had somehow been cursed. Surely she was being punished—for trying to claim something that wasn't hers. For trying to live freely and fearlessly, like Oscar Wilde.

In this world there are only two tragedies; one is not getting what one wants, the other is getting it.

She thought of her old conservatory flings, and Peter from her dormitory saying, "Now you've been deflowered," and supposed that she would never again have such carefree relationships. She recalled the joy she had felt that first night with Nicholas and in the morning waking up smiling. Seeing him again, that day on Boylston Street, she hadn't even cared, anymore, what Lesser said about her career. Standing naked before Nicholas, all she had wanted from life was *him*.

With Nicholas she had felt lit from within.

To live is the rarest thing in the world. Most people exist, that is all.

To break up with her last week he said, "Don't you see? It wouldn't be good between us."

They were in her apartment when he said it, standing at the door, and Remy had begun pummeling him. "Why? Because *you* decided it wouldn't be?"

"Look," he had said, when she grew exhausted with hitting him. "I'm going away. I leave next week, and I'll be far away. By the time I get back you'll have forgotten all about me."

"Don't give me that garbage! How dare you use a line like that on *me*!"

"I just mean . . ." But she could tell that he didn't have the slightest idea what he meant.

And now Remy was being punished.

She had told herself a music career didn't matter, that there was this other, better happiness—but that too had been snatched away.

Her wrists throbbed fitfully.

Well, what if she did give up the violin? She could grow her nails long, paint them magenta like Sandy's. Lose the scar on her neck. She thought of Samantha, off in New York getting a degree in music therapy. There was another musician she knew, a boy, who had quit the cello and instead was training to be an audiologist.

But could Remy really do such a thing?

No—no! She could not. Music was her life, the violin was her life, especially now, without Nicholas. If she couldn't have him. If she wasn't allowed to have him.

Lying across her bed as the little fan anemically stirred the air around her, Remy decided: I don't care what Lesser thinks. Music is all I have.

THE WEEK PASSED PLEASANTLY ENOUGH, AND NICHOLAS SOON FELT restored. His lecture was well attended. Lothar sat in the back, taking impassioned notes, and only one person, the man who had written a history of La Scala, asked an obnoxious question at the end. In response, Nicholas told a joke he had stored up for just such occasions. Afterward he couldn't help feeling confident—that he would return home to his old self, free of that spell that had gripped him. Life would return to what it had always been.

Since this was the final day of the conference, there was a picnic luncheon up at the castle. Nicholas shook hands with people he had met and wouldn't see until the next festival of this sort. A contralto from Sweden said, "I was so sorry to hear your news."

"What news?"

"There was an accident?"

"An accident . . ."

"Someone passed away? And yet you stayed."

"Oh, the posters." Amazing, Nicholas thought, how quickly rumors grow. "There was no accident. It was all a mistake."

"Some mistake!"

Again Nicholas found himself recounting how it had felt to see those flyers at the station, how his heart had nearly stopped. The episode had become a mere anecdote, he realized, when really he had never in his thirty-one years been so worried.

"Ah, you're here, good!" It was Anna, who appeared to have taken up with a fellow conductor. Nicholas had noticed the two of them walking arm in arm.

Now the closing ceremony was taking place. Some paid vague attention, while others continued to chat. Nicholas turned toward the platform where the town's mayor was thanking the participants. A young man lugged a bass fiddle over cobblestones, while next to Nicholas a baritone went on about a polyp that had grown on his throat. All across the grounds were musicians and singers exchanging telephone numbers and performance schedules. Anna wrote her contact information on the back of a Corelli program for Nicholas and said, "I'm going to go find Hans."

Nicholas stuffed the Corelli program into his jacket pocket and watched Lothar distributing the souvenirs. Everyone—men and women—received the same ugly brown and white silk scarf. Nicholas heard the Swedish contralto say, practically, "I will wrap my necklaces in it."

He helped himself to a glass of wine and wandered away from the ceremony, toward the north side of the castle, where the view was finest. The hills piled up against the horizon as if the world really was this peaceful. To the left, past the fields and sunflowers, the little train station awaited him.

Just glimpsing it, Nicholas felt his pulse quicken. Those posters tacked all over the place . . . Only now did they seem to him embarrassing, a public display of subconscious fears. In that way, it was as though he *had* dreamed it. Lothar was right, Nicholas nearly laughed to himself, though he couldn't, quite. He still felt the frustration of that unanswered question. *Who is that person?* He shook his head at himself—Freudian nonsense. Yet he could not dispel the residue of those panicked telephone calls, and the contralto asking about the "accident," so stupid . . .

The glass of wine fell from his hand, shattering at his feet. For a moment Nicholas just stood there, mouth agape, while the thought pulsed through him. Then he rushed back down the narrow street, to the café where there was a call box. An operator helped him complete the call, to the military station in Nairobi.

Once again his sister's voice came across a slightly crackling line. He told her, "It wasn't an accident."

"Are you all right, Nicholas?"

"When Mother drove onto the tracks. She knew the train was coming, don't you see? She meant to do it."

Silence on the other end, that other continent.

Nicholas was nearly tripping over his words. "Did *anyone* believe that piffle about the 'new electrical signals'? We just accepted what they told us."

Softly Glenda said, "We were children, that's why. You were a tot when you first asked what happened."

His father grumbling, "A stupid accident," and nothing more. Only years later had an aunt explained to Nicholas about the railway signals.

Glenda said, "You can't tell me you've never wondered before."

Nicholas found he was leaning against the wall of the call box. "You mean you knew?"

"Just look at her eyes in that photograph." Glenda's tone was annoyingly matter-of-fact. "It's clear she was deeply depressed."

"Postpartum depression," Nicholas heard himself say, to show Glenda he understood the implication. "Isn't that it?"

"Nicholas," his sister said, her voice sterner now, "you never did look up that therapist I recommended, did you?"

"Christ, Glenda, can't you for once . . ." But his voice caught in his throat. The posters, the phone calls. It really was too much.

Glenda waited patiently, a trained listener. When enough time had passed, she asked, in that insufferable way of hers, "That's not really what this call is about, is it?"

A know-it-all, that's what they had called Glenda back in school. Nicholas let his shoulders slump. Bloody hell. It didn't matter that

Glenda didn't even know what she was talking about—she was always so bloody incisive.

To Nicholas's stubborn silence, she simply said, "Now, what's *really* going on?"

Nicholas waited before answering, wanting to put off as long as possible what he only now understood he was about to say.

Chapter 7

*M*ORE COFFEE, GARY?" HAZEL BENT TO REFILL HIS CUP, TAKING care not to leave it too full; she hadn't forgotten about last time. Even though she knew that everyone made mistakes and that, in the scheme of things, spilled wine on your Persian carpet was relatively minor, she still found it somehow unforgivable.

"From you, sure!" Gary winked at her and then grinned at Nicholas, as if to prove how friendly he was. Hazel pretended not to notice. She couldn't help being annoyed at him for stopping by like this, completely unannounced and certainly not invited. For one thing, Nicholas was exhausted, had just returned from Italy late the night before. They had barely even had time to talk to each other, since today was the mother-daughter trip to the beach with the Junior League, and she and Jessie had only gotten back this evening.

"I see you've been holding down the fort," Gary said now. "Did you at least manage to have some fun while your husband was gone?" Hazel knew he didn't mean it in a lecherous way, but she also knew that he wanted her to think that he did.

Nicholas said, "She's already got a full plate. Plus she's been taking a course at Harvard Extension." He was wearing that paisley button-down shirt Hazel secretly wished he would get rid of, the one whose pattern, in light brown and pale red, looked more like a rash than a design.

"Just auditing," she corrected. She'd had to miss some of the sessions when she went down to help her mother.

Gary asked what subject, and Hazel felt like a college girl again. "Notorious Identity in Shakespeare's Plays."

Gary asked which ones, and she listed them off. Five in total. The truth was, even though she liked the course, she felt a certain disconnect in the classroom. While the instructor provided all sorts of interesting information, the connections Hazel would have liked to discuss never seemed to come up. The professor might spend a half hour on his theory of how *Richard III* was really a commentary on something he called "speech act violation," but the scenes Hazel had lingered over, the sections she had memorized, the lines she had questioned, were never noted.

It was as if she were concentrating on all the wrong things. For instance, three of the plays they had read included a female character who at some point emerged with "her hair about her ears"—always when these women were agitated, deranged, upset. Hazel thought this might be worth mentioning. But she didn't quite know what else to say about it, so she didn't say anything.

"I played Hamlet back in school," Nicholas said. "I was dire. I can still hear the director—he was our physics teacher—saying, 'You're the prince of Denmark, for Chrissakes. You've bigger worries than what tonight's pudding will be.'"

"Talk about miscasting," Gary said, while Hazel felt relief at Nicholas's chitchat. All evening he had been his fun, joking self. Not like last night, when he arrived home so tired. Not like this morning, when he waved good-bye in a distracted way as she and Jessie hurried to caravan to Ipswich with the other mothers. How did this sort of disjunction happen, between two people who loved each other? Even the time they'd had together before Nicholas left for Italy had been off. To Hazel it felt like water slipping through her fingers.

"Do you ever act out scenes in your class?" Gary asked. "I bet you're a good actress."

"No. It's mostly the professor talking." And Hazel jotting down ideas she hoped might be discussed. In *Troilus and Cressida,* when Troilus's sister Cassandra appeared with "her hair about her ears" everyone said she was crazy, but really she was prophetic. If Hazel had dared raise her hand, she could have framed her comment that way, in terms of public opinion and prophecy, and not even mentioned the part about the hair.

Nicholas asked if she would have to write any essays.

"Not me. Since I'm just auditing." But she wouldn't have minded writing about poor raving Cassandra, whose madness was in fact foresight. Hazel found the discrepancy, between delusion and pre-science, significant.

The fact was, Hazel herself had been feeling just the slightest bit crazy. No, she hadn't seen the woman, the doppel, again. Yet it seemed she was still perhaps . . . seeing things.

"Why is sex like a Shakespeare play?" Gary asked.

Hazel sighed, but he continued. "Because three inches is *Much Ado About Nothing,* six inches is *As You Like It,* and nine inches is *A Midsummer Night's Dream.*" Gary took another bite of cake, and Nicholas chuckled a bit, and Hazel gave a little "tsk" because she knew it was what they expected.

Delusion versus prescience, that was it, or at least part of it—caught somewhere between madness and insight. This was what made her want to cry out, to scream with frustration.

Still, she wasn't like those women in the plays, not really. Her hair was pulled up from either side of her face and fastened neatly at the back. A few strands had fallen in light curves at her temples, but even when she felt she might explode, the big plastic clip remained firmly at the back of her head.

"*Et tu,* cutie?" Gary gave her a little nudge, and Nicholas said, "We're boring her."

"No more than usual," she teased. She was used to making the best of any situation. Since finally settling in, though, the days had been falling into clumps: good days and bad days. On the good days things seemed to be coming together. On the bad days . . . she noticed things.

There had been a good day, before Nicholas left for Italy. They had taken Jessie swimming at Walden Pond, early on a hot, humid morning before the park became too crowded. Jessie wore little inflated doughnuts over her arms and was thrilled at the very fact of swimming. Hazel and Nicholas passed her between each other, swinging her through the water as she squealed gleefully.

"You should've seen the look on Duncan's face." Gary was describing a college production of *Macbeth* full of romantic intrigue and wayward props. "And even then the play seemed to go on forever. That was when I vowed to never see live theater ever again."

"That's a depressing vow," Hazel said.

"Not at all. Makes it easy to decline all sorts of invitations."

"You've truly not seen a single play since then?" Nicholas asked.

"Only when forced."

Hazel prevented herself from rolling her eyes. People like Gary, what were they trying to prove? She could tell that he purposely cultivated his lowbrow demeanor, while simultaneously hinting at expertise and connections, as if to suggest that life lessons were what allowed him to talk confidently about any topic at all. Hazel told him, "Some of what we've read in class I've found quite moving."

There was a day last week when they were doing a close reading of a section of *Richard III* and she had suddenly wanted to cry. Queen Elizabeth came onstage upset, and her lines took Hazel by surprise, even though she had read them herself the night before: "Oh, who shall hinder me to wail and weep, / To chide my fortune, and torment myself?" How Hazel would have loved to wail and weep: for her father getting worse and then better and then worse again, and the running back and forth with a three-year-old to tend to, and—there was so much inside her that she hadn't addressed. She had never allowed herself to rave, to scream, to throw a fit. *Enter Hazel, her hair about her ears.* The line didn't suit her at all. It simply wasn't the sort of thing she did. People who acted that way were selfish.

"Oh, here, please, have some more cake," she said, since Gary was reaching for the porcelain server and she didn't quite trust him with it. She slid another slice onto his plate.

He asked, "Any luck with the house hunting?"

"I've looked at a few places," she told him. "Just to get some ideas. Seeing what our options are."

Only for those few days before Nicholas left for Italy had they looked at anything together, but Nicholas hadn't shown the enthusiasm Hazel would have liked. He was so distracted. Even at home—his sleeping pattern was different. Usually he fell asleep immediately and slept soundly, but lately he was restless. Water slipping through her fingers . . .

There had been a moment when she walked into the living room and he didn't know she was there. His eyes began to close as though he were in pain—but then he noticed her and said, "How lovely you look!" as if everything were absolutely normal.

"If you don't mind some sketchy sections, the South End is up and coming," Gary was saying. "Give it a few years and it'll be prime real estate."

Hazel shook her head. Even parts of this neighborhood felt rough. "Nicholas wouldn't mind staying here in town, but I prefer something quieter. We saw some very nice houses in Brookline."

"It's pricey, though," Nicholas said. He had scolded her for allowing the realty agent to think they could afford some of the more spacious homes, while Hazel saw no harm in having a peek. Now Nicholas said, "We really don't need much space," and Hazel again felt chided. She looked down, and her gaze landed on the Persian carpet. How beautiful it was, always there for her. Although now it had that splotch in the corner.

"I want to stay up, too."

"Oh, sweetie, now when did you wake up?" Here was Jessie in her cotton nightie, standing at the entrance to the living room, rubbing her eyes.

"I want to stay up." Already she was yawning.

"But it's bedtime," Nicholas said, and went to her. He lifted her in his arms and kissed her on the cheek—and then the look came over him, desperate, as if he might not see her in the morning. "Come on, darling." To Gary and Hazel he said, "This is what happens when you trade the crib in for a bed," and carried Jessie back.

Gary said, "Her eyes are amazing. So green."

Proudly Hazel said, "She gets them from my father."

"Terrifyingly green," Gary added, as if fiddling with phrasing for some profile he was writing. Oh, shut up, Hazel wanted to say. Pretentious hack.

He said, "It's funny to see Nicholas so smitten."

Hazel turned to look at Gary. For a split second she wondered if he, too, had seen it. The elastic band. A hair elastic, the thick kind, not the little ones she used for Jessie's pigtails. She had seen it there on the floor beside the bed, before Nicholas left for Italy, when she was tidying up with the new vacuum from Sears; Nicholas of course hadn't cleaned at all. And there it was, lying on the rug innocently enough. Hazel paused, though the vacuum was still running loudly, and could have sworn she saw, caught in the little metal part of the elastic, a long, thick, brown, curling hair.

She had just bent down to examine it when Nicholas appeared at the bedroom door to say, "Phone for you."

Hazel sprang up and turned off the vacuum, not daring to look back at the elastic. She might have had a heart attack right then and there, but it was her mother calling with an update on her father's condition, so she couldn't.

The miraculous thing, though—the truly extraordinary thing—was that when she went back to the bedroom to finish vacuuming, the thick elastic band with the long curling hair was gone.

She had to wonder if her eyes were playing tricks on her. After all, there had been other confusing moments these past few weeks, ones that had nothing to do with Nicholas. Driving on the turnpike one afternoon, she saw the sign for her exit and immediately moved into the right-hand lane, but when she took the exit, she ended up on the wrong road entirely. She had to do an illegal U-turn and get back onto the highway, where it turned out that her exit was the following one. Yet even now she knew she had read the original sign correctly. So how had she ended up on the wrong road?

"Everything okay, Hazel?"

She looked at Gary with surprise. "Oh, I didn't mean to . . . I'm sorry if I— I think I'm just tired."

"Well, you don't look it. Nicholas's a lucky man to have you around."

Ah, flattery. There was also that sweet comment he made about Jessie's drawing on the refrigerator. But now he was looking at her with real concern, as if he honestly cared about how she felt. How surprising. People were like that, weren't they, as layered as artichokes.

She said, "I never realized how hard it could be to reunite with someone. I mean, after so many months of spending time apart." She hadn't meant to say it; it just came out.

Gary said, "Long-distance relationships—I stay the hell away from them."

Hazel said, "Sometimes you don't have a choice." To herself she said, He can't help that he's a buffoon.

"If you ever need anything, Hazel."

Now, why would he say that? She frowned.

He said, "I mean, if you want the advice of a native Bostonian. If you need any pointers from a local."

"I'll keep that in mind." She didn't mean to sound brisk. Really she was filled with relief: if Gary could show this gentlemanly side, then it proved she wasn't always right about things, that the craziness, the glimpses, could be wrong, too.

" 'To sleep, perchance to dream . . .' " Nicholas was back. "She was out even before I put her back on the bed."

Hazel found herself smiling at him, at the tenderness he showed their daughter. While they were swimming together in Walden Pond, she had been conscious of not knowing at all what he was thinking, yet she felt his energy all around her, in every splash of water. With Jessie they had held hands and done a sort of dance, ring around the rosey there in the shallow part. It was one of those perfect moments, like that vision she used to have, approaching the front steps of the beautiful house with Nicholas and their two children, the boy and girl, just ahead of them.

Swimming, Nicholas had sprung back in his happy backstroke, released, free, and after that let Jessie hang on to his shoulders, and Hazel had watched with pure joy before doing her own breaststroke after them. She had swallowed water just when she was about to reach them. One second she was smiling at how perfect everything was, and then she was gulping water, coughing, spitting it out. Moments like that always amazed her, how something could be so good and then so bad a mere second later. All it took was a split second. Once when she was a teenager she had laughed so hard that she threw back her head and hit the wall behind her with such force, she gave herself a mild concussion. Ever since then she had noted with awe the mere seconds that might separate pleasure from pain. There were so many degrees of this. A glass suddenly shattering, or a car hopping the median. A joke too honest. Wine on your Persian carpet.

Gary said, "I should get going. The cockroaches will be wondering what's happened to me."

Nicholas frowned, as if he didn't want Gary to go.

Stretching his arms, Gary stood, cracked his knuckles, and sighed loudly. "Thank you for the delicious cake and the magnificent company."

They walked him to the door. "Thanks for stopping by," Nicholas said, draping his arm around Hazel. She let herself relax.

"Good night," Gary said, stepping out into the hall.

"Good night, Gary."

Nicholas closed the door slowly, and Hazel went to clear the coffee table. She would have to stop questioning everything, analyzing everything. It wasn't healthy.

Nicholas said, "Thanks for the cake."

"You're most welcome." After all, it had been a perfectly nice evening. She carried their muddied coffee cups—the pattern she had picked out for their wedding—into the kitchen. That she had successfully trusted Gary with her best china felt like an accomplishment itself. Nicholas followed her into the kitchen, carrying the coffeepot and the trivet. He put them on the counter and, when she turned around, had a serious look on his face.

"What is it?"

He opened his eyes wide, as if suddenly caught. "Nothing." But it didn't sound that way.

Hazel waited a moment, sure that he would say something more. She knew better than to press him.

When he began to rinse out the coffeepot, she went back to fetch the cake plates and saucers. *Nothing.* There it was again, the feeling: her mind unraveling. Her world unraveling.

"Hazel." His voice came from the kitchen and sounded almost panicked. Now he was at the door, facing the living room. He cleared his throat and said, "I need to talk to you."

Her heart lunged, and she saw that her hands, holding the china plates, had begun to shake. But she walked carefully back to the kitchen and made sure none of the plates fell.

Part Two

Clairvoyance

Chapter 1

*H*AZEL GRIPPED HER LASHES IN THE FRIEZE OF A METAL CURLER and counted to three. On the bathroom counter were small tubes of corrective cream, two types of tweezers, a jumble of lip-sticks, and brushes and sponges of various shapes and sizes. At times the sight of so many tools oppressed her, but mostly she was grateful. She always made an effort; no one could take that away from her.

She released the curler, placed it back in the tray. Now she coaxed mascara onto her lashes with a tiny brush—though deep down she suspected all this effort was for naught. She almost shook her head at the thought, except that she had to be careful with the mascara. There. She blinked at her reflection and turned to the full-length mirror on the door. How odd that this reverse version of her face, of her body, should be the sole way she saw herself. Front view only, curvy waist, broad hips, bust propped cheerfully in an underwire bra. Yes, her makeup was fine. It took expertise to look natural and still hide the white patches.

As satisfied as she could expect to be, Hazel left the bathroom and officially began to wait. Hugh was coming to fetch her, and she couldn't help being a bit nervous. This was their first real date, and he was the only person in a long while to appeal to her. Handsome *and* a widower, not many of those around. Twinkly eyes flecked with green. A square, neatly shaven chin. The dignity of small lines framing the corners of his mouth. Kind, intelligent, polite. He was the communications director for a biotech company in Cambridge, which meant that while knowledgeable about science, he was easier to talk to than an actual scientist. Best of all, he was Hazel's age, early forties, not one of those paunchy older men her friends sometimes set her up with, the pear-shaped ones who wore those enormous plastic sunshades over their glasses.

She had met him that summer at a swim meet; his son Luke was a year ahead of Jessie and swam a slightly flailing butterfly. Hazel had been clocking the lane next to Hugh's when they began to chat; detecting the Carolina tinge to her accent (light as it was after a decade in Boston), Hugh asked where she hailed from. It turned out he had southern roots, had grown up in Macon before moving north. He still had family in Georgia, though he hadn't been back since taking Luke to see the Olympics in Atlanta last year. Even after their initial talk subsided, Hugh continued to address Hazel in an easy manner, as if they were already friends.

And so the summer had become an enjoyable one. For the first time, Hazel honestly looked forward to those hours at the public swimming pool, a place she had spent much of the past decade dreading, as it entailed uncovering herself and her mottled arms while Jessie ran blithely around with her friends, their eyes red from chlorine, their plastic swim tags fading from the sun. The water slippery with tanning oil, the retarded boy always lolling on the steps, sucking on a shoelace . . . At least the swim meets gave Hazel something to do— and Hugh had made everything more pleasant.

Then, just this week, she had met him by chance in the parking lot of the middle school when she was waiting to pick up Jessie from the first day of seventh grade. Hugh, too, had stepped out of his car, a shiny gray Civic, to catch some September sunshine. Hazel called to him. It was just as the children began to stream out of the school's doors that he asked if she might like to go to a movie with him.

As much as she had spent all summer hoping for just such an invitation, his offer surprised her. There were other single women to choose from, and though Hazel didn't think all that much of most of them, the fact was, you never knew what a man might find attractive. And, in her case, there were the white splotches. Although she could hide the two small ones on her face—one where her chin met her jaw and one below her right temple—they were still visible on her hands for anyone to see.

Ten years ago the first one had appeared, right when Nicholas moved out, when everything fell apart. The way Hazel understood it, just as some people's hair turned white from shock, she herself had blanched—but gradually, visibly, a living negative tattoo. "I really do wear my heart on my sleeve," she had joked to a doctor, holding out her arm to reveal a white splotch. The doctor, a humorless man with photographs of his basset hound displayed on all four walls, insisted it had nothing to do with her heart or with shock but rather with loss of melanin. "I can see how this would be troubling," he had told her, "but it's not a health concern. It's just something that happens." He seemed to think this a helpful thing to say.

Those were the days when Hazel wanted one thing more than anything else: for Remy and Nicholas to be as hurt and humiliated as she had been. Because there had to be some kind of retribution. In order to keep believing in God (for why would He punish honest, clean-living Hazel, who, as frustrated as she had been with Nicholas's constant travel and general thoughtlessness, had never, ever, cheated on him? What had she done to deserve the disgrace of being that most unpleasant of things, a divorced woman?), Hazel still clung to a belief that everything happened for a reason and that those who suffered would eventually be rewarded, and vice versa. She retained this belief even when the white splotches appeared, on her knees, her calves, her forearms.

Hazel had tried everything to even out her skin: the tonic that smelled of lye, tubes of cream the consistency of wet sand. She had even gone to an acupuncturist recommended by one of Remy's friends. That was a few years after the divorce, when the biweekly trading of Jessie back and forth had become second nature—though Hazel still dreaded having to glimpse Remy in the process. That day was the first time Hazel had been able to view Remy in a generous light.

"Mommy, what's that?"

Hazel had reached out to take Jessie's hand in hers, to lead her away from that happy, sloppy household whose contented disarray revealed a fullness of life Hazel couldn't help envying. And now Jessie was pointing at a big white splotch on the back of Hazel's hand. "Mommy, what's that?"

She was five years old. Only a reasonable, logical answer would do.

"It's loss of melanin." Hazel tried not to allow even a hint of resentment that so obvious a cruelty—the fabric of a wounded soul—had been thrust upon her. "Melanin is what makes our skin dark. It makes us tan when the sun activates it. People with dark skin have more melanin, and fair people have less."

"But why is it missing there?"

Hazel gave a little laugh. "Who knows?" She had wanted to sound lighthearted but instead sounded frantic.

Remy was still at the door, waiting to hand Jessie the purple backpack with the reflective stickers. "You know," she had said, timidly, "a friend of mine was having skin problems, and she went to an acupuncturist. It wasn't the same thing you have, but if you want to . . . I mean, if you're interested . . ." Remy let her voice trail off, as if already knowing there was no way to reverse the process that had overtaken Hazel's body.

But back then Hazel still believed she might halt the inevitable. She met with the acupuncturist, who also prescribed various herbal teas and, after a few months, when there was no change except in the opposite direction (more splotches of white on her thighs and arms), dared to suggest Hazel stop bemoaning what was happening and accept that she was changing. "You'd be amazed how much better you can feel when you accept change, rather than fight it. You have to embrace it."

Embrace this! Hazel wanted to say, and clock her, that petite woman with unblemished skin and a ponytail down her back. But instead she had just held her hands together and nodded stiffly.

The ironic thing was that after that, the white patches had slowed. Though each year one or two more emerged, mainly on her arms, it wasn't at all at the rate of those first two years. And though soon enough, probably, a good 50 percent of her skin would have bleached away, at least the splotches had stayed away from her face. As for the one that came up to her chin, and the one by her temple, she took time to blend her makeup so that no one would notice.

She wondered if Hugh had. She made a habit of wearing pants and long sleeves at the pool, as if sensitive to the sun. Well, if he were a real man, a good man, her skin wouldn't matter. So far he had proved to be the real thing, and gallant, too. Even tonight, instead of simply meeting her at the movies, he had suggested he fetch her at home. Hazel found that polite. At the same time, she couldn't help preparing herself for disappointment; it was what she was used to.

She glanced at the clock in the kitchen. As was her habit, she began to tidy up. She had read in one of those women's magazines that cleaning for just fifteen minutes a day was better than doing longer, less frequent cleanups; apparently people who waited too long to scrub the toilet bowl or dust the bookshelf spent a certain number of hours per month cleaning, whereas people who tidied daily never had to invest large blocks of time in the same activities. The truth was, Hazel had done the math, using the figures mentioned in the article, and it added up to the same amount of cleaning whether you did it daily, weekly, or monthly. But she had still followed the suggestion ever since.

With a sponge Hazel began to wipe down the kitchen counter. This room always pleased her, with its farmer's market bounty, the net sack heavy with speckled apples hanging from a peg above the counter, and the little clay bowl heaped with fresh bulbs of garlic. Heirloom tomatoes, skin spidery as if dipped in ink, lay in a woven sweetgrass basket, while firm shiny peppers, green tinged with purple, sat on a Shaker tray. Along the windowsill were miniature gourds whose contortions and warts, white and orange and green stained with brown, managed to look beautiful rather than deformed.

To Hazel these objects had the power of found art, reminders of what sort of shapes a miracle might take. With each year that passed, the importance of such things—beautiful things—became clearer to her. Domestic beauty, the subtle power of unassuming objects . . . Now she swiped the sponge lightly along the edge of the countertop, giving an extra scrub to the small stain near the corner; although it seemed to be permanent, Hazel always gave it another try. She sprayed a generous spritz of cleanser, guiltily wondering if some of the fumes might float over to the nearby terrarium to be inhaled by Freddie, Jessie's long-neglected pet frog. Hazel wiped away the cleanser and gave an encouraging glance toward poor, depressed Freddie. He seemed to want nothing more than to be put out of his misery.

"Oh!" Hazel hadn't expected the doorbell so soon. She walked briskly to the door to see Hugh on the front step. Twinkly eyes like Bill Clinton's. But there was a sadness there, too, a seriousness, in the lines of his face.

"Hi, there!" Hazel opened the screen door for him. "Would you like to come in for a minute? Or shall I just get my purse?"

"Actually," Hugh said, stepping into the foyer, "I double-checked the movie times, and it's a half hour later than the paper listed it. So we have some time to kill, if that's all right."

"Sure, come on in." Hazel closed the door behind him. They were going to see *L.A. Confidential.* She would have preferred to see *The Full Monty* but thought it might seem silly, so she hadn't suggested it.

"Would you like a drink? I have some wine open. Or a beer, if you'd like."

"I wouldn't mind a beer." He followed her into the kitchen, the faint smell of cologne, something sporty. Hazel opened the refrigerator, pleased to have thought ahead and purchased a six-pack of Sam Adams. Hugh said, "Nice frog you've got there."

"Want him?" Hazel closed the refrigerator door and reached for the bottle opener. "Please, take him!" She pried off the cap and handed the bottle to Hugh.

"You two not getting along?" He eased into a seat at the table.

Hazel had thought they could sit in the living room, where the light was less harsh. But she, too, took a seat. "Minnie van der Veer bought one for her son Brian, and she swore to me it lived all of two months. We've had this one for two years!"

Hugh laughed, and Hazel gave a little shrug. "I got him when Jessie was in fifth grade and Mrs. Klinman had the students write a poem about their pet. Jessie said how can I do the assignment when I don't have a pet? In science they had just done a whole unit on reptiles, and Jessie really wanted a snake, but I couldn't stand the thought of a snake in the house. And then I remembered Brian van der Veer's frog. Minnie said it just keeled over one day. Which I thought would be perfect, because you know Jessie: her attention span is almost non-existent."

Hugh was laughing harder now, and Hazel said, "Maybe I'll have a beer, too."

This just made Hugh laugh again. Hazel took another bottle from the fridge and flipped the cap off with a sense of power, as if she were suddenly alluringly comic and not just a beleaguered single mother— one who had even gone on to research the average life span of that particular species of frog. The book had said at most two years. *At most.* For all Hazel knew, hers was some sort of mutant that would live forever. To Hugh she said, "What she really wants, of course, is a puppy."

Hugh said, "Doesn't every kid? Unless they already have a dog, in which case they want a cat." He sighed. "Luke and I have an extremely aged cat. I fear we might have to put him to sleep soon, actually." He lowered his voice, as if confiding something. "He was one of the first things Teresa and I did together, back when we were in graduate school and moved in together. I was thinking the other day that that cat has known me longer than Luke has." His voice seemed caught in his throat. "And also that Teresa got to spend more years with our cat than she did with our son." He took a swig of his beer, swallowed, and asked, "Any pets in your past?"

"My former husband and I had a cat. A friend left it with us when he moved away. Well, he didn't say that. He asked us to watch him for two weeks, and then went to California and never came back." Hazel laughed, though at the time she had thought it abominable. "The ironic thing is that we were the ones who ended up moving around all the time. Poor thing was always being shipped here and there." It was the first time Hazel had really thought what it must have been like for Rascal, stuck in that plastic crate with the handle on top; back then it just seemed a huge hassle that only she had to deal with.

"In a way, the cat was one of the casualties of our divorce. He got left back home with my parents. But luckily my father really took to him. He was somewhat immobile in his last years, and that cat would curl up on his chest and just stay there for hours." Hazel took a quick sip of her beer. "To be honest, I'm not much of a pet person."

The truth, if she had said it more specifically, was that pets just left hairs all over the furniture and peed on the rugs. "I told Jessie I was allergic to dogs. Isn't that awful? 'Temperamentally allergic' is what I meant. It should be a crime, shouldn't it, denying your daughter a puppy for no good reason? But I just couldn't imagine taking care of another living being all by myself!" Hazel didn't mean to sound self-absorbed. "I thought her dad might let her have one, since he at least has a wife to help out. But they travel a lot, professionally. At least, that's *his* excuse."

Both she and Hugh were silent for a moment, both feeling wounded, she supposed. His wife had passed away just two and a half years ago, so his wound was surely deeper.

Hazel's own pain was now more of a constant, dull ache—yet there were moments when her wounds felt fresh. The worst was about a year after Nicholas left, when he was unable to pick up Jessie and Remy had arrived instead, with those narrow hips and straight shoulders and thin strong arms, her eyes avoiding Hazel as she waited on the doorstep. What had hurt the most was simply how very different Remy was from Hazel, so that Hazel felt newly rebuffed, at the understanding that Nicholas had chosen to be with someone not at all like her.

At that moment, Jessie had come running with her purple backpack and her favorite Dr. Seuss book and had cried out, "Remy!" with such delight that Hazel felt a knife in her chest. There really was a knife there, twisting.

Remy had appeared almost embarrassed by this greeting, said, "Hey, kiddo" in a soft voice as Jessie propelled herself into her arms. "Here, hug your mom good-bye," she had told her, pointing Jessie back at Hazel. That gesture itself had enraged Hazel—as if she needed Remy to tell her daughter to do that.

"Bye, Mommy!" Jessie had hugged Hazel and then went with Remy to the brown Volvo that Nicholas had bought after the divorce. Only as Remy helped her into the car did Jessie look back briefly, a sudden expression of complicit guilt on her young face. When the Volvo had driven off, Hazel's shoulders heaved as she sobbed silently, and she had to sit on the front steps to recover.

Since then Hazel hadn't sobbed in a long time, although every so often she felt all over again that something awful had happened to her. And it was true that as much as she enjoyed her life and her job at Maria's fabric shop, through it ran a thread of what could only be called loneliness. No matter how many activities she took up, no matter which new groups she volunteered for, there was always the sensation of being alone in the world. As much as she thought of herself as a strong independent woman, it was one thing to be independent and another to go through life without an ally, a partner, a hand to hold or to pat her on the back or massage her shoulders when the tension became too much.

She had so much love to give! Thank God she had Jessie. But even parenthood did not rid her of the drifting, lonely feeling, the residue of evenings spent on the couch across from the television, watching *Murphy Brown* while eating far too many low-fat Cheez Doodles and drinking a too-full glass of sauvignon blanc. At times such evenings felt intimate, at times decadent; other times it felt closer to something embarrassingly prurient, like masturbation. And then there were all the times she found herself in some public place looking around to discover that everybody else—everybody!—had somebody. When, last year, Jessie had let on that she had a crush on the boy in her class who played the bagpipes, Hazel had thought, horribly and against her own will, Even Jessie has someone to love. And I (because of Nicholas, because of Remy) have no one.

Now there was another boy in Jessie's life—her first boyfriend, though they hadn't as yet been on an actual date. They had met at a swim meet this summer, and although he went to a private school in Cambridge, Jessie talked to him on the telephone extensively, like a bona fide teenager. Hazel didn't feel at all jealous, since finally she, too, had someone to be excited about. And here he was, Hugh, sitting across from her, as if Hazel did such things—had handsome men over for a beer—all the time.

"Well," he said, "I suppose we should head over. Does that sound good?"

"It sounds great," Hazel told him, feeling fully content. Together they went into the front hall, where Hazel pulled on her autumn jacket and tied her silk scarf, wondering vaguely what the night held in store. Outside, the maples were just starting to turn, the evening's blueness propped between branches. In another month or so it would be cold enough to wear gloves, and Hazel wouldn't have to feel self-conscious about the splotches on her hands. Winter was good for her that way. Sometimes she wished it were olden times, so that she could wear gloves in the warm months, too.

Chapter 2

REMY STEPPED INTO THE BREEZY WARMTH OF AFTERNOON, HER violin case light in her hand, and turned toward Boylston Street rather than her usual route. Her mission this fine autumn day was both mundane and momentous: she must buy a training bra for Jessie.

Fetching her at Hazel's the other day, watching her sling her massive backpack over her shoulder, Remy had noted with ridiculous shock the new heaviness there, the faint outline, a girl-chest if not yet breasts. Perhaps because of Jessie's height and beauty and her comfort in her own skin, there was nothing awkward about it—but Remy remembered what it was like to be a thirteen-year-old, the body suddenly exerting itself in embarrassing ways. Though Jessie possessed the instinctive confidence of a natural athlete, though her skin still glowed with the infinite tan of a teenage summer, who knew what might in fact be going on inside her. There had been a day last month when she came home from the pool and burst into tears: How in the world, she wanted to know, could Remy have not taught her to shave her legs?

The thought had never occurred to Remy. To Jessie she explained that this was a choice a woman could make, and that Jessie's leg hair was so fine it was nearly invisible. "You could just leave it, if you want." She truly thought it the right thing to say.

Jessie looked at her as though she had suggested there was no need to wear clothes, either, if she didn't want to. "Meghan McGlough-lin has hairy armpits, and you know what people called her at swim practice? The Amazon. Because it's a total forest under her arms."

With that Jessie had stomped away, as if Remy were of no use to her anymore.

Until now, stepmotherhood had come naturally, a generally fluid progression she had never given much deep consideration. Rather, it was as if she and Jessie had always been in each other's lives. Remy was the one Jessie turned to with intimate questions, with whispered jokes and confidences—and until recently anything Remy did had become what Jessie had to do, too. It was why Jessie had taken up swimming, and had spent years loudly wishing for curly hair. She had even become a granddaughter to Remy's parents—another gift for Remy, after so many years of failing to have a baby.

But all summer Remy had felt something happening, as if all three of them—she and Nicholas, too—were in the throes of puberty.

"Hello, my dear!"

It was Yoni, in his running togs, hopping from foot to foot on the sidewalk before her. Tan from months of sunny travel, lines fanning from his eyes as if from so much time spent grinning. "How nice to find you on my way to the river!"

Remy gave him a quick peck on his moist cheek. "Long time no see." He and his girlfriend Patricia had been in Madrid all of August. Remy nodded at his training duds. "Nicholas said you were still on a health kick, but I didn't know if I should believe him."

"I've been trying to get him to join me."

"Are you kidding? He'd keel over!" The most Nicholas did in the way of sports was go over to Gary's to watch the World Series on television.

Yoni laughed. "Then what about you? It's beautiful, you know, running along the Charles. And I've never felt better. In fact, I just had my annual physical, and you know what? My heart has grown. The doctor said it's actually larger."

"I guess it makes sense," Remy said, "since it's a muscle."

Yoni said he found it wondrous that the heart could actually increase in size.

"It's a nice metaphor," Remy said.

"No, it's literal. My heart is actually bigger."

"I *know* that." Remy poked him in the chest. He was no taller than Nicholas, but there was something grand about the way he held himself, his hair dark and thick, his smile impervious. "I was trying to make it mean something."

Placing his arm lightly around her to jostle her a bit, the way he did whenever he teased her, Yoni said, "There's a 5K next Sunday, if you want to join me."

"You know swimming is all I'm good at." Remy nudged him away with her elbow. "You're much too healthy. It's disconcerting."

"It's for a good cause!" Yoni said. "We're raising money for . . . something or other."

Remy laughed. "Is it healthy for you to stop in the middle of your run like this?"

"A minute or two won't kill me. I'm glad to see you. How are you surviving the accolades?"

Remy gave a laughing sigh; she knew what Yoni meant. Lately with each of Nicholas's premieres came an inevitable shower of praise. This new piece, for woodwind quintet, was no different.

"You know what they say," she told him. " 'Nothing less than perfection.' "

It was a phrase from a review of Nicholas's last premiere, which both Yoni and Remy couldn't help finding hilarious. They still used it to tease him.

"It's all the conservatory's been talking about," Yoni said.

Remy suspected it bothered him, everyone so excited about Nicholas all the time, when Yoni too had tried his hand at composing. Only in the past year or so, though, had she noted on occasion, when the three of them were together, a little wince that sometimes crossed Yoni's face. "It stops meaning so much," she said, in concession, though it was true that as proud as she was of Nicholas, he seemed to be becoming someone others *had* to praise, to prove their own good taste.

"It's well deserved, though," Yoni said.

Remy sensed him wanting to say more but not daring to; it was not the first time she had sensed this. "But a lot of people deserve things." Why had she said that? She felt suddenly that she had told some dark secret about herself.

Probably it was because of the latest news at work.

But she didn't want to think about that now. To Yoni she said, "Well, I know you have to get back to your run."

Yoni started to hop from foot to foot again. "But it's so nice to see you."

"Come over for dinner one of these days," she told him. Yoni often dined with them, particularly when he was between girlfriends.

"I'd love to." He gave her a quick kiss good-bye.

She watched him run off. Beyond him the sky looked purged, just a few wisps of clouds stretched in the distance. Remy waited until his figure had disappeared, then continued on toward her destination.

AT THE DEPARTMENT STORE, SHE HAD JUST PASSED THE MEN'S TIES and made her way into the women's section, toward the lingerie, when she saw the most beautiful dark red blouse.

The blouse seemed to call to her. It was of densely knit silk, in tiers that billowed out toward the bottom. Though she usually wasn't one to pay much attention to clothes, Remy stopped and touched the fabric, substantial but soft. She took the hanger from the rack and held the blouse up against herself, then turned to see how it looked in one of the full-length mirrors.

The blouse was much too big.

Checking the tag for the size, Remy saw, with a sad little laugh, that it was a maternity shirt. She turned to look at the other racks around her and realized that she was in the maternity department. She shook her head at herself. Of course she would be drawn to this shirt, of all things. She held it up again, imagining what it would feel like to fill it out. Remy had a long torso, plenty of room for a baby. But she had given up that hope. Together she and Nicholas had decided not to pursue any of the recourses so many other couples took—no painful treatments, expensive surgeries, or complicated adoptions. No need to go down any of those roads; they had been lucky enough already. Remy returned the blouse to the rack and made her way toward the lingerie.

She meant to head straight for the training bras, but it occurred to her that she ought to buy some bras for herself, too. Hers were old and stretchy, to the point of barely performing their meager duty. And if she couldn't have that red maternity blouse, well, then, she might buy herself something else.

This thought was vague, more like a feeling. She found herself plucking up a short, sleeveless nightgown of creamy white satin and a flesh-colored bustier that hooked in a complicated way at the back. She imagined herself wearing the bustier under her orchestra blouse, transforming her chest so that there was more of it, propped up under the stage lights. But what solo was she playing? Which part?

Remy had been with the Boston Symphony Orchestra for nine years now—principal second, dutifully leading the second violin section. Along with the other principals, she played the occasional solo and was a member of the official chamber music group. Her seat was tenured, and she never had to play Pops. In a way, it was the perfect position for her.

But now it turned out the associate concertmaster was retiring. Auditions would be held for his seat: second chair of the first violin section.

For some reason, Remy couldn't help wishing that she would be offered the position—though of course that wasn't the way these things worked. There would be hundreds of applicants for the seat: a full-time position in a world-class orchestra, with a conductor as gifted as theirs, was a rare thing. Yet Remy couldn't help wondering if she, too, ought to put her name in for the slot. It could be rejuvenating to play the first violin part for a change.

Not that it would be any less routine than her current position, she told herself as she wandered through the forest of brassieres. Why, even the concertmaster had to play the same old solo in *Ein Heldenleben* or the *"Haffner" Serenade* again and again. The rehearsals, the performances, same old warhorses, same days and nights year after year . . . all of that would remain the same. Like the endless cycle of her long black skirts—the tiered crushed velour one, the narrow velvet one for cold winter nights, and the flowing rayon one for the hottest summer days—and nylon stockings that gradually laddered where the back of her shoes rubbed her heel. None of that would change, no matter which chair she sat in.

Next thing she knew, she was putting the bustier back on the rack; those little hooks were simply too much to bother with. Instead she found three new bras: a sheer one of nearly netlike taupe, a slinky one in a leopard pattern, and a lace one with padding. Each could be matched with a thong, but Remy left those on the racks—then thought better of it and went back for the leopard-print one. Though she supposed she ought to make sure the bras fit, she did not feel like stopping to undress and, at any rate, could always return them.

But that was the whole point, not to return them—not to return to her usual self, her same old ways! The fact was, she worried she had become complacent. Sometimes, recalling the pain she had felt in her wrists a decade ago, it seemed she had just barely escaped some awful fate and ought to serenade the gods each time she lifted her violin. Yet she had come to think of her playing as a job more than a gift, and no longer applied herself with such effort. Though she still practiced her scales daily and continued her swimming regimen, she no longer followed all the rules Conrad Lesser had sworn by. There wasn't always time to pay attention to every detail of a piece, not when it had to be performed after just two or three rehearsals. Often she had to resort to easier hand positions in order to perform adequately in time for performance night. It had been ages since she consciously chose to play something in the fourth or sixth position. Their schedule simply didn't allow time for such things.

She wondered if the leopard pattern would show through her lighter clothing—though if that were the case, the sheer bra, too, might show through thin fabric. But then the lace didn't make sense, either.

Remy replaced each of the bras on their respective racks. Since now the leopard thong would not have a bra to match with, she put that back, too. She kept the short satin nightgown, though, and scanned the area until she found the display of the same old brand of bra she had always worn.

Probably it was no good, she thought, to settle so easily back into—herself. But she *liked* herself. She liked her life! Of course it might be nice to play the melody for once. Sing the lead, emerge high above the others, soar supremely in the top register . . . But the middle voices were just as important. The seconds, the violas, the altos. The ones no one paid much attention to. They were the ones who added texture and depth, whose presence, if generally unnoticed, was absolutely necessary. And what did it matter, really, if she were associate concertmaster instead of principal second? She would still be Remy.

Quickly she plucked up three of the same brassieres she had been wearing for years. She liked knowing, without having to try them on, that they would fit, and was relieved to be so easily done with it.

After all, either way she would be second—second chair of the firsts, or first chair of the seconds. It was who she was, where she would always be. Always some version of second place.

For some reason she thought of Yoni, running rosy-cheeked toward the river.

"Runner-up" was the phrase she heard in her head. She nearly laughed aloud at her pun, picturing Yoni in his jogging outfit as she stood there with her handful of bras. Because Yoni never would come first at the conservatory, would he? Just as Remy would always be second violinist, second chair, second wife.

That was when she remembered: Jessie. She had completely forgotten her reason for coming here! How odd, how unlike her. Remy had to laugh at herself, and scanned the displays for the training bras.

Here they were. She selected the one she knew Jessie would like the best, beige cotton with a butterfly embroidered in white between the flat, flapping cups. Then she turned to join the line at the register.

But first she quickly went back to grab the leopard thong.

HUGH'S BIRTHDAY WAS NEXT WEEK, AND HAZEL HAD BEEN INVITED to celebrate with him: just the two of them, dinner reservations at Radicchio. She had thought hard about what to do for a gift, since this early on one couldn't risk anything too personal. She thought and thought, and then, during yet another slow afternoon at Maria's fabric store, came up with the perfect gift.

"What do you know about really good socks?" she asked Ginger, her coworker and best friend. Well, sometimes she thought of her as her best friend, and other times she thought of her as her divorced friend, since that was the main thing they had in common. Hazel had met her six years ago here at the fabric shop, where they each worked three and a half days a week, overlapping on Wednesdays. Sometimes Hazel wished Ginger didn't work here at all; then Hazel could do so full-time and become as expert as Maria, the Russian woman who owned the store.

"Fine quality ones," Hazel continued. "Woolen." When they went out this weekend Hugh had mentioned that he had just one pair of good wool socks, and that he always wished, during the cold winter months, that he would remember to buy some more.

"Do you mean for hiking?" Ginger asked, leaning against one of the enormous bolts of Spanish velvet, looking up from the magazine she was reading; since the store was high end, they had lots of gorgeous, overpriced materials and long stretches of inactivity in between clients. "You can get that sort of thing at REI," Ginger said, and turned back to her magazine.

Hazel was about to explain that that was not quite what she meant, but it was too early to mention Hugh Greerson; she couldn't afford to jinx herself.

"Right," she said, and busied herself with the fabric swatches. Socks would show him that she had listened, had heard what he had to say. Good, finely knit, high-quality ones.

As if holding such a specimen, Hazel ran her fingertips over the thickly embroidered rose pattern on her favorite fabric. She adored this shop, loved the way she felt here, surrounded by beautiful materials. She considered herself lucky to have a job that interested her and paid sufficiently. Between this, Nicholas's child support, and the money her father had left her, Hazel was able to live without financial worries.

She had even entertained the notion that she might open her own shop, one specializing in Oriental carpets. She had borrowed from the library every book she could find on the subject, had read about natural dyes versus synthetic ones, and the recurring symbolism of the various patterns, and the plight of the Afghani refugees who wove their initials into the edges. The careful craftwork and grand beauty, the combined elegance and domesticity of the carpets themselves, fascinated her. She drove around to various carpet stores and chatted with the men who ran them, thinking she might apprentice herself somewhere. But it was a male profession—heavy, dusty rugs lugged around huge warehouses, pure physical strength needed to roll them out and up again. In none of those shops had she felt quite welcome. And, of course, to become a buyer she would have had to voyage to all kinds of Middle and Far Eastern countries—and she had long ago lost her urge to travel.

She held the fabric up, to better examine the stitching. The embroidery of each rose petal was perfect. Such things really did make a difference. Even in a pair of socks, surely there was the equivalent of this gorgeous material. "Can you cover me for a coffee break?" she asked Ginger.

"Sure," Ginger said, pleasantly bored. "Take your time."

HEADING TOWARD THE DEPARTMENT STORE, HAZEL COULDN'T HELP thinking how wonderful it would be if things worked out with Hugh. That she might be part of a couple again, not just a lone divorcée in a sea of couples, was a thought she barely allowed herself to indulge in. It wasn't so much living one's life alone that was awful. It was that her aloneness felt like an element of her personality—as if her singledom were a character trait and not simply a situation beyond her control.

As much as Hazel abhorred this mentality, she herself sometimes thought this way. Take Ginger, for instance. Ginger was one of those busy single women who, because she had no children, was always participating in activities where she hoped to meet available men. Nothing ever came of it. To Hazel the repeated failures had become confirmation that there must be something wrong with Ginger—for being divorced, or simply for trying not to be. That was why Hazel joined Ginger in only one of her activities, the foreign film club (which consisted of five female coworkers from Ginger's previous job and two doughy-faced older men, one of whom still lived with his mother).

Surrounding her, all the time, like a cloud of gnats, was Hazel's awareness (everyone's awareness, she supposed) that there was something unseemly about being a divorced woman. Perhaps it was the mystery of what it was that was keeping an attractive woman all alone. Perhaps it was the unbecoming notion of a woman in her forties still going out on dates like a teenager. Perhaps it was the cliché of the desperate divorcée, bitter and on the hunt.

With a sigh, Hazel pushed through the front doors of Lord & Taylor—and there, just a few paces ahead of her, was Remy. Hazel could have caught up to her if she wanted to, could have said a friendly hello. Instead she slowed her steps, let Remy continue into the women's section. This city really was too small. Hazel was already in the men's section; there was no need to pretend to want to chat with Remy. Absently she picked up a packet of boxer underwear, but she couldn't help it: she looked ahead to where Remy was—and saw her fingering a big ruby-colored maternity blouse.

Hazel dropped the packet of underwear. She tried to retrieve it but her fingers wouldn't quite work. Again she looked over, to make certain she was correct. Yes, there it was, the sign overhead: MATER-NITY. Now Remy was holding the blouse up against her front, admiring herself dreamily in the mirror.

So, it was possible, after all these years. Hazel had assumed that was one thing that would never work out for them; after all, it had taken long enough for Hazel herself to conceive. The doctors had said Nicholas had a low sperm count, that his sperm were "weak swimmers"—well, something like that, was how she had understood why it had taken four long years for him to finally fertilize one of her perfectly healthy eggs.

"May I help you, ma'am?" The store clerk, very young, bent down to retrieve the packet of underwear.

"Oh . . . yes. I'm looking for a good pair of men's wool socks. The best you have." To Hazel's surprise, her hands were trembling. Ridiculous. Why should it matter to her if Remy was pregnant? Well, because her own daughter would now have a sibling. Hazel recalled the vision she used to have: the boy and girl in front of the steps to the beautiful house. Was this to be the boy, then?

Hazel followed the young man toward the socks.

"These are our most elegant ones," he told her, displaying a pair of dark gray knee-highs. "Merino wool. Made in Italy."

Ridiculous they looked. A skinny, droopy, overpriced pair of socks. She rubbed the long toe between her fingertips. What if Hugh thought a pair of socks like this piddly? On the other hand, what if he thought them extravagant, too much money spent on something unnecessary? The key to this thing with Hugh, she knew, was not to appear too invested, not to need him too much.

"The toe is double-knit," the man told her.

"It feels thin," Hazel said, concerned. Maybe this wasn't the perfect gift after all.

"If you'd like something thicker, we have these over here." The young man was turning toward a tree of socks atop one of the glass cabinets. "Or if you want something in between, we have these." He reached underneath, into the glass cabinet, where an array of socks were layered one over the other in a fan. "They come with a lifetime guarantee. When they wear out, you just send them in for a replacement pair."

Hazel felt her brow furrowing, her heart racing as the man handed her a pair to admire.

"Is there a problem?" he asked.

How could she explain? The problem was that only the perfect gift would do. Because it was all so difficult, and the chances so slim. Whatever she gave Hugh had to be just right, because if it wasn't, and things didn't work out, she would blame herself—for buying the wrong gift, for doing the wrong thing.

"I . . . I'm sorry. I need to think this through a bit more." It mattered now, somehow, so much more than she had thought it mattered.

"Yes, of course," the young man said, "take your time." But he took the pair of socks from her and put them back under the glass, as if to show her that she had missed her chance.

AT HOME, IN THE GOLDEN LIGHT OF AFTERNOON, NICHOLAS SAT AT his desk in the music room.

It was his favorite room, a former screened-in porch the previous owners had winterized, which now housed the piano, an incongruous flowered settee, a long glass coffee table, and an enormous couch Remy called "the miracle sofa" because it was covered in some tweedy fabric that managed to mask whatever was spilled on it—a frequent enough occurrence. So many friends and guests had sat there, wine or coffee in hand, listening, laughing, or joining in with their own music-making. Three walls of windows looked onto the trees and shrubbery that bordered the majestic house next door, and during the day, when the sun was at just the right angle, the room became part of the landscape, the brownish carpet (under which, the realty agent had repeatedly assured them, was a beautiful parquet floor) soaking up the warm rays, with flickering light and shadows of tree branches passing across it like a benediction. A twist of a handle tilted open each tall window, admitting the twittering of birds, the chattering of squirrels, and breezes adorned by neighborhood sounds—the postman chatting with a dog walker, or from Beacon Street the occasional screech of brakes or bleat of a car horn. Now Nicholas could hear the T conductor's ineffectual ringing of a tinkly trolley bell; the house, an ivy-covered brick one in Brookline, was just a block from the C-line.

Trying not to submit to distraction, Nicholas again faced his work in progress.

It was the large-scale piece he had begun the year he met Remy, the year that everything became complicated. Sometimes he allowed himself to suppose that was the root of the problem (although he didn't really believe that kind of psychobabble). Yet it was true that the point when he had begun having trouble was soon after his return from Italy—that his realizations about his mother and about Remy had somehow stymied his progress. It was as though the complexities of life had crept into the work itself, not in a way that might add texture or depth, but in a confounding way.

And so Nicholas had put the piece aside and for years not looked back at it. All the while, though, he intended to return to it, and when last year he finally took it up again, he found it as promising as he remembered. For nearly a year now he had been working on it—yet still it wasn't right. Though individual sections were quite good, the structure was too broad, almost meandering. It needed to be reined in—but to do so seemed to compromise all he wanted to convey. At times he thought the piece Promethean, in other moments, simply a mess. What had begun as an excursion into his youth in Scotland had taken a darker turn in the second movement and from there grew increasingly unwieldy.

He blamed various factors. As his finished pieces won increasing praise, he was continually receiving commissions for other, smaller works—ten-minute pieces, usually, nothing overly daunting—yet fulfilling these requests meant setting this larger piece aside for long periods. And while time away from a work in progress usually allowed him to view it with a fresh eye, with this piece it had been a struggle to find, again, his original impulse.

Yet he was determined to finish it. There was too much good in it not to.

Today, though, Nicholas had barely lifted his mechanical pencil. Hearing the front door click open, and the thunk of a heavy book bag, he called, "That you, Jess?" eager for distraction.

"Hey, Dad." There came the faint squeak of the refrigerator door, and Jessie pouring herself a glass of juice. Nicholas waited hopefully as she came to peer into the music room.

"There's a bunch of bands playing on Lansdowne Street Saturday night." Her tone was suspiciously nonchalant. "It's an all-ages show. Some kids from school are going."

The evasive "kids from school" made him wonder if that boy Kevin might be there.

Jessie took a swig of her cranberry juice. "So . . . can I go?"

Nicholas suspected he should say no. Hazel probably would have. If only Remy were home, she would know what to do. Shouldn't she be home now? Where was she, anyway? Suddenly everything felt precarious.

He tapped the mechanical pencil to his lip, weighing possible responses. "If there's a chaperone, then yes. I'll pick you up at ten."

"Ten! Dad, come on!"

"Well, eleven, then. As long as you all stick together."

"Dad! Some of the best bands won't even start playing until eleven!" Jessie stomped off in a way that let Nicholas understand he had been too lenient; clearly she was satisfied with the outcome, not to have wrangled for an extra hour.

"Ingrate," he muttered as the door to her room slammed. The girl he once knew had been replaced by this foreign creature who pouted and sulked. Nicholas blamed the teen novels she had been reading all summer—morbid tales in which the protagonist invariably had a terminal illness, a drug addiction, or multiple personality disorder. (Glenda the psychologist of course said they were "developmentally appropriate" and that Jessie was learning about the real world in a safe way.) The Barbies she and her best friend, Allison, once worshipped had been stuffed into a plastic bin in the hall closet; searching for something on an upper shelf, Nicholas would glimpse the mass grave of plumed heads, naked legs and feet in permanent demi-pointe, and recall cheerier times. These days Jessie and Allison spent hours locked in the bathroom, emerging with their hair tied in little twisting foam-rubber wires.

"She's thirteen," was how Remy explained it. "It's what thirteen-year-old girls *do*."

But to Nicholas a pouting female felt like an allegation against him. His daughter's new sensitivity seemed to him an indictment—yet what had he ever done to her?

Enough of this. He stood, went upstairs to her room, and knocked firmly on the door.

From the other side came harangued footsteps, and then, "What do you want?"

"I'd like to talk to you."

The door opened slowly, like a bridge lowered over a moat. "Yes?"

"There's a matter I've been meaning to speak to you about." But already he could feel himself faltering. After all, she was usually quite sweet, really.

"Fine, what?"

It wouldn't do to start a fight. He never did like to make trouble. Quickly he said the first thing he could come up with: "Wasn't Jasper to have returned to school along with you this fall?"

The guinea pig. Jessie claimed to have rescued the thing from a science teacher's menagerie last June, when students took the animals home for the summer. But Jessie still hadn't brought Jasper back.

"If I'm not mistaken, that poor, already sluggish creature is now nearly a month behind in his academic career."

"Dad! If you saw the conditions there, you would totally cringe. It's inhumane."

"Are you sure that's not an exaggeration?"

"Believe me," Jessie said, "we're doing a service."

"For . . . the guinea pig?"

"His name is Jasper."

"For Jasper." Nicholas frowned. "And his middle school education."

"Yes. Believe me." Jessie said this very seriously.

Nicholas thought for a moment. "Well, so. All right, then."

He couldn't help it, couldn't help his pride, that this girl was his daughter, the same one who had once been a mere frog-shaped newborn who fit in the crook of his arm, sucking on his pinkie, with eyes that sometimes crossed, listening to his singing with an involuntary, twitchy, blissful smile on her tiny moist lips.

"Is that it?" she asked, as if forever interrupted.

"Well, yes."

"Okay." The door was closing. Nicholas's panic returned, as if he were about to lose something.

"What are you doing in there, anyway?" he heard himself asking.

The door stopped moving. "I'm *thinking*," came the voice.

"Oh, well, yes, please, go on, cerebrate."

The door closed.

Nicholas remained there even when he had heard the lock on the door click shut. Something was happening, he just couldn't put his finger on it. If only he could regain control of the situation.

Chapter 3

A MONDAY, A NIGHT WITHOUT CONCERTS OR SYMPHONIES, THE first truly cold October night, dying leaves trembling, moon hanging like a shard of ice. None of Remy's sweaters was warm enough. She settled on a thick wool turtleneck the same brown as her eyes, and then she and Nicholas went to pick up Yoni. Nicholas was taking them to dinner.

"To celebrate!" he said now, steering the old Volvo down Huntington toward Yoni's building.

Remy asked what they were celebrating.

"Our anniversary!"

She raised an eyebrow. "And which anniversary would that be?"

"It's nine years ago that we took our first vacation together." Nicholas's voice was chipper and matter-of-fact. "As I recall, the sand on the beach was so hot you leapt onto my back and ordered me to carry you back to the hotel."

Remy had to smile as Nicholas continued. "It's six years ago that you cooked the best vegetarian bouillabaisse one could ever hope for, for the first and thankfully last time. It's—let's see—two years ago that you put on that polka-dot skirt for Vivian's opening. And it's twelve hours ago that I had the intense pleasure of lying next to you as you slept, watching your mouth twitch."

"My mouth doesn't twitch."

"Like a rabbit. Always nibbling."

That was Nicholas. He might forget your *actual* anniversary, but he could come through with some other one when you least expected it.

It was part of the bargain that Remy had agreed to—though at the time she hadn't thought of it that way. She had just followed her heart and found herself in this shared life. If she pondered it too much, their ending up together seemed haphazard. But really that was how most things in life came about—people just didn't like to admit it.

People were always looking for *meaning*. Remy knew better than to second-guess her luck. When her birthday went unrecognized, her haircut unnoticed, she reminded herself that none of it meant much in the long run. When during intense bouts of work Nicholas seemed, for days, to forget her existence, when he tossed off some comment that made her feel small, discarded . . . she knew he would make it up to her without even meaning to, in some other way. And sure enough, at some other point entirely, Nicholas would remark, with an enthusiasm close to disbelief, on her very presence, the taste of her tongue, the warmth of her palm in his.

At times this was enough for her. Other times she found herself wanting him to be someone else: the man who had come back from Italy to claim her, decisive and confident—not the one who was easily impressed by the simplest things, whether it was a colleague's supposed friendship with President Clinton, or Gary's risky sports bets, or Yoni's real estate ventures. Not the one who was suddenly so ineffectual in dealing with his own daughter.

Yoni was there in front of the building, and hopped into the backseat with an air of propriety. He asked about the restaurant. Nicholas wouldn't quite say what it was, only that it sounded intriguing, that they simply had to go. "A gypsy place," he added, as if it were a type of cuisine.

"What does that mean?" Remy asked. "Is it Czech? Rumanian?"

"We'll starve," Yoni said.

Remy was glad to have him along. He often came to them for companionship, and for comforting, when his romantic escapades went awry. The conspicuous absence of the moment was Patricia, who seemed to have disappeared shortly after their trip to Madrid. And though Remy had thought Patricia perfectly nice, it was good to have Yoni back to his old self, independent of any one woman, reclined in the backseat as if this were *his* car and Nicholas and Remy his drivers. He claimed to be happier as a single man, said he was now cultivating a "friendship" with his previous girlfriend, Cybil—whom Remy had preferred to his other women, and who might even join them at the restaurant tonight.

"They have palm readers!" Nicholas added. "But for some reason there's never anyone there."

Remy groaned. "I guess we'll find out why."

"We have to help them out," Nicholas insisted. "Who else is going to? Ah, here we are." He pulled up to the curb. "Go ahead, hop out. I'll find a parking spot. See, doesn't it look like a cozy place?"

The restaurant indeed looked cozy, perhaps too much so, more like someone's living room, into which they hadn't exactly been invited: through the window Remy could see a few tables, two of them occupied, as well as a couch and an armchair. Warm, dim lighting. Racks of wine against the wall. "Go on in," Nicholas said as Remy and Yoni stepped out into the brisk air. "I'll be back soon."

"Good luck parking." Remy pulled her coat tightly around her as Nicholas drove off. To Yoni she said, "He gets so excited about his own ideas." It was what she liked about him; you never quite knew where you might end up.

They entered the little restaurant, just one small room, plastic flowers along the ceiling as if forgotten from another season. From stereo speakers came folk music played on some wailing instrument. Remy laughed at Nicholas's enthusiasm, unworried by the way he had deposited her and Yoni in this strange place and then driven off without them.

The hostess, a small, gray-haired woman in a pilled sweater, looked shocked to see them. "Table for four, please," Remy told her, then asked Yoni, "Did Cybil decide she was coming?"

"I told her I'd call her at seven-thirty," he said but made no move to do so. "She wasn't sure if she'd have finished her project or not." Cybil worked at a high-end design firm near the waterfront.

They settled into a table in the corner of the room, near a small, square one where two men in wool caps were speaking a language Remy didn't recognize. At another table a man who looked like a bulldog and a woman who looked like a fashion model were sipping coffee and ignoring each other. Some of the tables were laid with linen and silverware, but others had no tablecloths at all. "Is this a café or a restaurant?" Remy asked.

"I think it's still deciding." Yoni picked up the menu, a brief, hand-written one, and squinted. "What time is it?"

"Time to call Cybil."

"Right. I'll go see if there's a pay phone." He stood and went to the back hallway.

When Yoni had disappeared, the man in the blue felt cap pulled his chair closer to Remy's. "You speak good English?" he asked.

"I like to think so."

"What you think of this?" He handed her a sheet of bright yellow paper with little tear-offs of a telephone number at the bottom. Remy skimmed the text—too long for a flyer—something about trading used cars for land in Costa Rica. There were numerous misspellings, but Remy didn't feel like correcting them.

"I give you some!" the man said brightly, trying to hand her some more flyers.

"No, no, thank you."

"Oh, okay," the man said, sounding hurt. Taking the flyers back, he turned abruptly away.

Yoni had reappeared. "She's not going to be able to join us," he said, and then, nodding his head toward the next table, "What was that about?"

"A business proposition. Used cars and oceanfront property." Yoni sat down across from her. "Too bad Cybil can't make it," she added as he unrolled his cutlery from the napkin. Really, though, she was content knowing it would be just the three of them, their little family.

Yoni didn't respond; he seemed to be thinking to himself. "So, what's new, how are things? How's dear Jess?"

"Oh, you know, she always manages to have a good time." Remy laughed. "I have to admit, sometimes I'm jealous of her. Or maybe just . . . envious." Of Jessie's ease, her endless summer, lying around reading those paperbacks, holding lengthy telephone conversations with that boy Kevin, and long sessions of giggling with Allison. "I mean, when I was her age, I was this anxious girl practicing my violin for hours. I watch Jessie at her swim meets and soccer practice, and there she is, always enjoying herself, scoring goals, *winning*. . . . Of course, she's completely unmotivated about anything other than sports."

The waitress, the same gray-haired woman, presented them with a basket of dark bread and a tray of olive oil and offered to bring a bottle of the house wine. Then she left them.

Yoni immediately began tearing at the bread though it had already been sliced. He always ate this way, Remy had noticed, zealously cracking things apart, so that when the dishes were cleared there was a ring of crumbs or seeds around where his plate had been. Sometimes Remy found herself watching his hands, entranced by the wounded one. It made her feel childish, the urge to stare at this deformity. Other times she didn't even notice it.

"Do you and Nicholas want to have a child of your own?" Yoni asked, dipping the bread in oil.

Remy watched him chew, heard the familiar pop of his jaw. Tonight his face was unshaven, so that he looked Mediterranean, tougher, his cheekbones more defined. Remy reached over and wiped some crumbs from his cheek. "I guess that's the one thing Nicholas and I can't manage to do together." She shrugged, to show that really it didn't matter. She had made a decision to stop trying; it was simply too painful. It surprised her now to realize that Nicholas had never mentioned any of this to Yoni. "To be honest, I've always found something slightly greedy in people having kids all the time. There are already so many children without families and homes."

"Oh, come on, cut the self-righteousness."

"I'm not trying to be self-righteous," Remy said. But she relented. "Look, I would love to have a baby. It's something I've wanted for a long time. It would be nice. Yeah. Really nice." It felt good to say it aloud. This was something she rarely spoke about anymore, though there had been a few years when she had spent tearful hours talking her friend Vivian's ear off about it, until she realized that Vivian was tired of hearing Remy complain. Even now she felt the need to add, "At a certain point I realized that everyone has something like this."

"What do you mean, 'like this'?"

"Everyone has something they want but don't get to have."

Yoni seemed to consider this. "Do you really think that's true?"

Remy nodded. "It's what makes us human. Or maybe what keeps us . . . moral." She thought for a moment. "What about you?"

"What's my unfulfilled desire?" He seemed caught off guard.

"No, I mean do you think you'll ever want to have children."

"Oh," he said briskly, relieved, "yes, I do. With the right person, yes, I would. Very much."

That he responded so quickly, and in the affirmative, surprised her. "I must say, Yoni, I'd assumed you were a perpetual bachelor."

"I believe in family," he said.

Remy thought about this. "The truth is," she told him, "Jessie really is more than enough for me. I don't mean that as a complaint, by the way. I'm talking about love."

Yoni smiled warmly. Feeling somehow embarrassed, Remy looked toward the door and said, "Nicholas appears to have vanished." And then: "Should we be worried?"

"Knowing Nicholas, no."

Remy smiled. "True."

Then Yoni's face changed. "Does everything really come so easily to him? I've often wondered that. It seems that way, but then I think it might just be the aura he gives off."

"He works incredibly hard." Remy heard how defensive she sounded.

"Well, of course, I know that, I just meant——"

"There's no struggle," Remy said flatly. "Believe me, I know exactly what you mean."

Yoni nodded, almost imperceptibly. "It's hard, isn't it, when one of the people you love most in the world doesn't quite understand what it feels like." He paused, as if revisiting some painful moment. "I mean that he maybe doesn't know what a certain kind of . . . frustration might feel like."

Remy supposed Yoni must be talking about himself, about how Nicholas made him feel, and felt a sudden tenderness toward him. She reached out to take his hand in hers. "He doesn't mean to do it. That's what I have to remind myself. He can't help it if he doesn't understand." Yoni's hand felt warm in hers. She heard herself say, "I do sometimes wonder what my life would be like with him if it hadn't been so easy. For him to win me, I mean. If he'd had to fight a bit more, to get me. If he'd had to fight for me."

Immediately she felt that she had told on Nicholas. Ashamed, she looked down at her plate, and brought her hand back to her lap. Yoni, too, was quiet, just thinking, perhaps, until the waitress arrived with the wine—a bottle already uncorked, as if pilfered from some lunch table in Italy. The waitress filled their glasses and, without waiting for their approval, left the bottle on the table and walked away.

"It's perfectly fine," Yoni said, somewhat awkwardly, after a small sip. "Could be fun to get drunk on it."

Now the man with the bulldog face approached them. "I draw you," he said, in another unplaceable accent, and held out a sketchbook into which he had scratched the image of a man and a woman who looked slightly like themselves. The man who was supposed to be Yoni was leaning toward the woman. Around them the artist had drawn the shape of a heart.

"Oh!" Remy said, and gave a little laugh—but Yoni was considering the drawing, not smiling. The bulldog man seemed suddenly nervous. "I leave you," he said, taking the sketch away, and went back to his table and to the blond woman, looking dejected. Yoni's eyes followed him.

Immediately the man in the blue felt cap at the next table pulled his chair closer to Remy's. "People give him a little money, you know." He nodded toward the man with the bulldog face. "For his art. People like to give him a little something."

"No, thank you," Remy said, trying to smile politely, and the man in the blue cap pulled his chair away again, back to the man in the black one. The air in the room felt suddenly sharper; Remy pulled the neck of her sweater higher. "I caught a chill, somehow."

"Here." From the back of his chair Yoni undraped his gray wool scarf with the short tassels and reached across the table, placing the scarf around Remy's shoulders. "How's that?"

"Thanks, Yoni." Remy readjusted her shoulders under the scarf. Quickly she asked, "What do you think's happened to my husband?"

"Let's see," Yoni said, repleating his napkin. "There are probably no parking spots, and the garages are full, and knowing Nicholas, he managed to get lost. Or something could have happened to the car. It broke down. No, let's see, Nicholas is driving, I would guess that he's had an accident." He said it not cruelly but reasonably, as if having given all possibilities equal consideration.

"With his driving record," Remy said, "it's probably all of the above. Should we order? Or should we call the police?"

Yoni raised his hand to call the gray-haired woman over.

"Yes?" she asked.

"We heard there was a fortune-teller."

"She has strep throat," she told him. "But that man over there will draw your picture for you."

Yoni blinked, a look of recognition, but shook his head. "No, thank you."

That was when Nicholas walked in. "Come here, you," Remy called to him, and kissed his cheek, feeling almost duplicitous, somehow, as he settled into the chair next to her.

Yoni said, "I congratulate you, Nicholas. This is truly the most bizarre establishment I've ever come to eat in."

Nicholas shook his head, looking exhausted, and said, "So many things have happened to me."

AT FIRST HE SIMPLY COULDN'T FIND A PARKING SPOT. HE MADE A slow tour of each square block, gradually at a farther and farther remove from the restaurant, until, quite suddenly, he was lost. In the darkness, nothing looked familiar, and he drove for minutes more before he found that he had arrived, somehow, near Back Bay. It was at that point that he believed he had found a space, directly across from a brightly lit hotel. But when he tried to park, the car wouldn't fit. He tried for a good few minutes while the boldly costumed hotel valets passively watched. Then, after attempting to pull back out into the street, he struck the corner of a passing car.

The car stopped, flicked on its hazard lights. A woman stepped out and walked to the front, where Nicholas's bumper had tapped it. Nicholas, too, had emerged from his vehicle. "So sorry. I hope there's no damage." Already he had noticed that her bumper was dented.

The woman didn't look furious, merely annoyed. "You'd better give me your insurance information."

"Oh, yes, of course." Nicholas went to find the papers in the glove box. To his delight, the papers were there. The woman took down the information, watched by the hotel valets in their long red cloaks.

The woman thanked him, returned to her car, and drove off. The street was suddenly quiet, lit by the shiny hotel and the bright shard of moon. As he opened the door to the Volvo, Nicholas saw a woman emerge from the hotel. Tall, with long limbs and a haughty, brisk stride. A name rose from the folds of memory: "Sylvane."

She turned to look. "Yes?"

He crossed the street, watched her face broaden in recognition. They kissed each other's cheeks. "What are you doing here?" he asked.

"Leaving," she said. "My flight is at eleven."

"Back to Paris? But I didn't even know you were in town!"

"Just briefly. A dear friend of mine was married this weekend. Otherwise I would have loved to see you."

His thoughts were adjusting now, readjusting—to Sylvane, the memory of who she was: a fellow composer whom he much admired. Physically, there was something elongated about her, the aquiline nose, the narrow gloved hands. Her neck and shoulders she held very straight, as if perpetually offended. She had always impressed him.

But she had not yet achieved the recognition she deserved. In the past five years or so this fact had become more and more pronounced, an element of her very being, of her Sylvane-ness, a certain fatigue behind her eyes, as if weighed down by disappointment. There was the visiting composer position that Nicholas had recommended her for, which, when the competition was finally narrowed down to just two, had gone to the other candidate. There was the post in New York that she had been selected for; at the last minute, due to a funding problem, the offer was rescinded. There was the annual composition prize for which she had been short-listed four years in a row.

With Remy, Nicholas had debated the reasons for this. He maintained it was just one of those things, some other composer always happening to win the judges' favor. But Remy pointed out that each one of those prizes had gone to a man (as had the visiting composer position). Well, of *course* they did, Nicholas nearly said in exasperation. Instead he simply explained, "You know how much it costs to maintain an orchestra. It all comes down to raising money. And men, dear Remy, as much as I hate to say it, are the ones with the money."

"Right, right, and they're more comfortable handing their money over to other, fellow, men—is that it?"

Nicholas nodded. "They trust men with their investment." But he did not think Sylvane a victim of the situation; she simply had not yet had her lucky break. Her music was lush, gorgeous. At times it reminded him of Rachmaninoff, something vast and sorrowful about it—yet too much sorrow could kill a living thing, and listening to Sylvane's work, Nicholas often felt the frustration of some heavy dark cloud always blocking one's view.

Even now, as they chatted on the cold sidewalk, the valets in their long cloaks half-listening with boredom, Nicholas heard the defeat in her voice.

"I hope you're having a good work year," he told her, wanting to be encouraging. "I'm always waiting to hear what you'll come up with next."

"You are very good at flattery," she said.

"I say what I mean." Sometimes when Nicholas heard her music he physically ached.

"Thank you for the compliment."

Something about her reminded him, quite suddenly, of Hazel. It flustered him as he asked her how her husband was, and their children. Even as she in turn asked Nicholas about his work, his life in Boston, his wife and daughter, he found himself overcome by the sensation that he was somehow responsible for this woman's disappointment.

The feeling was increasingly familiar these days, ever since his daughter's teenage sullenness, ever since Hazel's annoyed message at his work number last week, about forgetting to take Jessie to her dental appointment, ever since the other night when Remy had come to bed in a new creamy silk nightgown that Nicholas had immediately wanted to peel off. "What's this?" he had said, pulling it up over her hips, and Remy had sighed in a way that sounded less like pleasure and more like resignation.

"I'd like to conduct one of your pieces," Nicholas heard himself say to Sylvane. "At the conservatory next fall. I told them I'd conduct again while the director is on sabbatical."

Sylvane gave an odd smile. "How nice. Please don't feel you have to do that."

"I want to," he said. "The concerto for viola. It's a favorite of mine. I know just the soloist for it."

Sylvane's face had softened. "That's kind of you, Nicholas."

"It would be a pleasure." Really it was nothing much. But already he felt better. "Won't you let me take you to the airport?"

"Surely you have better things to do?"

"My car's right here."

"I cannot let you do that. There is a subway station across the street and I can go for just eighty-five cents."

Nicholas smiled. "Let me take you, please. That way we can continue our conversation."

She was going to relent, he could see, the way that she reached for the handle of her valise. But then she narrowed her eyes. "Are you not on your way to somewhere else?"

"Oh!" Nicholas remembered. "I can use the hotel phone," he told her, "to call the restaurant and tell them I'll be late."

Sylvane laughed. "No! You go where you're supposed to be! You're too kind, my friend, I'm happy to see your face. You make me laugh. Here, I kiss you." She kissed his cheeks. "And I hope to see you again soon."

MUCH LATER THAT SAME NIGHT, WHILE NICHOLAS SLEPT SOMEWHAT fitfully (the fault, he supposed, of that strange house wine), autumn sneaked in for good, the bone chill, wind like fangs. Nicholas woke with a mild headache, if not from the wine, then from the long, odd night. Service had been slow, the meal late, the conversation somehow awkward, not at all what he had envisioned—and then he had been unable to recall where he had parked the car. He felt disgruntled at the gods who usually protected him, that they had let his whimsy fail. As he peeled back the covers to begin his descent from the half-empty bed, his stomach made an unpleasant sound; that gypsy food hadn't sat well with him.

Remy had already left for rehearsal. Soon Nicholas, too, was on his way to work, feeling less than robust. All across campus, radiators were hissing with renewed effort, sputtering, clanking spastically, so that to Nicholas the entire place felt like an old car trying to start. He really would have preferred not to come to work today at all. But it was his job that afternoon to present an award to one of the students.

Now the award recipients were clustered with a small group of faculty and students eating rolled sandwiches and flat colorless cookies. Conservatory tradition had all award ceremonies followed by a buffet luncheon, to ensure a greater attendance.

"Bravo, Nicholas." It was his colleague George Frank, using a pair of metal tongs to pick through an enormous basin of salad. George refused to eat any exposed fruits or vegetables. Not tomatoes or zucchini or anything that hung off a vine or a bush. He would eat peas in a pod, but not shelled peas. Even after ten years, Nicholas didn't quite understand.

"I liked the introduction you gave there," George said. "Witty and brief, the way everyone likes them."

"Yes, brevity is key." Yoni had joined them, from out of nowhere, grinning as he always did, as if possessing a fabulous secret.

"Hello, Yoni," George Frank said. "I didn't see you at the ceremony."

"You know me: I only come for the buffet. How are you doing, George?"

"Very well," George Frank said. "And I've been following your latest success," he said, turning back to Nicholas. "What a wonderful article in the Sunday *Times*. I imagine you could paper a small bathroom with all the good clippings you're saving."

"Or just use them as toilet paper," Yoni said. Though he was clearly joking, George Frank raised his eyebrows. Only then did it occur to Nicholas that Yoni's tone might have been snide. He noted the feeling that, every once and again, pulsed between the two of them: a competition of some kind. Healthy competition, surely, since they had such different areas of expertise, yet sometimes there was an edge to it. Even last night, at the restaurant, he had felt some sort of tension.

He and Yoni had passed through such moments before. If only Yoni could understand that this was how things worked, the conservatory paying Nicholas for the simple privilege of having his name on the faculty roster. That Yoni shouldered more of a teaching obligation was only natural. Yet Nicholas understood that this fact might at times be a bother. Over the past few years his own professional life had grown more comfortable—less teaching and more time for composing—while Yoni's remained the same.

"Oh, there are only two sandwiches left," Nicholas said, nodding toward the buffet. "I'd better snatch one before they're gone." He moved toward the table, not at all hungry.

Like a fly Yoni followed him there. "Any chance you'll be up for another outing tonight, Nicholas?" His tone was hopeful; he must be wanting to make amends. "A pianist from Chile is playing at the club. He's supposed to be fantastic."

Though his stomach was still uneasy, Nicholas said, "Sure, sounds good," since he didn't want to sound sore. And anyway, Remy had the Symphony tonight.

"Good," Yoni said. "I think it'll be worth it. Now I'd better get back to business." He took his leave. Nicholas looked around the room, his eyes searching, though he couldn't think for whom.

ONLY A FEW OTHER PEOPLE WERE AT THE CLUB THAT NIGHT, COUPLES and some men in business suits—taking prospective clients out for a night on the town, Nicholas supposed. In previous years there wouldn't have been a free seat, just smoke swimming overhead and regulars shouting out in friendly support as the musicians burrowed in and out of their solos. But the club had come under new management a year or so ago, and the current booking agent had shifted focus to international talent. As a result the clientele had changed. The wooden tables had been replaced with glass-topped ones, and an air-filtering system had been installed. Still Nicholas and Yoni continued to patronize their old haunting ground, if less frequently and always with a pang of disappointment, as if their stubbornness alone might return it to the way it used to be.

Tonight they sat at their usual table, a small one in the corner. Yoni was drinking bourbon, looking slightly broody. "I'd have thought you'd be pleased with today's news," Nicholas said, referring to the record-breaking heights at which the Dow was soaring. "They say the New York Stock Exchange traded a billion shares today. Or something preposterous like that."

Yoni pointed out that the majority of his investments were in real estate—but to Nicholas, wisdom in any one sphere of business was surely transferrable across all realms. In the same way, when it came to Middle Eastern affairs, he liked to treat Yoni as a political analyst, due to his mandatory years in the Israeli army. Nicholas had always admired the photograph Yoni kept tucked on the bookshelf in his living room, of himself at age twenty, standing next to his mother, casually holding a rifle and squinting handsomely into the sun.

Now Yoni obliged him with insights regarding the U.S. economy, every so often readjusting his voice so that it didn't overtake the pianist. The piece, slow and loosely jazzy, was one of those seemingly tempo-less variations that, rather than gathering force, simply spread out like a blanket on a lawn. Nicholas thought the pianist quite good, but he could see that the other patrons didn't know what to make of it. On the other side of the room sat a couple that looked to be Nicholas's age, clearly tourists, who must have read a description of the club's former incarnation in an outdated guidebook and were now bewildered. At their right was a young couple obviously on a date, wrinkling their brows whenever they came to an awkward pause in conversation and were forced to attend to the piano. The young man looked embarrassed; clearly this was not what he had pictured when deciding what might impress his date. Should the relationship not take off, he would probably blame this place.

Now Yoni was watching the pianist. As always when in his presence, Nicholas couldn't help expecting that at any moment some slender young thing might walk in and join them. He wondered what had happened to Patricia.

Before her, until about a year and a half ago, Yoni had managed to remain with his girlfriend Cybil for a full two and a half years. Cybil was smart, in her midtwenties and, like many of Yoni's women, lanky and narrow hipped, with pouty lips, short messy hair, and compact buttocks; Yoni liked his women to look like teenage boys. But this one had been able to make Yoni laugh—not all of his girlfriends could do that. And so Nicholas had supposed that would be it, that Yoni had finally fallen in love and would get married, or at least pair off for life. But then, out of the blue, Yoni had announced that he and Cybil had broken it off. No explanation. Yoni claimed not to understand, and Nicholas supposed that might be the truth. Then, not long afterward, he had introduced them to Patricia.

They hadn't seen Patricia since midsummer. Now, strengthened by drink or perhaps by boredom, Nicholas decided to ask where she had gone off to.

"Oh, that didn't work out," Yoni said, swallowing bourbon. "Broke my heart a little bit, actually. She decided to take a job in Madrid. It was a last-minute decision."

"I'm sorry to hear it. You can tell us these things, you know."

"There's nothing to tell. I was surprised, myself."

The pianist had come to the end of an old standard Nicholas vaguely recognized. Applause like the last few drops from a tap. Nicholas and Yoni joined in. Yoni ordered another bourbon.

The voices of the businessmen rose and fell among the ting of glasses and the scrape of ashtrays across tabletops. The pianist played a version of "On Green Dolphin Street" that went on for a long time, lots of slow chords and twinkling runs, the melody nearly impossible to locate. Each time Nicholas thought the pianist was about to rein it in, the music wandered off somewhere new—and the middle-aged couple, trying hard, would sigh and readjust themselves in their seats.

It was when he had finished a third bourbon that Yoni said to Nicholas, quite suddenly and a propos, as far as Nicholas could tell, of nothing, "I sometimes find you careless with Remy's heart."

Around them the music drifted in billows. For a long minute Nicholas said nothing while a glint of candlelight swam in his glass. He watched it as one might read leaves in tea—as though it might explain to him what to make of this absurd statement.

The music stopped. A brief smatter of applause. Slowly Nicholas raised his head and looked at Yoni. "I am not responsible for Remy's heart."

"That's not what I mean," Yoni said testily. He picked up his glass, looked thoroughly affronted to find it empty. The pianist, desperate, had begun to play a calypso.

Nicholas took a gulp of Scotch, his one advantage. He placed the glass back on the table as calmly as possible. "Then what exactly do you mean?"

In a low, drunk voice Yoni said, "You have a treasure you don't appreciate."

Again Nicholas looked down. "What do you know about my appreciation?" he said softly, to the table. "What do you know of what I do or don't do?" But he wondered if in fact Yoni did know something, like about the times he had forgotten Valentine's Day (as if such things mattered!) or had been late meeting Remy and she had to wait . . . or when he missed the flight to Ohio for her father's birthday dinner, was she still angry about that? It was true he wasn't one to say "I love you"—but he had never been that sort of person, it was such a fatuous expression, so unoriginal. Remy knew he felt that way.

The light twitched in his whiskey. He wondered if Remy might have told Yoni something—something that he himself didn't know.

"I only know what I see," Yoni said. "I'm trying to tell you."

"Tell me what?"

But in stubborn drunkenness Yoni refused to elaborate. He looked suddenly exhausted, a man roughed up by thugs. With effort he said, "I suppose you'll figure it out."

Nicholas turned his head in rebuff, saw the young couple, and the tourists, and the now-drunk businessmen. The music had become lively and easy to follow. But Nicholas's ears rang with Yoni's words: "Careless with her heart." What did that even *mean*? It was true that there had been moments when Nicholas hurt Remy's feelings without knowing it, times when Remy told him in a bruised voice that she felt neglected. There had been a big fight after a visit from her parents, once, where she said that even when he thought he was doing something for others, he was really just thinking of himself. But Nicholas had taken note and rarely erred that way now. And though they still bickered, at times, Remy no longer seemed to feel the need to make a scene, the way she had in her twenties. It was years ago, now, that she had thrown that teakettle at him.

"I've overspoken," Yoni said, having regained his strength. He shook his head at himself. "It's time I dragged this drunk man home."

Nicholas nodded, his mouth tight. But he managed, after Yoni had forced himself up from the table and they had told each other (as if nothing had happened) good night, to add, "Take care of yourself, now."

As for what Yoni might have meant, by "careless with her heart," Nicholas still didn't understand. By the time he returned home it was very late, and Remy was fast asleep.

Chapter 4

*T*HIS IS THE FIRST HALLOWEEN JESSIE ISN'T GOING TRICK-OR-treating," Hazel told Ginger. "There's a party at her new friend Kevin's house instead. " *Boyfriend* was the word, though it was still a bit of a shock even to think it. Jessie and two friends were dressing as flapper girls, long strands of plastic beads draped over dresses from the local vintage shop, and flat bands of fabric around their heads, and leather shoes from jazz class with buttoned straps and Louis XIV heels. "They have to look feminine," Hazel continued, checking the tag on a swatch of pale linen. "No more green face paint. Suddenly they're young women, when just a few months ago they were kids." She shook her head, still not quite believing. "I just bought Jessie her first bra."

Ginger, who had been practically reclining on a pile of translucent fabric, straightened up. "Well, now, that's a big deal!"

Hazel decided not to mention how it had come about, Jessie turning up at home wearing a training bra that was too small. Immediately she had modeled it for Hazel, the minute she walked in the door, peeling off her T-shirt right there in the foyer. And though Hazel was proud of Jessie's comfort in her own skin, she was also horrified— that she herself had not noticed her own daughter having grown this way. In fact, the bra strained to stretch across Jessie's rib cage, the straps barely long enough for her broad shoulders.

"Sweetie, it barely fits you," Hazel had told her.

"That's what Remy said. She said we could exchange it."

"But not if you've been wearing it around!"

"I like it," Jessie said.

"Well, we'll just have to get a bigger one. I don't think I ever realized what a strong upper body you have."

"Remy says it's from swimming," Jessie said, unfazed.

After work the next afternoon, Hazel had gone to Saks and bought the most expensive brassiere she had ever purchased, pale pink lace with a little pearl at the center and expandable straps of silk ribbon. Yves Saint Laurent, size 36A, a truly exquisite piece of equipment. That Remy had harnessed her daughter in something as ugly as that Warner's thing . . . The beige elastic reminded Hazel of the sanitary belts her mother had worn. No, for this awkward moment in time, while Jessie's body became, briefly, something bewildering, Hazel wanted her to have only the best, to be proud of her body, to adorn it with beautiful things. No need to feel constantly embarrassed, to cover up, to hide—the way Hazel did.

"Sometimes I look at her and I can see the woman in her," Hazel said now. "And at the very same time I see her the way she was when she was a little girl." Hazel unrolled a new import, damask, the faintest green with yellow threads. "I was remembering, the other day, the sweetest thing, from when she was still little. She was always very protective of me, and I remember one day, it was the year that Nicholas and I separated, Jessie seemed to know that something was wrong. She looked up and asked me, 'Mommy, what's the matter?'" Hazel paused, remembering Jessie's tiny voice, the concern in it.

"I'd vowed to myself never to complain in front of her about the situation; I wanted her childhood to be as normal and happy as possible. So I said, 'Oh, I was just thinking about some things that have been difficult.' And she asked me why things were difficult, and I said, 'Sometimes things can be a bit hard, that's all.' And Jessie thought it over for a moment, and then she shrugged her shoulders and said, 'Well, then, let's just play.'"

Ginger laughed and said, "That's sweet," though Hazel could tell she didn't appreciate how much it had meant at the time. Those early days had been so painful, all the more so for having to hide the pain and never complain about Nicholas lest she color her daughter's impression of him. Back then Hazel still wanted him back. And as, with each passing week, it became more and more clear that he wasn't coming back, her pain only grew.

The worst part was that she didn't understand *why* it had to be that way, why there could be no other outcome. If only she could *understand,* she kept saying. Other husbands strayed, she knew, but returned to their wives and regretted their mistake. Nicholas, though, was adamant; he had "fallen in love" was how he explained it that horrible night in the apartment, when he decided to break the news. It was nothing he could control; he had no choice.

"Oh, right—no choice!" Hazel felt her pain turn to anger. Standing there enraged, looking down at him while he sat limply on a chair in the kitchen . . . "As if you have no ability to make decisions or do the right thing!"

Nicholas shook his head, eyes bloodshot, cheeks wet. He kept wiping his tears on the sleeve of his shirt, as though he were the one whose heart had been broken. "I'm so sorry, Hazel. I don't know what else to say." It was true, nothing he said helped. They had been talking in circles for hours, during which Hazel had gone through an entire spectrum of emotions: shock, hurt, hate, fear, desperation.

"You made a vow, and making a vow means sticking to it." She was trying another approach, gathering up her strength. "How can you just turn around and give your love to someone else?"

"I don't know," he whispered. "I don't understand it myself. All I know is what I have to do."

Yet she kept asking, throughout that long night and the tearful days that followed, as though it might have helped: Why?

He could not say.

And then Jessie told her *Let's just play* . . .

That memory had reemerged last month, after Hazel glimpsed Remy in the department store. At home afterward she must have been furrowing her brow, because Jessie asked, "Are you okay, Mom?"

Hazel had looked at Jessie and felt two things simultaneously: gratefulness, and a wish to protect her. "I'm fine, sweetie," she said, forcing herself not to mention what was most on her mind—and looking into Jessie's green eyes she could see that her daughter knew nothing of Remy's pregnancy. It even occurred to Hazel that perhaps Remy wasn't pregnant at all. Perhaps she had imagined the whole thing. But no, that would be too easy an escape; this pain felt inevitable.

Since then, Hazel had been bracing herself daily for Jessie to learn the news and relay it to Hazel.

Until she had confirmation, she didn't dare mention it, as much as she wished to confide in someone. Twice she had nearly said something to Ginger. But she had stopped herself, knowing Ginger disapproved of that sort of lingering, unnecessary grief.

"I am come back from lunch!" Maria announced. She was a woman without embarrassment; no lack of vocabulary or shakiness of grammar ever stopped her from conversing with complete freedom. Ginger turned away, annoyed, but Hazel smiled. Maria was a wonder, a self-styled businesswoman whose glamour always looked slightly out of place. Hair dyed unnaturally black, and bright eyes with too much green eye shadow glittering above. Her earrings were always large and matched her necklaces, and though she carried herself with hauteur and owned the most expensive fabric store in the Back Bay, she never hesitated to cough extravagantly or blow her nose loudly into a dirty Kleenex. "Let me tell you what I eat. So delicious!"

Maria's lack of self-consciousness was so different from the way Hazel had been when she lived abroad, always trying to slog her way through some foreign language. Only now did she see that there was something beautiful in the incongruity of an alluring, cultured woman speaking incorrectly, something fabulous in the harsh accent and brazenly improper syntax. Why was it, Hazel wondered, that what she found lovely in another woman she could only abhor in herself?

If Maria had been the one to see Remy in the department store that day, and Remy were the wife of her ex-husband, Maria would probably have gone right up to her and asked, "You expecting?" in a loud voice. She wouldn't have huddled behind a tie rack, fumbling a packet of men's underwear. Even if Maria hated Remy, she wouldn't allow herself to feel envy; she would simply revel in thoughts of a pregnant Remy nauseated and puffy and having to pee all the time.

Now Ginger was trying to look busy, as if she didn't have time to chat with Maria. Hazel suspected that Ginger was in fact jealous, since Maria had such a successful business, money for all kinds of gaudy jewelry, and a loving husband and children and grandchildren. After all, here was Ginger, who made such an effort to keep fit, stay on top of things, was educated and polite and easy to get along with—whereas loud and at times uncouth Maria let everything hang out and had no curiosity about things that didn't directly affect her, and still everything seemed to go her way.

This was precisely what Hazel found so fascinating about Maria. Yet it did confuse her—about how to behave in the world. She herself was more like Ginger. And though she liked Ginger and was closer to her than most of her other friends, Hazel sometimes couldn't stand her.

For that reason she still hadn't mentioned Hugh Greerson to Ginger. Since Ginger lived in Arlington and didn't know the people from Jessie's school, it was easy for Hazel to keep the whole thing with Hugh under wraps—though surely some of the other parents had noticed what was going on between them. Hazel herself had taken note when, a year ago, she glimpsed Hugh at First Night with Roberta Plotnik.

Hugh. He had looked so thrilled when he finally kissed Hazel, the night they went to dinner and he dropped her off at home and then just leaned in so naturally, his lips soft, pleasant. Since then things had progressed beautifully. The socks had gone over very well. Yet even now Hazel knew to be wary. Experience had taught her that even the most charming man could surprise you. There had been Jerome Thau, for instance, whom she met back when she signed up with the matchmaking service, the one that advertised on the classical music station. Jerome Thau had been kind and polite, with a bashful laugh, and then, after three lovely dates, on a night when Jessie was at Remy and Nicholas's, Hazel had gone to dine at his house and told herself that, if the occasion arose, she would spend the night with him. And just when the best part was beginning and Jerome Thau had removed most of Hazel's clothing, and she most of his, and things were moving forward as she had hoped, Jerome Thau had donned a pair of weight-lifting gloves and asked Hazel to do something so odd and improbable, she still hadn't brought herself to tell even Ginger about it.

Next week Ginger would be leaving for another continent, trekking in Nepal, away for the entire month. Hazel was relieved at this; it allowed her a full four weeks to proceed with Hugh without the constant deception of withholding it from her. And if things continued to go well, Hazel would have a surprise for Ginger when she returned. It would be a miracle, perhaps—but why not? Why not a miracle, for once?

Hazel felt her hope, tucked under her lungs, blooming again. There were times when she had thought it was gone for good, when she sat on the couch watching television, drinking her sauvignon blanc, certain that the very last of her hope had been killed off. But there it was, growing again, as unlikely as that might be. Even when she thought it had abandoned her forever, Hazel's hope, hidden away, lived.

THE WEATHER HAD TURNED FOR GOOD, NOTHING BUT COLD, THE trees naked and shivering. But the rehearsal room was warm. Remy was comforted by its familiar fuggy smell. This was one of the airtight Wenger rooms down in the basement of Symphony Hall, where, along with Christopher, a clarinetist, and Nora, the pianist, she had been rehearsing a piano trio for a fund-raiser for the Museum of Fine Arts.

Now that they had finished, Remy placed her violin back in its case and carefully loosened her bow—well, not *hers*. She was trying it out on loan, not sure she would purchase it, though she longed to own something so beautiful.

She had first tried it out two years ago. Just on a whim, while her luthier, Daniel, tallied up the fee for a violin repair. When she glimpsed the bow—silver and gold, the frog made of tortoiseshell, the adjuster bead of malachite—its beauty made her want to touch it. After discovering how good it felt in her fingers, and the gorgeous sounds it coaxed from her violin, she dared ask the price. Which made her hand it right back to Daniel.

The bow was still there last week, when she entrusted Daniel with the latest bout of repairs. Her violin's sound post had slipped, and then Daniel found two hairline cracks Remy hadn't noticed. "It's like a car," Remy had said to him. "You think you just need a tune-up, and then it turns out the entire air-conditioning system has failed."

Daniel, a quiet, almost oddly serious man, had said nothing, and Remy worried she had insulted him. But then he said, so softly it was barely a suggestion, "That Melustrina you liked is still here."

The gorgeous bow—of course Remy had to try it again. She played a few of her favorite concert passages, and then an Irish jig, to test its responsiveness. She tried a bouncy *spiccato,* and then porta-mento. The bow was exquisite.

Daniel had let her borrow it on loan.

She told herself now, as she placed it in its slim slot in her case, that the bow would be more than a professional investment. It might even make a difference in her audition for associate concertmaster. Well, if indeed she were to audition . . .

There was a sudden influx of air as the door to the rehearsal room opened. Nora said, "Oh, good, you're here!"

Remy looked up to see Yoni, his cheeks rosy, as if he had sprinted from the conservatory. "Hello!" he said in his confident way. He didn't look surprised to find Remy there.

"Hi, Yoni." Remy had forgotten that he and Nora knew each other. She watched him introduce himself to Christopher, who sidelined in historical performance and even in his daily life looked like a character in a costume drama, with a long curling mustache and ankle-length cloak. Remy no longer recalled having found him odd. She watched Yoni shake his hand and, carefully buttoning the Melustrina into its slot, thought she might just go ahead and buy the bow, to hell with the price. It was a beautiful thing, and so little about her daily work was glamorous. For some reason she thought of the leopard-print thong.

"We're planning a little going-away party for a friend of ours," Nora explained. To Yoni she said, "I'll be right with you. Christopher and I just have to work out some scheduling." She had taken out her datebook and was paging through it.

"Oh, and I have to show you my latest discovery," Christopher told Nora, who hadn't yet seen the seventeenth-century flageolet he had apparently discovered in a bin at a garage sale in Concord.

Remy shut her violin case. But instead of leaving, she found herself lingering by the piano, and played a few chords. Yoni stepped up beside her. "How are you, dear?" He played a little melody on the keys beside her.

"Fine. How's school?" Her hands pressed into the piano keys, another chord resounding.

"The students are wonderful," he said, "though sometimes, some of them, you know . . . they plop down a solo like they're plunking a bag of groceries down on a table." He laughed, while Christopher played Nora a little tune on the flageolet. To Remy it sounded like the call of some small, asthmatic bird. Yoni picked out the same tune on the piano.

Remy moved her left hand down an octave and played the same chord in a lower register.

"It needs a melody," Yoni said, and then she felt his body almost behind her, an arm around one of her shoulders, his other hand alongside hers on the piano keys. Every hair on her body seemed suddenly to be standing on end. "Go ahead," he said, "give me a chord."

She pressed into the keys, and Yoni improvised a little run, up and then down, right over her right hand, a loopy little melody, his playing not affected at all, it seemed, by the maimed finger and thumb. As his skin touched hers, something flashed inside her—but Yoni easily followed Remy's lead when she switched keys altogether, and allowed himself to doodle around on the keyboard. His head was beside hers; it seemed that if she turned her head her mouth would be on his chin.

Remy could hear Christopher telling Nora, "It's an amazing find," as Yoni lifted his hand and placed it directly over Remy's, his fingers over hers. A flame coursed through her, straight down to her groin. Remy bore down into the keys, a loud, rumbling chord.

Yoni, his arms still encircling her, didn't lift his hands. She could feel his pulse, and now his chin grazed the side of her head. His mouth came toward her ear. "I would fight for you."

The words were so soft, she might have dreamed them. She let the last groans of the piano strings reverberate into silence.

Nora was blowing into the flageolet, trying to muster a tune. Remy took a deep breath, felt Yoni stepping back, his arms lifting away from her. Nora handed the flageolet back to Christopher.

"I should have the *Antiques Roadshow* people appraise it," Christopher said, and Remy laughed. But the laugh felt wrong.

"I'd better get going, guys. Have a good afternoon." She pulled on her jacket, feeling utterly confused.

"See you at the museum," Christopher said, and Nora gave a little wave.

"See you." Yoni, unsmiling, leaned in to kiss her good-bye. She kissed him quickly, still hearing his words in her ear—though by now they might have been a breeze, or her own thoughts.

She took her violin case and left the room. Even as she stepped out of the building her pulse raced.

＊—＊

THE NEXT MORNING, IN HER LONG WOOL CARDIGAN AND GRAY sweatpants and fuzzy slippers, Remy waited for Vivian.

She was alone in the house, sipping black coffee in the kitchen. It was a small room, old and high ceilinged, with an ancient stove and a floor layered with linoleum; encountering it when they first viewed the house, six years ago, the realty agent had offered a panicked onslaught of suggestions for renovation. But it was a warm room, cozy despite the high ceilings, with a back door opening onto a patch of backyard.

Remy sipped her coffee and thought. Another sort of woman would not be the least bit troubled by any of this. Another woman would not attach such significance to each small flurry of her heart.

Whatever it was she was feeling was different, very different, from a few years ago, when she had gone through what her friend Vivian had informed her, with perfect math, was the seven-year itch. That was when Remy finally confided to Vivian, tearfully and with embarrassment, that she felt she was crawling out of her own skin. "I need something new so badly," she had told Vivian. "Maybe I need to be away from Nicholas. I don't know how people do it." Vivian, who had never been married but seemed to possess an overall wisdom about the world, had assured her that this was a normal phenomenon and that the feeling would eventually dissolve. "Just make sure to never, ever, put yourself in a situation where you can follow through on your urges. It's one thing to feel lust. It's another to act on it."

The itch had indeed faded away. But this new feeling left her heavy, tumid with recollections—the murmured words in her ear, and the pulse of the piano beneath their mingling hands. She asked herself what in the world she could possibly want that she did not already have.

The doorbell rang. "Hey, you." Remy kissed her, Vivian in her tall fur hat and matching muff, a heavy embroidered coat that reached her ankles. "Let me in out of this *weather*," Vivian said, the only person Remy knew who could dress this way and not look ridiculous.

Just as Nicholas had his friend Gary, the one person completely outside his circle, Remy had Vivian, who lived off of a trust fund and owned an art gallery and sometimes called herself a photographer. Other times she called herself an art dealer. Now she lifted the fur hat off her head with two hands, up high, a champion displaying her trophy. Her hair rose with static. "It's so cozy here." She placed her hat on the table; it looked like a stuffed animal. "All right, what's going on?"

Remy spoke without pause, described what had occurred with Yoni in the rehearsal room. Vivian listened without question or comment, nodding like an expert.

Finally Remy said, "I don't know what to do."

"Nothing, silly." Vivian always made things sound so simple. "Feelings like that are normal. You've been through this before."

"No, this is different."

"Well, okay," Vivian conceded, "I don't mean to belittle it. But don't you think it's natural, too, when you've known someone so well, for so long? To have a sudden surge of affection? You two are very close. And let's face it—he's a very handsome man."

"It's more than physical," Remy told her. "Sometimes I think he understands me better than Nicholas."

"Well, come on, so do I."

Remy laughed.

Vivian asked, "Have you thought about seeing a therapist?"

Remy gave a loud sigh. Music was her meditation, her daily practice; she did not covet Vivian's $100-per-hour psychoanalyst, just as she did not covet her fur hat and muff, her artist lovers in their East Boston lofts, or the rich clients who sent top-quality champagne at the holidays and tried to match the paintings they purchased with the fabric of their sofas.

She said, "I take everything too seriously. It's from being a musician. I'm used to trying to get every little thing just right. I can't just let something be, and not examine it, or ponder it. I can't *not* think that this really matters. It *does* matter."

Vivian's eyes opened wider. "Remy. Are you falling in love?"

Remy felt her own eyes widen. "Oh." She thought for a moment. "I don't know." Pulling at a few of the woolly pills on her sweater, she asked, "Why can't I be one of those women who don't obsess about these things? Who don't feel bad about it? You know, the ones who don't read into every little thing?" She was recalling the time when she had wanted to live like Oscar Wilde—insouciant, decadent, her candle burning at both ends. "I wish I were one of those carefree, witty women. The ones who don't take love so seriously. Who don't let these things overtake them."

Vivian looked puzzled. "Who *are* those women?"

Chapter 5

THEY WERE AT HUGH'S HOUSE, SITTING BEFORE THE FIREPLACE, watching flames wrap themselves around logs. Hazel had kicked off her shoes and folded her legs to her side, propping herself up on one arm, aware of the curve of her body. Next to her, Hugh was leaning back on his arms, his legs stretched out ahead of him in corduroy pants, his feet in thick socks, one over the other. Caves of ashes glowed beneath the grill.

Luke was at a sleepover. Jessie was at that Halloween party (and in Nicholas and Remy's charge). Hazel watched the infinitesimal adjustments of each collapsing log, each dripping ember, and felt all around her the luxury of a night alone with Hugh. She was awash in ripeness, in possibility. Beyond the windows was an incredible blackness.

"I can't remember the last time I roasted chestnuts."

"I never have, actually," Hugh admitted. "I saw them at Bread & Circus and thought it might be a nice treat."

Hazel smiled; she adored this man—how could she not adore him, with his honesty and goodness and spur-of-the-moment chestnuts? At last she had found someone right for her, just when it seemed there was no hope left. "Sometimes I think that's the most wonderful part of life," she told him. "Not the big, fancy things. It's the little, hidden treats."

Hugh nodded, a bit gravely, Hazel thought. "It's funny, isn't it," she continued, "how life gets tossed into baskets that way? I mean, there are the days that people assume are the most important ones, like your wedding day, or the day your child is born, the few defining events, the tragedies, too—that's one basket. And there are the tiny wondrous moments that barely anyone else will ever know about, that's another basket. And then there's everything else."

"I never thought of it that way," Hugh said.

"I don't, usually." She thought again and added, "Sometimes I feel like I'm passing through the days, and other times I feel like the days are *mine*."

Hugh reached over to run his fingers through her hair. "And which kind of a day is this?"

"It's mine, but I'm sharing it with you."

He gave her a very serious look and leaned over to kiss her, longer this time than the good night kiss last week. The fire was stronger now, bright scarves of flame whipping at each other. Hugh kissed her again, and this time he did not pause except to say something brief and meaningless, so sweet and surprising that Hazel at once forgot what it was. Nor was she sure of what she said back. They continued this way, saying things in little bursts, moving closer, Hugh's fingers working open the top few buttons of Hazel's blouse.

He would see the white splotches, she knew. She felt herself shrinking back, told herself not to, told herself that in this light, the spots would not be noticed. But suddenly, just as she had feared, Hugh pulled away.

The chestnuts had caught fire. There was the smell of scorching while with tongs Hugh rescued the blistered foil. Hazel was re-buttoning her blouse, her fingers fumbling. The logs leaked orange ash. Hugh turned to look at her just as she secured the top button, then looked down at the burned foil as if it meant something. His face changed, and he tugged open the wrinkled folds of foil. There they were, little chestnut brains, some of them brown, some of them blackened. Hugh said, "I think they're okay."

Hazel gave a laugh to show that it didn't matter. But it sounded wrong. Why did that always happen to her—even a genuine emotion, when it most mattered, sounding false?

Hugh, too, looked disturbed. Hazel said, "We should probably wait for them to cool."

Hugh was looking into the steam that rose from the chestnuts as if it contained a private message. Hazel saw him swallow, saw the pensive movement of his throat. She decided it was better not to say anything more.

After what felt like a very long minute, in a quiet voice, Hugh said, "I've been thinking. . . ."

Hazel felt a wrenching inside of her. Whatever Hugh was about to say would have to do with her; it might be wonderful or it might be terrible. And as much as she supposed that it might be something good, what her heart felt was more like terror.

"I've been having such a good time with you," Hugh said, and swallowed again. "A really wonderful time."

Hazel's heart sank. That was it. When they began with something nice—when they began by praising you—that was when you knew they didn't want to be with you anymore.

"It's hard, though," Hugh continued. "Because as much as I enjoy my time with you, as much as it feels comfortable, even tonight, even now, something's off."

"What do you mean, 'off'?"

Hugh frowned. "I suppose it's that I'm wondering if I'm truly able to do it."

"Able to do what?" Hazel asked, though she knew perfectly well what he meant. But she refused to make this easy for him.

"To be with you."

No matter how prepared she was, her heart still plunged. Now Hazel was trying to hold her face in place, her heart diving, falling. Thinking to herself: Of course. Really she had expected as much. Supreme disappointment was the only thing in life she knew she could truly count on.

"I don't know why I'm saying this," Hugh said. "I'm having such a nice time with you. I mean to say, I've been having a wonderful time with you. You're a wonderful woman."

Hazel looked down at the abandoned chestnuts. It hadn't been this way back before Nicholas; before Nicholas, she had been the one brushing people aside, trying not to lead anyone on. But since her divorce, the power she had once had . . . it had slipped away. The few times she found herself at all interested in a man, it had been utterly different from when she was young, when she never had to wonder whether he would like her back. And though she could still, sometimes, turn heads, her old allure somehow always eventually failed her.

Hugh was saying more now. The truth was, Hazel barely heard him. Nothing could explain it in any helpful way. Hugh himself was saying so, right now, saying that he himself didn't understand, he was confused. His confusion looked genuine, and Hazel supposed he truly didn't understand how he could want to be with her and not want to at the very same time. He tried again to explain, more familiar phrases. To Hazel it was all a bit tiresome. She looked past Hugh, through the windows, into the blackness, thinking that so many other fateful things must be happening on this same night, things that had nothing to do with her, things that surely mattered much more than this. Significant, meaningful, perhaps wonderful things. When Hugh stopped speaking for a moment, and poked despondently at the chestnuts—as though he and not Hazel were the one being rejected—Hazel leaned over and lightly kissed his cheek. "I think I should go now," she told him, before the explanations could continue.

REMY HAD THE SYMPHONY THAT NIGHT, AND JESSIE WAS OUT AT A party, leaving Nicholas home alone.

He sat, lethargic, at the grand piano. The room was dark, just one lamp lit, and the tall windows closed against the cold. Nicholas wished Remy were here—that they might play together, just for fun.

It had been some time, he realized, since the two of them had made music together. Those evenings were a chance for Remy to enjoy a turn as soloist, front and center, with Nicholas accompanying on piano. Her favorite was the Franck sonata, the one she had been learning the year they met, which Nicholas loved for its swaying beauty, and for the wonderful interplay between piano and violin. Nicholas made a good accompanist, knew when Remy might want an extra moment to fill out a rubato phrase, or hold a tenuto, knew to slow down, almost imperceptibly, in those brief moments where she had to slide into a glissando, or replace one finger with another. Conducting had developed in him an instinctual understanding of musicians' needs—from having to be aware, at each moment, of what each one of them was experiencing.

He had learned from Remy, too, over the years—about the violin. She would point out passages that made the most of the instrument, so that Nicholas saw more broadly its range of capabilities. And over time he had come to understand, too, the sorts of technical challenges that could excite and motivate an experienced player like Remy.

She had a particularly good ear, could identify any borrowed phrase in a piece, even the smallest conceptual echo, and understand what that echo might be harkening to. Sometimes when Nicholas improvised he tossed in little riffs from other pieces, to see if she might recognize them. Now, though, alone at the piano, waking his fingers with a Bach prelude, he thought despondently of the big symphonic piece.

It was incoherent as a whole, was the issue. Kaleidoscopic changes within movements, this grand sweep from the earthy to the ethereal, the terrestrial to the spectral . . . He wanted his symphony to contain galaxies. Of course that was different, he knew, from just being all over the place. He needed to return to that first, most basic impulse, to see again in his mind's eye—and hear again—his long-ago home.

> Pu' Scotland up,
> And wha can say
> It winna bud
> And blossom tae

Yet he barely had the will to work on the piece. Was this what it meant to be "midcareer"—as he had found himself recently, gall-ingly, referred to? It was true that one grew tired of oneself, some-times. That one wished, sometimes, to take some kind of leap, far away to some other place.

Perhaps this was what was happening with Remy, too. She had been standoffish lately, even about the associate concertmaster slot. Nicho-las thought she ought to try for it, if only to avoid a slump. The other night, after a performance, she told Nicholas she felt she had played lazily. "Well, maybe not lazily, but at one point I realized I was think-ing about which soup I wanted to make tomorrow, trying to remember which ingredients we had in the fridge!" Laughing. "I used to try to al-ways remember what Julian said, that the rehearsal *is* the performance. But you know, sometimes, when you're playing the *William Tell Overture* for the hundredth time, even the *performance* isn't the performance!"

She had laughed when she said it. But when Nicholas suggested she try for the upcoming open slot, Remy seemed bothered, pointed out that the work would remain basically the same.

It was true, Nicholas knew. Remy's work was physical, the con-stant wrist and neck injuries, and every summer the travel back and forth to Tanglewood, where they played outdoors whether it was forty degrees or ninety, and only the woodwinds were allotted space heaters (so that the wood of their cold instruments would not crack from their breath). Often Remy had to learn an entire symphony in just two or three rehearsals. "Anyway, lots of people have repetitious jobs," she had added. "What matters is your attitude." But Nicholas sometimes worried about Remy's attitude, her self-deprecation. "I'm just one fiddler among the many," she had said at one point. Well, it was one way of looking at herself, a mere pat of color on the orchestral palette—but that did not diminish her importance. Not at all. She was a necessary and significant member of what Nicholas viewed as the greatest musical instrument of all: the symphony orchestra itself.

Back when he met her, she had been so determined. But it was hard to sustain that degree of commitment, he told himself now. Success demanded the proper mind-set, and if one hadn't the right attitude, well, even the most gifted musicians burned out. Like that girl Lynn, who had played first chair when Nicholas first arrived at the conservatory. Nicholas had looked for her to make waves as she matured, yet nothing seemed to have become of her. A few years ago he heard that she had abandoned music altogether and become a Graphoanalyst. Apparently she lived in Bali and had a job at a fancy resort, analyzing guests' handwriting.

The recollection of Lynn, and of Remy sitting next to her, her hair pulled up into a big curly tuft, blew through Nicholas.

Yank oot your orra boughs, my hert!

He pressed into the keyboard, a bright C major chord, that most simple and satisfying affirmation. The chord resounded, and gradually faded. Keep it simple, Nicholas told himself. That was what he usually did—what pleased him so elementally. Simple manipulations that created something new. Just keep it simple, the way you like to. . . . He knew that. He *knew* it. Why, then, did such a thing no longer seem possible?

HAZEL AWOKE EARLY THE NEXT MORNING, FEELING HUNGOVER, AS if the previous night had been one of celebration rather than disaster. Heavily she made her way to the bathroom. It was as she washed her hands, when she happened to glance at herself in the mirror, that she saw the splotches. Three new ones, large as quarters, on the right side of her face.

Hazel dropped the soap, didn't even think to turn off the water as she leaned toward the mirror. She flicked on the vanity lights, to inspect the new pattern on her skin, while water fell uselessly from the tap. The spot below her eye looked like a fava bean. In the space that went from the side of her nose to the apple of her cheek there was the shape of an artist's palette. And above her jaw was a white crescent, a waning moon reclining on its back.

Hazel's hands were shaking now. She managed to turn off the water, then stood and stared. How had three of them come at once, overnight, right on her face?

She covered them up. It took a long time, but she was able to do it, her makeup thicker than usual, and a finishing coat of translucent powder from the big plastic tub with the twist-off top. All day at work she waited for Maria to say something, certain that the foundation would wear off and the splotches show through. But Maria spent the day as usual, talking about herself, humming loudly, eating pastries that she kept offering Hazel, as if hoping to make her fat. For a long time she was deep in concentration, tying maroon and green fabrics into elaborate holiday bows. Now she was singing a Whitney Houston song, pronouncing the words all wrong.

"How your Friday night was?" Maria asked, giving up on the song. She had begun weaving strands of holly and pine branches together for the new display.

"Oh, it was fine." Hazel heard herself talking and was amazed at her voice—that it sounded the same as always, no trace of what had happened last night, or during the horrible hours between night and morning. "How about yours?"

"We saw a movie, you know that movie, what it's called?" Maria began to attempt to describe it.

Hazel's thoughts leapt back to the chestnuts, to what might have happened if they hadn't caught fire. It seemed things might have gone completely differently if only the chestnuts hadn't burned.

"The star, she so beautiful, what her name is? You know. That girl, the blonde." Maria began to describe the other movies the blonde had starred in, since she couldn't recall those titles, either. Now she was describing one that took place in California. "In San Francisco. You know . . ." Hazel had trouble listening. Her thoughts had fallen into the same old loop: How could he not be "able" to be with her? What did that mean? The more Hazel thought about it, the more it seemed that this had to be a lie, that in fact he was "able" but had somehow decided against her.

As Maria talked, Hazel readjusted the window display, dark curtains of a fabric imported from France. Only their wealthiest clients could afford such stuff. She glimpsed herself in the glass, made certain that her makeup had not faded, told herself that she was still prettier than most of the other mothers; as biased as she might be, this was still a fact. Sure, there was Sonia Fajed, who was half Pakistani, half Danish and so had that alluring combination of dark skin with fair eyes, but she was in another category altogether, and probably even Hugh wasn't classy enough for her. When it came to single women in their circle, Hazel's only real rival—if one wanted to use that word—was Roberta Plotnik, whose daughter was a year below Jessie. Roberta had been widowed when she was in her twenties and still wore her husband's wedding band on a gold chain around her neck—a gesture Hazel found a bit precious. Yes, Roberta was younger than Hazel, she had that going for her, but she was small and dark-eyed and rarely smiled.

Hazel dusted off the folds of an Egyptian import. What was it that had caused Hugh to hesitate? All that Hazel could come up with was her skin. Wasn't that what these new splotches were trying to tell her? Hugh had sat close enough to her, and spent long enough hours with her for her makeup to fade, kissed her enough for it to rub off, so that already he must have seen the mark where her neck met her chin, or perhaps the one by her ear. No matter how generous a disposition he might have, she supposed it was inevitable that Hugh would find such a thing repulsive.

"We was so cold!" Maria said. "I never forget, I thought it's California, it's spring. I bring with me my T-shirt! No sweater but the one I wear on the plane! Then they tell me, June in San Francisco is winter."

Unless, thought Hazel, stepping back down from the window display, it was the same old thing, the most basic reason of all: that such happiness—the kind that came from love—simply hadn't been allotted to her. Hugh must have somehow picked up on this, glimpsed it in her eyes, or in a splotch of white on her hand. The tattoo must be her bitterness, her grief.

The fury of this realization nearly caused Hazel to lose her balance. She leaned against one of the large bolts of fabric.

"You all right?" Maria asked. "You tired, I think."

"I had a bad night," Hazel told her. "But I'm all right." That her old, old grief had gotten the best of her again was more painful than the feeling itself. Still, she believed what she told Maria, that it would all be all right. She had her own kind of happiness, a diluted one that was nonetheless real. She had a job that interested her, and friends to talk to. Jessie would be coming home with her tomorrow and would give her one of her long, warm hugs.

For a moment Hazel thought she might burst into tears. Sometimes things were hard, she reminded herself, that's all: being told you were unable to be with, it was just a bit hard, especially when she had wanted so badly for things to work out, and thought they might, thought there might be a joy for her that was something beyond herself. And so it was a bit hard, that's all, let's just play.

Chapter 6

REMY PULLED UP THE COLLAR OF HER COAT AS SHE MADE HER way along the avenue, her steps brisk, as if to escape the weather. Instead of heading straight to the pool for her postrehearsal swim, she had decided to stop by the conservatory, to pay a surprise visit to Nicholas.

They needed to reconnect, to find again the easy rhythm of a shared life. These things take effort sometimes. She had been confused the other day, with Yoni, in the rehearsal room—but now she knew it was just hormones. What a relief. Vivian said premenstrual syndrome caused all kinds of odd thoughts and behaviors. And for Remy it was of course always an unpleasant reminder. . . . She could use some cheering up. And if nothing else, try to be nicer to Nicholas.

But when she arrived at the conservatory, Nicholas was not in his office. Momentary despair—as if not just her little plan but an entire future had been dashed. Well, she might catch him on his way out. Remy hurried back down the hallway.

"He just left. I don't know where he went."

"Oh, hi, Yoni." She said it in her same old voice but felt strange as they kissed each other's cheeks and stood facing each other. "Are you on your way out, too?"

He had looped his scarf like a noose and wore a knit wool cap tight on his head. Gruffly he said, "I'll walk you out."

They stepped out into the chill, the air moist and cruel, a slap from a clammy hand. "Where are you off to?" Remy asked, as lightly as possible.

"Heading home. I'm done for the day."

"Me, too. I thought Nicholas might want a coffee break."

Yoni nodded slowly. "Where were you thinking of going?"

"Oh, I don't know. Maybe just take a walk. Though it's not really walking weather, is it? Have a cup of tea, maybe."

"May I join you instead?" he asked. "I'll take you to my favorite place."

Remy knew the place he meant, the cramped English tea shop that had every kind of tea leaf and not enough seats. "All right."

The tea shop was full, customers huddled at the little shelf by the window and lingering on the damp bench out in front. From the sidewalk, Remy and Yoni watched all the people warm inside. Remy wanted, quite suddenly, to press her face to his, to feel the smooth cheeks he must have shaved just this morning. He said, "I know a better place."

Remy followed him. She wanted to think of him as someone who understood how to handle such situations.

He was beside her, had taken her free hand. It wasn't anything he hadn't done before, but this time it was with a certain determination, almost as if she had become an annoyance. He turned a familiar corner, and she realized that they were heading toward his home. Her grip tightened in his hand. She was frightened, but not enough to turn in the other direction.

They arrived at the apartment she knew so well. Large abstract paintings on the wall, books stacked in haphazard towers here and there, an upright piano laden with sheet music, the many horns—trumpet, trombone, euphonium—in their various cases, the wall of stereo equipment, the half-kitchen full of cheap cooking implements. "It's cold," she said.

"Here, let me turn on the heat." He put the kettle on to boil while Remy removed her coat and folded it over her violin case. She wrapped her arms around herself. She had made a mistake, she realized: the mistake of being alone with him.

"Here, have a look at all the teas I have." Yoni's voice sounded strained, as if trying to find its old tone. He opened a cabinet containing various tins and boxes, which Remy supposed must have been purchased by past girlfriends.

"You know," she said, "I don't think I need tea after all."

"Okay," he said, frowning. "All right." He turned off the kettle. Then he stepped toward Remy and put his hands on her arms, which were still folded around her. It was a gesture he had made so many times in the past, in conversation, or to make a point. But now it felt acknowledged. The flame whipped through her, and she closed her eyes. If he kissed her, that would be the end of her.

"You're trembling," he said, with surprise.

"This apartment is an icebox."

To her relief, Yoni stepped back. "Wait here." He walked away, down the short hallway and into the bathroom. Remy heard the squeak of faucets, the crash of water. She stood and waited, pleased that at least now her pulse had slowed. She looked around the room, at the Indian fabric on one wall, the bamboo stalks by the window, the photograph of Yoni with his mother and his rifle, grinning and squinting at the world.

Yoni came to her, looking relaxed, purposeful. He reached out and took her hand. "Come here."

He led her down the hallway and into the bathroom, where the tub was half full, the water tumbling into itself. He closed the door behind them.

"What's that smell?" she asked.

"Sandalwood. It was a gift."

Remy found herself laughing. "I bet it was. It smells nice."

"Here," he said, and untied the scarf around her neck.

"Oh, this is brilliant," she said. "This is just so smart of you." Yet she was laughing; the nervousness, the racing pulse, the fear, was gone.

"You said you were cold," he told her, placing her scarf on a hook on the door. "Here, raise your arms."

Off came her sweater, and her silk chemise. At her bra, Yoni paused, seemed to question his rights. When Remy reached out to unbutton his shirt, he looked pleased, and even, perhaps, surprised. She unbuttoned the shirt in a diligent, efficient manner, not allowing herself to touch the skin of his neck, his biceps, his torso. She removed the shirt and tugged his T-shirt out of his pants, over his head, and let it drop to the ground.

Reaching behind her back, he unhooked her bra and peeled it slowly away, let it fall to the floor. He cupped her breasts in his hands. When he brought his mouth down, the flame shot through her. Remy said, "Oh . . . no."

He stepped back. As if to convince himself that nothing had occurred, he began unhitching his belt, unsnapping his pants as though Remy weren't even there. Remy removed hers, too, and her underwear and socks, and stepped into the tub as if it were her only refuge.

What am I doing? What am I *doing*?

Was she really doing this? It seemed to her almost like a daydream, or a mere consequence of the weather. The water, silky with sandalwood oil, slid itself around her.

In stepped Yoni, sending waves around the both of them. When he sat down, his legs made a vee around hers, her feet at the sides of his hips. They fit there as if they did this all the time, the water containing them, warming them, so that it almost seemed to Remy that what they were doing was perfectly natural.

"I never think to take baths," he told her.

Remy rubbed her toes up and down his side; to speak would make this fully real. Yoni's hand encircled her calf and moved up her leg. He said, "I haven't stopped thinking about you. I don't want to have to stop. To have to try to make myself stop."

It was what she wanted to hear, and yet she could not bear it.

She reached out for his bad hand, the wounded one, and held it.

Touching the darker patch of skin, she felt fully the realness of this moment—that, without giving it much thought at all, she had allowed herself to move beyond the merely precarious. She rubbed the darker patch with her thumb. "Where did this come from?"

"The graft, you mean?" Yoni took her hand and brought it down to his hip, toward his buttock. "They took a swatch from here."

Remy thought she could feel a scar. "You've never told me what happened. Just that it was an accident." Despite what he had always said, part of her had imagined him in a Green Line skirmish, or maybe detonating a suspicious package.

Yoni leaned back, frowning, dislodging Remy's hand. He was quiet for a long time, and Remy felt her heart drop.

"I had a friend," he said, and his voice seemed to catch. "His name was Elan. We grew up together. We were even born in the same week. But Elan was taller and smarter. Beautiful, actually." The words had a rusty, halting quality. "He was very funny, always playing practical jokes. That's not how the accident happened. It was when we were in the army, when we were eighteen. We were off duty, and we were setting off fireworks. It was just the two of us. We wanted to get away. It was hard being in the army, you were always in groups, never alone."

His voice cracked, and Remy feared what he might say. She had done something awful, she realized, in making Yoni recount this. She told him, "You don't have to."

But he did not seem able to stop. "In a way it's a fluke, what happened. Not to my hand. But a piece of metal ended up in Elan's arm, and then it got infected. They didn't stop it in time. He died."

Remy watched the shift in his face, first an awful twitch and then a horrible softening she had never seen before. In a broken voice he said, "I think he was my first love, actually."

"Oh. Baby." Remy moved closer, reached over and held him, his head on her shoulder. Of course—of *course*. The stream of young girlfriends, perpetually slim-hipped and flat-chested, forever eighteen years old . . . Was Yoni even conscious of this? Remy could not help kissing his moist face. She leaned her forehead against his and imagined this other boy she had never known.

"I want you to know," Yoni said. "I really want you to know——" It seemed he could barely continue. "You're precious to me."

Remy thought she might cry. Yoni reached up to stroke her shoulder. He was running his other hand up and down her thigh. Remy closed her eyes, melting into the water.

That was when he leaned over to kiss her, his face moist with heat. Remy tasted his lips, his tongue. They moved toward each other with their limbs and with their hands. For a long while they were entwined, their breath in each other's mouths. She didn't know how much time had passed when they unpeeled themselves from each other, only that the water had cooled. A sudden shiver coursed through her. She said, "We should get out."

"Right," Yoni said. And then briskly, "Please don't leave."

It seemed to her that if only she were out of the tub, she wouldn't have already made an enormous mistake. Water fell from her as she stepped onto the natty bath mat and reached for a big, wide towel. She dried herself and draped the towel over her shoulders like a long cape. Yoni stepped out of the tub, toward her.

He had already lost one person he loved. At eighteen years old, Remy thought to herself, I was just heading to the conservatory, just beginning my new life. When he was eighteen, he was burying his best friend. His first true love.

Slowly he ran his fingers through her hair. Remy nodded to him, to let him know that it was all right; she had decided to stay.

She saw the relief in his face. He leaned into her, kissed her cheekbones, her ears, her forehead. "I love you so much. Thank you for allowing me to say it." Then he led her across the hall into his bedroom, where she had never been.

When she left, it was without plans for another meeting. Silently she pulled on her coat and retrieved her violin case. She thought to herself that she would take a long walk, in order to return to normal.

"Okay, see you," she told him, as she often did.

"I love you," Yoni said, almost desperately, as if sensing her un-ease.

Remy realized that she was looking at the floor. "I love you, too," she said, without looking up. As she stepped out the door, Yoni said, "See you soon, I hope."

Chapter 7

I N JUST ONE WEEK, THREE MORE WHITE SPLOTCHES APPEARED ON Hazel's face; the next week, three more. She briefly considered seeing her doctor, but there was no point, really; she had been assured, years ago, that her condition was purely aesthetic, no threat to her physical health. She had been told, too, how these things usually progressed, knew that this proliferation was, like so many other things, inevitable. After all, remissions always come to an end, she found herself thinking, and recalled the homeopath telling her, so easily, to "embrace" what was happening to her body—as if Hazel did not hate, truly hate, the mottled person she had become.

That Monday night she spent a full thirty minutes reapplying her makeup. There was a meeting at Jessie's school, and Hazel couldn't help thinking she might possibly run into Hugh.

A midterm report had arrived explaining that Jessie was having trouble in her Earth science class, which was why her parents were being called in. This would not be a private meeting, the letter explained; each term the school held "open classrooms" for parents whose children were not excelling in a particular topic, as "a chance for the teacher to address in a more comfortable manner the main problem areas and typical points of contention."

We find this a nonconfrontational way for teachers to communicate more generally their own expectations as well as the ways parents might help their children improve personal performance in a specific class.

Hazel had telephoned Nicholas about it, but he hadn't been at all worried by his copy of the letter. He pointed out, as he always did, that Jessie would have other talents; she possessed them already, within her, just waiting to make themselves fully known, like the scent of baking bread. And really (he always reminded Hazel) these talents—athleticism, her good nature, her physical beauty—would propel her further than even the best grades. For now Jessie was simply waiting out seventh grade, where, Nicholas explained (based on some sort of journalistic knowledge from his friend Gary), all the worst teachers were employed, the ones with unchecked psychological disorders, the ones who had been reprimanded by administrators, who spouted extreme politics, and whom the high school teachers couldn't bear. If she could just make it through this awkward time, Nicholas told Hazel, he was sure Jessie would make something wonderful of herself.

Hazel supposed this was Nicholas's way of convincing her that there was no need to attend the meeting.

"I can't, at any rate," he had said, explaining that there was a concert at the conservatory that night. In retaliation, Hazel informed him that she was to help Maria with an event at the fabric store that same evening. And though she knew deep down that she would end up going to the school instead, she told Nicholas that it was time he stepped up and took more interest in Jessie's academic life, hoping he might at least feel briefly guilty.

Really, though, she was less worried about Jessie's scholastic record than about the possibility of crossing paths with Hugh. She hadn't seen him since the night of the chestnuts, and who knew if she might bump into him in the school parking lot, or the corridor. Already she had planned how she would act if that happened: calm, content, glad to see him. As if he had not crumpled her heart in his palm. After all, she told herself, he had suffered his wife's untimely death and was better than those other men, who just wanted someone younger than themselves. In fact, even now it seemed to her that there was still a chance he might become "able." It even seemed possible that if she wore just the right thing (the green silk blouse, with her black pencil skirt and narrow sling-backs), that alone might be enough for him to see, finally, that she, too, was lovable, she, too, could be (had once been) a person accorded happiness.

Hazel shook her head at herself. Pathetic, to think that could ever happen for her. Her aloneness was part of who she was, part of her daily embarrassment. Especially at these school events, couples all around, so that each year she told herself that *next* time she would not show up alone. Worst of all was the annual holiday performance. Already she was dreading it, as she did every December, arriving alone while Nicholas and Remy and the rest of the parents all had each other, their own small circles of love, as if there existed only so much joy to be ladled around, and none left for Hazel.

Two years ago had been the worst. Hazel had been making her way toward Jessie after the concert, pushing slowly forward among the throng of parents, when Nicholas and Remy had somehow ended up just a few paces ahead of her, chatting happily, their arms swung casually around each other, and Nicholas had leaned over to spontaneously place a kiss on Remy's cheek. At that moment, the parents of one of Jessie's classmates had recognized Nicholas and Remy, and while the two husbands began chatting, Hazel heard the wife tell Remy, "Your daughter's a real firecracker, isn't she?"

Hazel had stopped in her tracks, horrified by the error. Mistaken identity, as if she were a minor character in some British farce—only now her very motherhood had been usurped.

And to think that Remy might be having a daughter of her own now! And that her pregnancy might be visible by the time of this year's holiday concert! As if the usual spectacle were not painful enough.

Hazel added one last dab of foundation. To think that she had allowed herself to imagine that this year she might not have to go there alone! That she might have gone there with Hugh!

Even now, though, as she finished her makeup with a protective layer of powder, she permitted herself a fantasy, just briefly, that Hugh might come running up to her in the parking lot tonight. In a low, desperate voice he would say that he had been wrong, that in fact he *was* able to be with her. He simply hadn't realized it until now, the chestnuts had thrown him off. . . . He might even kiss her right there, unworried should anyone witness them, so sure he would be of his love for her. Things like that happened, sometimes. At least to other people they did.

Hazel let the fantasy slip away. The truth was, Hugh might not even be there tonight. Luke was surely a responsible student. Probably Hugh hadn't received any school letter at all.

REMY ARRIVED AT THE SCHOOL EARLY, A VESTIGE OF HER LONGTIME effort to make a good impression wherever other parents were concerned. She made her way down the brightly lit, oddly quiet halls to the science classroom, where three other people sat: in the front row an oldish man whose face looked familiar (perhaps his child had been in Jessie's elementary school) and toward the back a blond couple she hadn't met before. "Hello," Remy said, and all three said hello back, with little enthusiasm; it was nothing to be proud of, this visit. The oldish man introduced himself and said the name of his daughter, and Remy did the same, shaking his hand. The blond couple mumbled their names quickly, as if not wanting to be recognized.

Remy took a seat near the windows and immediately felt like a student in detention. "Kept after school"—that was how they said it, though of course she hadn't ever had to "stay after." Now, though, she felt real guilt. No matter that she had made it clear to Yoni they couldn't let such a thing happen ever again. Nothing could erase what she had allowed to happen.

"I'll do what you say," he had mumbled into the phone when she called him, two weeks ago now. Before that she had spent a full week dreading what she might again do with him. "I didn't know I could feel this again," he said when she called. "I'm here. For you, I mean. I'm yours." And through it all she had told herself that no matter what he said, she could not allow herself to be alone with him again.

She looked down at the freshly waxed floor, at her feet in her scuffed shoes, and then up at the walls with their curling posters of aerial views of various fissures in the earth. At her left was a low shelf on top of which sat three murky tanks of greenish water. Remy's eyes searched and found a few glum goldfish. Another tank, containing wood shavings instead of water, housed two gerbils, also inactive.

Now Remy smelled a familiar scent, subtle and hovering, somewhere behind her. Hearing the others saying hello, she turned to find Hazel standing a few desks away.

"Oh, you're here!" Hazel sounded oddly delighted.

"Oh—well, yes, Nicholas said you couldn't make it." She didn't mean to sound accusatory; she was just confused. But Hazel always made her stumble like this, made her sound like a worse person than she really was.

"I was supposed to help Maria at the shop. But since Nicholas said he couldn't make it . . . Well, good of you to come." She smiled in that terrifyingly civil way of hers. It was always this way with the two of them, Hazel so polite, Remy cowering a bit. It had something to do with Hazel's briskness, her crispness. Probably it was simply that, deep down, Hazel still hated her.

Well, why shouldn't she? Remy shifted uncomfortably in her seat. The first few times their paths had been forced to cross, Hazel had looked at her with such cold, sad eyes, Remy was sure she had been cursed. And yet there had come—quite soon, actually—a period when Hazel, Nicholas, and Remy were all three perfectly cordial, exchanging Jessie back and forth every two weeks until that transfer itself became second nature and Hazel seemed (but perhaps just *seemed*) to have forgotten to feel the awful things she had surely felt, just as Remy forgot to feel that constant heavy remorse. By the time

Jessie was seven, eight, nine, Remy had often taken a moment to chat with Hazel about television rules and homework habits, and to briefly update her on Jessie's accomplishments and minor offenses. That was parenthood; there was no way around it.

Perhaps to prove that there were no hard feelings between them, Hazel took the desk just one seat away from Remy. Her perfume billowed over, delicately sweet, like something edible only in brief seasons. In her younger days, Remy had been in awe of Hazel and her perfume, of how elegant it must feel to be the type of woman to wear scent, to be recognizable by it. Now the scent made her feel ill. Surrounding Remy, like some awful odor of her own, was a cloud of guilt—so strong Remy was sure it must be visible.

She looked down again, suddenly ill. She really was a wreck: exhausted yet sleepless, hungry yet without appetite, every part of her—breasts, skin, heart—throbbing, as if permanently bruised.

A few more parents had joined them in the classroom. Apparently they already knew the blond couple; a lively conversation had started up. Remy wondered if Hazel knew them, too, but Hazel hadn't even looked back. She was extracting from her purse a small spiral-bound notebook, which she opened to a blank white page. Next to it she placed a black pen. Remy looked down at her own bare desktop; it hadn't occurred to her to bring a notepad, probably because she had been so focused on herself. She scolded herself for not planning ahead. Not to mention that she must look like a schlump, in her wrinkled pants and baggy purple sweater. In fact, Hazel was staring at the enormous sweater as if its very bagginess were an affront. Hazel saw that Remy had noticed, and quickly pulled her eyes away, but Remy couldn't help putting her hands where Hazel's eyes had been, across her midriff, as if to protect herself from that stare.

Well, who could blame Hazel? She must resent the very fact that I'm here. . . .

Of course Hazel was perfectly arranged, makeup on her face and spray on her hair. Her foundation and blush were exactly blended, as if she were about to go on live television or have her portrait taken. *Impeccable*: that was the word.

They were just very different people, that was all. That was why Nicholas was with Remy now, instead. With this thought, Remy became newly horrified: here she was, sitting next to the woman whose husband she had stolen, when for weeks all she had thought about was another man, about the things she had done with that other man. Ashamed, Remy turned her head away—and found one of the goldfish staring at her.

On the telephone with Yoni, telling him that she could not continue with him, she had said that she knew he would understand. She couldn't help it: as much as she cared for him, her heart belonged to Nicholas. That was what it came down to. She was devoted, she explained, and could only remain devoted; it was her nature.

"So, have you met the teacher?" Hazel asked.

"Oh!" Remy turned back. "No. He hasn't been here yet." She lowered her voice. "I'm feeling a little wary, though," she added, "just seeing the state of these fish tanks."

Hazel swiveled her neck to look at the shelf next to Remy. The expression on her face became one of horror. "It's *disgusting*," Hazel whispered back. Remy felt bad for having pointed it out; Hazel looked like she might be sick.

Quietly Remy said, "Now I understand why Jessie refuses to bring Jasper back here."

"Jasper?"

"The guinea pig."

"Oh." Hazel seemed to be thinking about this. "When did she bring him home?"

"End of last year."

Hazel still looked deep in thought, her brow wrinkled. "Is he in her bedroom?"

"The guinea pig?" Remy wondered if this was some sort of hygienic issue. Irritated, she said, "No, he's in the family room."

"There's room for him there?"

"Well, I mean, it's just a big glass cage with a wire thing on the top. It's not like we don't have any free space." Their house was smaller than Hazel's, but it wasn't tiny.

For some reason this information seemed to be of great interest to Hazel. She was nodding, as if imagining. "I suppose he's more interesting than Freddie. Jessie's frog. To be honest, I'm not sure she even remembers that he belongs to her. Or even that he's alive."

Remy gave a smile. "She's actually been pretty good about cleaning out Jasper's wood chips and making sure he has enough food. Of course, when she's at your place, I'm the one who takes care of him. Nicholas has never touched the thing."

"He doesn't help much, does he," Hazel said.

Remy just laughed.

That was when Hazel leaned in and, with a strange intimacy, asked, "How are you feeling?"

Was it that obvious, Remy wondered—guilt splayed across her forehead? No, it must simply be that she looked tired, exhausted, from so many sleepless nights; probably she looked ill. As if on cue, a chill ran across her shoulders, and her stomach churned briefly.

"Oh, I'm all right," Remy said, "just tired. Thanks for asking."

Hazel seemed to be waiting for more. Remy looked away, flustered.

"I remember Nicholas wasn't always as understanding as I needed him to be," Hazel said, as though fishing for something. "I remember I thought he'd figure out when I needed his help. I didn't realize I'd have to tell him everything I needed."

Remy gave a little laugh. "Every single thing." But she felt she had been tricked—tricked into saying something against Nicholas.

"I didn't even have the energy to stay angry with him," Hazel said, almost to herself. "Whenever I got mad at him, I'd just picture him eating peas."

Remy let out a small yelp; she couldn't help it, envisioning Nicholas stacking peas neatly on his fork, orderly colonists overcrowding an island.

"You know how he piles them up in rows?" Hazel asked. "I used to find it so charming."

Remy knew exactly, said, "It must be something they taught him in boarding school." Poor Hazel, having to imagine Nicholas with peas on his fork. Remy preferred simply to throw something at him.

"Hello, my friends!"

The science teacher had arrived. A small man, dark hair plastered to either side of his head. Brown slacks, matching blazer, and fastened to his lapel a large round pin of one of those happy faces that when you looked more closely was making some other expression. "Welcome to the fun house," he said, and laughed nervously at what he must have thought was a joke.

"This is my world," he began. "A world I've created. In my classes, we call it Polaris. It's a magical world, completely separate from the rest of this building."

Hazel gave a barely audible sigh and flipped shut her notebook. The oldish man in the front row let his head drop to his chest.

The teacher didn't pause in his narrative, went on for long, painful minutes. Remy let her eyes slowly roam the room, tried to stifle the panic that had begun, yet again, to rise within her. It didn't matter that she had told Yoni they could not continue, or that he had said, "Yes, I understand," in the most mature and kindly way. It didn't matter, because the mistake was already made, and there was no way to erase it. She had been disloyal to Nicholas, and she had hurt Yoni.

"Any questions?"

A man in the back row had a few. Everyone else waited patiently, thanked the teacher, and filed out of the room as swiftly as possible. Remy felt the relief of knowing she didn't have to go back there ever again. Even as they wished each other good night and made their way out of the building, no one dared to say anything about the teacher.

"Oh dear," was what Hazel said to Remy, when they had stepped out into the parking lot.

"'Oh dear' is right. Do you think there's anything we can do to help Jess get through that?"

Hazel was looking distractedly around the parking lot, as if someone might catch them there. "I think we're just going to have to write this one off."

"I think you're right," Remy said.

Hazel was looking at her again in that oddly expectant way. When Remy said nothing, Hazel turned toward her car. "Well, good night," she said.

"Good night." Remy watched her walk away, sure that there was something she was forgetting to do, some new way she had disappointed her. "Oh, wait," Remy called, thinking of a possibility.

Hazel turned. "Yes?"

"I've wanted to ask you," Remy said, approaching her. "What do you think of Kevin? The ninth-grade boy."

"He's seems perfectly nice," Hazel said. "I've only met him a few times, but he was very sweet." She looked suddenly concerned. "Is there a problem?"

"No. No, not at all. It's just that, you know he asked Jessie to come with him to the holiday dance; Nicholas keeps acting worried about it, since it's at another school." She thought for a moment. "Well, I suppose it's not the dance. I guess it's the idea that she has a boyfriend."

Hazel gave a small laugh. "I think for a man it's more of a challenge. After all, you and I were girls once, we've gone through everything Jessie's going through—going on a first date, wearing our first gown to a dance. But to Nicholas it's foreign territory. Watching his little girl become a woman. It must be disconcerting."

"You're right. I hadn't thought about it that way."

Proudly, Hazel said, "Well, it's just a theory." She looked again somewhat nervously toward her car.

"Okay, well, have a good night," Remy told her.

"Good night," Hazel said, and added in that bright, cold voice, as if suddenly remembering who the two of them were to each other, "Give Jessie a hug from me."

THE FOLLOWING AFTERNOON, NICHOLAS SAT ALONE IN THE COURT-yard of the Gardner Museum. It was his new routine, coming here one day each week. On Thursdays he was gradually making his way through the MFA, and yesterday he had made a visit to the Fogg. Last week he had gone to the Sackler and next Friday he planned to visit the new exhibit at the Boston Public Library.

It was his new push to broaden his horizons, to be "an artist *in toto*," as his university mentor, Gordon Winthrop-Hayley, had put it. An expert in clerical music, Winthrop-Hayley was a Renaissance man who spoke eloquently not just of music but also of architecture, sculpture, poetry; he attended the theater, read novels—had even written one—and, having married a ballerina, claimed to love dance. Nicholas had never been particularly keen on dance, nor did he pretend to be, and other than poetry read just nonfiction, occasionally. The only time he had ever enjoyed standing around looking at things in museums was when Hazel was there to explain everything to him.

Yet for the past hour he had been squinting at portraits in the wearily lit Isabella Stewart Gardner. It was part of his new initiative to nudge himself into some new creative space. His hope was that it might bring new insight to the big orchestral piece. After all, of all possible modes of creative output, music just happened to be the one at his disposal. Not words arranged on a page, or color swept around by a brush. What the Dutch masters had used oil paints to portray, or what a sculptor expressed in physical shapes, Nicholas could imagine only as sound and silences. Who knew why that should be, why his talent should be for "surprising harmonies" (as one of the critics had put it) and rhythmic invention. Even when he was so young that when he sat on the piano bench his feet didn't reach the floor, he had loved playing with chords and cadence, finding beauty in dissonance, teasing new aural patterns out of any tonal landscape. In a way, that was all it came down to, really: discovering new combinations of sounds that pleased him.

The big orchestral piece, though . . . he really had hit a wall. Perhaps he ought to talk it out with someone, have a fellow composer take a look. The thought came to him: Sylvane.

Of course! Why hadn't he thought of her earlier? She had already wrestled with her own lengthy orchestral work—the sprawling *Day of the Kings*. That one in particular had impressed him, the broad space she managed to cover, the way she seemed to paint with sound, with light and shade.

It was what Nicholas wanted to do in his own piece, reaching back to his youth and all the things he didn't quite know, to his lost mother, to the brief wisp of a human being's time on earth.

Well, even Sylvane struggled and faltered. Sometimes an almost phlegmatic heaviness dampened even her loveliest work. That piece she based on Monet's water lilies hadn't impressed him much; there was something too pretty about it, and then it became sort of muzzy, and seemed to disintegrate toward the end. . . .

Well, either way, he ought to talk to her. Yes, that's what he would do. Call Sylvane.

Chapter 8

*I*T TOOK A FULL MONTH UNTIL REMY DECIDED THAT SOMETHING was truly wrong. When at last she allowed that she felt worse than ever before, and that her body was not behaving correctly at all, she decided she must be dying. That would be her punishment.

She skipped a morning chamber music meeting and instead made a visit to her doctor.

Two days later, at Vivian's, on the dark red divan draped with a chenille throw, Remy slouched, her forearms on her knees, and said, aloud for the first time, "I'm pregnant."

Vivian's face lit up. "Oh, Remy!"

Through the tall windows the afternoon sun was weak, a wash of chamomile over the floorboards. Remy shook her head and burst into tears. That was when Vivian understood and said, "Oh, Remy," in a completely different voice.

Remy leaned her head into her hands. "I'm like a character in a fable. Or one of those awful Greek myths."

"No, just a soap opera," Vivian said, placing a kiss on the top of her head.

"Thanks for putting me in my place." But she still pictured the immortals on Olympus having a good laugh.

Vivian slung her arm around Remy's shoulders. "Come on, tulip, don't be too harsh on yourself."

"Why not? I've behaved abominably. Multiple times."

Vivian gave a small, blasé shrug, indicating that she was not necessarily of the same opinion.

"I just wish I knew what to do."

"Well," said Vivian, pragmatically, "there are only so many possibilities."

But already Remy's imagination had produced a host of horrible outcomes. She had confessed to Nicholas and then miscarried, losing husband and child. She had ended the pregnancy but been caught out in her lie. She had told the truth and made the three people she most loved—including a girl at the precarious age of thirteen—miserable. And many other configurations of catastrophe.

"Do you even know for certain it's Yoni's?"

"Ha. That would be a fun bet." Remy shook her head again. "No, it has to be his. . . . But I haven't told him."

"Does he even want a child? He doesn't strike me as the sort."

"He once told me he wanted a family." Remy's heart sank, again, at the thought of that other boy's life cut short. "I think he would be a wonderful father. More than Nicholas, even." And there was that other thought, too: that Yoni loved her.

"Then why not have a modern relationship," Vivian said, as if none of this were terribly complicated. "A baby with a mother and two fathers."

"Don't joke."

"I'm not. There are lots of ways to live, Remy. There are all kinds of families."

Remy thought about this. "You have to be a certain kind of person to do that."

"What makes you think you're not that kind of person? You're already part of a less traditional family."

Remy shut her eyes. "Because I'm scared." The very range of possibilities frightened her. So many unknowns. Her fear was as great as her guilt.

We never know what life might toss at us. Conrad Lesser making her sight-read in front of the class, holding down the page so that she could not see what came next . . .

"I can't believe what a mess I've made! It's ridiculous. I think of myself as this unassuming person who just works hard, does her job, doesn't overstep her bounds—"

"What bounds? No one's binding you."

What she meant was that she did not seek out trouble; she took what she was given, and was grateful for it—and yet she had created such trouble!

Vivian said, "I think you're losing sight of the bigger picture here, Remy. You finally got what you wanted."

Remy tried to envision that she might somehow be the person Vivian thought she was: a woman who could have everything she desired, all at once. Could it be, after all these years, that she really was that person?

I want you to feel limitless. Sleek and floating and free.

Perhaps she already *had* been, all this time, but simply hadn't realized it.

No, surely not. She told Vivian, "I gave the bow back."

"The bow . . . The *violin* bow?"

"I don't deserve it. I'm probably not even going to try for the associate concertmaster spot, anyway—"

"Remy! What does your violin have to do with this? Oh—you mean you're planning on taking maternity leave. So you won't need the bow. Is that what you're saying?"

Remy sighed. "I mean that I'm not a person who can just blithely have this modern ambiguous family, or pull the wool over my husband's eyes, or Yoni's, in order to get what I want. And I don't *need* anything more than I already have. Not a baby or a job or a new bow."

Vivian gave a little exhale through her nose. "Maybe you don't actually want it."

Irked, Remy said, "I've been dreaming of that bow for two years."

"I'm not talking about the *bow*!" Vivian lifted one of the little sofa cushions to give Remy a light bonk on the head. "Is it possible you just *thought* you wanted a child?"

Appalled, Remy said, "Of course I want it!" But she paused to consider.

You are learning to play without fear.

Her fear was immense—fear of the calamity she had created. Who knew what might happen, should she upset the delicate chemistry of their world?

And yet she had believed, those years ago, that she might learn to be fearless!

Conrad Lesser pinning the pages down, knocking the music off the stand. Yet she had played on, impromptu, intuiting what might come next. Couldn't she find that intuition within herself again? After all, what other choice was there? Impossible ever to know what new fence of notes might be thrust before you.

SHE ASKED HERSELF WHAT TO DO, WHAT TO DO, OVER AND OVER AS she swam her afternoon laps—at the high school pool, where the public was allowed during certain hours each day, presided over by a pair of teenaged lifeguards who, despite the seven lanes separating them, managed to flirt with each other, Remy had noticed, across the expanse of chlorinated water. Jessie was here, too, in the "fast" lane with her friend Allison. It was part of Remy's weekly routine, bringing the girls to the pool with her—one of those little customs that settle in by default until one day you realize that the custom itself has become precious to you.

With an ease that belied the strife inside her, Remy swam backstroke, gliding along the surface, the water pleasantly obliterating other sounds. Though she always chose the "medium" lane, she realized that she was pulling the water faster today; she kept nearly running into the woman sharing the lane and had to repeatedly slow herself down. But then she would accelerate again, as if fleeing something—until she realized, as she completed another rapid lap, that what she was fleeing was herself.

She wanted to escape herself! The thought caused her to lose her breath, and at the end of the lap she paused to dangle at the edge of the pool, resting her chin on her arm. She looked out over the wet tile floor, then turned to find the lane where Jessie swam freestyle, in a blue swimsuit and white cap identical to Remy's. In their goggles, their hair stuffed into the rubbery caps, they were masked versions of themselves.

Jessie had come to the end of a lap and did a quick flip turn, launching herself from the wall, shimmering underwater like a glittering fish until she burst again through the surface. Amazing creature. How untroubled she looked, speeding through the water, when really her entire world might be about to capsize. And only Remy knew—Remy who was the cause of all the trouble that had ever happened in this girl's life.

Weak with the thought, Remy pulled herself out of the pool, stepped into her flip-flops, and went over to the bench where her towel lay next to Jessie's. She hadn't the strength to dry herself, just wrapped the old green towel around her shoulders and sat watching Jessie and Allison complete their laps. When a wave of now-familiar nausea surged through her, Remy bent forward and focused on the wet tile floor, waiting for the queasiness to pass. Already she felt, incredibly, a protective impulse for this other child inside her. Amazing, how automatically that happened.

When she looked up again, Jessie had finished swimming and was chatting with Allison, the two of them bobbing in the water like seals. Then something must have struck them as funny; they shook in paroxysms of laughter, the physically grueling kind that only happens when you're thirteen. Remy laughed at the sight, then felt the stab inside her, her own awfulness. To disrupt such hilarity, the warmth of this very routine, this pool, this laughter . . . How could she even consider such a thing?

Now Jessie and Allison had climbed out of the pool and were padding wetly toward her. Remy saw again, if with diminished shock, how Jessie's body was changing—the budding breasts, the discernible hips. Like Remy, she had pulled her goggles up onto the top of her swim cap. Allison didn't wear goggles; her eyes were tinged red.

"What were you two cackling about over there?"

"Jessie's going on a date!" Allison said.

Jessie was grinning so widely, the silver band of her retainer showed. "Kevin invited me to go see *The Nutcracker* with him. His parents are taking us." Though she was clearly trying to appear nonchalant, her eyes shone.

"That's a pretty suave Christmas present," Remy said.

Allison said, "We were trying to figure out what she should get for him."

"Why don't you bring him to the Symphony for our Christmas concert?"

Jessie rolled her eyes. "That's so *gay*, Remy."

"Oh, and going to the ballet isn't?" Remy couldn't help laughing.

Diplomatically, Allison explained, "It's different if the guy is inviting the girl."

Remy gave each of the girls a pinch on the shoulder. "C'mon, you two, I'm getting cold."

As they headed toward the locker room, Remy thought how odd life was. She would not even be here with Jessie if Nicholas hadn't made up his mind—if he hadn't returned from Italy saying he knew what he had to do. He might just as easily have decided to stay with Hazel, to turn away from Remy instead.

The mere thought caused a small flip of panic inside her as she stepped into one of the shower stalls. She let the blast of water warm her. Jessie and Allison were showering on the other side of the locker room, jabbering away.

This time, Remy told herself, the decision was hers to make. This time she was choosing. Yes, this time *she* would decide.

But across from her the girls had begun laughing again—reminding Remy that, really, she already had decided.

☙───❧

AT GARY AND ADELE'S THAT EVENING, NICHOLAS AND REMY ATE Adele's angel food cake and listened to stories from their trip to South America.

Nicholas found it charming the way Adele urged Gary to tell his various anecdotes. They had been married last May, during a hailstorm, by a priest who kept calling Gary "Greg." Theirs had been a quick courtship. In fact, Nicholas and Remy had made bets on how long the marriage would last. Remy said a year and a half; Nicholas said forever. When he asked why she had made such a cruel prediction, Remy explained that Adele didn't know what she was getting in to. "She's stepping into a life that has just barely enough room for her," Remy had said, though she spent much less time with Gary than Nicholas did and couldn't fully know. "That *apartment* barely has enough room for her. It's only a matter of time."

Now they sat across from them on a lumpy couch and ate rubbery wedges of cake. Normally Nicholas would have enjoyed such a visit. He liked to relax with a beer or two and discuss local politics or some other subject on which Gary was an unofficial expert. But this evening he was unable to fully relax; his mind kept returning to Sylvane.

"We thought it was some mistranslation in Spanish," Gary was saying, weaving his way through an anecdote set in Guatemala. "So then the guy tells me that he *did* work there, but he was on his lunch break."

Though Nicholas hadn't bothered to follow the story, he was pleased to see Remy laugh. She had looked so worn-out earlier today. But Remy had always found comedy in Gary and his household— the newspapers and magazines in piles everywhere, the television always on, the random books splayed open to whatever esoteric subject Gary was currently researching, and now Adele's exercise equipment tucked in the living room corner.

Now Adele asked, "So how's Jessie liking middle school?"

"She has a boyfriend!" Nicholas hadn't intended to say it aloud.

"No longer a little girl, huh?" Gary said.

"She's even going to her first dance," Remy said. "The Holiday Gala."

"With an older boy," Nicholas added, astonished again by the very fact.

"All of fourteen years old," Remy said. "It's very sweet, actually. His parents are taking them to see *The Nutcracker*."

"It's a big deal," Nicholas said, to explain his own alarm. "Her first boyfriend."

"Well, don't make too big a deal of it," Adele said. "My parents always turned everything into an issue, you know, and as a result I just became rebellious. It can all change, no matter how well you've done in the past."

Now Remy was looking down, somehow distraught. Such an odd, troubling day. Just a few hours earlier, Nicholas had opened a letter from a composer who mentioned—as a casual aside, in the gossipy, one-upping manner he was known for—that "our mutual *amie* Sylvane" had attempted suicide.

They're calling it "exhaustion," the friend had written, *but Benjamin Sittinger tells me pills were involved. She's doing better now.* . . . And then he had gone on for a whole paragraph about his carpal tunnel syndrome.

Nicholas had read the tucked-in sentences over and over, trying to understand. Well, that explained why she hadn't returned his telephone call. Though he had left a message, weeks had passed. Now he had to wonder: Had the attempt already been made when he called? And there he was blathering on about himself, how he hoped to chat with her when she had a moment, don't worry about the cost, I have unlimited overseas calls on my telephone plan. . . .

How could Sylvane have tried to do such a thing? What about her children, and her husband? And her music, the lush, dark tangle of her music. They might have lost that, too.

Or perhaps that was the very source of her despair. The repeated small failures. In the past Nicholas might not have understood; but lately, wrestling with his own symphony, he knew how it felt to experience pangs of hopelessness. The pangs were brief, and always passed, but he could imagine how it might feel to be caught inside. Why, his own mother must have felt that, when she drove onto the tracks. And now Sylvane . . . Had she been feeling that way even during her visit to Boston, when he saw her last?

"You all right?" Adele was asking.

"Oh, well, I had a disturbing bit of news this afternoon," Nicholas said. "A composer friend of mine tried to kill herself."

"What?" Remy turned to face Nicholas. "You didn't tell me that."

"Sylvane," Nicholas said. "I only just found out. I suppose I'm still processing it."

"How awful," Remy and Adele said at the same time.

"She's apparently recovering just fine," Nicholas said. But what did that mean, really?

Gary said, "Sounds like a cry for help."

Adele said, "I always wonder what could drive a person to do that."

"Sometimes you feel stuck," Remy said. "Sometimes it feels like there's no way out. Maybe that was how she was feeling."

"But that's just a feeling," Adele said. "Believe me; I know. There's always a way out."

"Still," Remy said, "there must be plenty of situations where the right decision doesn't feel right. I mean, where nothing you can do seems right."

Thinking aloud, Nicholas said, "It's odd, but when I heard the news, I first felt shock, you know how you don't want to believe something horrible has happened. But then I felt something else. And, you know, I think it was shame."

Remy frowned. "How do you mean?"

"At not having noticed that anything was wrong," Nicholas said. "I saw her just last month or so. Only briefly, but I didn't think anything was wrong. Not that she seemed happy, but she didn't seem any different than usual."

"But how could you have known?" Remy asked. "Doesn't she live in France?" She was looking into his eyes, as if searching for something.

Nicholas said, "I suppose I'm ashamed that I didn't notice anything."

Remy touched the side of his face with her hand. "How *could* you have noticed?" Her eyes continued to search his, and then it was as if she had found what she was looking for. She began laughing, if in a sad way.

"What's funny?" Nicholas asked.

"That you think you're that observant——" She laughed again, shaking her head, so hard that tears came. Adele and Gary had begun laughing, too. "Sweetheart." Remy cupped his face with her hands. "There's so much you don't notice!" Still laughing, tears streaming, she was quick to add, "It's not a . . . fault. It's just who you are." She laughed again, wiped her eyes, and kissed his mouth decisively.

In her kiss Nicholas felt, just briefly, like a sting, the familiar surprise—that she had agreed, all those years ago, to love him.

TWO WEEKS LATER, REMY STOOD IN THE KITCHEN, STIRRING A POT of stew, her one winter talent, while Jessie sat across from her, flipping through a magazine, just the two of them silent together. Remy basked in the silence, the normalcy of it, the relief of having put things right again.

That she could have disrupted this—the clumsy perfection of their life together, she and Nicholas and Jessie alive and well, without illness or tragedy, just the easy flow of day after day. That she might have hurt this girl she adored. She thought again of Sylvane, of how everyone had some painful dark thing hidden inside them. Sometimes the pain was visible, like Yoni's mangled hand, but for most people it was tucked away somewhere.

"Your dad will be back soon. How about setting the table?"

"I don't want to!"

"Whoa, where did that come from?" Remy turned around.

"I'm mad at him."

"*Again?* What is it now?"

Jessie was silent; she looked somehow embarrassed. "I just get mad sometimes."

"But why? Why be mad at him?"

Jessie shrugged her shoulders. Then she said, "For making Mom the way she is."

Remy took a breath. That Jessie had never blamed *her*—that Hazel had never sat Jessie down to explain the exact sequence of events, and Jessie had not on her own come to any accusatory conclusions—was a reprieve Remy supposed would not last forever.

"What do you mean, 'the way she is'?" She pictured Hazel at the parent-teacher meeting last month, cheery and put together as always. But, then, that was probably exactly what Jessie meant: that escutcheon of good cheer, that pained—painful—brightness.

Jessie said, "It's his fault. It's his fault she's . . . that way."

"Is something going on?" Remy asked. "Is something happening that your dad and I don't know about?"

Jessie was shaking her head, as if unable to explain.

"Oh." Remy felt something stretch inside her rib cage. "Come here, baby." She put her arm around her.

Jessie must have decided it was too much. "And then he's being so weird about Kevin," she said in her usual manner, as if the two offences weren't very different at all.

Remy wondered if she ought to allow the conversation to be so easily derailed, or if she should try to find out more concerning Hazel. "Your dad's just discovering what it's like to be the father of a teenager," she said. "None of us have ever done this before, remember. We're all figuring it out. I know it's a burden, to have him so concerned about you going out with a boy." It was true; it really wasn't like Nicholas to worry, especially about something so innocent. Really it was Remy's mischief he ought to have worried about. Instead he was focusing on Jessie, as if she were the one about to misbehave.

Remy stood up straight at the realization. Of course. Nicholas *had* sensed something. He wasn't as immune to these things as she had always assumed. He knew, deep down, perhaps not even consciously— but had worried about Jessie instead. "I'm sorry, Jess," Remy said again. "I feel responsible."

Jessie's voice sounded calm now. "I'm not really angry at him anymore. Just sometimes."

Because of me, Remy thought.

As if to punctuate this, the telephone rang. The sound made Remy jump.

It was Allison calling for Jessie.

"I need to talk to her in private," Jessie said. "I'm taking this call upstairs. Hang up when I tell you, okay?" She ran up to the study and called down to Remy, "Okay, you can hang up now."

Remy could hear Jessie's voice upstairs, her tone chatty as always, as if no emotional confession had taken place. The thought of Jessie worrying for her mother made Remy want to cry. As though to put a thorough end to any contemplation, the doorbell rang.

There was Yoni, looking weather-beaten, the scruff of his cheeks that of a nomad. "Oh, good, you're home," he said, as he had so many times in the past, whenever he was in need of comforting, each time a romance ended or a relationship derailed. No matter that this time it was *their* relationship; still there was only Remy and Nicholas to come to for comfort. Remy understood this.

"I was in the area and thought I could use some company."

He knew Nicholas wouldn't be home yet, of course. Remy said, "Come here," and held out her arms. He stepped into them, and gripped her firmly. She felt his shoulders moving, and, almost imperceptibly, silent sobs. All over again she was horrified at what she had done. He had already suffered—why, his entire being was defined by that suffering—and now she had caused him to suffer again. She stood unmoving, pummeled by her own heartbeat. Then Yoni released his arms, as if aware that it was too much for her. "I'm sorry," he said, wiping his reddened eyes. "I'll stop now."

Remy felt her own tears. "Come and have some hot cocoa," she said, as naturally as possible. She called out, to make it all feel more normal, "Jessie, want some cocoa?"

"I'm on the phone!"

"The secrets of middle school," Remy said as they walked to the kitchen, still trying to convince herself that they could find their way back to the way it had once been. Her tears had receded. "I do wonder what they're discussing, actually."

Yoni said, "She'll come down when she smells the chocolate." The bags under his eyes were nothing Remy had ever seen on his face before.

"We'll see." Remy poured milk into a saucepan, stirred in sugar and cocoa powder, watching that the flame wasn't too strong. Meanwhile her chest clenched. She had made her decision. It was over now. She would stop feeling sorry for herself, stop berating herself. All around were the huge, shifting movements of the planet, its daily avalanches, while her own worries were small enough to fit into this room.

The cocoa began to steam. "This will make you feel much better," she said.

"I already feel better," Yoni told her, though really he looked worn-out. Remy turned away, concentrated on the cocoa. Yoni said, "Tell me something funny."

Remy thought for a moment, and poured the cocoa into two mugs. "I used to want to be Oscar Wilde."

Yoni said, "The poor man ended up in prison!" He took one of the mugs from her.

"But he lived richly," she told him.

"So do you."

She thought about this. "It's true."

Yoni said, "Here I am, in the middle of the afternoon, drinking

Dutch cocoa with the woman I love. What could be richer than that?"

Remy sat down heavily, feeling the pain inside her. "I know we're spoiled. But why does it always feel like other people are doing more exciting things? Sowing their wild oats. Living large." She looked down at her mug of cocoa. "I always wanted to have a big life."

Yoni said, "Even the grandest lives come down to a few people and places. Loved ones, your daily work, your neighborhood. I don't mean that in a belittling way. I've been realizing that lately. How complete our lives can be with just the few people and activities you most love."

Remy nodded. "So many evenings every week I put on the same skirt and blouse. I go play beautiful music and come home and take off the skirt and the blouse. Over and over. But it doesn't feel ceremonious." In a way her life was a blur of repeated gestures, twisting the pearly end of her bow and watching the horsehair straighten, slacken. Blowing lightly at a faint layer of rosin, wiping the excess with a chamois cloth. If she were to calculate how many times she had repeated these small movements, the number would surely floor her. And yet this was what she had chosen to do, keeping her fingers limber with the same scales she had been playing since the age of nine. It was why she still wasn't sure she wanted to try for the associate concertmaster slot. Because even that would be just another version of the same thing.

"Why is it that repetition dulls things?" After all, wasn't that what this was all about, these small flailing attempts at change? Switching from the second violins to the firsts . . . really it was just some sort of protest against time, a tiny fist railing at the face of time itself.

Remy sipped her cocoa. "I sound like I'm complaining. I'm not. I love my life. I just always wanted to live it to the hilt. To not waste anything." She thought for a moment. "To love fully."

Yoni was frowning. He had taken her hands, had leaned over to kiss her, his lips on her cheek, slowly, below her ear. Remy felt her body turn to fire.

"I can't, Yoni. It's too much." But she couldn't quite pull away. And so she said again, in a whisper, "It's over now."

"Hey, can I ask you guys something?"

Jessie was there. A funny smile came to her lips. She stopped midstep.

"Hey, beautiful," Yoni said, sitting back as if nothing had happened. "Finally I get to see you. You're never around these days."

"She's been conducting top-secret phone conversations," Remy said, surprisingly calm, despite the heat in her face. She reached out to give Jessie a little pinch on the elbow, but she was too far away. "What's up, kiddo?"

"Nothing." Jessie paused awkwardly, and her face looked suddenly unfamiliar, almost that of a grown woman. Remy braced herself for what this new being might be about to say. But all Jessie said was, "Allison's parents are wondering if . . ."

Remy didn't even hear the question. She still felt the fire inside her, her face burning. It would take a long time, she supposed, for the fire to die. But she had made her decision, had followed through. With Vivian, she had gone to her appointment at Planned Parenthood, where Christmas decorations hung obstinately on every wall and the oddly cheerful staff made sure everything went smoothly. It hadn't taken long. No reason for anyone but Vivian ever to know.

Yoni sat across from her, listening to Jessie, looking intent. Remy felt another wash of pain, at what she had done, and at what he had already been through. But she managed to find her way back into the conversation, and then it was the three of them, Jessie the same as usual, Yoni behaving as if nothing had happened. He had left by the time Nicholas returned.

Chapter 9

*E*VEN AS SHE DRESSED FOR THE CONCERT, HAZEL PRACTICED THE bright, positive things she would say to Hugh, should they cross paths. She hadn't seen him, not even from a distance, since the night with the chestnuts, though sometimes, when she arrived home after work in the black evenings, she checked to see if he might have called. It still seemed possible that he might do that, might have a change of heart.

Almost two months had passed since the night of the chestnuts. How odd, that until that night she had known precisely what was happening in his life, his daily schedule, and now, nothing. Hugh's absence, and the dark December afternoons, and the Christmas songs littering the air—on some days Hazel found these things painful. Other days they didn't bother her so much.

Now she tried to muster some enthusiasm for tonight's concert, though really she was, even more than usual, dreading it. As much as she loved to watch Jessie and the other children, all that lay ahead of her was an evening of pretending: that sitting alone in the audience didn't bother her, that the couples all around her had nothing she envied, that the visible happiness of Nicholas and Remy and their baby-to-be did not offend her. The effort of appearing unbothered was itself exhausting.

Jessie was still in the bathroom, using Hazel's curling iron, wearing a red velvet dress that didn't suit her. She had insisted on having the red dress, because Allison Rupka had a similar one. Hazel had tried to explain to Jessie that bright red was fine with Allison's coloring but all wrong for hers, but Jessie hadn't listened, even when Hazel found her a beautiful green satin dress with a scoop neck that had looked beautiful with her eyes.

"Are you almost ready, sweetie?" Hazel called to her, when she had dressed and spritzed herself with perfume and was making sure that her makeup was in place, the splotches thoroughly camouflaged. Two more had cropped up, across her forehead.

"Yeah," Jessie said, somewhat glumly. She had sounded this way, morose, ever since Hazel picked her up from Nicholas and Remy's two weeks ago. Hazel had at first assumed it was her usual pubescent angst, but now it struck her that perhaps there really was a problem.

"Sweetie, I'm worried about you. You've looked sad all week. Is something wrong?"

Jessie twisted her mouth, considering. Clearly something was up, though she didn't necessarily intend to share it with her mother.

"It hurts me when you keep secrets from me," Hazel said. "Especially if I might be able to help."

"There's nothing you can do about it," Jessie said.

"But what *is* it, sweetie?"

Jessie scrunched her lips together, chewing on them. "Something I think I saw."

Something she thought she saw . . .

Though Hazel rarely thought of the doppelgänger, whom she had last glimpsed a decade ago, she swallowed hard, wondering if something similar might have happened to Jessie.

It had been ages since she had thought of the woman at the hospital, and in the airport. And though she had wondered, at one point, if Jessie, too, had seen her, gradually the memory had faded. She considered that vision, or whatever it was, a remnant of the past, of the stressful time right before everything fell apart. After all, that was when the split had occurred—between Hazel's notion of who she was, of what her life was, and what it actually turned out to be.

Yet now Hazel felt a shiver between her shoulder blades, recalling how it had felt to watch that other Hazel, the happy one, hand her plane ticket over and walk contentedly away, to some other, better life. It had been ten years, and still Hazel hadn't found her way through that gate.

"Never mind," Jessie said.

"Sweetie. You can tell me. What did you see?" Really Hazel was wary of what Jessie might tell her.

"It doesn't have to do with you."

Relieved, Hazel said, "Well, it does if I'm the brunt of your pouting every day for two weeks straight."

Jessie scrunched up her face and said, "Why are there spots on your face now?"

Hazel's heart seized. "You can see them?" Even Hazel couldn't see them through the makeup.

Jessie let her shoulders slump. "Not *now*. In the mornings, before you put on your makeup. I can't see them at all, now."

"Is that what's worrying you? Oh, sweetheart." Hazel was touched. "Please, don't worry about me, all right? It's the same thing as always, nothing scary. I'm not sick. No need to worry at all."

But Jessie didn't look reassured. In fact, she looked sad. Hazel said, "That's not all that's worrying you, is it?"

Jessie looked up. "I think something's wrong between Dad and Remy."

Hazel felt her eyes widening. "Why would you think that?" she asked, tentatively, aware of her limits.

"Something I saw." But then Jessie seemed to recognize the power she held, and said, "Let's just go, okay?"

It has to be Remy, Hazel thought to herself: something must have happened with the baby. Maybe she had one of those tests and had gotten bad news. Or she had miscarried. It happens often enough. Still, it surprised Hazel to feel her heart sink. "I wish you would tell me these things."

"There's nothing you can do!"

"Sweetie, really, I'm sorry." For some reason, Hazel felt tears collecting in her eyes. How odd, when she had thought it one more affront, that Remy, too, would have Nicholas's child. Now, though, she felt no relief. She would keep an eye out for Remy and Nicholas tonight, to see if her guess was correct.

IN THE AUDITORIUM, HAZEL SAT NEXT TO MIDGE AND TRENT DAVIS, with Nina and Rob Altschuler on her other side and Mary-Claire and Christopher Coviello in front of her. Behind her, Gayle Boudreau and Helen Wynetsky complained about how they could never get their husbands to come to these things. The room smelled of fresh floor wax, and of pinecones decorating the walls, and of musty winter coats retrieved from the far reaches of hall closets.

The orchestra had emerged, filling the stage with the proud, creaky sounds of tuning instruments. The students grinned at their conductor, Mrs. Brody, knowingly and a bit smugly, as if they were all in on a dirty joke. Below, on the risers, the choir lined up, the boys in their beige slacks and button-down shirts, the girls in their dresses of velvet and plaid. There was Jessie, in the red velvet. She nearly blended in with the others, despite her height, and the shine of her hair, and the green of her eyes.

When Hazel spotted Luke Greerson among the tiers of skinny boys, her heart snagged at the thought that his father was somewhere nearby. She pulled her shoulders back, tried to smile as if all was well in her little world. She told Midge and Trent that Simon must have grown a full head taller since she had last seen him. She told Nina and Rob that Morgan was absolutely blossoming, right in front of her eyes. She told Gayle and Helen yes, she would indeed be heading down to North Carolina for the holidays. Now she could see Nicholas and Remy sitting together near the front, just the backs of their heads. She had not glimpsed Hugh.

All through "God Rest Ye Merry, Gentlemen" Gayle explained a complicated cheesecake recipe to Helen, while Rob Altschuler scribbled things into a thick, ratty-looking datebook; Nina kept brushing at his pencil as at a housefly. Then came a song where the children appeared to be singing in Russian, and everyone looked down at the photocopied program notes to figure out what they were saying. Midge told Hazel that Jessie looked lovely up there with her hair in ringlets. Hazel told Midge about the green dress she had found, how it suited Jessie so much better than the red one. "But you know how it is when they decide on something," she whispered.

She wanted the songs to end, the orchestra's anemic accompaniment, the choir director much too serious about it all, scowling at the students and even at Mrs. Brody, as if every one of them had somehow failed him. Hazel shifted in her seat, trying not to slouch. The effort of retaining a pleased expression had begun to tire her.

Afterward, everyone moved toward the lobby. Hazel went quickly to the restroom, to make sure her makeup was still in place. She dusted on another layer of powder and freshened up her lipstick. When she stepped back into the hallway her pulse began to race, from fear of seeing Hugh and of the way her voice might sound, should she find the strength to speak to him. She wondered what the other parents thought, if any of them had, in earlier weeks, noticed her together with him, and then apart.

In a blur, she searched for Jessie among the drift of red velvet dresses. There she was, with a small group of friends. Hazel held back, knowing not to interrupt at such a moment. She nodded at the principal and at the vice principal, and clutched her purse at her side, as if holding a partner's hand. She was waiting for someone she knew to pass by, so that she, too, might become just one more chatting parent with her coat slung over her arm.

Remy and Nicholas had spotted her; she saw their glances and approached them, feeling a certain relief at finally having an activity to occupy her. "Hello, there."

Standing side by side, tucked into their winter coats, they looked the same as always. Still, Hazel searched for a sign of strain between them, for a hint of what had happened. Nicholas's eyes showed just his usual fatigue. Remy looked gaunt, though, her eyes slightly puffy; they hadn't been that way when she saw her in the science classroom.

"Hello, Hazel, don't you look beautiful," Remy said in a soft voice. Hazel thanked her, thinking, Yes, Remy has had bad news. She has lost the baby. She no longer looks pregnant at all.

"So, we made it through," Nicholas said, with a wink. "How have you been?"

"Fine, thanks." It occurred to her to wonder if they might have somehow heard about Hugh. "And thank you for taking Jessie tonight." Since Hazel was invited to Ginger's annual holiday party, Nicholas and Remy had agreed to take Jessie a day early.

"Oh, it's no problem. In fact, she's sleeping over at Allison's."

"Ah, here she is," Remy said, with that devoted pride that Hazel had witnessed before but that never failed to shock her. "Congratulations, kiddo."

Jessie was beaming. "Did you really like it?"

"It was beautiful," Hazel told her.

As if in an effort to cheer herself up, Remy said, "I loved that Scottish ballad," and turned to Nicholas. "You said you thought you recognized it from when you were little, right?"

Hazel watched them as they spoke. Yes, something had indeed gone wrong, though they were doing their best to cover it up. Then again, anyone looking at Hazel would not have guessed that, trapped inside her rib cage, her own heart was wilting.

"I loved the Russian one," Nicholas was saying. "You all sounded perfectly drunk. Slurring your words. Tripping over them."

"That's my favorite one!" Jessie said, laughing. "That, and the one about the tropical elf."

"That was cute," Hazel told her as the Rupkas approached, Allison at their side, her velvet dress a deep red, her hair in a matching bandeau. The Rupkas greeted them, and all five adults talked easily. Hazel felt herself relax.

"Bye," Jessie was saying now, reaching up to embrace Remy, who kissed her hair and gave her a smack on the behind. "Bye, Mom," she said to Hazel, who told her, "Be good, sweetie," and hugged her.

"Bye, Dad." Jessie reached up to Nicholas, too. He kissed her cheeks and said, "I love you."

It was right after that, as the Rupkas were shepherding the girls away, that Hazel spotted Hugh. He stood near the auditorium doors with his coat buttoned tightly, his scarf tied in a knot, preparing to leave. Next to him, holding on to his arm like a girl in an old-time movie, was Roberta Plotnik. Her coat was open, revealing the trim, youthful figure, the unlined neck. Her smooth face, with the full, rosy cheeks of a woman still in her early thirties, was radiant.

Hazel felt herself cringe with abhorrence of Roberta, of her needy hand on Hugh's arm, like a little old lady crossing the street. To remind herself of just how insufferable Roberta was, Hazel looked for the familiar gold wedding band, the widow's medal hanging coyly, hypocritically, as it always did, around her neck.

To Hazel's shock, the ring was no longer there.

Hazel grabbed at her coat, which was sliding off of her arm. "I'd better run to Ginger's," she told Nicholas and Remy, hoping her voice was not shaking. "Before the eggnog's gone."

"Have fun. Happy holidays."

"You, too," she told them, her heart imploding. She pushed her arms into her coat as if it might somehow protect her, and turned away.

RUSHING OUT OF THE BUILDING, NOT BOTHERING TO PULL ON HER gloves, she wondered how she could go to Ginger's party now. A mixer, Ginger called it, when really it was just another holiday party with a hill of coats on the master bed, a tangle of scarves braided with unfamiliar perfumes, abandoned plastic cups on every surface, the meaningless chatter of people Hazel had met before but whose names she had to be reminded of each subsequent year. Never had Hazel skipped this party, even in the years when she had felt truly blue, as she always did over the holidays—even that time when she had not quite recovered from the flu. Always she went, to support Ginger, and to prove to herself that she had not given up, because you never knew when or where you might meet that special someone.

Tonight, though, she drove straight home, her bare hands trembling on the steering wheel, and left her car shuddering itself to sleep in the garage. Stepping into the foyer, she dreaded the silence that awaited her. She opened the closet and was suddenly too exhausted to pluck out a hanger. Instead she dropped her coat onto the wooden settee, where it lay like a hobo in a park. She kicked off her shoes with something close to anger; they fell onto their sides at an uncouth angle, lying there as if stunned. Straight to her bedroom she went, where she undressed quickly and pulled on her flannel pajamas. In the bathroom she removed her makeup, massaging it off with cold cream until the splotches gradually revealed themselves like a drift of clouds. It didn't matter that she had managed to cover up the spots; it didn't matter, because she was still, beneath all the makeup, not the person she wanted to be.

Her mascara she rubbed off with Albolene, leaving shiny dark circles around her eyes. In the mirror she looked as though she had been punched. Angry thoughts knocked at her: What did Roberta Plotnik have that she didn't have? What made Roberta such a candidate for love, for romance, for happiness? What had she done that Hazel hadn't?

Hazel dreaded her cold sheets, the empty pillow next to her head. She went back downstairs, to the credenza in the dining room, and fetched the bottle of Irish whiskey. Prudish Roberta with her wedding ring around her neck . . . And now the necklace was gone, as if to prove that her new love was genuine, the real thing.

Hazel brought the whiskey with her to the kitchen, where the light felt harsh, a spotlight on her pain, on her ugliness. Was that all Roberta had to do to get what she wanted: toss away her old ring to get a new one? Hazel poured milk into a mug, placed it in the microwave to warm, and was about to press the Start button when she realized that she was indeed right. That was exactly what Roberta had done. She had done what Hazel hadn't managed to do: stepped past her grief, found her way out of sadness.

Hazel stood that way for a long time, her finger on the Start button. Was that all it took, then, a simple tossing away of a wedding ring? Tears rolled from her eyes, mixing with the Albolene. Something had happened, something had broken inside her. But no, it wasn't just inside her; it was in this room, she felt it, the air itself felt different. She looked carefully, farther along the counter, holding her breath. Then she walked over to give a few pokes in Freddie's glass tank, where the body lay oddly flat, a puddle of its old self. It was true, finally. He was dead.

Chapter 10

OUTSIDE THE SCHOOL, THE NIGHT WAS COLD, THE AIR DRY AS chalk. On their way to the car, and even as they drove to the Prudential building for the conservatory's annual holiday party, Nicholas and Remy were silent.

Nicholas's mind raced as he joined the stream of traffic toward downtown Boston. These mandatory assemblies always left him restless. Too much time to think—of the little things, the things he usually didn't have time for. He needed to follow up, for instance, on Sylvane's viola concerto for next term. Though he had ordered it nearly two months ago, the music hadn't arrived. The publisher claimed it must have been lost in the mail. This sort of complication . . . he was not used to it. Meanwhile he had sent a politely reticent note to Sylvane, saying he had heard that she had been in hospital and hoped she was feeling better. It was all he could muster. And tonight, for some reason, during the concert, that odd guilt had floated up again, though he knew in his heart that he wasn't guilty of anything.

Yet the feeling had reemerged when he saw Hazel there in the lobby after the concert. The way she gripped her coat had seemed nearly desperate—and caused Nicholas to notice, as he hadn't for so long, those pale spots on her hands. In the many years that had passed since they first appeared, Nicholas had nearly forgotten about them. But the way Hazel held her coat tonight, gripping it tightly, he couldn't help noticing them. Desperately putting on her coat, quickly turning away her perfect, hidden face . . .

Remy broke the silence. "It was sweet tonight, wasn't it?"

"Yes, well, the kids were sweet." Nicholas readjusted his thoughts as he took the exit off of Storrow. "The choir director seems a terror."

Remy laughed. "Allison and Jessie were so cute in their matching dresses. You could see how proud Jessie was."

In his mind Nicholas saw the ridiculous red velvet, a fabric too heavy and old-fashioned for Jessie. Hazel must have selected it. "She'll never be quite like this again, will she?" Nicholas heard how obvious his question sounded. "I mean, the way she was tonight, still a girl— even though you can tell this is the last of it. Her young girlhood, I mean."

Remy said, "I didn't think of it that way. But you're right. It's the end of an era."

Nicholas nodded. "Even though we're still in it." He saw in his mind Jessie walking off with Allison, her back to them, the matching red velvet, walking away, away from him.

The car lurched, came to a halt, its engine puttering and then silent.

Remy gasped. "Nicholas, what happened?"

He might have lost her forever. He might have been one of those fathers who never saw his child again. The ones without custody or visitation rights, the ones who have to fight just to see her. Or whose wife kidnaps the child. Or a weekend father, no normal parenthood at all, just Saturdays at the movies, the park, the zoo. Or the father whose child has been told all manner of horror stories, about how awful her father is, what a horrible man.

Wasn't that what he had feared, those ten years ago, when he realized that he wanted to be with Remy? There had been moments when the idea of not seeing Jessie every waking morning had nearly paralyzed him, the fear of not knowing how it would work, not a conscious thought or conscious fear, but now here it was, belatedly, and the realization that he had been saved. Jessie had not disappeared from his life. Nor had Hazel. How lucky he had been, without even knowing it.

"I-I seem to have let the car stall." Nicholas was leaning on the steering wheel. He tried to catch his breath, but he might have been socked in the stomach. Behind him a car was beeping, though the light ahead of them now turned red.

"Honey, what's wrong?"

"Nothing, it's all right." Nicholas turned the ignition key and pressed the clutch, and the car sputtered back to life.

THEY PARKED ON DARTMOUTH STREET. REMY'S HANDS WERE COLD through her knit gloves. For years she had accompanied Nicholas to this party, which she looked forward to not only for the fully catered buffet but also for the view of the city, always magical to her, which made her feel a part of something beautiful, that this was indeed her city, a place she had come to love. Tonight, though, she couldn't help feeling uncomfortable, knowing what she and Yoni would have to do: put on their old act, play their same old roles, as if nothing had happened.

She and Nicholas were among the last to arrive. Already the dessert had been laid out, and soon the dancing would start; the student band was setting up noisily on a raised wooden platform. Nicholas went off with one of the new faculty members to line up at what was left of the carving station, and Remy found herself in a conversation with George Frank, something about the new miniscreens in the audience seats that the Metropolitan Opera had instituted to display translated lyrics. Remy wasn't really listening.

"My God, don't tell me Yoni's dating the babysitter." George Frank said this suddenly, breaking off from his own narrative, chuckling.

Remy's heart pounded as she turned to look in the direction of George's gaze. "Oh, that's Elizabeth and Steve's au pair," she said, with relief, recognizing the tall, skinny blonde Yoni was chatting with. "They're really good to her. They want to make sure she experiences as much of Boston as possible while she's with them." Remy had met the girl, a twenty-year-old from Serbia, back at Steve and Liz's Summer Solstice party.

"Don't they feed her?" George Frank asked. The girl's plate was heaped with pasta and sliced meats. She was laughing at whatever it was Yoni was telling her.

It was then that Cybil sidled up to him. She looked the same as always, delicate-boned like a dancer, with a Tintin haircut that apparently cost a hundred dollars every five weeks. Clearly she had noted the Serbian girl, too close to Yoni, younger and blonder than herself; Cybil made a small proprietary gesture, swiftly dragging her hand across the back of Yoni's shoulders, a cat marking her territory. Something tight seized Remy's heart.

"Hi, Remy!" Cybil must have seen her watching them, and waved, beckoning her.

"Excuse me," Remy said to George Frank, and forced her feet to move forward.

She greeted the au pair and said, "Cybil, what a surprise." She leaned over to embrace her, and gave Yoni an equally equivocal kiss. The au pair took her heaped plate and moved away, toward the cakes.

"How are you?" Remy asked Cybil, hearing the tightness in her voice. "I wondered what you were up to."

"Working insanely, and feeling sad. I missed Yoni so much." A brief, luminous smile overtook Cybil's pristine face. "We're giving it another go." Bashful, her eyes radiant, she looped her arm around his. He looked awful—tired, almost pale, eyes downcast. Remy, too, looked away. She was embarrassed for Cybil, for this effusive display of desire. Cybil turned her head to call, "Hi, Nicholas!" and waved ebulliently as he approached.

Yoni's cheeks reddened. Remy looked toward the windows, but the sparkling lights dizzied her. Sweat was running from her armpits.

"Hello, Cybil," Nicholas said, giving her a kiss. "It's been a long time, if I'm not mistaken."

"Too long," Cybil said, with a loving glance toward Yoni. He smiled, but it was not his usual grin, the one that made his eyes crinkle at the sides. His gaze met Remy's. *I did this for you. I did it for*

Nicholas. Remy felt a tremor rising inside her. She turned to look at Nicholas, to help pull her from these drowning waters.

He was chatting happily with Cybil.

Yoni stood beside Cybil, a martyr. Perhaps he thought of himself that way; this young woman holding on to his arm, as much as he cared for her, was a gift to Nicholas, after all. A gift to preserve their own oddly knotted friendship.

I would fight for you. But he hadn't fought at all.

The thought caused Remy's cheeks to burn—with shame, at only now understanding. She looked at her husband, and at Yoni watching him, the one Yoni loved more than he had ever loved Remy.

Of course. Of course! Was that what all this was about?

A sudden peal burst from the speaker system. With a jerk of her head, Remy looked toward the makeshift stage. The amplifiers had been plugged in, and the big band was warming up, already showing off, as eager as Remy had been at their age to perform.

Now Nicholas was teasing Cybil about something, making her laugh.

"Hey, we only get this one shot at life," Cybil said, still laughing. Remy felt chided and kept her eyes on the stage. In her mind she heard her old teacher Julian, his admonition from ten years ago. *The rehearsal is the performance.*

Maybe Vivian was right. I could have had what I always wanted.

But it was too late. There was a crash of sound, and the band began to play.

Part Three

Déjà Vu

Chapter 1

"H EY, YOU." REMY SOUNDED RELAXED AS ALWAYS, NEARLY monotone, as she stood from the little café table. Hazel heard her own voice rising in a singsong way, as if to counter it.

"Well, now, what do you know!" Too cheerful. At once she felt ridiculous in her paper-plate shoes. And with the cup of coffee in one hand, and her bag across her shoulder, suddenly encumbered.

Remy had reached over to give a delicate hug. Hazel let herself be briefly squeezed, and said, "It's been a long time."

"It has, hasn't it? Do you have time to sit down?"

"I'd love to, for a minute. I'm just finishing up my break." Hazel put down her coffee and her bag with the ballet flats and felt less awkward. "I thought I'd get my nails done to celebrate the warm weather. Mi made me these little sandals."

"Like hospital slippers," Remy said.

Hazel knew they looked silly. Yet she managed a breezy, "And what are you up to?"

"Oh . . . I just had a rehearsal and thought I'd walk a bit." Remy didn't look very happy about it. "And in a little while I'm meeting a friend." She seemed to Hazel somehow smaller there at the little outdoor table. Now she was forming that small half-smile of hers. "You're looking well."

"I'm feeling cheerful," Hazel told her. "I love this warm weather. And I'm of course so happy for Jess."

Remy's eyes smiled, a warm brown. "Me, too—what a relief. Of all those guys, Josh just shines so much brighter."

Hazel had to agree, though she didn't like the way Remy said "all those guys" . . . even though there had been, in fact, quite a few guys.

"She was so cute when she called with the news," Remy said. "I was picturing her at home after a long romantic evening, but when I asked when he'd proposed, she said, Just now! They were still in the restaurant, that dive Josh took us to—oh. A little place near Pike Place. She said she'd called you first but you weren't home."

"I was, actually, but we were asleep. Robert turns the ringer off at eleven."

With a nod, Remy said, "She never does bother to convert West Coast time."

Hazel laughed. "Robert has had enough of her one a.m. phone calls."

"That's what this was." Remy smiled, but her eyes looked tired. In an almost wistful voice she said, "She sounded so happy."

"You know, she was thinking of having the wedding this summer," Hazel said. "I told her how much planning it takes. Thank goodness she agreed to wait until fall."

"You think she'll make it till then? She's got the patience of a parking clerk." Remy laughed, and Hazel joined her, though she didn't think it a very nice thing to say about a person. But it was true, Jessica had approached her romantic life with the same enthusiasm and easy confidence she brought to most activities. Just twenty-three years old. Clearly Hazel and Nicholas's breakup hadn't done much damage, for Jessica to want to launch into her own marriage at a young age.

Remy said, "It still surprises me how quickly she's grown up. Sometimes I could swear it was yesterday that she came home with that pink lace bra you gave her. She was so proud. She immediately took her shirt off and went prancing around the kitchen, showing it off."

Hazel smiled at the thought of Jessie parading around shirtless in Nicholas and Remy's kitchen; for a moment, it was as if Hazel, too, had been there in that warm little room. She had noticed this before, the way she and Nicholas and Remy shared respective memories, like vacation photos swapped back and forth.

With Jessica in Seattle now, Hazel no longer had any reason to see Remy or Nicholas. Those days were so long ago, when Jessie had arrived for her two weeks with Hazel bearing delicious—if cryptic—pronouncements ("Daddy says it's not always his fault," or "Remy's tired of having to say everything five times!"). Tiny glimpses of that other couple's life together. "Remy threw the teakettle at Daddy!" Jessie had announced one day, her green eyes sparkling. And Hazel had felt something near to glee: *I knew it wouldn't last*. But it had.

Then came a day, five or so years ago now, when Hazel and Robert went out to dinner with friends in the South End, and as they stepped into the restaurant, who was exiting but Nicholas and Remy? The four of them had greeted each other with such pleased surprise that Hazel had felt proud. How honestly cheery they had been, like old friends, so that when Nicholas and Remy went on their way and Robert's friends asked how the four of them knew each other, it had felt wonderful—sophisticated, even—to say, so lightly, "Oh, that was my ex-husband and his wife."

"So how are things?" Hazel asked now.

Remy seemed to weigh her possible answers. "They've been better."

The small shrug of her shoulders suggested Hazel simply offer a small nod in return. Looking out at the black clouds that huddled in the distance, she considered making some diverting comment about the weather.

But the day seemed too beautiful to complain about anything as benign as clouds. Even the surprise of finding Remy here felt like a gift of sorts. In a way, after Jessica left for college, Remy, too, had been lost to Hazel, along with that nearly conspiratorial feeling they had once, if briefly, shared. By then Hazel was married to Robert, and her time with Nicholas had become no more than a brief blip; she was finally able to agree with what everyone always said, that she and Nicholas were utterly mismatched, a perfect example of opposites attracting for no good reason.

Robert, on the other hand, valued what Hazel valued, was much more comfortable as a "we" than as an "I." Friends had set them up, soon after Robert's divorce, and it had been easy with him. Robert worked at an educational foundation and was good at balancing his work and leisure time. Their relationship had moved forward smoothly, speedily, and a new generosity had infused Hazel's vision of the world: Nicholas had found his soul mate, and now she, Hazel, had found hers. The failure of her first marriage had been a necessary step toward this ultimate, mutual, contentment.

"I suppose your season is finishing up," she said.

Remy nodded. "Just one more performance and then we're done." She looked down into her still-full mug of tea.

Even when she stopped talking, the fine lines at the sides of her mouth were visible. This was new, Hazel noted, and glanced over at the hairdressers from the salon next door, who had burst into loud laughter at something. These young women in their skimpy outfits— Hazel had real sympathy for them, with their bare midriffs and body studs. Luckily Jessica had escaped all that. She may not have been a stellar student, and yes, she had gotten into trouble enough, but she had never mutilated herself in the name of fashion. She was tall and tan and could care less, with green eyes and lashes out to here and only her earlobes pierced. At a soccer match a few years ago, visiting her in college, Hazel had overheard a boy talking about her: "Look at her, man, she does me in." And Hazel had found herself thinking, knowing, certain of it, She doesn't even know he exists. Because Jessica rarely paid much attention to anyone, not for long. And so Hazel had worried: How would her daughter focus on any one man long enough to discover if theirs was a bond that could grow and stretch with time?

And yet sweet Joshua Staughton had managed it just fine.

Thinking this, Hazel said, "I have to admit, I'm hoping she'll let me shop for her gown with her. Though I don't want to be pushy. I'd hate to be one of those mothers-of-the-bride who take over all the wedding plans."

Musingly, Remy said, "I wonder if she even wants a gown."

"Oh—good point." Hazel gave a sighing laugh. One of the hairdressers, a young man in tight pants and a shirt open to his navel, was loudly berating the others in a teasing way. His eyebrows were painted on, Hazel noted; she wondered if it were fashion or hair loss that had prompted him to do that.

She had spent so many years camouflaging her mottled look, with thick foundation and a makeup sponge. There was the day when she realized it was no longer the white patches that needed hiding; she had come to the point where the leftover dark parts seemed wrong. Yet only in the past few years had Hazel finally traded in the corrective cream she had at one time bought by the bagful for plain old daily sunblock. She was now, finally and completely, pure white.

The odd thing was that her new skin suited her better. She was beautifully pale, clean and crisp, and her look, like her current life, agreed with her. She had finally become the person she was meant to be.

"She said you'd been away."

Remy nodded. "Symphony tour, Budapest and Vienna. Vienna is always a big challenge. We worked really hard to prepare for that."

From behind them came the wail of sirens, two enormous fire trucks fighting their way down the street, past double-parked Range Rovers and delivery trucks and sporty convertibles with their tops down. Hazel plugged her ears at the loud whistling. Her gold earrings were hot under her fingers. Remy didn't seem to notice the sirens.

"Did you take any pictures?" Hazel asked when the fire trucks had passed.

"Of?"

"Budapest and Vienna."

"Oh—no. We've been before."

She really did look tired. Her eyes, wide set and deep brown, seemed to pull down at their corners. Well, she would have passed forty by now. Finally, thought Hazel, another reward for patience, for surviving the relentlessness of life: Remy was aging. Soon she, too, would have a slight jiggle to her arms; she, too, would gradually pale.

Now an ambulance was howling its way past them, followed by a police car, lights flashing, siren whining.

Remy looked at her watch. "I'd better get going. I told Vivian I'd meet her at two."

She hadn't even drunk her tea, Hazel noted.

Remy squinted at the sky and again at her watch. "I'd planned on walking, but I don't know about those clouds." She stood, and slung her tote bag—which needed a wash, Hazel noted—over her shoulder. "She's not near a T stop."

"Take a cab," Hazel said.

The suggestion seemed to surprise Remy. "You're right. I never do that." She reached down for her violin case, then bent to give Hazel another little hug, and this time Hazel was able to embrace her. Pulling away, Remy said, "It's good to see you."

"Oh, you, too, Remy. Take care now." She gave a little wave as Remy turned away, aware that it was true: it *was* good, this brief reunion. Hazel felt warm and full with the thought, and through the paper plates on her feet absorbed the sidewalk's heat. Taking a last sip of her coffee, she reveled in the contrast of the cool ice in her mouth and the hot wind that had begun gusting around her. She would have to get back to the shop.

Remy had stepped off the sidewalk, looking for a taxi, her batik skirt billowing around her legs. She was like Jessica that way, Hazel thought—her own private energy always stirring things about her.

Her eyes, though, had looked so tired. They didn't used to look like that.

Hazel gave a little shake of her head. Sometimes you just sense things aren't right. Like that day, decades ago, when something made her look in on Jessie one last time, and sure enough she had somehow managed, at age one and a half, to climb up to the low bedroom window, not yet aware that the apartment was six stories above the ground. And Hazel had known to move swiftly but calmly, had somehow not screamed, sensing, again, that this was the right thing to do. It was only after Jessie was safe in her arms that Hazel had cried and cried, at the fact that she could not control anything in life, and that she might not have breathed that sudden whiff that told her to turn around and, for no good reason, look in on her daughter once more.

Like the moment when Nicholas cleared his throat, and Hazel knew that something devastating was about to come from his lips.

The thunderclap came not from the sky but from within.

Hazel tore off the paper plates and jammed her feet in her shoes, not even thinking about her nails. Had a cab come yet? No. There was Remy, standing a few feet from the curb, her skirt still dancing around her, the storm swilling inside it. A taxi slowed beside her, and Hazel was sure Remy would disappear before she could reach her. But Remy didn't notice the taxi, just stood there staring out at the street, so that Hazel, feeling dramatic, yelled "Remy!" as if to prevent her from throwing herself in front of a moving car. Remy didn't seem to hear her, and Hazel yelled again, pushing past two tourists reading from a guidebook.

"Remy!"

Now she heard. Remy turned around sharply, and the wild billow of her skirt made sense now. That individual storm cloud had finally burst. Her face shone, wet and brilliant with grief.

IT BEGAN ON A COLD, CRUEL MORNING IN FEBRUARY, THE MONTH that people cannot wait to be rid of. It was one of the rare days when Nicholas sensed, lurking within him, the possibility of becoming old. Preparing to leave for the conservatory, he glimpsed himself in the bedroom mirror and noted how his physique, often described as sprightly, might at some point become something closer to spindly. For so long his litheness had allowed him an air of permanent youth, a seeming agility (though he sometimes felt aches in his shoulders at night). That at some point he might not be so nimble hadn't ever worried him before—and yet, on that cold winter morning in the two thousand seventh year of Anno Domini, he had rearranged the bedroom door so that the mirror was hidden against the wall.

Downstairs he pulled on his parka and hat, knotted his scarf, and grabbed the container of leftovers for lunch. "I'm off."

"Look at you!" Remy had said, laughing. "You look like an immigrant." She was standing in the kitchen wearing her long flannel shirt and the woolly slippers that had been a birthday gift from Jessica.

"Well, I am an immigrant, my dear." He leaned over to kiss her.

"I mean the way your pockets are bulging—like you've crammed them full of your worldly possessions. It's like you're about to step onto a boat and head off to some completely new place."

"It's these gloves Jess gave me for Christmas. They're enormous." Nicholas plucked one from a pocket of his parka. "Boxing gloves."

"They're for skiing." Remy laughed. "Put them on, it's freezing out." She gave him another kiss, and he stepped out into the frigid day, closing the door quickly to keep out the cold. The frozen snow crunched underfoot, a wincing sound. Nicholas pulled his scarf a bit higher; he was recovering from strep throat, still a bit infirm.

He tried to adopt a sense of recovery as he went through the motions of the day. He still loved his work, continued to teach his one class per semester with genuine enthusiasm. The conservatory's administration prized him. He was that rare creature, an artist both critically revered and publicly embraced. Not only had his *Elegy* won the Pulitzer, but it had figured prominently in the soundtrack of a Hollywood movie about Afghanistan. The movie had broken box office records, and then came all sorts of Oscar nominations. Since then Nicholas had enjoyed the luxury of eminence, could afford to be affable and generous in a slightly aloof way, to forget people's names, to doze briefly as he sat stage-side awaiting this or that award. (He had dozed through the Afghanistan movie, too.) Bashful students asked him to autograph their copies of his music, from which royalties reliably came rolling in.

And yet none of this could prevent a more troubling development of late. Fear was what it was—that he would never complete his finest work. This was the big piece for orchestra that he knew in his heart might be better than anything he had yet composed. Better than the *Elegy,* better than his *"Millennium" Chorus.* It mattered to him terribly, for he knew deep down that his newest works weren't as good as earlier ones, and that audiences and critics, too, must know it, though no one had dared say so. Instead his premieres were reliably greeted with the gently fawning reviews reserved for those artists thought to be unassailable. Only when Nicholas went online and Googled himself (in private, while Remy was at work) did he find anything critical. A blog by someone at the Royal Academy of Music described his *Aubade* as "more of the same," while a review on a Web site Nicholas had never heard of called his latest chamber work "very similar to his *Music for Two Pianos,* though lacking the energy and playfulness of that earlier piece." Well, it was true, Nicholas supposed—but that's what happens, he wanted to explain, when the commissions keep coming, and with them the unspoken assumption that the commissioned work will be in the same vein of previous pieces. That was the price of popularity.

Despite his usual rhythmic experimentation, Elko seems too comfortable working within the stricter rules of musical construction. Fans call him a neo-Romanticist, and it's true that his musical daring has always fallen within safely recognizable borders. But with few real risks taken, there can be no great payoff.

And then there was some insane person in an online chat room railing about how all of Nicholas's work was overrated, "facile," and part of a larger conspiracy to keep truly original composers out of the fore.

Well, his symphony would change all that. It was almost done, finally—twenty years in the making. For a long time he hadn't even thought of it as a symphony per se, just that it was expansive and still taking shape. But it was indeed a symphony, his only one. He comforted himself with the knowledge that he was in good company, thought of Brahms, his hero, who had spent twenty-one years completing his first symphony.

But the piece was a big unruly thing that just kept growing. He wanted to say something about the fragility of life, its tenuous magic . . . but the thing wasn't yet cohering. What had begun in his mind as sound and vision was now a pattern of dots along horizontal lines, and while it always surprised Nicholas that such conversion ever succeeded, in this case the piece still wasn't quite there.

And so he had worked for hours that day—that cold, bright day in February—until, desperate for some sense of accomplishment, he decided he might as well take the car, which was badly in need of servicing, to the auto repair place.

This was in a neighborhood outside of Boston; it was cheaper and the service better, but it was also a bother because of the location. Remy would be pleased at his taking care of this task.

The sun was still out, and Nicholas had to squint against the glare of hardened snow; he had no sunglasses. He dropped off the car and, facing a long wait, walked to the shopping plaza next door, to a store called Sunglass Hut; he thought he might buy himself a pair.

There was a girl there, at the big tree of sunglasses. She looked familiar, in her midtwenties or perhaps older, tanned skin and long dark hair, briskly trying out various styles. Nicholas took his place across from her, where the men's styles were.

"Hopefully the men's ones are better than these," the girl said.

She had a slight accent, something Hispanic. "I can't find anything half decent."

Nicholas told her he had never owned a pair.

"Really? Never?" Her tone made this fact sound fascinating. Nicholas began to ask lots of questions about sunglasses, in case there was something he ought to know. The next thing he knew, the girl was next to him, guiding him through his many choices. Nicholas heard himself keeping up a continuous, diffident commentary, as though he had never before undertaken such an overwhelming task: "Well, now, these are like mirrors, aren't they? Might be a bit troublesome, people trying to get a glimpse of themselves. These, though—well, why *not* look like a fighter pilot?"

The girl was standing close, her brown eyes laughing at him, her straight dark hair gleaming. "Or you could just go retro," she said of the pair he now put on. "Do the Buddy Holly thing."

She made encouraging comments when Nicholas modeled a wire-rimmed pair. As he went back and forth between a darker and lighter version, the girl hummed along with the dance song on the stereo.

"I like this music," Nicholas said. "What is it?"

"You don't know Joe Arroyo?" She said it with exaggerated disbelief, teasing but also serious.

"Should I know him?"

"He's one of the biggest names in salsa."

The music was jubilant, and the girl did a few steps, singing along. "Do you dance?" she asked, and did a few more steps.

"Not salsa," he said, and then, "Not anything, really." The tag on the sunglasses was hanging down over his nose. For fun, he began to mimic her steps.

"Not bad," she told him. "You catch on quick."

He told her that he was a musician and had no excuse for rhythmic ineptitude. Then he stopped dancing and removed the sunglasses he had chosen. "Well, thank you," he said, for her help as much as for the compliment. "And I suppose this store should thank you, too."

The girl told him, "They suit you."

"What about you?" he asked. "Didn't you find any?"

"Oh, I'll stick to my same old pair. I always take a peek at new ones, thinking I'll come up with some new look, you know? But in the end I just stay the same."

Nicholas took a good look at her then, as the girl reached into her bag for something. For a moment it seemed she might be about to offer him her telephone number, and Nicholas's heart gave a small, terrified lurch. But then he saw that she was writing on the back of a business card, in thick, sparkling green pen: *Joe Arroyo y la Verdad*. "The band that's playing," she said, handing him the card. She looked away, as if suddenly embarrassed. "Since you said you like it."

Nicholas said, "I like it very much." He glanced at the other side of the business card—thin, from one of those template machines—to see her name. "Paula," he said aloud, and told her his. Also on the card were the words HANDMADE TEXTILES, and below that, WEAVINGS, KNITS, & CROCHETED DESIGNS.

"I made them before I'd ever even sold anything," Paula told him, "because you know what they say, you have to be ready." A woman on the T had complimented her bag, she explained; when Paula told her she had made it herself, the woman asked Paula to make her one. "My first commission. And the next thing I knew, all her artsy South End friends wanted one."

Nicholas glanced at her bag, a square woven thing in orange, pink, and red. "So, you're a businesswoman, too."

"Well, I always make sure to have my card on me. You never know who you might meet. I have luck with people like that—outside my circle, you know? Like you."

Nicholas put the card in his coat pocket.

"There's dancing tonight," Paula told him, as if just remembering. "You can come along, if you like."

To take up an invitation was always a pleasure. And Remy would be at work, another evening of just Nicholas home alone. Dancing might be just the thing he needed to pull himself out of this winter funk. "That sounds like fun."

And indeed it was lightly thrilling when, later that evening, Nicholas accompanied Paula in her dented Kia with rosary beads hanging from the rearview mirror. Her hair, long and gleaming, smelled of something floral, as though it were summer and not the coldest month of the year.

"I thought we could go to Nestor's," she told him. "I usually only go there on Saturdays, with Philomena."

"Philomena," Nicholas said.

"My best friend," Paula said. "We go dancing every weekend. I sometimes go on Thursdays, too. The only problem is we might run into José."

"José," Nicholas repeated, this time darkly, comically.

"He's this Colombian guy I sometimes dance with. Apparently he's decided he's going to marry me."

"But surely you can dance with someone else?"

"Yeah, that's the way it usually is. Everyone dances with everybody else. But José . . . I don't know why he's so possessive. He barely knows me." She seemed to be reflecting on this. "Let's go to Nestor's, anyway," she said. "It'll be a little more quiet on a Thursday. And people there dance New York style. It's more difficult, but it's more fun to watch."

Nestor's was small, just one square room with huge inflated beer cans depending from the ceiling. The place was full of young, glowing people—different from the hopefuls at the conservatory. Paula and Nicholas ate snacks at the bar as the lesson began. A man with a long, sleek ponytail was telling a small group of couples that Latin dance was a mating ritual, and that the best dancers never even looked at each other. "In fact, the really good ones manage to look completely bored. But they always, always, know exactly where their partner is. They feel the other person's energy, that's how."

As they ate their buffalo wings and celery and cucumbers with dip, Paula told Nicholas about her work. Her grandmother had taught her how to knit when she was still a little girl, and later how to weave. She had a loom at home—the one that had belonged to her grandmother—and wove her own fabrics, which she sewed into bags and pillowcases of her own design. A store in Brookline had started purchasing her knit skirts and sweaters, which apparently were a big hit with the Orthodox women. And a gift shop in Wellesley had recently picked up her weavings. When she saved up enough money, she would buy a bigger loom and open up a workshop of her own, with a few employees to help her increase her output. That was the plan, at least.

"Sounds like a good one," Nicholas said, trying to wipe the last of the hot sauce off of his fingers. The man with the ponytail was motioning to them to join the class, but Nicholas wouldn't have minded just sitting there at the bar hearing about Paula's hopes and dreams.

"Are you ready to dance?" she asked, and took him by the hand, leading him off the barstool and onto the floor.

To his surprise, Nicholas found that he was a fast learner. He was proud when the other couples looked to him and Paula as an example, while the instructor yelled at them over the music: "Maintain your distance! When he approaches, she retreats! When she approaches, he backs away!"

Nicholas was conscious of the fact that he was having a new experience, and that it had been a very long time since he had had such a thing. He felt joyful, and though at first he supposed this was due to the syncopated rhythms and the strangers all around him, soon the truth of it dawned on him: it was the freedom of becoming a beginner again.

He could make mistakes, try and fail, and it didn't matter. Because no one here thought of him one way or another; no one respected him in that obliging manner. No one knew him at all—or thought they knew him, who he was, "pleasing melodies threaded through with texture-building atonalities" . . . "signature patterns of augmented chords and appealing lyrical repetitions that gradually merge to create a denser, if now familiar, field of sound."

Rhythmically complex yet lyrically accessible . . . Playful musical puzzles, at times self-consciously clever . . . What a crime, the way these critics reduce one's body of work to a mere phrase, as if "pleasing melodies" were simply out there for the taking, as if "appealing lyrical repetitions" just happened out of thin air.

Nicholas forced these thoughts away and focused on the dance steps. This one was a cha-cha, the next one a salsa. It wasn't until an hour or so later, when the dance floor filled with boys who were all young and women who were all ages, that Paula apparently saw someone she knew: a boy named Danny, in baggy pants and leather sneakers, with a baseball cap on sideways. Paula danced with him briefly before Danny went off with someone else. "Danny's the type who likes to dance with every woman in the place," Paula explained. "You should have been here a few Saturdays ago, when Carlos came out of the men's room and found him with Liz."

"Oh, dear," said Nicholas.

" 'Oh dear' is right. Some friends had to take him outside to cool off."

Danny returned to request another dance with Paula. In her absence, an older woman approached Nicholas. She was dressed elegantly, with strappy heels and a skirt with a slit on the side, and her hair arranged high on her head. Her very walk was graceful, that of a professional dancer. Reluctantly Nicholas followed her onto the dance floor, holding her long, slightly veined hand as loosely as possible. As he danced, he turned his gaze elsewhere, in expert salsa style, feeling something like mild indignation. Paula, dancing with Danny, nodded at Nicholas in an encouraging way. With envy, Nicholas watched Danny spin Paula this way and that, her legs moving so easily, and a smile on her radiant face. She was a natural.

When the song ended, Nicholas thanked the older woman and quickly walked away. He didn't want to dance with her anymore.

"You looked so absolutely free just now," he told Paula when she came back from the dance floor. "The way Danny was spinning you around . . ."

Paula said, "Next time you'll be spinning me like that."

Nicholas was unconvinced. "I've never been a great fan of dancing. Until tonight, that is. My wife and I are sometimes given tickets to the ballet, and the dancers, well, compared to the music they just seem so . . . superfluous."

Paula raised her voice over the music. "Your wife?" She frowned at him. "Why don't you wear a ring?"

"Oh, we never did that," Nicholas said, almost lightly. "I suppose we thought we were being different. That we didn't need to do that." Then he understood why Paula was frowning and said, "I'm sorry I didn't mention it." The thought truly hadn't occurred to him.

Now Paula squinted at him. "Does she know you're here with me?"

Nicholas shook his head.

Paula raised her eyebrows. "We should go, then."

Nicholas dropped his shoulders, irked.

"I'll drive you to the subway," Paula said.

Nicholas took his coat and followed Paula into the frigid night. The parking lot was nearly full. When Nicholas had again taken his seat in the Kia, and Paula had slammed shut her own door against the cold, she asked him, "And if your wife caught you cheating on her?'

"Is dancing cheating?" Nicholas was annoyed. He had done nothing wrong; she had misunderstood.

Paula looked at him coldly. "And if she *thought* you were cheating on her?"

"She would kick me out, I guess." He reconsidered. "Or maybe just kill me."

Paula rolled her eyes. Nicholas gave a little shrug, to show that it was all hypothetical. Then the car rumbled to a start and they were driving away, not speaking. When she dropped him off at a T stop, Paula sat back, her neck straight, her gaze proud. Nicholas decided to state his case. "Dancing isn't cheating, you know. It's a beautiful thing. It doesn't have to be . . . sexual."

Paula nodded. "I hear ya."

Relieved to have made his point, Nicholas stepped out of the car and thanked Paula for the dancing.

"You're welcome," she said, and it sounded true.

"Well, good night." Nicholas closed the door and waved good-bye through the window. When Paula gave a little wave back, he felt pleased at having brought things to a happy conclusion. At home, it took him a hot bath and a mug of tea to relax.

FOR A WEEK HE THOUGHT OF PAULA AND THE SALSA CLUB WITH A pleasantness that felt almost nostalgic. The following week his thoughts became something more like longing. At the conservatory's music library, he looked up Joe Arroyo y La Verdad and in his office played over and over the CD he borrowed, until he thought he had even begun to understand some Spanish. By the third week, though, the image of Paula was beginning to fade.

That Saturday night, shortly after Remy had left for the Symphony, Nicholas sat down at the piano to tackle, yet again, his composition. Though he felt optimistic enough when he first lifted his pencil, he soon worked himself into the same corner as always. Truth be told, every so often a suspicion crept in: that the thing might never really come together. Sometimes he even suspected that what he needed to do was to start all over again, scrap entire sections and return to that original burst (though already he had had his graduate copyist formally notate two entire movements, thinking them complete). Lately an even more troubling idea had besieged him: that he might die before finishing it—this work that he had already begun, quite consciously, to think of as his magnum opus.

As he sat at his piano that cold Saturday night, he felt again the threat of defeat. He told himself he was in a rut, that was all. He just needed to shake things up. Find a new path. And so he rose, changed into a clean button-down shirt, black slacks, and leather shoes, and brushed his teeth and his hair. Then he bundled himself into his parka and drove past the city limit, to Nestor's.

The club was much more crowded than before, and Nicholas had to search for a minute or so before he found Paula. She was standing near the bar, with a few young men and a plump, dark-haired woman. Philomena, Nicholas supposed, proud at remembering. He removed his parka—the room was already hot from so much dancing—dropped it on a chair, and made his way over to the bar, aware that the young men were looking at him. Paula saw him and raised an eyebrow. "Addicted to salsa after all?"

"I suppose so," Nicholas said, relieved that she seemed about to laugh. He nodded hello to her friends. "How do you do."

"Here, let's dance." Paula swept him away, and Nicholas was momentarily hurt. Perhaps she was ashamed of him. Perhaps he looked old and odd.

"Lucky for you José's not here tonight!" she said, tugging him away by the elbow. "Those guys are friends of his. I didn't want you to talk to them, in case they start something."

Nicholas felt suddenly, delightfully, embroiled. But Paula looked serious as she pulled him over to a corner of the dance floor.

"Why do you even talk to them," Nicholas asked, "if they're like that?"

"We're all a group here, you know? Dancing friends. It's its own little world. You have to follow the rules while you're in it." Paula shrugged. Then she looked at Nicholas with wide eyes. "I can't believe you found me."

"I knew where to look," Nicholas said.

"But you looked for me. All the way out here, and you came to find me." Her eyes told him no one had ever done such a thing for her before.

At once Nicholas felt horrible. "You know I'm married. I just wanted—" He thought how best to formulate it. "I meant what I said last time, about dancing. Look, I'd love if you could teach me."

"Teach you." Paula raised her eyebrows.

"To dance. And about the music, the groups you know. I found a CD of the band you told me about. I'd love to learn more."

Paula looked skeptical. "Is that all?"

"If it makes you uncomfortable . . ."

With a little toss of her head, Paula said, "No, no. Sure, I'll teach you." Then she laughed, in a close-mouthed way that made her nostrils flare. With her hand on his elbow, she pulled him out from the corner and took her place across from him on the dance floor. "Ready to rumba?"

"*Is* this a rumba?"

"Problem is, you're the one who's supposed to be leading." Paula gave a look of mock frustration. "Here, I'll show you the basics."

Nicholas watched, and quickly joined in. Again he felt the absolute freedom of a novice, the relief of this place where no one knew him, where there were no expectations to uphold. Beyond Paula's shoulder were girls clustered hopefully around tables covered in cocktail glasses, and young men at the bar eating fried mozzarella sticks, and women fiddling with the straps of their high-heeled shoes, adjusting their skirts so that the slits were just so on their thighs. And here in front of him was Paula, showing Nicholas the steps of a merengue. She moved, and Nicholas followed.

BY THE TIME REMY RETURNED HOME FROM VIVIAN'S, IT WAS EVEN- ing and the rain had let up. Battered leaves and petals lay in puddles along Beacon Street, and storm dregs purled in the gutter. Turning onto her block from the T, Remy came upon another dead baby bird. Every day, it seemed, she found a squashed robin's egg or some newly hatched creature so mangled it was barely recognizable. Well, that was May—the month of dead baby birds. Remy knew she was being morbid, but it suited her mood.

At the house, the front door with its old brass knocker, Remy paused, wondering if Nicholas had dared come back.

It was just this morning that she had told him to get out. If he wasn't going to act guilty, then at the very least she could inconvenience him.

Vivian had laughed at that. But Remy still felt stabbed in the heart. That their home stood waiting as usual, lovely as always, seemed somehow wrong. Especially with its new fresh face. They'd recently had to remove all the ivy and repoint the bricks, so that the facade was clean and elegant, no longer hidden by vines. Seeing it now, Remy thought again of Hazel's face, skin soft and white, newly luminous like a child's.

Running into her on today of all days . . . As if she'd been sent as a reminder.

Vivian said not to read into it, but it was hard not to.

Inside, the house was silent. Remy placed her violin and bag on the floor. Already she had turned to check the answering machine and, seeing that there was indeed a message, wondered if it might be Nicholas. But it was Jessica, saying she and Josh would be coming to visit next month.

Remy pressed Save. She would have liked to call Jessica back, just to hear her bubbly voice. But she worried she might allow herself to say too much.

"Hellooo!"

Remy turned to find Cybil on the front stoop, peering through the screen door. She was carrying a large shopping bag, along with a closed umbrella and—snuggled into a patterned sling on her chest—a sleeping Ravit.

"Oh, hey, come on in." Remy wondered if Nicholas had gone to stay at Cybil and Yoni's. Perhaps he had sent Cybil as a messenger. She certainly looked the part, her always-neat hair in a short, severe pageboy. She stepped lightly inside and kissed Remy's cheeks. Though it had been just six months since she had given birth, she was already back to her skinny, flat-stomached self. With long limbs and rosy skin, her eyebrows tweezed into a permanently bemused

expression, Cybil was both naturally beautiful and carefully maintained. She had the straight posture of a dancer, a doll-like mouth,
a perfect nose with small round nostrils, and each neat little earlobe
punctuated by a stunning black pearl. Her wedding ring was a block
of half-polished amethyst, like something just excavated from a mine.
Holding her shoulders perfectly straight, she managed to convey ease
and lightness despite the weight of her baby in the sling.

Gently, careful not to wake her, Remy touched Ravit's soft, fine
hair. She asked Cybil if she would like something to drink.

"Oh, no, thanks. I won't stay long. Where's Nicholas?"

"In the doghouse."

"Uh-oh."

"Never mind," Remy said, as if it were simply a nuisance. "What's up?"

"I was hoping I could leave something with you. This backgammon set—here, I have to show it to you, it's absolutely gorgeous.
I just bought it at McPherson's." The antiques dealer. Remy hadn't
been there more than once or twice, it was so unjustly expensive.
"It's for Yoni's birthday," Cybil explained. "This way he won't find it
before then."

"Of course, no problem." Of course it would be something like
this, something for Yoni, of all people, something elegant and expensive, and for Yoni. There had been a time when Remy's heart still
winced at the thought of him and of the child they might have had,
and then gradually she had told herself that was all behind her—and
eventually it really was.

In a way, Remy still felt personally responsible for Yoni and Cybil's union. At first it had seemed like a sacrifice of sorts, Yoni resign-
ing himself to a future with Cybil—but he had embraced marriage
wholeheartedly. And now, with Ravit, Yoni had turned out to be, as
Remy had always suspected, a doting, enthusiastic father. That was
the wild and wonderful thing; Yoni and Cybil's life together was an
unqualified success. Yoni, a man who might never have married, had
become a faithful and loving husband.

Of course Remy had pangs of jealousy. She hadn't quite realized the reprieve she'd been given, all those years when Cybil had put her career first and never even mentioned wanting a child. But so many women waited until their midthirties, or even older, these days. . . . Really, Remy should have known this was coming.

"Isn't it beautiful?" Cybil was asking. She had peeled back the bubble wrap, to reveal a folded wooden case.

"What a find." Remy didn't reach out to touch the smooth wood, as Cybil had. Never in her life had she been given a gift like this, something purchased with premeditation and a great deal of money, and hidden away as a surprise. Nicholas wasn't that sort of spouse. Well, lots of husbands weren't.

Thinking this, Remy said, "Oh, guess what? Jess is getting married."

"Whoa, that was quick! Josh . . . right? What a sweetie." Cybil and Yoni had met him once or twice last year.

Remy told Cybil about the phone call last week, how excited Jessica was.

"That's fantastic," Cybil said. "A wedding! My friends never have them, they just move in with their partners— Are you really all right, Remy?"

"Oh, I'm okay." She wondered if she had the energy to tell Cybil. "Here, are you sure you don't want a glass of water or something?"

"No, no, thanks, I should get going, actually. The princess could awake any moment and turn into a monster. Thanks for keeping this for me." Cybil gave Remy a quick kiss on each cheek and told her to feel better. "Let me know if I can help." Taking up her umbrella, she stepped lightly out into the drizzly evening.

The backgammon set lay against the wall. To Remy it looked reproachful, a reminder that she, too, had slipped. But she had paid for her lapse. That was the problem; paying for a mistake was nothing Nicholas had ever done.

Her mind whirred through the revelations of today. Hard to stop the whirring. Her fury came and went in bursts. The thought came to her again that she could leave him, leave here, start anew. She could, if she wanted. There was even a job she might try for, with a new orchestra in Barcelona. Her friend Christopher had been telling her about it.

Enough of this life—these secrets and lies.

She went back inside and dialed Jess's number. She simply wanted to hear her voice, to be reminded of the other people she loved.

Instead there was the recording of their golden retriever barking and Jessica saying, "Hey, leave us a message," as if it didn't really matter to her one way or another.

"Hi, sweets, it's me. Just calling you back. Glad you're coming to visit. I'll call again soon." She hung up and waited, as if Jess might call back any minute. She was unaware of exactly how much time passed, just that at a certain point she found herself marching angrily through the French doors into the music room, as if she might find Nicholas there as usual. The room looked beautiful as always—more beautiful, now that they had finally pulled up the carpet and polished the parquet floor. Why had they waited so long? Remy saw that she had left the windows open, but luckily no rain had gotten in. She twisted a handle to open one of the windows wider. From the next block came the hooting of the trolley's horn.

Remy turned to Nicholas's desk. It was messy as always, covered with scattered pages of his manuscript—*the* manuscript, or "the beast," as they had called it, for a long time now. How odd, to see it there without Nicholas hunched over in contemplation.

He had gotten on with it recently—gotten past whatever had blocked him. Remy had noted the change in him, the way his mood had lifted despite the increased hours at his desk. Lately, when she returned home from Symphony performances, he would still be up, working, but instead of fatigue in his eyes there was a glow.

She looked down at a page of the score. It was in its final stage, she could tell, because instead of pencil Nicholas had used ink. He was old-fashioned that way, still wrote out his next-to-final copies by hand, on sleek staff paper with preprinted clefs, before handing them off to his copyist. Seeing his handwriting now, Remy felt oddly moved, at the thought of him having drawn all these dots and stems. The many staves were stacked one upon the other, rows and rows, for each instrumental voice. A single page contained so much; it was nothing a simple glance could easily make sense of. The only reason Remy was able, at all, to comprehend the thing was because of Conrad Lesser, all those years ago, insisting his students understand not just their parts but the orchestral scores, too.

She could almost hear him now, explaining how to approach new work: first look the thing over and suss out the piece as a whole, its form, its mood, its principal idea. . . .

But even this one single page—the woodwinds up top, and below them the rows of brass, and then the percussion, and on down the busy page—was really too much for Remy. Though she could read well enough the individual lines, she wondered at the fact that composers managed to hear internally how the piece would sound as a whole. Here was the oboe's part; there was the trumpet's. Here came a piccolo. Remy could hear individual parts in her imagination, but to synthesize these varied voices, to mentally weave them together all at once, was too difficult. It struck her now how odd it was, that this man she lived with had for years been listening to these harmonies and melodies in his mind, without Remy ever hearing more than a scrap here or there on the piano.

Her eyes continued down the page, to the string section. There was the first violin part, and the second. Above, tucked between the harp and the violins, was a word in capital letters: "SOLO."

A violin solo.

Remy flipped backward through the movement, to see where the solo began. With only eight or so bars of score per page, the pages made a thick stack. Ah, here was the beginning of the solo; it was quite an extended one. But how was that possible? Nicholas had never mentioned it. Surely he would have asked for her input—or at least mentioned what he was doing.

Remy's heart sank all over again, to know that he hadn't even bothered telling her. Really that was what hurt the most. Not just the other woman. It was how easily he had excluded Remy from the most important parts of his life. A violin solo, and he hadn't even thought to consult her, hadn't thought she might have something to offer. So that now this solo, too, was yet another thing he had kept from her— the very thing she had always thought they shared.

Remy read the opening few bars to herself. But then she had a better thought.

She spread the pages out along the piano so that she wouldn't have to keep flipping them quickly, and went to fetch her violin. When she was ready, she raised her bow and began to play.

Chapter 2

"J ESSICA CALLED," ROBERT ANNOUNCED WHEN HAZEL ARRIVED home from work. His eyes smiled from behind small wire-rimmed glasses. "They're coming to visit next month after all. The third week of June."

"Wonderful!" Hazel said, leaning in to kiss his smooth mouth. "I'm so glad." And then: "What's *that*?"

"That," Robert said grandly, gesturing toward the corner of the foyer, "is my new acquisition."

"But what *is* it?"

"It's art!"

Heart sinking, Hazel asked, "Are you sure?"

"It's a sculpture," Robert said, but his face had lost its glow. Quietly he asked, "Don't you like it?"

"*Like* . . . is not the word." Hazel tried not to let anything show on her face. She walked closer to the "art," which sat on a large steel gray pedestal lit from behind. It was a sculpture of sorts, in what might have been crystal or imitation crystal, a carving of a curling frothy wave, and inside the wave, reclining (sleeping? dead?), the figure of a naked, nubile young woman. She was slim waisted and smooth skinned, utterly expressionless, with long flowing crystal hair that melted into the curl of the wave. Her limbs, too, were long, unnaturally so, one leg bent slightly so that her crotch was concealed. There was, of course, no pubic hair, and her face was devoid of emotion, eyes closed and the mouth, with perfect, lush lips, just slightly open, making her look comatose or perhaps mentally retarded.

"Cooper says it's a collector's item."

"Really?" Hazel heard the tension in her voice.

"Or it's going to be. He said it was a good investment." Robert paused. "And I think it's nice."

"Nice." The girl (nymph? prostitute?) lay there incapacitated, light shining up on her from below. With trepidation Hazel asked, "How much did it cost?"

The number shocked her.

"The artist is famous," Robert explained, and picked up a big, glossy magazine to prove it. "See, right there. A whole article on him." The magazine, thick with advertisements, was open to a two-page spread, photographs of more crystal waves, and a tan, fit, gray-haired man posing at the prow of a boat.

"It says here that people from all over the country order pieces from him. He'll even customize them for you." But Robert's voice was wavering a bit, which made Hazel feel even worse. Not only was she horrified by this blemish he had brought into their home; now she had made Robert—kind, generous Robert—doubt his own judgment. This seemed to her the crueler of her crimes.

She looked at her husband, saw how badly he wanted to please her. It was one of the qualities she loved in him, this willingness, for it made him open-minded and adaptable; he liked to laugh, even at himself. Sweet Robert. Though a few years older than she, he still cut quite a dashing figure, lean and fit, with a kind face, and hair that had been silver since his twenties. Now he glanced back at the sculpture. "I don't see why you think it's so awful."

Worried, she asked, "Did I say it was awful?"

"I can tell by your face."

"I'm sorry."

With real curiosity he asked, "But what's wrong with it?"

Where to begin? Hazel wasn't sure she could even articulate her thoughts. "It's a bit tasteless," was what she said.

"Well, I suppose you would know," Robert said in a bruised way.

After all, Hazel spent each workday in a shop filled with only the most elegant of objects: hand-worked gold earrings, woven sweet-grass baskets, Shaker sewing trays. "It's true," she said, "I'm not used to tackiness."

Robert said, "Well, not all of us devote our time to tchotchkes."

"Tchotchkes!" Hazel felt her face heating up. "Do you know what I sold today? A necklace of pure Austrian crystal." She tried not to let her voice rise. "My store is one of only two in Massachusetts that carry authentic Navaho woven carpets. I have blankets hand-quilted in the Ozarks." Hazel dealt in hand-carved chessboards, black-and-white nature stills, photograms by a local artist, no two alike. Every one of those "tchotchkes" had the mark of a human hand. Not like the plastic woman in the wave of spittle here in the foyer. This really *was* a disgrace—so smooth and flawless, there was no mark of craftsmanship at all.

Robert looked sadly toward the sculpture. "I can try to sell it back, I suppose."

"No, no," Hazel heard herself saying. "I mean, I do hate it, but maybe I'm wrong." Why was she saying that? She wanted it gone. And yet she wanted to be tolerant. The wave-girl had done her no harm. Perhaps Hazel was having a negative reaction to the subject itself. After all, here was a young woman with all the physical qualities Hazel herself no longer possessed, lying expectantly with her mouth half open. Just because it bothered Hazel wasn't enough of a reason to make Robert return it to the dealer.

And yet . . . If only she were able to explain precisely why it was awful, then maybe she could ask him to take it back.

"I'm going to read that article," she said solicitously. "Maybe he's someone I should know about." In order to not have to look at the wave creature, Hazel went into the kitchen, where a big calendar hung on the wall. "I'm so glad Jessica's coming," she said, to end the conversation. "Did she say what day their flight gets in?"

"That Sunday," Robert called back. He had gone to his sofa chair in the corner of the living room, where he kept a pile of word puzzles to exercise his brain. "I think it's the eighteenth."

Hazel marked the date on the calendar. "We should throw an engagement party," she called, over the din of pouring rain. It had started again, the second big burst since this afternoon. Outside the window, thick vines streamed down.

"What did you say, honey?"

"We should have a party for them. An engagement party." She was aware that she and Robert were doing what her parents had done, yelling back and forth from two different rooms, slightly mishearing each other—one of those unattractive habits old marrieds slide into. But now that she herself had begun to do it, she didn't quite know why she had thought it wrong in the first place.

"Did they say they wanted one?" Robert was asking.

Hazel went back out to the living room. "No, but you know Jessica loves a party. And they're only here a few times a year. Oh, Robert. That . . . *thing*."

She wondered, was Robert having some kind of late-blooming midlife crisis, where instead of a new car he had gone and bought a . . . girl? Probably his age was on his mind; his older sister's sixtieth birthday was tomorrow. They were to celebrate with her family in Framingham for dinner.

Sixty years. The number wasn't all that far off for Robert—nor would it be, one day, for Hazel. She used to think she would be frightened as it approached, but lately she found that she worried not so much about age as about bad things that might accompany it—cataracts, Alzheimer's, colon cancer. At the same time, she had always sensed, hidden within her, a certain wisdom she associated with older women.

And luckily Robert had healthy ways, ate lots of salads and whole grains and went to the gym a few times a week. On weekends he played racquetball. Hazel liked the way he would come back from the gym, bathe and shave in minutes flat, and emerge perfectly dapper in slacks and a crisply ironed shirt. He was kind and thoughtful and considerate. That was what had most impressed Hazel when she first met him: that he would never hurt her. It was why, with confidence, she had been able to marry him. No risk of again finding herself in the situation she had suffered through decades ago—and that Remy was apparently in right now.

Or was she? Hazel had been so sure, today, that something was wrong. Those brown eyes streaming tears . . . But then Hazel blinked and Remy's tears were gone.

Even as Remy stooped into the taxi, Hazel stood there, confused. She felt like a fool, had just muttered, "Oh, I thought . . . never mind. Please go ahead."

A splatter of raindrops had started, and as Remy looked up at her from the backseat, the taxi gave a small, impatient lurch.

Her face a torrent of tears . . .

Hazel had seen it, so clearly—and then, nothing. All afternoon the thought had troubled her. She had even allowed herself to mention it to her coworker, Laura.

"Maybe you were seeing a moment from the past," Laura had reasoned. "Like déjà vu, you know? But instead of a feeling, it was an image."

Hazel considered this. "I guess it's possible—but has that ever happened to you?"

"No. I sometimes dream things before they happen—just little things. Like a certain color that was in my dream, or the shape of a bird flying by. Actually, once I dreamed that a bird went to the bathroom on my window, and then that morning I went to get in my car, and a big splash of bird shit came down just as I got in."

Hazel laughed.

Laura said, "I do believe people can have psychic powers. Ones they aren't even necessarily aware of. I remember reading about this guy in India who helped people by physically embodying their traumas. If they were sick, he would become sick instead, and the patient would get well. Even if they didn't tell him what the specific ailment was. It was called . . ." She closed her eyes. "Empathic assimilation. I think that's it. He internalized their ills."

"What a crummy job." Hazel had to laugh. "*Empathetic assimilation.*"

Laura laughed, too. "But I do think we have more powers of intuition than we realize."

Hazel said, "My friend Ginger took a course called Tapping into Your Third Eye. She wanted to, you know, 'harness the hidden insight within.'"

"And? Did it work?"

"Not that she ever mentioned. I guess I don't really believe in that kind of thing." Hazel thought for a moment, then decided she dared continue. "A long time ago I had a sort of vision. I saw my double. Not just another woman who looked like me. It *was* me. She was even wearing the same clothes. It happened twice."

"You mean like a doppelgänger?"

Hazel explained to her about the woman in the hospital corridor, and at the airport gate, making a point of sounding as sane as possible. "I haven't thought of it in a long time, actually. I used to worry about it; I mean, you know they say that seeing your doppel is a bad omen. But it never happened again. And I still don't know what it meant!"

Laura considered this. "You know, in Judaism, it's not a bad omen. It means you've reached a prophetic state."

"Really?" Hazel thought for a moment. "Well, I have to admit, it was right before my husband left me."

Laura nodded knowingly. "Maybe you do have some kind of second sight."

"Oh, I don't know about that." And yet she knew for certain what she *had* seen: Remy's cheeks wet with tears.

Even now, back home with Robert, the feeling clung to her—that something was amiss.

But she didn't dare tell Robert. His mother had slid into dementia in the years before her death, and the first clues of deterioration were just this sort of remark. Visual confusion, logistical impossibilities, contortions of memory. The first sign was when she said she had been chatting with someone everyone knew was dead. Then came recollections of things she had never actually experienced. Things that sounded fine at first but didn't quite make sense. For that reason, Hazel didn't even consider telling Robert what she had seen, or not seen, that afternoon.

IT WAS THE MORNING AFTER HIS SECOND TIME WITH PAULA THAT Remy asked Nicholas, "What did you do last night?"

"Oh, you know, wrestled with the beast." Nicholas had said it automatically, with no real forethought, since it was what he usually said. Ever since Christmas he had been working exclusively on the symphony.

"Oh." Remy paused. "I thought you went out. The car was wet when I got home."

Nicholas could have said, with unfeigned surprise, "Oh, that's right, I did go out." Because it had felt so odd and unlikely to be there at Nestor's, dancing again—which must have been why Nicholas heard himself say instead, "Hmm? I guess it's just so damp in the garage."

Immediately an icky feeling overtook him. But now that he had evaded the truth, it became all the more awkward to mention when he went dancing again the following week. That time he took the T instead, and Paula gave him a lift to Nestor's. It was afterward, as she drove him back, that Nicholas noticed the many skeins of wool in the backseat of her car. Piled to the side were big woven tote bags— stripes and zigzags in all sorts of colors. "I dye the yarn myself," she told him. "I can't always get the colors I want. I see them so clearly in my mind, how I want it to look, you know? But the stores around here are pretty limited. And the more subtle colors, they cost a lot. Luckily my grandmother taught me how to work with dyes, so I can mix whatever colors I need." The very best was New Zealand wool, she explained. She hand-dyed it in batches. Her current project was a pattern she had worked out based on some Polish pottery she had seen. "But I haven't been able to afford the good stuff for a while now."

Nicholas vaguely recalled his first mother-in-law—Hazel's mother—who had knitted in an automatic, soul-less way, as if it were a mere necessity, like breathing.

Paula said, "I'm hoping it'll make me rich someday."

Something about the way she said it, so earnestly, made Nicholas wish he could lift her up and present her directly to the gods.

Instead he thanked her for the lesson, and the ride, and, now that they had reached the T, told her good night.

"Here," she said, "before you go." Reaching into her purse, she found a pen and an envelope, from which she tore off the flap to write something on it. "For your continued musical education," she said, handing him the scrap of paper.

He looked at the words, in that same loopy script, only this time in dark purple ink. *The Latin Brothers.*

"Another band for you to research," she said, "since I can see you take this seriously." She winked.

La Sonora Carruseles was the name she wrote the following week, this time at the other dance club, which had disco balls and a cover charge. She wrote the words on the back of a piece of cardboard she tore from the packaging of a new hairbrush. The brush was a big cylindrical one with many tiny bristles, like something for cleaning machine parts. She dropped it back into her bag and told Nicholas, "They're one of my favorite groups." He was looking at the scrap of packaging as if it were a password or secret code. On the other side were the equally foreign words "Salon Styling at Home."

Nicholas found more CDs at the library. This, too, was freeing, listening to something with simple curiosity, not as a composer or critic or teacher. The propelling rhythms, the lyrics in Spanish so that he didn't even know what the singing was about, energized Nicholas at the same time that something deeper within him relaxed.

And then, on a cold night in March, something wonderful happened.

It was one of Remy's Symphony nights. Nicholas met Paula at the dance club, and instead of the usual DJ, there was a band playing. Six young men with slick dark hair and matching button-down shirts. Their energy reverberated throughout the space as they sang and played their instruments as if their lives depended on it. The percussionist and horn player were particularly good, as was the lead singer. By the time Nicholas was ready to leave, the place was packed, and Nicholas was sweating from all the dancing and bodies and the excitement of having live music on the premises. He thanked Paula for his lesson and, watching her happily go off to dance with another partner, elbowed his way out the door.

The parking lot was quiet. As Nicholas was unlocking his car, some other patrons exited the club. The band's music slipped out the door with them—a brief buoyant affirmation, the singer's voice soaring above them, hailing the night. And then the door slid shut, and all that was left was a throbbing box of tamped sound.

Nicholas stood in amazement.

The gypsy music on the sidewalk.

A visitation. A call. Nicholas waited, shivering in the cold, for someone else to leave the dance club, so that he could hear again that burst of joy punctuating the air.

This was what he wanted. The feeling of that moment, the bewildered awareness of the divine. That simple burst—an unfettered voice.

For that was what was missing from the symphony—the voice that hadn't been allowed to shine through.

> A miracle's
> Oor only chance.
> Up, carles, up
> And let us dance!

Don't let go of it, he told himself when he eventually started the car up and set out toward home. He felt the two moments merging in his memory—the sidewalk gypsies and the salsa band—and knew that if he could just keep the sensation alive he would figure out what to do. Already he had an idea, felt that rare clarity of vision. He drove fast and didn't wait to turn at the two NO RIGHT ON RED stoplights. He had to get home.

Less than an hour later, as he sat down eagerly at his desk, he saw, in one sweep, the entire thing, his symphony, from beginning to end. The full arc of the whole unruly mess—the places that didn't belong, the ones that needed to be cut, a whole section that would need to be moved. And embroidered through the entire piece, breaking out intermittently in interpolated bursts, that one voice soaring above. Yes, *that* was what he needed, the surprise of it, sound cutting through the stillness, the gypsy musicians, right there on the sidewalk. . . .

He began to work, keeping at it long after Remy had returned from work, and he rose early the next morning to continue. There was much new composing to be done, to create this new conception out of the existing fabric. He composed in long bouts, until his fingers were cramped, his hand tired from gripping the pencil. Why hadn't he thought of this before?

Because I was stuck, he told himself. I needed a nudge out of that rut. That must have been what drove me to Paula in the first place. I was driven to her—to the dancing—for a reason.

He told her this when he returned to the salsa club the following week. His left wrist still tingled from the long hours of notation that day; he hadn't wanted to stop working, had quit only so that he could see Paula and thank her. As they sat out a cha-cha, leaning wearily on a table in a dark corner not far from the bar, he told her, "I feel very lucky, actually, to have met you."

Paula gave a big grin. "I feel that way, too." Looking suddenly bashful, she added, "I've never met anyone like you."

And then she was leaning toward him and his lips were on hers.

How lovely, her soft lips, and the tip of her tongue, the taste of her. It was hard for him to stop—but soon Nicholas pulled away, sat farther back in his chair. The slightly icky feeling returned. Paula shook her head at him, her nostrils flaring in that laughing way. She rolled her eyes and let them close for a moment, but then she exhaled loudly and reached for his hands. "Fine, then, come on. Let's dance."

Even as they danced he felt her electricity, as if some connection between them had been finalized. Her hands were warm as he led her, spun her around. When he told her good night, outside in the cold, they kissed again.

The next morning he set immediately to work, to prove that it was all in the service of art. Though he had much new writing to do, his confidence kept him afloat. The days, and then weeks, blurred one into the other, hours passing as if mere seconds while Nicholas worked. No time for anything else. In fact, he stopped going to the dance club altogether. He simply had too much to do, now that he knew what was needed, how to finish the symphony.

SHE STAYED UP LATE PRACTICING.

The violin solo wove through much of the first movement. A lithe, winding tune in F-sharp major—no open strings, which meant fewer overtones ringing out. What resonated instead was the touch of Remy's fingertips on the strings, the warmth of physical contact; without open strings vibrating, the sound of each note was more audibly human, almost voicelike. It seemed her fingertips themselves were singing.

In very brief moments, a wisp of melody seemed to recall something, some tiny sound-memory within her—but it was too brief, too quick. Remy could not hold on to whatever the recollection was, though she listened hard as she worked through that first run-through. She loved how it felt to move freely along this unfamiliar path. The solo was full of melismalike embellishments and rapid downward spirals that at points were nearly dizzying. Falling in love—that was what Remy's first-year theory teacher had said fast downward scales represented. When our ear hears that wild tripping down the scale, he had explained, we can't help being reminded of what it feels like to tumble headfirst into infatuation.

Was that what Nicholas had been writing about all this time, falling in love?

With her—or someone else?

Her heart seized once again at the thought of that other woman, and again she thought of what she might do—leave him, hurt him. She would call Christopher about that new orchestra in Spain . . . go somewhere far away from here.

Yet she did not want to stop playing. When she arrived at the end of the first movement, she immediately retuned her violin and flipped back to the beginning. This was one of those rare parts that made the most of her instrument's lyric qualities, its ability to portray human emotions. Not just the falling in love, but the excitement and trepidation (Nicholas had even included a *sul ponticello* section, that spooky sound that came from drawing the bow right across the top of the bridge) and the moments of pure joy. She loved the drama that leapt from the page through her limbs, through her violin; when she played those spirals, she felt a tumbling sensation, as if she, too, were falling in love.

She realized it had grown dark. Forcing herself to take a break, she went to the kitchen and scrounged for leftovers in the fridge, suddenly ravenous. It was the first time that day that she had had an appetite. She ate quickly, eager to return to the score. But first she closed the windows and fixed her heavy practice mute on the violin's bridge, so as not to disturb the neighbors.

Chapter 3

NICHOLAS AWOKE TO A VIOLENT HONKING—GARY BLOWING HIS nose into a paper napkin, which was then tossed past Nicholas's head in the general direction of the wastepaper basket. Gary had spent so much of his life alone, he thought nothing of gargling with the bathroom door open, burping loudly at whim, walking from room to room in nothing but his underwear. Though it was not yet seven, he was already at his computer, wearing a slim telephone headset, its mouthpiece curving like a tiny garden snake toward his chin. From the lumpy couch where he had slept poorly, Nicholas watched with half-opened eyes as Gary typed madly, one window on his computer connected to the Internet (for firing off pithy e-mails and letters to editors) and the rest of the screen filled with an article he was negotiating to sell to a magazine.

Nicholas tossed off the musty blanket, produced a deceptively jolly "good morning," and went to rinse his face at the stained bathroom sink. He had decided to take his breakfast at the diner down the street, the one where the waitresses call you "honey." He was in great need of affection; even the indiscriminate kind, from thick-ankled women in aprons, would do.

He washed in a halfhearted way, slapping suds onto his cheeks and neck, sloshing palms of water under his armpits. He reached for a towel that wasn't there, then squeezed some toothpaste from the messy tube onto his fingertip and rubbed it around his gums and teeth. He caught some water in his cupped palm, brought it to his lips, swooshed the liquid around in his mouth, and spat it out. Again he reached for the absent towel. Gary had lived in this apartment for decades, and though it accommodated the occasional guest, it did not welcome anyone with sincerity. All around were the subtle signs of neglect that, Nicholas realized, must accompany so many homes of a certain type of single male. Mildew speckled the bathroom ceiling; a bouquet of dried flowers was netted with cobwebs; in the small refrigerator sat half-wrapped deli sandwiches, a twelve-pack of Busch, and a carton of curdled milk. From those few years of Gary's marriage, all that was left were a series of blurry watercolors, covered by a faint layer of dust, that Adele had painted. Gary didn't seem to think it odd to have kept them. Neither had he seemed particularly distraught at becoming a bachelor again, though Nicholas knew it had been a painful time.

Nicholas took his jacket from the hall closet, eager to leave. He would go to that diner, eat a big breakfast, and think, hard, until he figured out what to do about Remy.

"Okay, I'm off," he called to Gary. But doubt gripped him, and he added, "I might possibly be back this evening, if that's all right."

Gary spun his swivel chair and nodded, his lower lip jutting out a bit, as if in the midst of contemplation. The telephone headset gave him a mildly absurd air of importance. "Okay, buddy. Maybe we can go to the pub." When he spun back to face the computer, the chair gave a loud sigh.

"NEED MORE COFFEE, HON?"

The Day Shift, populated mainly by elderly widowers and young college students, had a nice, warm greasy smell. The widowers took entire booths for themselves, forcing newcomers like Nicholas to sit at the counter, where heaped breakfast plates were passed, steaming, overhead. From behind the swinging kitchen door came the crashing sound of cutlery landing in soapy bins and the heavy chink of ceramic dishes being stacked. Nicholas found himself watching the cook, a stocky man named Marty, flip pancakes on the wide dark grill where pork sausage had been frying mere seconds earlier. The waitresses shouted their orders to him, so that there was a sense of urgency about the place, as if it were all quite dire, cups of coffee and bowls of oatmeal handed hastily back and forth. On the wall was a mute television tuned to CNN.

The man next to Nicholas ordered steak and eggs and wished Nicholas good morning. His name was Harvey. He was eighty-seven years old and had been eating at the Day Shift every morning for the past eighteen and a half years. They were already planning the party for his twentieth anniversary, he told Nicholas, explaining that he lived around the corner, and about the party that would happen two years from now. There would be news spots on Channel 2 and WGBH, and the *Globe* would do a piece in the Living section. He described it as if all this were just days away. Nicholas, though, couldn't help wondering if Harvey would make it to his own celebration. He was wheezy and intensely wrinkled, his face patterned with liver spots.

When Nicholas had ordered his eggs and allowed the waitress to take his menu away, Harvey asked, "You new here, or what?"

Nicholas said, "I don't usually eat here, no."

"No, I mean in town. You've got that accent, and I've never seen you before."

"Oh, yes, well, I've lived here for twenty years, actually."

Harvey was still peering at him. "Got any kids?"

"A daughter, yes. Jessica." Nicholas heard the absurd pride in his voice, as if it were his love alone that had nudged her into what she had become: strong, beautiful, lucky. Upon graduation from college two years ago (she had a BA in Hospitality Management), she had led cross-country bicycle tours for a summer before being offered a position at the West Coast branch of a company where she had interned, organizing travel incentive packages for business corporations. As the liaison between corporate clients and tour providers, she was brightly professional while retaining the aura of someone perpetually on holiday. Though her own vacation preferences were strenuous ones (biking across Tuscany, hiking Machu Picchu), her business travels were to ensure that the most popular tour packages—Malaysian spas, European ski chalets, Alaskan cruises, and Hawaiian beach resorts—maintained expected standards. She was also good at wrangling freebies—had sent her mother to Costa Rica, Nicholas and Remy for a long weekend in Turkey, and Remy's parents on a cruise to Argentina.

"She lives in Seattle," Nicholas told Harvey. "In fact, she's just gotten engaged." Even her voice on the telephone last week had been ebullient, describing how Joshua had bent down onto his knee to propose.

"Careful, honey, the plate's hot." The waitress, with reading spectacles low on her nose, handed Nicholas his runny eggs with wheat toast on the side, while the men to his right debated how the United States could ever get out of Iraq.

Shaking his head, Harvey said, "What a mess."

For a brief second Nicholas allowed himself to think that Harvey somehow understood what had happened yesterday. But Nicholas hadn't discussed it with anyone, not even last night when he asked Gary if he could sleep on his couch. Gary had just said, "Big fight, huh," as if he, too, went through such things all the time and they were nothing more than a headache.

The problem was, Remy felt betrayed. And so it was up to Nicholas to figure out what to do. He felt suddenly wild with panic—but forced himself to take a slow sip of coffee. Twice already he had tried to apologize. Now he said, "What do you think we ought to do?"

"What do I know?" Harvey said. "I've got one foot in the grave, the other on a banana peel."

At that moment an anorexic woman, so thin her shoulders poked at her shirt, fit herself onto the stool next to Nicholas. A sour smell came off her. Nicholas turned his face away and looked up at the television. Images flashed: a bombed-out city, children on hospital stretchers, wailing women. The anorexic woman ordered a coffee mixed with hot chocolate. So much foulness in the world, Nicholas found himself thinking—though he had never before thought of the world that way.

REMY ROSE EARLY, UNABLE TO SLEEP. AND THOUGH HER BACK ACHED from practicing late into the night, she returned to the music room. It felt good, this fatigue—not just physical but cerebral, too. The fatigue of hard work. She had forgotten, over the past years, what it felt like to study something with intensity. She had forgotten that sense of discovery.

The violin solo, it turned out, wove throughout the entire piece; variations reappeared in each movement. There were even cadenza-like sections, as in a concerto—though Remy could see that the *tutti* parts were still the main thrust of the piece.

That all this time, Nicholas had been writing a symphony with solo violin . . .

How could he have kept this from her?

Now Remy was teaching herself the second movement, which started out quietly but grew big and blustery, nearly roiling; the solo parts were full of wild runs and sudden furious chordal stops. This was a storm, Remy realized quite suddenly, her fingertips powerfully stopping the strings as she used a whiplike bow stroke. The section was marked *colossale,* so that she couldn't help wondering if it was one of Nicholas's private jokes.

As she moved through the notes Nicholas had written, there came again that tiny burst of recollection, a reminder of something—it must be some other piece, some other melody—but she could not find the memory. Odd. She was usually so good at locating motifs, quickly identifying aural allusions. If there were a "Name That Tune" for classical music, Remy would be the reigning champion. Nicholas used to try to stump her when they played together, improvising little mutations of recognizable themes—but she always managed to figure them out. Now she searched the score for a visual clue as to what this one might be, but found nothing.

Well, it would come to her, surely. In the meantime she worked to perfect the solo parts, attending to details she rarely had time for at the Symphony, making sure to substitute one finger for another on repeated notes, working to shape certain phrases without crossing strings. The second movement called for a range of timbres, using the back of the bow for *col legno* in the calm right before the storm, and snap pizzicato—plucking the string so hard that it slapped the fingerboard—where the first splatters of rain started. At least, that was what Remy pictured in her mind, recalling what Nicholas had once described to her: a brooding ocean, and dimming light thrown from wave to wave, and the plaints of gulls incising the sky. How strange it was now to see in her mind's eye what had once been in Nicholas's imagination.

And yet he hadn't told her about the violin solo. Had he intended to surprise her with it?

Had he been thinking of her at all?

Again Remy found herself scrutinizing each page, searching for hidden meaning, as if the answers to these questions might emerge from the notes themselves. It had been years, she realized, since she had studied a new work this way.

Maybe it hadn't even occurred to him to share the piece with her. Or maybe he meant to, when he began it all those years ago, but then forgot.

He did that sometimes, forgot about her, like some absentminded professor. One time he had neglected to give her the address of a friend's picnic out in Concord where they had planned to meet up; Remy didn't even know the friend's last name, kept calling Nicholas's cell phone, but of course he hadn't turned the thing on. And it hadn't occurred to him when she didn't show up to call her and see what the trouble was. Hard not to feel, when he made that sort of blunder, that perhaps, if subconsciously, he didn't really want her with him anymore.

But he had always been flighty that way, hadn't he? Well, yes, but . . . She thought back to her brief time with Yoni, that sudden reckless connection. Even then, her confusion had not diminished her feelings for Nicholas, had not diminished those things she shared with him. Music had remained the bond between them.

Now that, too, was lost—no different, she saw now, from any of those other activities people do together and then separately, when unable to resist the wear and tear of growing apart. That was what made his betrayal all the worse. It didn't matter how many times he apologized or tried to explain about that other woman. The slow growing apart that overtakes so many had reached them, too, without Remy even realizing it.

AT WORK, HAZEL ASKED LAURA IF SHE KNEW OF AN ARTIST CALLED Trent Rafael.

"The name sounds familiar."

"Here." Hazel held the magazine article out to her. The magazine was fat, heavy with colorful photographs intended for people with so many homes, they had to constantly search out new things to put in them.

Laura lifted her reading glasses from their little silver chain. "Oh, right," she said, at the photographs of the pastel-clad man and his sculptures. "I've heard of this guy. How is it this kind of thing gets a following?"

Hazel said, "Now there's one in my house."

"You're kidding." Laura let her reading glasses drop on their chain. "I'm so sorry."

"A friend of Robert's said it was a good investment. I was sure he must have been hoodwinked."

"Not according to this article. Jesus."

Hazel said, "I don't have the heart to make him return it. It's the only 'art' he's ever bought." In another time, another mind-set, she might have pinned some terrible significance on the awfulness—the falseness—of the wave-girl. But now Hazel knew enough to understand that in the grand scheme of things it didn't matter.

Laura was again looking at the photographs in the magazine. She began laughing, hard. "Of all people to have one of these in her home . . ."

"I know." To her relief, Hazel found that she, too, was laughing. "This is good," she told Laura when their laughter had at last subsided. "As long as I can joke about it with you, Robert won't have to hear me making fun of it. I hate to hurt his feelings."

Still, a heaviness hung on her for the rest of the day. It couldn't be the sculpture; it must still be Remy. It had all been so clear, for one brief moment. And yet—this was the oddest part—what Hazel had once wanted so badly (for Nicholas to hurt Remy, for there to be irreparable damage) was now, she realized, something she dreaded.

It just wouldn't do, if Nicholas and Remy fell apart, she told herself as she flipped through the past month's invoices.

"I hung those new mobiles up for display," Laura said, nodding toward a corner of the shop.

"Oh, they look lovely. Thanks." Hazel took a deep breath, told herself everything was all right.

Because if it wasn't, and Remy and Nicholas fell apart, then why had Hazel been humiliated like that? What was the reason for all that misery? To have been put through such an ordeal, when none of it was ultimately necessary . . . That didn't make sense at all.

"Cognitive dissonance," she knew from the psychology class she had taken at Harvard Extension. She knew that was what this was. But, she told herself as she put the invoices away, there had to be a reason. Otherwise, what was the point of those years of suffering? Why had she been hurt that way? She went over to the wall and straightened one of the framed photograms. Why had any of it happened, if it wasn't even meant to be?

ভ৹᎒᎒ᠣᢆᠣ

HE LEFT THE DAY SHIFT AND GLANCED AT HIS WATCH. REMY WOULD be headed to rehearsal now, not thinking of him at all, perhaps—or perhaps still as mad as yesterday. If only she would let him explain. If only nothing at all had happened. If only he knew what to do . . . He headed to the conservatory and knocked on Yoni's office door.

This he did even though he knew Yoni would not approve, that in Yoni's eyes Nicholas had already—always, somehow—failed Remy.

This fact was long acknowledged between them, though it was never spoken outright. There had been that night, years ago, back when the two of them still went to the jazz club, when Yoni had scolded Nicholas. "Careless with her heart." Yoni across from him too full of whiskey . . . That was during the rough patch with Remy, when something had happened, Nicholas never quite knew exactly what. Two months later the club had closed down, as though permanently contaminated by their conversation. (The following year, as if to consecrate the tragedy, the entire building had been gutted. In its place was a tall, shiny glass-and-metal structure with million-dollar condos reaching into the sky. On the ground floor, in approximately the spot where the jazz club had been, was an overpriced raw bar.)

No answer came when Nicholas knocked on Yoni's door. Nicholas made his way to his own office, on the fourth floor of the new building, Treenan Hall. A few stalwarts continued to call it "the new building," though it had been there four years now and already had its own tradition of jokingly obscene graffiti in one particular bathroom stall. Unlike all the other buildings, Treenan had no distinctive smell, no clanking radiators or flickering ceiling lights. Nicholas's office was graced with a skylight and continued to welcome him with a cheery cleanliness that his many stacks of papers and cardboard mailing boxes and even the occasional lump of wet raingear or snowy boots could not dispel.

"Hey, there, Nicholas."

He looked up to see Justin Fiori exiting the office next to his. "Oh, hello, Justin. Congratulations."

"Thanks, wow, I didn't realize word traveled so fast—oh, right, you mean about the grant." Justin readjusted his expression so that Nicholas understood there was some other accomplishment about which Justin felt even more excitement. "Yeah, well, there's still a lot of work to do there."

Justin was the school's youngest hire, just twenty-seven years old, and though he looked even younger, he had already won almost every prize available to a young composer. Last week it had been announced that Justin had secured an enormous development grant to purchase state-of-the art equipment for the conservatory's Digital Composition department. The department had barely been on the national radar ten years ago; Justin, a "digital whiz," had been brought in specially to revamp it. With rapidly increasing enrollment and the well-publicized success of some recent graduates, the department had apparently already gained national attention (although Nicholas didn't see what all the hoopla was about).

"How's it going with you?" Justin asked, locking his office door behind him.

"Fine, fine," Nicholas grumbled. An entire page of the school's Web site described the many radical developments Justin had instigated since his arrival.

Nicholas had reservations about these so-called advancements. For one thing, he had never particularly liked digital compositions. And when it came to technology . . . he simply didn't find it an improvement. His composition students now turned in electronic files of their assignments, so that the computer played back accurate yet soulless renditions Nicholas couldn't help thinking of as . . . well, not cheating, exactly, but cheapness. And unnecessary. After all, Nicholas could tell what a piece would sound like simply by reading the score; these computer playbacks were inferior versions. He himself still wrote everything out in long hand and always composed in full score. He saw what happened when students used those computer programs, the way the fixed pages and measures confined them, so unlike the freedom of blank staff paper. He saw how quickly the students worked themselves into corners, stumped by the orderliness of the programs themselves. Nicholas's work was untainted by all that.

"Well," Justin said, "I'd better run. I've got a commission that's overdue and . . . well, I'm just adding final touches, but you know how much time that takes. Plus I'm off to Rome tomorrow night and haven't packed."

"How nice," Nicholas told him. "Have a wonderful time."

"Thanks, see you in a week." Justin turned and went briskly on his way.

Nicholas let himself into his office, the familiar view of the wall busy with photographs and plaques. On the other side of the wall was another recent hire, Sarah Pagent, chair of Guitar and Harp; Nicholas could hear her yelling into the telephone at her teenage son.

Nicholas tried to find pleasure in the sight of his crowded office—the welcoming messiness his colleagues teased him for. On the floor near the door was a big plastic bag filled with wool: the best kind, from New Zealand, skeins and skeins of it, natural and undyed.

He had bought it a month ago, on a whim, when he passed a store not far from here during his lunch break. It was a store he had never taken note of before though it was just around the corner. He recalled Paula mentioning how expensive real wool and real silk were, and how she hated to use synthetic yarn.

By that time it had been weeks since he had gone dancing. Ever since that lightbulb had gone off in his head, he had spent his evenings at home with his symphony. And so, when he came upon the yarn shop, it had struck him as an appropriate way to thank Paula. He had bought a whole bag of wool for her, the size of a big black garbage bag—and the bag was still on his office floor. It had been here so long, it had become part of the landscape of the office, though Nicholas still fully intended to stop by the club and drop it off.

Seeing it now, he hung his head at how angry Remy was, and for some reason felt Justin Fiori was to blame. " 'Final touches,' " he muttered to himself. " 'Off tonight and haven't packed . . .' " The telephone on his desk blinked at him, and his heart gave a small skip. With a mixture of trepidation and hope, he lifted the receiver, filled as he was with the notion that Remy might have left word for him.

Instead he heard his daughter's voice. "Dad, hey, I left a message at home but thought you might be here. Just wanted to let you know we'll be coming to visit next month—we get in on the eighteenth. Just want to make sure you'll be in town. I'm pretty sure you said you would be. I'll e-mail you our flight info. Love you!"

Nicholas took his seat in the bouncy rotating desk chair that the school had recently splurged on in an effort to become more "ergonomic." He sorted through the mail that had come into his department box, most of it ignorable—but one envelope, a big, thick one, caught his eye. Noting the return address, he slit the thing with a pair of scissors. Paper-clipped on top was a note:

My friend,

It seems to me a long time I haven't seen you. I hope you are well as always. I write you now because, as you know, I value your help. I hope therefore you will allow me to take you up on your offer of critiquing my latest work. It is one that has preoccupied me for years—yet it seems for once I have managed to capture what I hear between my ears.

I hope you do not find it presumptuous that I enclose a recording here; it is the Lyon orchestra, in their "New Works" performance. My hope is that this work might be nominated for the Felster Prize (as if I might have any more chance this year than in the past! But one continues to try . . .). Please let me know if you think this possible, if you would do that for me.

And you are doing well, I hope? Life is good, is it not? For some reason it took me a bit long to see that. (Well, because sometimes it isn't, quite.) But even so—en avant! I have so many other pieces I want to write.

    Je t'embrasse très fort,

                                      Sylvane

Nicholas took the CD up to see if it had a title. He had twice before nominated Sylvane for the Felster Prize and would be happy to do so again. Yet as curious as he was to hear her new piece, now was too risky, while he was still making final alterations to his own work. And so he wrote a quick e-mail to Sylvane: "I've received your piece. How good to hear from you, will get to it next week at the latest, as soon as I finish some outstanding projects I have right now."

Probably it would be something marvelous. She was the real thing—not an overconfident kid, like that Justin Fiori. *Final touches . . .*

Nicholas settled back to his work—returning phone calls he had long put off, taking care of this and that, anything to keep busy. Morning became afternoon, and Nicholas stood from his desk. Remy would be finishing rehearsal soon. He left his office, ready to try once again.

Chapter 4

WHAT HAPPENED WAS THAT SHE WAS LOOKING FOR THE STUB for the dry cleaning. Instead she found, amid the various slips of this and that, a scrap of paper—cardboard, actually. Remy was crumpling it up as trash when she saw something written on the other side, something in loopy, feminine script. For a moment she thought it might be Jessica's, except that Jess always wrote in sloppy block print, as if never having learned cursive. And this was, she realized, Spanish. Remy looked at the mysterious words for a good few seconds, wondering. It was not just the unfamiliar handwriting—it was the scrap of paper itself, taken from what must have held a hairbrush. PROFESSIONAL, the package said, and SALON STYLING AT HOME—nothing that Remy or Nicholas would have purchased. Perhaps that was what stopped her from throwing the scrap of paper out. Instead she put it in the pocket of the cardigan she was wearing, as if it might be useful at some point in the future.

Thinking back to this now, Remy realized she must have known, subconsciously, what had happened. Why else would she have kept that scrap of paper? A clue, evidence. She hadn't thought of it that way at first. She had simply put it in her pocket and forgotten about it. It was days later, when she was eating breakfast and Nicholas was fixing himself a cup of tea, that she reached into the pocket of her cotton sweater and found the scrap of paper there.

Reading the words again, she had felt herself take a deep breath, somehow aware that she held in her hand the key to a mystery. And yet she asked her question in a calm voice: "What's this?"

"Hmm?" Nicholas had leaned toward her to look at the writing. He shook his head, confused. And then his face had softened, remembering something. "Oh, a young woman I know, she gave me that. It's the name of a band she wanted me to listen to." He said it lightly enough that Remy might not have worried.

But the phrase "young woman" caught her, the unspoken meaning it carried. "What young woman?" she asked, though she knew she was pressing into a dangerous place.

"She's no one, really," Nicholas said.

Being lied to infuriated her. "Who is she, Nicholas?"

Nicholas began to explain: it wasn't what she thought, it was nothing at all, just salsa lessons, at a dance club.

"Salsa lessons? When did you start that?"

"Oh . . . February."

Four months ago. "You've been going to dance classes and didn't even tell me?"

Nicholas looked equally surprised, as if unclear as to how it could have happened.

"Why didn't you tell me?"

"I don't know," he said. "I don't know why." Remy saw that it was true. It must have been the "young woman" there, the need to see her, to admire her, or to be admired. . . . He must have done something illicit—otherwise he would have told her. "What else aren't you telling me?"

"Nothing. Really, it isn't like that at all."

"Really?" Even as she asked this, full of dread, she recalled her own confusion, back when she had been unable to keep herself from Yoni. But any empathy she might have mustered flew away when Nicholas said, "Well, no, I mean, not really . . ."

"Nicholas! Is she your . . . lover?" Saying it, she felt her heart crack in two. Never had she felt such a thing, her heart being cracked in half, like a nut.

"No—no!" But the twitch of his cheek told her there was something.

"You lied to me."

"I didn't lie."

"Four months." Without me, she was thinking. A whole experience he had that he didn't want me to be part of. A whole part of his life he didn't want me to touch. He chose to do this without me. Whatever it is he actually did. She couldn't bear to imagine.

And so she told him to get out, while the cereal in her bowl became mushy and dejected. It was the first time in her life with him that she did not, in anger, throw something. Instead she sat there behind the *Boston Globe* and pretended that she was through with him.

These moments played themselves out again in Remy's mind as she came to the end of the Symphony's final rehearsal of the season—an open rehearsal, with a small audience of retirees and music students dotting the hall.

It had been something of a letdown today, to find herself back with the second violins. Not that she usually minded. After not winning the associate concertmaster seat (a good ten years ago now) she had resolved to make the most of the one she did have. Indeed, she had become the best principal second she could be—had even been praised in print a few times, and warmly thanked more than once by her colleagues. To herself, she had resolved to try to embody those principles she had once abandoned, reminding herself of what Julian had said, that every time she played, no matter the occasion, was a performance.

Yet it had been a long time since she felt ignited, as she had while playing last night.

Rehearsal ended. As the others hastily packed up their instruments, and the makeshift audience applauded and then shuffled out of the hall, Remy wiped away the rosin dust that had collected on the face of her violin. Carefully she fitted the violin into its satin bed and rested a silk kerchief across the top. Twirling the little adjuster, she loosened her bow and plucked off a broken horsehair. The dedication of these small movements, the endlessly repeated gestures . . . Sometimes it seemed her life was one never-ending rehearsal. Even her violin was showing signs of age, its C-bout worn in the place where her bow sometimes brushed against it, as was the varnish of the upper rib shoulder. Her bow, too, was worn down, at the spot where her thumb met the leather cushion.

It was the gorgeous bow, the wildly expensive one from Daniel's shop. She had purchased it ten years ago, when she didn't win the associate concertmaster slot. No, the bow hadn't consoled her, but it was a beautiful daily presence in her life.

The youngest musicians were already heading off together, and now the brass clique was noisily making its way out the door. Over in the first violin section, the concertmaster was joking about something. Although they both played the same instrument and were both section leaders, he made five times Remy's salary—even though he sometimes played only half a concert, if it was one that included a long solo.

"So, have you given it any more thought?" Christopher had come over from the woodwinds. He spoke in a whisper though Remy's stand partner had already left, and nervously stroked his theatrically long mustache.

"I haven't had time to really research it," Remy told him, almost as quietly, as she placed her music back in her tote bag. "But I—I'm definitely interested. Have you gotten any more information?"

A good friend of Christopher's was helping to start a new orchestra in Barcelona. Apparently there was generous funding, and the music director was soliciting musicians from top orchestras all over the globe. Interested musicians were to send recordings and résumés, and auditions would be held in July. It all sounded potentially wonderful. In fact, Remy had begun to wonder, late last night, when her mind was still turning angry circles, if part of the reason she was so furious at Nicholas had to do with this—if she wanted an excuse to try out for the new orchestra.

Because there were things she no longer loved so much about her job. Some of the musicians she had most liked, the ones she had counted as friends, had already retired or moved away. Gone—just like the affable security guards whose names Remy had known and who had greeted her, too, by name; they had been replaced by a management company from out of town, an endless rotation of random agents who didn't know any of the orchestra members by sight. That was something Remy certainly wouldn't miss. . . .

She recognized what she was doing, mentally preparing herself, telling herself there were things she wouldn't mind leaving behind. Yet at the same time she wished she could say, as she would have in the past, No, thank you, I don't need a new job or a new place to live. I'm perfectly content with my life here. Though how could she pretend that now?

"I'll check my e-mail when I get home," Christopher told her. "See if there've been any new developments. I'll get back to you soon."

The stage had emptied out, but a few other friends lingered behind and suggested lunch at a new noodle shop. "No, thanks," Remy told them as she shut her violin case.

That was when Christopher turned toward the wings and said, "Hello, Nicholas!"

"Christopher." Nicholas nodded hello as the rest of the little group greeted him.

"How are you?" Christopher asked, but Marina, another friend, said, "Come on, folks, I'm hungry." The little group made their way out the door, the last to leave except for a timpanist who was still in the back, fiddling with something.

"Remy," Nicholas said, making his way toward her through the rows of chairs until he was in front of the conductor's stool. He looked tired, said again, "Remy." His voice sounded different here on this stage renowned for its acoustics. He said, as he had too many times, "I'm sorry."

Remy felt oddly bored.

"You have to know that what happened really was nothing," he continued, "and that nothing like it will ever happen again."

To have these lines delivered in such a place, center stage, made them sound like a performance—and like most performances, insincere. All the while, Remy could hear the timpanist fiddling at the back, like some sluggish stagehand late with a scene change.

In a low voice Nicholas said, "I know you don't believe me when I tell you it was just dancing. But that's basically the truth—"

"Basically!"

"Really, Remy, it was nothing, please believe me—"

"I do believe you! That's just it! That's exactly it!" For Remy the very notion that "it was nothing" made it all the worse, the fact that Nicholas could have betrayed without sacrifice—without giving anything up, not even a sliver of his heart.

When she herself had slipped, the connection *meant* something— and the pain remained with her even now. Whereas Nicholas could cavort with some "young woman" and then move on, without any trouble at all.

"Look, I'm really sorry," Nicholas said, with a desperation that was new. He must have heard how hollow his words sounded; he went down onto his knees to say, "I'll never hide anything from you again. I promise. Please, Remy."

"Jesus, Nicholas, get up off the floor."

Nicholas hunched his shoulders like an old man.

Remy said, "I think I've seen enough of you for today."

Nicholas narrowed his eyes at her. The muscles of his jaw twitched. He stood, and for a long second waited, then turned and negotiated his way past the empty chairs.

Remy watched him leave. The timpanist dropped something, and a loud, clanging sound reverberated across the stage.

❧— —❧

BY THE NEXT MORNING, NICHOLAS COULD NO LONGER STAND IT. ON his way to the Day Shift, he made a phone call.

"Hello!" came Yoni's chipper voice.

"Oh, good, you're there. Have you got a minute?"

"Nicholas, how are you?"

"I was hoping we might meet to discuss something, if you're free."

"I have time this morning. But I'm meeting Justin Fiori at noon."

"Well, if you're free now, how about breakfast?"

"That works."

Nicholas asked him to meet him at the diner and felt both relief and apprehension when Yoni said, "I'll be right there."

At the Day Shift, Nicholas took a seat at the counter and slung his jacket over the stool to his right; there were no free booths at this hour. A plump, blond waitress said, "Hi, honey," and asked if he had gotten a good night's sleep.

"I did," Nicholas lied, so as not to sound like a complainer. "And you?"

"Oh, on my feet all day, you know, I fall into bed like a log."

The old man, Harvey, hadn't arrived yet. Nicholas found himself glaring at a college couple nearby who addressed each other with a shy complicity, the girl smiling at the boy in a glib way, the skin under their eyes puffy from a night of drink and sex.

"Here you go, hon," the waitress said, handing him his coffee.

Nicholas took a gulp and shook his head—at the couple, but also at himself. Never before had he been so judgmental. He had always been open to everything. Wasn't that why everyone liked him?

"You again," Harvey wheezed, easing his body onto the seat to Nicholas's left.

Nicholas nodded hello. "How's life treating you?"

"It doesn't treat me at all. I treat myself. Otherwise I'd be completely neglected." He gave the hollow snort that was his laugh. Nicholas could see the skin tags on his right eyelid, the deep wrinkle in his earlobe, the crease down the middle of his cheek.

"Hello!" It was Yoni, grinning.

"Yoni, thanks very much for coming." With reservation Nicholas introduce him to Harvey.

"Pleasure to meet you." Yoni shook Harvey's hand firmly, and Harvey said, "Yeah, yeah." Nicholas indicated Yoni's seat for him, and swiveled his own toward it, away from Harvey's, to show that this would be a private conversation. The waitress, understanding, briskly took their orders.

Settling onto the stool, Yoni leaned forward on his forearms in a gung-ho way. Nicholas couldn't help admiring how successfully Yoni retained his youth, with ease rather than desperation. At fifty he remained dashing and fit, the lines in his face suggesting wisdom. Age had dignified him, outwardly as well as inwardly, and he brandished his little rectangular reading glasses with aplomb, squinting into the narrow slits of glass as if detecting secrets available only to the old and wise.

"So . . . ?" he asked Nicholas as the waitress filled his coffee cup. Nicholas saw her do a quick double take at Yoni's stunted finger and the thumb with its patched skin. Yoni didn't seem to notice. "What's up?" he asked.

Nicholas made a long grumbling sound. He realized he didn't know what to say.

"What is it, Nicholas?" Yoni's brow creased.

"I've screwed up."

Now Yoni frowned, like a parent accustomed to nothing but trouble. He didn't speak, and it occurred to Nicholas that perhaps he would rather not know. And so Nicholas said nothing, just waited for Yoni to ask what had happened.

Instead there was a long silence—so long, it began to feel like a contest. Yoni spent a good minute looking down at the Formica countertop, and then the waitress was there with their toast and eggs.

Nicholas took a long, preparatory swig of coffee. The idea of not discussing this, of having no one to talk to, was too much. "I've hurt Remy's feelings," he finally let out, when he was sure Harvey was well into another conversation with the waitress and wouldn't hear. "I don't know how to make it up to her."

Now Yoni seemed to be gritting his teeth. "Is it what I think?" he asked softly, barely moving his mouth.

"No!" Nicholas gave a frustrated shrug of his shoulders. "Well, there's another person, but—" Quickly, seeing Yoni's face, he added, "It's not *that*! I mean, not really. The problem is, Remy still insists I've cheated on her or something." He stopped, aware that it sounded awful. "Look, I realize I've made a mistake. Now I need to know what to do."

Yoni's face had reddened. "And you're sitting here eating fried eggs?"

Nicholas let his eyebrows rise. He looked at Yoni imploringly. "I don't know what to do."

With a tight jaw Yoni said, "You have no idea, that's for sure."

"Yoni, look, I realize I've made a mistake. If I'd known it would hurt her . . . You know more than anyone how much I love Remy. You of all people know that I can't live without her."

Yoni's nostrils flared. Very slowly, he nodded.

"Need a refill, honey?" The waitress poured more coffee, then swiveled her hips to squeeze behind the counter. Nicholas's heart was beating fast.

Yoni pursed his lips, shook his head. In a low voice he said, "Just how much damage can you do?"

Nicholas felt his heart sink. "What's that supposed to mean?"

"Here you are with the most amazing woman, and look what you do. To her and whoever else."

Quietly, angrily, Nicholas said, "I'm perfectly able to berate myself. That's not why I asked you to come here."

"You want me to fix things for you, is that right?"

"No, I—"

"You want someone to clean up after you."

"Not at all! I simply—"

"I can't listen anymore, Nicholas, I'm sorry." Yoni's voice sounded almost weak. "I want to help you. I would love to be able to help you. But I've already done all I can." He nodded slowly. "Believe me, there's truly nothing more I can do."

"I just wanted some advice," Nicholas said feebly, but Yoni had already stood and thrown a few small bills on the counter. He turned and walked out.

Heart racing, Nicholas looked down at his plate of runny eggs. He heard the door swing open and then shut. The stocky waitress was saying something to Harvey in a teasing voice. Harvey said, "Don't look at me. I've got one foot in the grave, the other on a—"

"Yeah, yeah," the waitress said, refilling his coffee mug.

IT WAS A SLOW AFTERNOON AT THE SHOP, NO ONE THERE BUT ONE OF the regulars—an old woman who always spent hours examining every single object but had never bought a thing. Hazel lifted the telephone and called Nicholas at work.

She had been wondering how long it would take for him to contact her about the wedding. The two of them really ought to confer about it; they were Jessica's parents, after all, plus everyone knows that the bride's father is supposed to foot the bill. Jessica would be here in a few weeks, and Hazel wanted to make sure that when it came to wedding plans, they were all on the same page.

When Nicholas's line stopped ringing and clicked over to an answering machine, Hazel decided to leave a message; someone had to get the ball rolling.

By the time he rang back it was evening and Hazel was on her way home, on Storrow Drive, in thick traffic. For safety, Hazel made a point of never answering her cell phone while driving. Not until she had arrived home and changed into more comfortable sandals and opened all of her windows wide to let in the spring air did she press the Return Call button.

Waiting for the line to connect, she fetched the feather duster and began—automatically more than consciously—to tidy up a bit.

Now the phone was ringing as Hazel flicked the duster here and there. Just when she decided that no one would answer, a voice came on: "Yeah?"

"Oh, I'm sorry, I must've— I'm calling for Nicholas Elko. This is Hazel—"

"Hazel! Whe-he-hullo there!"

"I'm sorry, who is this?"

"It's Gary Schmid!"

"Gary. Well, what a surprise." Hazel could feel her eyebrows arching. Gary was so far off in her past, she barely remembered him. A few times she thought she had glimpsed him on the streets of Boston, but if anyone had told her she would ever have to converse with him again, Hazel would have laughed out loud. He was simply a reminder of a time when Hazel had been too miserable to see any good in him, when his very presence made her own small world seem that much worse.

"How are you?" She heard how businesslike she sounded.

"Hazel. Now, that's a surprise. How're you doing?"

Already she felt perturbed. "Fine, thanks," she said, surprised at how foreign Gary's voice sounded in her ear. She wouldn't have recognized it. "I just wanted to touch base with Nicholas about something."

"Sure, no prob." Hazel could hear Gary moving about, heavy footsteps, the groan of a testy old window being raised. She had completely stopped her tidying and was holding the feather duster limply. "But he's not here right now."

"Will he be back?"

"Seems likely."

"Well, if he could call me, I would appreciate it."

"Okay, I'll pass that along."

"Thanks very much."

Then Gary coughed loudly, and Hazel held the phone away from her ear. She heard him say, "Listen, it's great to hear your voice again. I hope you're well."

"Oh, yes. You, too. Bye now."

But even after the call had disconnected, Hazel felt shaken. Something *was* definitely wrong.

Wasn't that really why she had called? To find out if her hunch was correct? Her hand trembled as she ran the feather duster over the wooden plant stand and the large oval mirror and—she sighed—the fake crystal wave-girl. She barely allowed herself to glance at it.

She put down the duster and went out to the back patio, for a restorative breath of fresh air. She gazed out at the potted geraniums that presented themselves so brightly, and the flounce of nasturtiums lining the edge of the house, and the cabbage butterflies flitting about industriously. Her world continued on as peacefully as before. Robert would be home any minute now, and they would grill the pork tenderloin she had left marinating this morning, and eat out here on the patio, with the citronella candles lit in their clay lanterns, and go to sleep together in the big four-poster bed. This was real, this was her life, not that other, old, world she had breathed, so briefly, moments ago. She rose from her chair to go back inside, reminding herself that she could not—it was impossible—slip back into that long-ago place.

FOR HOURS THE SECOND NIGHT, AND AGAIN THE NEXT MORNING, Remy practiced the violin part. She knew the solo's reappearance in each of the movements must *mean* something—this timbral presence, this protagonist of sorts. But what was its meaning, what was this voice *saying*?

The third movement required scordatura—quickly loosening the G string down to an E—so that the sound became as soulful as a viola's. A mournful sound. Remy recalled what Nicholas had told her back when he was just beginning the piece, that first year of their life together, after his realization about his mother. Recalling the despair of that discovery, Remy felt again (she could not help it) a genuine sympathy. The violin solo had become so achingly sad, it shocked Remy to think this could have come from Nicholas, this man who loved to proudly declare his affection for the key of C major. . . . Remy experimented with the cadenza, taking greater liberties each time, finding within it a sense of freedom and improvisation, and concluded with a resolutely melancholic four-part chord.

The final movement was the most beautiful of all, very calm and still. The violin solo remained prominent, and Remy played without vibrato, moving her bow slowly, barely touching her fingertips to the strings so that they scarcely held each note. She wanted to convey a sense of peace that was real yet hard won. The purity of rest that comes from deep fatigue. A letting go of life's effort and pain.

Even in this movement she heard, if ever so lightly, the scant re-verberation of some familiar air. Not the air itself . . . At that first tickle—the shiver of recollection—she stopped and scrutinized those specific measures on the manuscript page. Just a small string of notes had done this to her, caused some deep auditory resonance, and yet even seeing the notes here on the page she could not think where they might have originated.

It did not matter. She lifted her violin again and played on. It had been a long time since she had worked with such intensity. None of the contemporary works the music director at the Symphony selected had ever struck Remy this way—*le coup de foudre,* her stand partner, Carole, sometimes called it. Yes, a long time it had been since she had fallen in love with a piece of music.

It was on the third day that she noted something even more sur-prising. She was *improving*. She could hear it and could feel it in her fingers (which had creases in the tips from playing so much these past days). After years of upkeep, and the never-ending struggle to maintain her technique, always trying her best despite that inevitable plateau, something *new* was happening. It wasn't simply the mastery of a new piece, that gradual familiarization of the unfamiliar. No, something was growing within her as she struggled with various interpretive problems, making sense of Nicholas's notations, creating her own reading of the work—not following that of a conductor or a teacher. It had been a long time since she had figured out something like this on her own.

She even found herself taking issue with a few decorative flourishes Nicholas had written into the third movement. She decided they got in the way—and after some contemplation, edited them out. As Julian used to say, a musician was more than an interpreter; the musician became its coauthor. It was the musician's imagination that fully realized any new work.

Remy had never fully understood what that meant. But as she experimented with these notes Nicholas had written, she felt the full bloom of her imagination. For in Nicholas's pages she saw, to her surprise—and unlike in real life—so many possibilities.

She thought of the Barcelona orchestra. A possibility, but was it what she wanted?

When, as she began the final movement once again, the telephone rang, Remy wanted simply to continue playing. But the ringing continued, and here came the recorded message, and now a familiar voice. "Hey, it's me, I've been meaning to call you back but things have been kind of crazy at work and then by the time I remember to call it's three in the morning your time and—"

Remy snatched up the telephone. "Hey, kiddo."

"Oh, good, you're there! Sorry to only just be calling now, but—"

"It's all right, I was just calling to say hi. You've been busy, huh?"

"Good busy," Jessica said. "I had to write a whole proposal, and you know how long that kind of thing takes me. What about you?"

It was clear from Jessica's voice that Nicholas hadn't told her anything, that she knew nothing of their stalemate. But somehow, today, with music still coursing through Remy's limbs, the thought didn't seem to matter so much. She heard herself saying, "Oh, you know, same old, same old." She closed her eyes against the dissimulation. "Just one more BSO performance, and then I'll be free."

Knowing what those words might mean, she added, almost before she had thought it, "In fact, I had an idea I wanted to run by you."

The idea had just now come to her. "A proposition, actually."

Remy didn't allow herself to worry about the implications, or that she hadn't yet worked out a plan. She thought for a moment, took a breath, and improvised.

Chapter 5

AT HAZEL'S BOUTIQUE, A WAFT OF LAVENDER OVERTOOK NICHO-las like a cloud.

Hazel was behind the counter and looked businesslike in a way that made Nicholas ask, "Is this the right time?"

"Yes, Laura can cover for me. Give me just one second."

"Of course." Nicholas surveyed the shop, the ceramic clocks and marble sundials, paperweights embedded with malachite, silk patch-worked scarves, batik prints sewn into throw pillows; he had been here just once before, for the grand opening. Hazel stepped out from behind the counter and said, "Here, we can talk in the back."

Nicholas followed her to the rear of the store into the storage room, where Hazel's coworker—petite and plump, a pair of reading glasses hanging from her neck like a stethoscope—was fishing through a pyramid of boxes. All along the walls, towers of cardboard and thick rolls of bubble wrap leaned precariously. Nicholas marveled: everyone, even Hazel, had some sort of clutter in a back room somewhere.

"This is Laura," Hazel told Nicholas while Laura buried her arms in crinkled paper that she began weeding out like great tufts of cotton candy. Barely looking up, her eyeglasses swinging on their beaded chain between her breasts, she said, "I'm looking for more of those paperweights."

"I can take care of that," Hazel told her, "if you'll cover for me up front."

"Sure." Laura disappeared back to the other side of the curtain. Hazel peered down at the pile of boxes and, as if after judicious selection, reached into one and pulled out a wrapped paperweight. "Good, here they are." To Nicholas she said, "Have a seat. It's good of you to stop by."

"Well, you're just around the corner, really." Nicholas sat down on one of the folding chairs.

"School's still in session, then?"

"This is the last week."

"I wasn't sure you were still going into the office, so I'm glad I caught you at Gary's." She said it in a fetching way; clearly she was wondering why he had called her from there. Already Nicholas sensed what Hazel often caused him to feel, that he was supposed to be offering up all kinds of information about his life. She looked at him almost as if she knew what had happened. But there was no way she could know, he reminded himself.

"It was odd hearing his voice," Hazel continued. "I didn't recognize it, I hadn't spoken to him in so long."

Nicholas smiled and said, "You never could stand him, could you? I always thought it was because he had a crush on you, that you must have sensed it. Or perhaps you two had more in common than you wanted to admit."

"I doubt that," Hazel said, clearly offended. "And I doubt I'm the only one to react that way to him."

"I suppose you're right," Nicholas said. "I don't think Remy has ever taken much of a shine to him, either. I remember a long time ago she was so upset when he spilled something on the carpet. Red wine, I think it was. She tried to pretend it was fine, but for a while there she could barely look at him."

Hazel opened her eyes wide and looked at him oddly. It made Nicholas uncomfortable, so that he added, as jollily as possible, "Practically banished him from the house."

Hazel was pursing her lips. What have I done now? Nicholas wanted to ask. Not just Hazel—Yoni, too. He still heard his voice, wondered what Remy could have told him. And now, with Hazel . . . the whole room felt suddenly perilous, the boxes potential avalanches all around them. I'm sorry! he wanted to say. I've made a mistake, and I'm sorry! Instead he took a casual breath and said, "So, our girl's getting married."

Now Hazel's face relaxed. Quickly she listed ideas for the wedding—and what they could expect to pay. Nicholas watched the way her hair bounced lightly, so in contrast to the messy towers of boxes behind her.

"And I'm planning an engagement party," Hazel was saying now. "For the third Sunday in June, since she and Josh will be here. I just have to finalize the time with her. I'll make sure to send an invitation to you and Remy as soon as I do."

"Oh, good," Nicholas muttered. "Very nice of you."

There it was again, the look in her eye—of concern, of worry—so that he could not but feel she wanted something from him.

"Well," she told him, "thank you for stopping by. I appreciate it."

Together they went back to the front of the store, past Laura polishing the collection of glass mobiles. At the door, Hazel said, "I hope everything is okay." She sounded surprisingly earnest. "I feel like we haven't spoken in a long time."

"Yes," Nicholas said. "The years go by like minutes sometimes, don't they?"

"Indeed they do," Hazel said, as if waiting for something. Her face was a different version of the face he had once loved—a pale, creamy one—and her hair lighter, too, as if she were only now being allowed to fully glow.

"Okay, talk to you soon," Hazel told him.

But instead of saying good-bye, Nicholas heard himself say, "I still see you sometimes when I'm asleep. It sometimes happens in my dreams. Usually we're still young, and Jessie's very tiny, just born, and your hair is long, cascading down your back. And then I wake up and for a moment I don't know where I am anymore." The words came out in a rush.

Hazel leaned against the doorframe, as if suddenly weak. Quietly she said, "I have that dream, too, sometimes."

Chapter 6

WHEN NICHOLAS ARRIVED AT THE DAY SHIFT THAT MORNING, the waitress with the heavy walk was fitting herself behind the counter. Shaking her head, she said, "Bad news about Harvey."

"Oh no," Nicholas said.

The old man had broken his hip; it took hours before he found help. "I guess that's what happens when you live alone," the waitress said. "I keep expecting him to walk through that door."

Instead the anorexic woman had come in. She wore her hair in two low ponytails, and as she ordered her coffee with hot chocolate, her hair itself struck Nicholas as abhorrent. It was abhorrent that she should try to look youthful, when in reality she was just ill.

"With old people," the waitress continued, "these are the things that do them in. Here—do you want to sign this card for him?"

Nicholas wrote his name into the card, adding a jaunty line about the twentieth-anniversary party. But his hand was shaking. How could he be so upset, when he barely knew the man? Well, he was still smarting from his conversation—if one could call it that—with Yoni. Hard not to keep puzzling over what Yoni could have meant. Even Hazel seemed to want more from him somehow. And now this. He looked to the mute television screen, where a perky-looking blonde was giving a report on what was apparently a new trend: beauty spas for dogs. Nicholas felt a surge of disgust.

Everything was rotten. And he still hadn't figured out what to do for Remy.

On the television a little dog wore pink sneakers—four of them—

and a matching bow in its hair. The newscaster nodded in conversation with its owner. Normally Nicholas found humor in such things, but today all he saw was one more indication that the world was going to pot. What an abomination, he thought. The crappiness of it all. He had little appetite when his eggs arrived and shifted them around on his plate; by the time he tried to eat them, they had gone cold.

HE WENT TO HIS OFFICE AND WORKED THERE INTO THE EVENING. IT was Friday, a Symphony night—Remy's last performance of the season. She would be heading there right now. What he would do, to not have hurt her.

He stood, his legs stiff, and took Sylvane's CD and manuscript from the envelope. He couldn't help being curious. *That* at least he could count on; *that* he knew would be beautiful. He opened to the first page of the score, placed the CD in the stereo, and pressed Play.

At first he was simply reading along as he listened. The opening was sparse, mere daubs of color, the woodwinds lightly touching the air. Then a slow repeated knell rose from the tuba, was caught by the French horn, increased in speed, and was lifted by trumpets until it became a siren skirling. But instead of whirling out of control, the trumpets were absorbed by the orchestra *tutti* and, after a long calming diminuendo, a lovely air emerged, a flute's whispered wisdom, one of those runic melodies Sylvane so excelled at. Nicholas pictured a shady bower, a trickling bourn, blossoms dandled by a breeze. Gradually the music's tracery widened, first into shimmering rills (the tremolo of the second violins), then broad ribbons of sound, and the woodwinds' counterpoint against the first violins. The sound grew luxuriant, the brass a haunting chorus as the strings came together densely, a jungle of deep green vines. The thick tangle of the vines, the bright voices of the woodwinds . . . It was a gorgeous, luscious jungle, but he was lost.

He began to weep.

For the entire first movement he wept, sobs that tore at his chest.

His lungs were exhausted by the time the second movement began. Nicholas became quiet, managed to flip ahead in the score to find his place. At the third movement, he rested his forehead on his desk and simply listened. Sylvane's music crept up from the dale out toward the glade—the piping of a piccolo, its sunny tinctures. The brass and strings continued to weave their patterns, numinous harmonies, a panoply of voices.

For the finale, Sylvane had done something unusual—quite unlike her signature conclusion, that melancholic swell and gradual fading out that often left Nicholas with a feeling of quiet sadness, some dark effluvium hanging over everything. This time she had used a higher register, so that the sound was lighter, brighter, and there was an angular lilt from the violins, and the clarinets' sudden bright accents, rooted by the cellos' modulations. The sound became lucent, as if emerging triumphant from some hidden shadow. Yes, it was as though Sylvane had at last cleared her way through that forest, cleared out the knots and the darkness. What remained was vibrancy, without the lurking danger. Instead there was brilliance. As the woodwinds carried their melody up toward the sky, Nicholas felt his own heart lift.

He opened his eyes. She had done it, after so many years. She had made it through. Nicholas wanted to call out to her, Sylvane, at last, you did it! So much was possible, then.

He listened as the last reverberations died out, the tremolo of the violins like heat glimmering on a desert clearing. I've been saved, was his thought. I must tell Sylvane, You saved me.

But first—the thought came to him with clarity—I must make amends.

He stood from his desk. Yoni was absolutely right: How had he let these days pass by? So little time. These people in his life, the people he cared for . . . Only a few hours remained until Remy would have finished up at work. Time enough. Nicholas went to fetch the big, full plastic bag by the door.

❧ ⎯ ❧

AT NESTOR'S IT WAS STILL EARLY AND NOT MANY PEOPLE WERE ON the dance floor. Nicholas spotted Paula easily, amid a small group of young men, and waved.

She looked up from her beer and a made a surprised face, as the others followed her gaze. The young man next to her frowned and said something to Paula, then headed briskly toward Nicholas. Paula called, "You're kidding, right?"

But the young man had already grabbed Nicholas by the shoulders and was pushing him toward the side door. "We don't need you here." He was taller than Nicholas, his bones thicker, his hands large.

"Please," Nicholas heard himself say. "Pardon me, but——"

"Just use her and then disappear, is that how it goes?"

When Nicholas raised his hands in protest, the man simply grabbed one and dragged Nicholas outside, where the sky was now dark and the asphalt twinkled beneath the parking lights.

Nicholas said, "You're hurting my wrist."

"*You're hurting my wrist,*" the man whined in a mocking voice, and in one fluid movement wrenched Nicholas's arm back, twisting his wrist until something popped. Pain leapt from Nicholas's left shoulder down through his forearm. He heard a cry and realized it was his own.

"Oh my God——stop it!" Paula was there, pulling furiously on the young man's button-down shirt. "What the hell's wrong with you?"

"He won't bother you anymore."

"He wasn't *bothering* me! Are you insane?" The young man looked offended as Paula added, "God, Nicholas, are you okay?"

With surprise Nicholas said, "I can't move my arm."

"José, you idiot." Paula reached for Nicholas's arm but stopped when she saw that his wrist, too, was injured.

José put his hand on Paula's shoulder and said, "Come on, girl——"

"Get the fuck away from me!" Paula's face was red with anger. José turned, moping, and headed back into the club.

"Shit, Nicholas, does it hurt?"

"Well, yes." He felt, incredibly, tears in his eyes. "I'm not sure how I'll drive home."

"You're not going home. I'm taking you to the hospital. I think he dislocated your shoulder." She exhaled loudly. "Jesus Christ. Where are your keys?"

"In my pocket. The left one."

Paula reached into his pant pocket, swearing under her breath, and followed him to the car. "That creep just confirmed every suspicion I had about him."

Only when he had sat down in the passenger seat, and Paula had closed his door and taken her place behind the wheel, did Nicholas realize that his legs were shaking.

"What are you even doing here?" Paula asked. "I thought you were through with dancing."

"I was. But I never thanked you. I saw some wool, and . . ." He took a sharp breath, because a new, searing pain shot through his wrist.

"And you thought of me? That's sweet." Paula said it in a way that Nicholas couldn't tell if she was being sarcastic.

"That bag of yarn, in the backseat. It's for you."

Paula gave a quick look toward the back. "All that's for me?"

"I hope you'll take it. I certainly don't know what to do with it."

"Are you serious—you really bought all of that for me?"

"It's New Zealand wool. I remember you said that was the best."

Paula had reached back to look inside the bag. "Wow." She gave a loud exhalation and, glancing at his arm, said, "Your wrist is already starting to swell."

It was red, throbbing. "It's all right," Nicholas told her, weakly, because it was all he knew to say.

BACKSTAGE, DURING INTERMISSION, REMY TRIED TO IMAGINE THAT this could be the last time. Next season she might be far away, no longer next to Carole at the front of the second violin section. Well, who knew what might happen. This morning, practicing the violin solo, she had felt something from long ago, from when she was still a girl. Aspiration. A furious *wanting*. It had stunned her, this determined yearning, so that she had to wonder: What had happened to the girl she had been, the one who wanted everything?

Now here was Christopher, with his carefully teased mustache and serious air. "Did you get my e-mail?"

"I haven't checked it yet."

"Just some more information. It looks really good, Remy, it's an amazing opportunity."

"I know. I looked up the m.d. again. She sounds terrific." Thrilling, what could be a world-class orchestra, and directed by a woman.

"I'm telling you, she's wonderful to work with. And she's open to all kinds of new music."

"I appreciate it, Christopher, really." Remy recalled how she had felt back when she was a student, learning new work every week, that continuous self-renewal. And now, after so many years, she was feeling it again. She had practiced for so long yesterday, the bruise on her neck had developed a rash.

That she could capture again what she hadn't felt since her student years, that sense of constant discovery, left her with a feeling of hope mixed with dismay. Hope that she might find again what she had sworn all those years ago never to lose: commitment to her own talent. And dismay for what she had allowed herself to become: some lesser version of herself.

"We'd better get back," Christopher said, and he and Remy returned to their seats.

THE CALL CAME AN HOUR LATER, WHEN SHE WAS LEAVING SYMPHONY Hall. Cybil's voice through the cell phone was hoarse, explaining that she was at the hospital. "Mass. General. Yoni's had a heart attack."

Remy said, "No," as if she could simply refute it.

"I just left you a message at home. He needs surgery."

Remy had stopped walking and stood on the sidewalk, feeling lost. Despite the late hour, the avenue was busy, cars crowding past, their lights suddenly alarming in the dark of night. A stormy breeze swept Remy's long skirt into an angry billow while Cybil said, "If you could come here."

A taxi was passing, and Remy frantically waved him over. "I'm on my way," she said, but her voice sounded funny; only when she had shut the taxi's door and huddled, terrified, back in the seat did she realize that she was crying.

Chapter 7

SHE FOUND CYBIL IN THE WAITING AREA, HER FACE VERY PALE.
Cybil explained what had happened, and that Yoni was sleeping
now. Though still somehow neat, Cybil looked diminished, like a wet
bird.

"They need to do emergency surgery. Normally they would wait
until he was stronger, but they think—" Cybil slouched, something
Remy had never seen her do. Remy wrapped her arms around her.
Cybil whispered, "I'm so frightened!"

Remy clung to her tightly. "Where's Ravit?"

"Trude's with her." Gertrude was Cybil's sister. "Is Nicholas here?"

"I was going to ask you."

Cybil shook her head. "I left him a message. Yoni asked for you.
Earlier, before they had to rush him in. He really wanted to see you."

"I want to see him."

"He looks awful!" Cybil began to cry.

A doctor came up to them then, to ask Cybil to fill out some paperwork, and Cybil allowed herself to be led away.

Fluorescent lights gave the room a bluish tinge, and as Remy sat,
alone, she felt sick to her stomach. She stared at her hands in her lap,
clasped them, unclasped them. She changed the cross of her hands,
right over left, which felt unnatural, and looked down at her thumbs
crossed one over the other. When she was very young, she had looked
at her hands one day while washing up for dinner and, seeing the
tap water fall over them, thought to herself, These are my hands,
and they will be my hands when I'm old, but they'll be different,

they'll be older hands. And the thought had seemed profound and overwhelming, and had been followed by one of those unanswerable questions: Are they still the same hands?

A year or so ago, her colleague Carole had accidentally sliced the tip of her left-hand forefinger while cutting a cucumber—and had refused to be rushed to the emergency room for stitches, terrified that surgery might compromise the sensitivity in her fingertip. Instead she had some kooky ultraviolet light contraption that a friend had rigged up, under which she placed her fingertip for hours each day, to help the skin of the sliced section rebind itself. After a week, like magic, the fingertip was fully healed.

If it could happen for Carole's finger, all back to normal and good as new, then it could happen for Yoni, too. Remy clasped her hands the other way. Though it was nothing she had been brought up to do, she decided to pray. Please, please, let him be all right.

And now she found herself making a pact with a God she had never really thought much about: If you let him live, I will forgive everything. I will forgive Nicholas, forever, no matter what he did with that woman. Just let Yoni live, please.

As if hearing this, Nicholas materialized. He walked up to Remy briskly, pale, frowning. His left arm was in a sling, the wrist bandaged. "Have you heard anything?"

"My God, what happened to you?"

"Let's just say I avoided a fight. Is Yoni all right?"

"What? Jesus." Remy felt her heart plunge all over again, at the life Nicholas must lead without her. Just how many secrets did he have? But all she said was, "We've been waiting for you. He needs surgery. Right now he's sleeping." Then, feeling furious all over again, she couldn't help asking, "Why didn't you answer your phone?"

He nodded toward his arm. Then he sat down and asked, "Is Cybil with him?"

"She's with the doctors. There are lots of . . . decisions." Remy realized her jaw was shaking. The quick thumping in her chest seemed suddenly faster. "What the fuck, Nicholas?" she asked quietly, but he just shook his head.

They waited.

"Well, here we are," Nicholas announced after many minutes, as if they had already completed long laps.

Remy said nothing, just looked down at her hands until a nurse finally came and told them they could see Yoni now.

THEY WERE USHERED INTO A SMALL BRIGHT ROOM. "HEY," CYBIL SAID weakly, and then, "Oh, no—what happened?"

"Never mind," Nicholas said, "I'm fine," and then nodded hello to Cybil's sister, Trude, whom he and Remy had met a number of times. She was holding Ravit, who was awake yet oddly peaceful, grabbing onto some small purple fuzzy thing. Yoni lay in the bed, motionless, eyes closed, asleep.

Nicholas watched Remy go to Yoni and say, "Hey, you," in a low voice. Her kiss on Yoni's pale gray cheek met no reaction other than a tiny twitch of his face. "Jesus. Look at you." She burst into tears. "I'm sorry to cry," she said, turning her head away.

Her face was wracked, as if Yoni were *her* husband and not Cybil's. Nicholas felt suddenly confused, nearly dizzy—from the painkillers, probably. And from the fact that this was *real,* this awful scene before him was actually happening.

He dropped down into one of the plastic seats, overwhelmed.

"We have just a few minutes," Cybil's sister said tightly, absently rubbing the baby's back; Ravit had begun to squirm, and Cybil reached for her. "They have to prep him for surgery."

Nicholas nodded, because he found he couldn't speak. He felt panic coming on, though he told himself it would all be all right, of course Yoni would be fine. But the panic was still there, rising. He hadn't felt such a thing in years, in decades, not like this—not since that day in Italy, at the train station, when he hadn't known who had died.

He wanted to reach out for Remy, hold her, but did not dare; instead he stood and moved toward the bed where Yoni lay, gray-looking, not right at all. No mischievous smile, no flicker in his eyes. Nicholas still heard the echo of their breakfast conversation, Yoni's quiet anger, the way he had nodded his head so slowly, as if to prevent himself from bursting. *I've already done all I can. There's nothing more I can do.*

A thought whipped through Nicholas: that the episode might have somehow triggered this attack. But no, these things were common enough. Every winter Nicholas read in the paper about men not yet old keeling over from the mere effort of shoveling snow. Even the ones who seemed fit, who rode bicycles and, like Yoni, jogged and went on hikes and drank protein shakes. They, too, succumbed. Sometimes it was simply congenital; you can't help what goes on in your heart.

Yet a horrible guilt clung to him. "I'm sorry," Nicholas mouthed, but no sound came out. Leaning down, he managed to whisper, "I love you, Yoni. Please. Get well, hmm?"

He waited, as if Yoni might speak. Despite the nearly imperceptible movement of his eyes beneath their lids, Yoni simply lay there while everyone stood watching him, this man they all loved, except that it was no longer the same man.

WHEN THEY RETURNED TO THE WAITING ROOM, NICHOLAS DROPPED carefully into the seat next to Remy. After long, awful, silent minutes, he said, "I guess this is what it means to grow up."

Remy turned to look at him. "For you. The rest of us grew up a long time ago." She let her head drop into her hands. How can I stay so angry, even now? What does it even matter? I made a worse mistake. I broke up a family. Who am I to feel wronged? Other people can turn the other cheek. Look at Hazel the other day, so kind to me. I turned her life upside down, and in return, she has been nothing but kind to me, really.

But, of course, Remy reminded herself, that was who Hazel was: a person who gave. She had shared, if unwillingly, her life with Remy—her daughter and her family—with all the grace she could muster. She had given, and had forgiven.

To be able to do that. What Remy would give to be able to do that.

She looked up to see Cybil's sister standing in front of them, her face pale. "They've stopped the surgery, there was a problem. Cybil's with him, but they won't let me in with her. It looks . . . It's not good."

Remy began to shiver. That small sentence—"It's not good"—those short, benign adjectives that people use to deliver the most deadly of news.

Nicholas was asking questions now. Surely there must be a way, he was demanding, almost belligerently, as if it were Cybil's sister who had caused all this trouble in the first place. "Surely there's something they can do!"

Remy didn't hear the response. She was biting her lip so hard that she tasted blood. "It's not possible," Nicholas said, angrily, when Cybil's sister had left them again.

Remy thought of Cybil, what a good mood she had been in the other day, Ravit a neat little package there on her chest, and the backgammon board in its bubble wrap. Remy could practically see it now, leaning against the wall.

A new kind of pain crashed through her. This very moment, Yoni was in a room somewhere fighting for his life. Impossible, that they might have to live without him. And yet it was what people did, of course. Continued.

"It's not possible," Nicholas repeated, in a murmur.

But yes, Remy told herself, of course it was possible. Yoni was a casualty of something beyond health or illness. It seemed clear this disaster was something she and Nicholas, their own misdeeds, had led to, inevitably.

Remy held her arms around herself, to try to stop the shivering. Then she let go, because nothing would do.

The pact she had made, her pact with God . . . It was the wrong pact. She saw that now. It was too easy. A selfish pact. One where she could keep everything for herself. But a fulfilled wish was not a reason to forgive. It was the unfulfilled wish that was the reason. Forgiving *despite* that.

A fullness came over her, a furious clarity.

Yes, that is why we forgive: because we live only so long, and love only so long.

She said none of this to Nicholas. But as if hearing her, he made a small motion with his arm, as though to lift his hand to hers, before his face broke into pain. Remy reached for his other hand and curled her fingers around his. She continued to hold on, for what felt like a long time, and prayed in a silent, ashamed way.

They were still sitting like that when Cybil came toward them, dreadfully slowly, her face as they had never seen it, so that even before she had reached them they had begun, already, to understand.

IT WAS VERY LATE WHEN THE THREE OF THEM ACCOMPANIED CYBIL and Ravit home. Nicholas felt he was moving through someone else's life. Cybil made the first call, to Yoni's brother in Haifa, but the effort was too much; after that, Trude and Remy took over while Ravit slept in her crib. Nicholas sat on the sleek gray sofa and held Cybil as best he could with just his right arm. His other arm hung in its sling, wrist bandaged, useless.

If I had known, he wondered, that would be the last time I would speak to him . . . But what would I have done differently? What could I have done that would have made it any better? In a way, he's always been cross with me.

Well, I could have run after him. Told him how much I love him, and that I forgive him.

Forgive him. Where did *that* come from? Really there had been an opposite dynamic, as if Nicholas owed Yoni something, always the sense that Nicholas was in the wrong somehow.

Well, there was something else. It had to do with that odd period years ago, those uncomfortable months when something had gone on with Remy. Whatever it was, Nicholas never quite understood, only that it was something she must have told Yoni, something he held over Nicholas—because for a while there had been such uneasiness around him.

Cybil fell briefly asleep on Nicholas's good shoulder, but then awoke and cried again, great loud sobs that became hiccups. Nicholas had to fight himself not to join her.

Night had begun to turn to day. Remy scrambled some eggs. Nicholas was amazed that although he had no appetite—surely none of them did—all four of them ate, swiftly, automatically. Nicholas had to hold his fork with his right hand, making him feel even stranger.

Ravit ate, too; the three women took turns feeding her some green puree with a baby spoon.

When Cybil's sister asked, in a hoarse, tired voice, "So, what exactly happened to you, again?" Nicholas just said, "I got my comeuppance. Let's leave it at that. I'm too ashamed to admit how this happened." The wrangle at the club seemed something from days ago—from another lifetime.

That was when Cybil stood, quickly, and ran to the bathroom. They could hear her vomiting. Trude went to help her, and so it was just Remy and Nicholas, sitting across from each other, and Ravit in her swing seat, as the sun rose. Remy spooned some more green mush out of the jar, and Ravit played with the purple spoon. Remy touched Ravit's plump cheek. Then Remy's face crumpled; she began to sob.

Nicholas watched, paralyzed, as Ravit reached out for Remy's hair. He still heard the anger in Yoni's tight, furious voice: *You have no idea, that's for sure.*

And yet Nicholas *knew* how much Remy loved Yoni, and that Yoni cared just as deeply for her. He wanted to scream at Yoni, I know, I know!

From the bathroom, the sounds came again, Cybil retching into the toilet, while Remy reached down and wrapped her arms around her own abdomen, her face collapsing all over again. The pure physicality of all this grief was horrifying.

You have no idea.

But I do! I know I've always failed you, somehow.

And yet it did seem, now, that there was something he did not know, something that kept him apart from the vast grief in this room. He pictured Yoni's face in the diner, the familiar frustration suddenly too much. Well, that sort of anger could happen when you were close the way they were. And there had always been envy, of course—Yoni always wanting what Nicholas had.

Nicholas sat up straighter at the thought. He turned to look at Remy. She had put her hands up over her eyes, like a grieving widow.

Cybil was still retching into the toilet. "I'm sorry," Nicholas heard himself stutter, "but I think I have to go home now."

Remy nodded. "Go and get some sleep. I'll stay here as long as Cybil needs me."

Shaking, he stood. Even his legs felt weak. But he managed to walk away from her, this woman grieving for her other husband.

IT WAS HOURS LATER WHEN REMY HEADED HOME. SHE HAD FALLEN asleep on Yoni's hard gray sofa, awaking to find Cybil's closest friend and a neighbor setting up trays of food, taking charge for the next shift.

Carrying her violin case as if it were any other day . . . The air was sweet with springtime. Yoni, what happened to you? But she knew, of course: his heart had broken. Of course it had. An entire life spent trying to refind that one true love. How long could a heart stand it? Missing someone, yearning. It was just that combination—loss and desire—that had been Yoni's very essence.

At home, the house was quiet. Nicholas had fallen asleep atop their bed. Seeing his wrist in its bandaging, Remy bridled again at how separate the two of them had become, how little she understood him, and could not bring herself to lie down beside him. Instead she went downstairs to sit in the light-filled music room. The air sifting through the windows made her feel briefly stronger.

Nicholas's pages were still spread atop the piano. Remy didn't even need them anymore, except for the final movement; the others she knew by heart. Just glimpsing the manuscript, she itched to play the piece again, to be back inside that alternate world, instead of here in this room on this horrible day.

She took her violin from its case, tuned the strings, tightened her bow. Closing her eyes, she thought back to the opening bars. Her bow met the string, and soon she found herself among those mysteries she was still trying to understand, those questions still taking shape. Playing from memory always held this quality for her, as if inhabiting a nameless space whose light and shadows became gradually—with each playing—more clear to her. Already she sensed, this time, a leap forward in her comprehension, her playing no longer a matter of mere translation. The music had become a part of her, so that she felt, this time (though tears streaked her cheeks), its meaning.

Yes, she heard it now. Those measures that had been haunting her—the wisp of something she almost recognized. Notes she had already examined closely. She stopped and, this time, instead of playing them as written, reversed them. Played them backward, just like that.

It was a riff from the Franck sonata—the one she and Nicholas loved to play together, the one she had learned in that long-ago summer with Conrad Lesser.

She laughed out loud.

Then she went over to where the pages of the manuscript lay and took them up, seeing anew these marks her husband's hand had made, this code whose secrets she only now understood. She turned ahead to the next movement to see what he had done.

This time he had inverted the notes, had them going down instead of up, but again with the original rhythm intact. And in the third movement he had used the same notes and rhythm but rearranged their order, like an anagram. She looked ahead to the fourth movement, where he had shuffled them yet again. How amazing—how stupendous! To see in this pattern of dots and stems the constellations of another soul.

Just a little string of notes. But to Remy they were a secret message just for her. She saw that now, as she began to play the solo section of the final movement. With each stroke of her bow she felt Nicholas's love course through her, immense and many colored, nothing he could have put into words, nothing he could speak aloud. Its expression was *this*.

"That was gorgeous."

She looked up to see Nicholas, and was surprised all over again by the bandaged wrist and the sling. His nose and eyes were red from crying. Remy went to him, leaned into him, and felt him lift his right arm around her.

"Thank you," she told him. "For the violin part."

"It's the first time I've heard it played. I thought I'd surprise you. It's . . . You've made it beautiful."

"I've been working hard on it!" Remy gave a little laugh—her first laugh, she realized, since the events of last night. Not even a day had passed, and already she had laughed. She felt she had betrayed Yoni.

"I can tell," Nicholas said. "I'm honored."

"Well, I wanted to use it for an audition, actually." She stepped back, paused just briefly before telling him about the orchestra in Barcelona. As she spoke she could see that she had shocked him. "I mean, who knows if it's even a possibility, who knows if I'll really want . . . well, I mean, I want to be sure of at least getting an audition."

"I'm sure you'd be selected," Nicholas said, as if in a trance. The expression on his face prevented Remy from saying more. In a slow, heavy voice, he told her, "Barcelona was the first city I ever visited in Spain."

"I remember you telling me about it."

He said, "I don't suppose you want me there. Not that you even asked, I mean, I don't mean to suggest—but if you did—"

"Honey," Remy said, taking his good hand in hers. "Honey." There was so much she wanted to say. But a lump had formed in her throat. "Here, come help me. Let's try the final movement."

Nicholas nodded at his sling. "I'm afraid I can't accompany you."

"I mean to turn pages," Remy told him. "I don't have all of it from memory yet." She laid the stack of pages before her, and Nicholas came to stand at her side.

She began to play.

Since this was the full score, the turns came quickly. The lilting music filled the room, Nicholas following along beside Remy, each turn of the page taking them forward in time.

She felt herself floating within time, the way she often did while playing, that suspension of time that is the peculiar alchemy of music. Just as Nicholas had said on that very first day, twenty years ago. *Not just how fast or how slowly the music moves. It's about how fast and slow* life *moves.*

Now they were approaching the thick dark vertical line that signaled the conclusion of the movement. And there at the end were the penned instructions, which Nicholas had abbreviated to "D.C."

Da capo. Remy felt herself preparing for the shift. And with perfect timing Nicholas flipped back to the first page, so that she could start again from the beginning.

Chapter 8

⟡────⟡

*T*HE ENTIRE YARD WAS BLOOMING, BRIGHT NEW PETALS AND THE green of youth, nasturtiums by the front steps, petunias happy in their big clay tub. Among the shrubs, chipmunks ran busily, stashing seeds, and from all along the street came the hum of lawn crews mowing, blowing, raking.

Hazel stepped out onto the veranda and breathed the smell of wood chips and fresh peat—her backyard, her world, where sycamores formed a protective awning over the healthy lawn. With so much rain last month, things were growing like mad; already a few stubborn tufts of onion grass had reemerged, along with a smattering of clover flowers, their messy heads soon to be lopped off by the mower. But what a gorgeous afternoon it was turning out to be, Hazel thought as she sponged off the glass-topped table and made sure there were no spiderwebs or dead bugs on the chairs. Marta was fetching the folding ones from the garage. Everything was in place.

With a little shake of the sponge, Hazel returned to the kitchen, where an array of thick paper napkins, plastic cups, and shiny disposable plates waited to be freed from their wrappers. Her good china teacups would go on the credenza with the punch. On the counter, covered with a glass dome, was a homemade chocolate cake with marshmallow icing. The marshmallow oozed over the sides and had coagulated in shiny puffs. It looked disgusting, but it was Jessica's favorite, ever since she was a little girl.

Marta shouted, "The chairs are all there!" She always shouted. "For the dining room, do you want the linen or the lace table runner!"

"The linen sounds nice. Thanks." Hopefully people would spend most of the party outside.

Marta shuffled into the dining room as Hazel dumped a frozen brick of raspberry sherbet into a cut-glass bowl. She tipped a plastic bottle of soda water over it, watched it glug, then gave the concoction a stir with the matching glass ladle. Immediately the sherbet began melting in its fizzy way. Why was it that some of the most delicious things looked so revolting?

"You know, I think the lace is fancier!" Marta called.

"All right, then." In such matters, Hazel always let Marta have her way. Sloppy and increasingly deaf, Marta had been Hazel's cleaning lady for sixteen years and, though she continued to arrive twice a month without fail, now missed entire swaths of dust, and dirt, due to failing eyesight and aging in general. Hazel always had to go over windowsills and corners with a wet rag after Marta had gone. Well, what was she going to do, fire an old lady who had spent much of her adulthood pushing dirty water around with a mop, who had helped Hazel prepare for some of the most important parties (Jessie's graduation, Robert's promotion) and had witnessed her daughter transform from a girl into a woman, in and out of braces, in and out of phases? If in the end it came down to this, cleaning up after the cleaning lady, then so be it.

"Ah, *that* looks nice!" Marta announced. "I put the daisies in the middle!"

Hazel stepped into the dining room to look. "Beautiful." They were Jessica's favorite flower; hopefully she would at least notice them. "I figure we should keep the cold cuts in here," Hazel told Marta, "so the bugs don't get to them."

"Right!"

The guests were due in a half hour. Jessica had sworn she and Joshua would arrive earlier, but you never knew with her. They had been staying with Nicholas and Remy; their dear friend Yoni had passed away. It happened last month, very suddenly, and Hazel could see that Jessica was still torn up about it. Yesterday they had taken part in a memorial service at the conservatory. And though Jessica had insisted she go ahead with the party as planned, Hazel knew it had been a rough time for all of them.

She looked at her watch. Robert, just back from racquetball, was upstairs showering.

Hazel took the feather duster from the broom closet and stepped into the hallway to glance around appraisingly. The living room looked especially nice, brightened by the many colors of the antique carpet. She and Robert had purchased it the year they married; the old, smaller one was up in the study now. Hazel shook her head, re-calling Nicholas's mix-up—as if Remy would ever have even cared about a thing like spilled wine on a carpet. But Hazel understood: to Nicholas, the recollection concerned his friend and his wife, and he could have only one wife at a time. It would therefore have to be Remy.

From upstairs came the squeak of the shower taps being shut off. Truth was, Hazel thought to herself as she dusted lightly at the end tables, she couldn't imagine reacting quite so strongly, now, to a spill. She smiled at the sounds of Robert upstairs dressing in his speedy way, the drawers quickly opened and shut, a crisp clean shirt plucked from a hanger in the closet. In the foyer she sighed, from habit more than emotion, at the nude crystal girl lying in the curl-wave on the pedestal.

The fact was, the "artist"—Hazel could not even think the word without quotation marks—had died. Just last week. He wasn't even old. Midsixties. It was a yachting accident; she read about it in an article Laura had clipped for her from the *Times*. Robert told her that, according to the dealer who had sold it to him, the sculpture was now worth three times what he had paid.

"Then can we sell it now?"

Robert had laughed at that. "Well, all right. Although I've already grown rather fond of it."

"I'll bet you have."

Supposedly he was negotiating its sale this week. Hazel felt herself relaxing at the thought; soon the imitation crystal wave-girl would be gone.

"It's art!" she could still hear Robert insisting, the day he brought it home. It had taken her a full two weeks to finally find a way to explain why it could not be art: because it wasn't *true*. But Robert had just replied, "It's one artist's vision."

"Yes, but it's a fantasy," she had corrected him.

"But isn't that what art is meant to do? To posit another possible world? Create something more beautiful than our pedestrian lives?"

Hazel had been frustrated at that, because she couldn't find the words to explain why this plastic girl's beauty was not real. "This is a fake woman with no thoughts or emotions," she had told him. The girl's face did not reveal a psyche at all; her perfect, slender body might as well be a pinup or an inflatable sex toy.

To that Robert had said, "It's not *pornography*."

Maybe not, but the fact that it passed as art was a crime.

"This isn't art," she declared now, to herself, with conviction. After all, she knew true beauty when she saw it. It was thanks to her that so many local craftspeople were able to sell their work, and to find a following. She had been a godsend for the woman in Somerville who made those clay beads, and Sam the silversmith out in Wellesley. Just yesterday she had put in another order for those woven bags from the pretty Hispanic girl. The girl had sounded delighted; Hazel had felt good about it all afternoon.

Of course, few people thought of her as a curator. Many thought her work nonessential. Jessica, in her college years, during her anti-materialist phase, had referred to Hazel's wares as "rich people thingies" (phrasing that must have come from Remy). Yet even Nicholas had marveled, the first time he saw the Newbury Street boutique, at the fine workmanship Hazel had managed to cull. He was the one who, at the shop's grand opening, had said, as if just realizing it,

"You're an artist, too. You're the one who brought all of this together. It's your imagination that orchestrated this entire arrangement."

His words had touched her. He was one of the few people secure enough in his own accomplishments to be able to truly praise the talents of others. It was the insecure artists whose anxieties left them clinging to the notion of certain arts as somehow more noble than others. To them, the fine arts would always be of a higher calling than mere arts-and-crafts. Even this atrocity . . . Hazel looked down at the sculpture. A lie that pretends to be the truth is not art. That was all it came down to. The fact that Hazel had ever put up with this thing surely deserved some sort of award.

Yes, there was a lesson in it, she decided as she dusted one final time around the girl. In fact, it seemed at this moment the only real advice she might be able to hand on to Jessica now that she was engaged. They always say marriage is about compromise, about accepting the bad with the good, the happy with the sad. Well, sure, Hazel would tell her, that's all perfectly true—but what it boils down to, really, is having a tacky nude statue backlit in your foyer.

"Let's turn the display light on!" Marta had emerged, a bottle of Glass Plus and a roll of paper towels in her hands.

"Ugh, Marta, I don't know. I hate to call attention to it."

But Marta loved this statue, had proclaimed to Hazel the moment she first saw it that it was beautiful. Hazel had asked her to explain what made it beautiful, thinking that then she herself might be able to see what Robert saw. Marta had just said, "She's pretty, and the glass is so shiny, like a big diamond!"

Now she was polishing the thing, somewhat heedlessly, and Hazel couldn't help smiling: though it might pose as art, it couldn't escape Glass Plus and Marta's rough hand.

"I think we should turn the light on!"

Hazel laughed. "All right, then, fine."

Marta flicked the switch, and the naked girl glowed.

Funny, Hazel thought, how separate this was from the real thing.

Jessica, for instance—now, there was real beauty. Of course Hazel would think that about her own daughter, but Jessica truly *was* more than a pretty face. She was a force of nature. Next month she and Remy were going to Spain for three weeks, just the two of them, while Joshua took a month-long intensive teaching certification course back home.

"It's just us gals for the first week," Jessica had said, when Hazel asked if Nicholas would be going with them. Remy apparently had professional business there, and Jessica, too, had decided to mix business and pleasure. "A reconnaissance mission. I'm going to scope out some hotel packages for work, so that I can write it off."

Hazel laughed to herself, at Jessica's notion of a business trip, picturing her on the Andalusian coast in some newly purchased bathing outfit. Hazel was able to hold completely different images of Jessica in her mind at the same time: in her soccer uniform in college; in her ice skates with the pom-poms in middle school; swimming in Walden Pond when she was still a toddler; and strapped into her collapsible stroller when she was one year old, bouncing along the bumpy cobblestone streets that summer when Nicholas had the fellowship in Belgium. It was amazing, actually, the way that, in Hazel's mind, Jessica could be all those things at once.

Hazel glanced at herself in the oval mirror above the side table. From the little drawer she took a plastic comb and made a few brief adjustments to her hair. Then she opened a small compact and lightly powdered her forehead and nose. That was all she needed.

Here came the springing steps of Robert descending the stairs to join her.

"Hey, there!"

The voice came from outside.

Hazel turned to the screen door to see Jessica hand in hand with Joshua, the two of them smiling broadly as they approached the front door.

"Look who we brought along."

Behind them on the curving path were Remy and Nicholas. They were walking unhurriedly, side by side, with Jessie and Joshua just in front. The door became a frame, then, the crosshatch of the screen muting the four of them, making them look soft, ethereal, so that for a brief second they were a picture, stepping forward, and Hazel nearly lost her breath, so taken she was by this movement toward her that was her family.

Glossary of Musical Terms

ARPEGGIO: (Italian: "like a harp") A broken chord in which the individual notes are sounded one after the other in rapid succession (usually ascending) instead of simultaneously.

BADINAGE: (French, *badiner*: "to jest, joke") Term used to describe a piece of music with a lighthearted, playful mood, as in a bantering conversation.

BAGATELLE: (French: "trifle") Term used as the title of a short lighthearted piece of music, in no specific form, often for piano. The term was first used by François Couperin in 1717 and was employed most notably by Beethoven in a series of such compositions for piano.

CADENZA: (Italian: "cadence") An ornamental passage, often improvised, usually leading to the last section of a movement or composition (most often an aria or concerto), in which the virtuosic ability of the soloist might be shown. Cadenzas are now more often written by the composer, although some modern performers continue to improvise.

C-BOUT: The "waist" or C-shaped indentation of a stringed instrument's body. The upper bout would form the instrument's "shoulders," and the lower bout its "hips."

COL LEGNO: (Italian: "with the wood") The strings (for example, of a violin) are to be struck with the wood of the bow, making a percussive sound.

DA CAPO: (Italian: "from the beginning") The letters D.C. at the end of a piece of music or a section of it indicate that it should be played or sung again from the beginning (*Da capo al fine*) or from the beginning up to the sign (*Da capo al segno*).

FERMATA: (Italian: "finished, closed") A notation (sometimes called *bird's eye*) indicating that a rest or note is to be sustained for a duration that is at the discretion of the performer or conductor. A fermata at the end of a first or intermediate movement or section is usually moderately prolonged, but the final fermata of a symphony may be prolonged for dramatic effect, up to twice its printed length or more.

FOUR-PART CHORD: A combination of four notes played simultaneously.

FOURTH POSITION: Placement of the left hand on the strings at the fingerboard, where the forefinger is placed on the E string at G. Musicians may choose a different position to produce a particular timbre; the same note will sound substantially different depending on what string is used to play it.

FUGUE: (Italian, *fuga*: "flight") A contrapuntal composition. A short theme (the subject) is introduced in one voice (or part) alone, then in others, with imitation and characteristic development as the piece progresses. Generally the voices overlap and weave in and out of each other, forming a continuous, tapestrylike texture.

GLISSANDO: (French, *glisser*: "to slide") This Italianized word describes a continuous sliding from one note to another. On the harp or the piano this is achieved by sliding the finger or fingers over the strings or keys; on a stringed instrument each semitone would be sounded as the finger is slid up or down the length of a string.

MARCATO: (Italian: "marked") Execute every note in an accented, stressed, or emphasized manner.

MELISMA: (Greek: "song") In vocal music, especially in liturgical chant, the technique of changing the note (usually at least five or six times) of a syllable of text while it is being sung.

OPEN STRINGS: For stringed instruments, a pitch (note) played on a string that is not stopped (held down) by the finger.

PARTITA: (Italian, *partire*: "to divide") *Partita* is another word for *suite,* used first in the eighteenth and nineteenth centuries where it referred to a multimovement composition consisting of dances and nondance movements or entirely nondance movements.

PIANO: (Italian: "soft") This notation is generally represented by the letter *p* in directions to performers to play gently. Pianissimo, represented by *pp,* means very soft. Addition of further letters *p* indicates greater degrees of softness.

PORTAMENTO: (Italian: "carrying") A smooth, unbroken gliding from one pitch to another, where the intermediate pitches are audible. This term is used primarily in singing and string instruments. Often called glissando for other instruments.

RITARDANDO: (Italian: "becoming slower") Often abbreviated to rit., this notation directs players to slow down or decelerate the tempo. Opposite of *accelerando.*

RUBATO: (Italian: "stolen time" or "robbed") Short for "tempo rubato." A direction to perform music more expressively, faster, or slower than strict adherence to the basic tempo would indicate, by taking part of the duration from one note and giving it to another. This tasteful stretching, slowing, or hurrying thus imparts flexibility and emotion to the performance.

SCORDATURA: (Italian: "out of tune") An alternative tuning used for a string instrument, generally used to extend an instrument's range, or to make certain passages easier or more possible to perform, or to achieve certain special effects. Scordatura was popular between 1600 and 1750 but is used rarely now.

SONATA: (Italian, *sonare*: "to sound") Designates music that is to be played on an instrument rather than sung, by a soloist or ensemble, usually in three movements.

SPICCATO: (Italian, *spiccare*: "to separate") A way of playing the violin and other bowed instruments by bouncing the bow on the string, usually with the point of the bow, giving a characteristic separated, detached sound.

STACCATO: (Italian, *staccare*: "to detach") A style of playing notes in a detached, separated, distinct manner.

STAVE: Staff, stave, or pentagram. A framework of five lines on which musical notation is written such that the higher the note-sign on the staff, the higher its pitch. Note symbols, dynamics, and other performance directions are placed within, above, and below the staff.

SUL PONTICELLO: (Italian: "at the bridge") A direction to string players to bow (or sometimes to pluck) near the bridge (the small piece of wood that raises the strings away from the instrument). The tonal resonance is reduced, producing a characteristic glassy and more metallic sound.

TENUTO: (Italian, *tenere*: "to hold") A directive to perform a certain note or chord of a composition in a sustained manner for longer than its full duration, but without generally altering the note's value.

TIMBRE: (Old French: "bell") The quality of a musical tone that allows one to distinguish voices and instruments; that component of a tone that causes different instruments (for example, a guitar and a violin) to sound different from each other while they are both playing the same note.

TUTTI: (Italian: "all") A directive to perform a certain passage of a composition with all instruments together, not specifically by solo instruments.

VERTICAL PIZZICATO: Musical direction denoted by a circle with a vertical line going from the center upward beyond the circle. Known as the Bartók pizzicato, it was invented by the musician Béla Bartók and is used extensively in his compositions. This technique is achieved by plucking the string far from the fingerboard, using the right hand, using enough force to cause the string to snap back and strike the fingerboard. This snapping sound has its own pitch.

VIBRATO: (Italian, *vibrare*: "to vibrate") Vibrating; a rapidly repeated slight alteration in the pitch of a note, used to give a richer sound and as a means of expression. Since the nineteenth century, vibrato has been used almost constantly because of its enhancement of tone.

SOURCES

E-zine articles, http://EzineArticles.com/6816626.

San Francisco Classical Voice, www.sfcv.org; through Naxos, www.naxos.com.

Virginia Tech Multimedia Music Dictionary, www.music.vt.edu.

Wikipedia, www.wikipedia.org.

Acknowledgments

THANK YOU TO THE MACDOWELL COLONY AND VIRGINIA CENTER for the Creative Arts for support in writing this book. I'm deeply grateful to the friends and readers who helped me from draft to draft and to the composers, conductors, and musicians who read these pages with critical expertise or simply shared their knowledge with me:

Eve Bridburg, Faye Chiao, Jessica Berger Gross, Hubert Ho, Michelle Hoover, Jill Kalotay, Leah Kalotay, Jhumpa Lahiri, Jean Layzer, Judith Layzer, Don Lee, Margot Livesey, Chris McCarron, Tom McNeely, Emily Newburger, Rishi Reddi, Bruce Reiprich, Julie Rold, David Schmahmann, Elizabeth Schulze, Jennie Shames, Mandy Smith, and Anna Weesner.

About the Author

DAPHNE KALOTAY is the author of the novel *Russian Winter*, which won the Writers' League of Texas Fiction Award and has been published in twenty languages, and the fiction collection *Calamity and Other Stories*, which was short-listed for the Story Prize. A MacDowell fellow, Daphne holds a PhD in modern and contemporary literature and an MA in creative writing, both from Boston University, and has received fellowships from the Christopher Isherwood Foundation, Yaddo, and the Bogliasco Foundation. She has taught literature and creative writing at Boston University, Skidmore College, Middlebury College, and Grub Street. Copresident of the Boston chapter of the Women's National Book Association, she lives in Cambridge, Massachusetts.